Giving In

Awakenings 4

Michele Zurlo

Lost Goddess Publishing

Giving In (Awakenings 4)
Copyright © May 2020 by Michele Zurlo
ISBN: 978-1-942414-65-0

Editor: Nicoline Tiernan
Cover Artist: Pyroclastic

Published by Lost Goddess Publishing LLC
www.michelezurloauthor.com

This book is a work of fiction. While reference might be made to actual historical events or existing locations, the names, characters, places and incidents are either the product of the author's imagination or are used fictitiously, and any resemblance to actual persons, living or dead, business establishments, events, or locales is entirely coincidental.

Warning: This book contains sexually explicit scenes and adult language and may be considered offensive to some readers. It is not meant for underage readers.

DISCLAIMER: Education and training are necessary in order to learn safe BDSM practices. Lost Goddess Publishing LLC is not responsible for any loss, harm, injury or death resulting from use of the information contained in any of its titles. This is a work of fiction, and license has been taken with regard to BDSM practices.

About Giving In

Evan—A Dom in love with his vanilla best friend and enamored with a quirky older woman who enjoys submitting to him.

Alaina—Burned by love and tired of masking her true nature, she doesn't want to risk her heart with two passionate younger men.

Daniel—He doesn't see why he can't have them both.

Daniel and Evan have been together—without being *together*—for nine years. The best friends share everything—except their lovers. When Alaina Miles walks into their lives, all of that changes.

Alaina isn't on the same page. Over a decade older, she has things they don't—a cheating ex, a child, and autism. A second chance at love isn't part of her life plan.

Queen of BDSM Michele Zurlo brings you a scintillating tale of compromise, self-acceptance, and taking a chance on love even when it could cost everything.

A Note to Readers

Longtime readers will recall Alaina, Daniel, and Evan from Time to Pretend. As with almost all of the other Awakenings novels, I've rewritten this story completely. I hope you enjoy this new version of events even more than the original.

Chapter 1—Daniel

Rubbing a towel over my wet hair, I checked the security feed for the cameras downstairs in my martial arts studio. Living above it in a loft made it easy to go home and use the shower after teaching a grueling class. That last session had been a private lesson for a student who'd graduated from my highest-level class. Kendra was hitting the competitive circuit, and I was serving as her mentor and coach. It was my first time on that side of things, and I was looking forward to learning a lot.

While that had been going on, my sister, Sophia, had been finishing up a grant-funded self-defense class we offered every other Wednesday. To a one, the people in the class were all victims of violence, and they wanted to regain a sense of control over their lives. Learning self-defense was one way to increase a victim's confidence, and the counselor that conducted therapy sessions afterward helped with issues you couldn't punch away.

We'd lucked out with that grant, and we'd been fortunate Doctor Alaina Miles came with it. She wasn't a resident looking for contact hours. She was a bona fide, board certified psychologist with more than a decade of experience. I'd seen dozens of women walk in here with their heads hanging low and walk out with their shoulders thrown back. Alaina had a no-nonsense attitude and a quirky personality. She was completely genuine, and the people she was helping knew how much she cared.

The security camera showed that the session was over. Alaina was down there alone, putting away the chairs they used for their meeting. She bent down to retrieve something from the floor, pointing her ass at the camera because she hadn't bent at the knee. Her skirt tightened over those delightfully rounded cheeks, and I gave myself permission to look, but just for a moment. Alaina was about twelve years older than I was. She had a doctorate. She was a professor in charge of a whole department at a very prestigious university. Beautiful, smart, and so far out of my league that I couldn't even see where she was camped out.

And off-limits.

She was the reason our program was so successful. I liked to sleep around, but I wasn't stupid enough to go after Alaina. If I ruined this with an unwelcomed, or even a politely rebuffed, advance, not only would Sophia and my whole family be pissed at me, but dozens of people would not get the help they needed.

I was a slut, not a greedy bastard.

I glanced at the clock, noting the time was later than I'd thought. I tossed my towel over the top of the shower curtain and ran a hand through my hair so that it wasn't so messy. Then I went downstairs to help the doctor. I'd told her a dozen times that she didn't have to clean up. Her time was valuable, and Sophia and I appreciated every moment she spent in my studio. Plus, I always walked her to her car. My place wasn't in a crime-ridden area, but I was a slut with manners.

The bell over the front door chimed as I came down the stairs, and I frowned. While I was okay with Alaina leaving before the room was cleared, it would be out of character for her to do so. I fully expected to pry her hands off chairs and push her out the door.

An unfamiliar male voice came from the lobby, and I hurried down the hall.

"Where is she?" The guy sounded pissed.

"The studio is closed right now. Please come back during normal business hours." Ever the professional, Alaina's tone was calm and even.

"I know she's fucking here!"

I didn't need to see the guy to know he was most likely trying to physically intimidate Alaina. I emerged from the hall and into the lobby.

"What's your name?" She didn't seem to notice the way he was leaning over her short, curvy frame. Alaina was tiny, maybe five feet tall, but her officious demeanor made it seem like she was unaware of being at a disadvantage.

"Get out of my way, bitch." He went to shove her to the side, but I'd be damned if he was going to lay his hands on anyone in my presence.

Without breaking my stride, I grabbed his arm and twisted it behind his back. I pressed his face against the glass door where he'd entered my place of business. "She asked for your name."

2

I understood why she wanted it. She needed to contact the woman he was seeking to warn her, and she needed to inform the authorities that he was on the loose.

"Glen."

"Glen what?"

He hesitated, so I twisted a little harder, putting painful pressure on his shoulder and elbow joints.

"Simpson."

"Glen Simpson, who are you looking for?"

He tried to kick out behind him, but his attempt to break my hold was laughable. I altered my grip on his arm to target a nerve, and I took him to his knees while he screamed. Nothing I did would cause lasting damage, but it hurt like a bitch.

"You've got two choices, Glen. You can tell me who you're looking for, or I can see if I can make you scream louder. Pick one."

"Ashley. Ashley Langhorne. She's my girlfriend."

Names seemed like enough information. I couldn't think of anything else we might need, but this was not my area of expertise. "Doctor, do we have any more questions for Glen?"

"No. I'm sure the police will follow up with some, though."

"Okay. Glen, I'm going to release you. You can get up slowly, and then you need to leave. If you try anything, you'll find out why I have three national titles."

Using his better sense, Glen got up slowly, and he shot a scowl in my direction before leaving. As I watched him get in his car and drive away, I noted the make and model, and I took down his plate number. I also realized the nasty look he'd lobbed had been focused over my shoulder.

I turned the lock on the door, and I faced Alaina. "Are you okay?"

"Yes." Abruptly, she went back into the meeting room. Really, it was a smaller practice arena with a rack of folding chairs for people who wanted to watch lessons and a bank of storage cupboards along one wall.

Her reaction didn't seem right, so I didn't believe she was actually okay. I followed her into the room with the intention of telling her it was normal for that scene to have shaken her up. But I found her on the phone, reporting the incident. I handed her the paper where I'd written the vehicle information, and cleaned up as she navigated the law enforcement bureaucracy.

"Yes, I understand no crime was committed. However, he has a history of domestic abuse, and she has a restraining order against him. Perhaps you can add an extra patrol in her neighborhood tonight? Yes.

3

That would be helpful. Thank you." She called Ashley next, and then she slipped her phone into her purse.

At the counter, she bowed her head and exhaled.

I finished stowing the last chair, and then I approached her. "Alaina, I know that was intense."

She offered a brief, false smile. "It comes with the territory, and it's nothing compared to what Ashley has to deal with."

"That doesn't make it less intense for you." I leaned my hip against the counter next to where she still faced her purse.

Staring straight ahead at the white door of a cupboard where I kept cleaning supplies, she looked like she was deep in thought.

I recognized someone who didn't quite know what to do next, so I tugged on the long sleeve of her blouse. "Come upstairs and have a drink. Take some time to get your wits back."

Now she looked at me, a frown marring her cute chin. "I'm sure you have better things to do than to entertain me."

"Nope. I was going to have a glass of wine and flip through channels to see if anything catches my eye." I stopped leaning and held out a hand to herd her toward the door. "Come on. Have a drink with me. I also have leftover chocolate mousse cake you can help me polish off. Then I'll walk you to your car."

My mom had baked the cake for me, and I was supposed to share it with Sophia, but I hadn't. She lived with a chef, so she had access to lots of great food all the time. I felt like Mom's chocolate mousse should mostly go to me.

Of course, I'd felt that way before Sophia had hooked up with Drew. I wasn't generous where baked goods were concerned, but I didn't mind sharing with the good-hearted doctor with the fine ass and alluring, honey-brown eyes.

Okay, I needed to stop thinking of her that way.

She was much older than me. So what if I had all kinds of librarian and hot-for-teacher fantasies about her? That was on me.

She was cultured and refined. She wasn't the kind of woman who would be up for me licking chocolate mousse from her breasts.

I shut off the lights as we headed toward the stairs that led to my loft. I gave my best effort to avoid looking at the sexy ass sashaying from side to side right in front of my face as she went up the stairs ahead of me.

But I'm only human.

Just a man.

A man who was immensely glad to get to the landing before he said or did anything stupid or inappropriate.

My urges illustrated exactly why Alaina would never be interested in me. On my best day, I was immature and constantly horny.

I'd left the door to my loft open, and I gestured for her to enter. "Welcome to my humble abode."

I was a fucking dork.

She went inside and set her purse on the island counter. Then she looked around, sweeping her gaze from left to right. She noted my kitchen, the cutout where the bathroom was located, the corner that was my bedroom, the living room area with the resistance trainer off to one side, and a French Provincial dining table to her immediate right. While my furniture was nice, it was modern. The antique table with the parquet surface and cane-backed chairs stuck out like a sore thumb.

Alaina made a thoughtful noise.

"I know. The table doesn't quite fit the décor of the rest of the loft. It belonged to my grandparents, and I love it."

She peered closer at the table. "It's a beautiful piece and a great way to remember them."

"They're not dead." I went to the cabinet and selected a bottle of red, which was the only bottle of wine I had. "They downsized when they retired to Florida."

"Oh." A light blush traveled up her neck and stained her cheeks. She clasped her hands together. "I misunderstood."

"I worded it badly." I flashed a grin to put her at ease. "How about you grab the mousse from the fridge?"

While she did that, I got glasses and forks. There was only a third of the cake left, so we could eat straight from the tin. Then I looked at Alaina again. Beautiful face. Minimal makeup. Hair in a bun. Long pencil skirt. Long-sleeved blouse with a bow at the neck. Smoking hot body clad in silky librarian clothes. She wasn't the kind of person who ate cake from the pan.

I grabbed a couple plates from the cupboard, and in the spirit of maturity, I got out the wedge-shaped cake cutter. I measured out a good-sized slice and rested the cutter where I intended to cut. "Is this good, or do you want a bigger piece?"

She looked from the round cake to me, a short laugh tinkling from her. "Daniel, that's much too big."

"It's my mother's chocolate mousse, which she makes from scratch. Trust me—you're going to want a big slice. I've been known to sit down and eat the whole thing by myself."

She laughed again. Sliding between my body and the counter, she set her fingertips lightly on my wrist. While the heat of her touch made me want to lean in and put my lips on her exposed neck, she guided the cutter to a different spot. "This is plenty."

5

Then she returned to where she'd been standing, well out of my personal space. I was reeling from the lingering scent of her perfume, and she didn't seem affected. She was not at all interested in me.

Which was a curious development. Women of all ages tended to throw themselves at me. I did not lack for female companionship. Maybe she was a lesbian.

Or maybe she looked at me and saw a man who was too young and unsophisticated?

I chose to go with the lesbian angle. Maybe we were both pussy hounds.

"Are you a lesbian?" I was a dumbass. Nobody who knew and loved me would tell you differently. "Sorry. That's none of my business."

She laughed as she opened the wine. "I've slept with a couple of women. Sexuality is a spectrum, and where people fall on it is a rather fluid situation."

I did a double take, mostly because my brain was playing a naughty porn video. "I hadn't heard it expressed quite that way before. Do you tend to choose to be with women over men?"

She poured the wine. "I enjoyed it, but I just didn't click with those particular women. I mostly date men, though that's probably because society is set up that way. What made you ask that? Are you thinking you'd like to experiment with men?"

While I'd slept with too many women to count, I'd only had sex with one man, and we got together on a fairly regular basis. He was also my best friend, so it was more like a friends-with-benefits situation. In my whole life, I'd never had the urge to have sex with any other man, just Evan.

"No. I'm just—I'm stupid sometimes. Ignore me."

"It's perfectly normal to question your sexuality and experiment at your age." She laughed again and sipped the wine. "At any age. This is good wine."

"Thanks. Sophia brought it over." I didn't know much about wine. I was more of a beer connoisseur. "But we finished off my beer instead."

I plated two slices of chocolate mousse and carried them to the table. Alaina brought the wine.

"So, what plans did you cancel to be here tonight?"

She peered at me strangely. "I had planned to be here tonight. I've blocked off every other Wednesday for the next six months. Except there will be two instances when we'll need to cancel or reschedule. I was planning to email you about them."

"No, I meant did you have plans for afterward?"

6

"Oh." She waved away my concern. "Nothing exciting. I'm working on a book, so I was going to finish outlining a chapter."

I had no idea she wrote books, but I wasn't surprised. "What's your book about?"

"Issues in advanced genetics research." She put a forkful of mousse into her mouth and moaned like she'd just had an orgasm. Her eyes were closed, accenting their catlike slant and the flutter of her delicate lashes. She pulled the fork out slowly, her luscious lips clamped down to make sure she got all the chocolate.

I knew exactly how she felt about the cake, but seeing her reaction left me uninterested in the cake—unless I could lick it from her bare skin.

Her eyes popped open, and their honey color sparkled as she grinned at me. "You weren't kidding about this mousse. It's divine."

A distraction would be nice right about now. It would be nice if a phone dinged with an important message or rang with a ring tone that couldn't be ignored. Or an unmanned aircraft could crash in my parking lot. It needed to be repaved anyway.

But nothing happened, so I scrambled for a way to get my mind away from the idea of picturing her lips on my cock.

Genetic research, she'd said. I'd read a few articles about that topic. "Like the ethics of cloning?"

"Yes. Or in selecting traits for offspring. But also more technical problems associated with genetic research, like contaminated samples, inconsistencies with using DNA for diagnosing illnesses, the complexities of gender identification, the ethics—or lack of ethics—of how the health care industry could use genetic testing. Things like that."

Yeah. Majorly out of my league. I was using a tee to bat, and she was in the Hall of Fame.

"I didn't know you were interested in genetics." My degree in political science seemed inconsequential right about now. If I'd become a lawyer like my dad wanted, I might've be able to impress Alaina with something.

But I'd rejected that path in favor of owning my own martial arts business.

"My first doctorate is in genetics. That's mostly what I do at the University—teach, research, and write about genetics. I only got a second doctorate in psychology because it was interesting, but I find it pairs well with genetics."

Two doctoral degrees. I shoved aside my inadequacies because I knew she liked me as a person, and I didn't mind being the farthest moon in her orbit. "They both study why we are the way we are."

She brightened. "Yes. I'm trying to understand the extent to which our DNA determines how we interact with our environments." She explained more, going into detail about some of her theories.

I can't say I understood everything she said—though it was easier when she explained some of the technical terms—but her passion for the field came through loud and clear. I could relate to passion. I was passionate about martial arts.

We finished off the cake—I was right about her wanting more than just that paltry, normal-sized slice—and had a second glass of wine. I did participate in the conversation, and I thought a lot about the theories she posed.

About an hour later, she stopped suddenly.

I tilted my head, asking a silent question.

"I'm doing most of the talking. I'm sure you don't really care about most of my theories. It's not suitable for light conversation." She pressed her fingertip to the table, and that's where her gaze centered. "I kind of suck at casual conversation, in case you haven't noticed. Thank you for being nice about it. I should go."

She got to her feet, an abrupt move that had her knocking her thigh into the table.

I jumped up to catch her, which was stupid because she wasn't falling. "Are you okay?"

"Yes. I'll help you clean up before I go. Your loft is very clean. I hadn't expected a bachelor pad to be this tidy. My house certainly isn't this clean. Of course, I just moved in, and most of my boxes aren't even unpacked. But I'm still not a fastidious housekeeper."

Before she could grab the plates, I closed my hand over hers. "Alaina, I find your theories fascinating. I don't know enough about the field to have much to contribute, but I enjoyed listening to you talk. I think you've said more to me tonight than you have in the year you've been coming here."

She stared at my hand, shades of surprise and confusion washing over her face, but mostly she looked uncomfortable.

I eased my hand away, and she relaxed. "Sorry. You don't need to clean up, and I know it's getting late, but I wanted to show you something before you go."

Straightening up, she smoothed her palms down her skirt, but she looked intrigued. "Oh?"

"Yes. That guy was just one of many assholes in this world. You don't participate in the self-defense class, and I wanted to walk you through a couple moves before you go."

Her brows furrowed. "I took a self-defense class in college, but that was twenty years ago. I could probably do with a refresher." She met my gaze and nodded. "Okay. Should we go downstairs?"

"That's not necessary." I led her to the open space behind my sofa, so nobody would inadvertently knock into anything. "Let's start with a similar scenario to what happened in the lobby."

I positioned myself in front of her, and I put my hand on her arm the way Glen Simpson had done.

She brought her arm up counterclockwise, knocking away my hold. Then she leaned in and brought her knee up.

Part of me wondered if she was going to put force behind the groin kick. The rest of me knew her skirt and height were factors working against her.

The kick stalled less than halfway up.

"Your skirt is too tight for that kind of move. It hinders your ability to use your thighs."

Before I could talk her through an alternate plan, she hiked up her skirt, wrapped her leg around mine, and pushed me while pulling at the weak point at the back of my knee.

I didn't move because I was a lot stronger than her. "That's not a good defensive move, not unless you've got a lot of weight and more moves to back it up."

She took a step back and stared at my knee, frowning. "It should work. You should go down, and that should give me time to kick you in the face and run away."

"Physics, Alaina. I'm bigger and stronger." I could tell she was about to argue, so I showed her what I meant. "Even if you did get me down, I could pull you with me."

I went down as she'd intended, and I pulled her with me. I thought she'd fall to the side, but she landed on top of me, and she pinned my arms under her knees. She leaned forward, pressing all her weight into keeping me down.

"Ha! See, it does work."

She straddled my chest, and her skirt was up around her hips. It wasn't enough to flash me, but it definitely gave me a view she hadn't anticipated. I now knew her panties had a floral print.

"It works if you're planning to ravish me."

She blinked, that frown line wrinkling her chin, and her gaze seemed centered on my neck. "No, I'd be punching you, and then I'd hop up and run away."

To show her how much she wasn't in control, I lifted my arms, which meant I lifted her entire body. "I could toss you off me." Wiggling my arms out from under her knees, I gripped her hips. "Or I could bump and roll, reversing our positions. You don't want to get closer to your assailant, Alaina. You want to slow him down so you can run away."

"What about if I did this?" She leaned forward and pressed her forearms into my chest. "Wouldn't that keep you from moving?"

The knot of fabric that had been tied at the top of her shirt had come unraveled, and I could see even more of what she normally kept covered. Her bra matched her panties, and I estimated her breasts at a little less than a handful. The rounded tops were in shadow, and I had to rip my attention away.

"If you were bigger than your assailant, then, yes, you could use these moves. But, Alaina, you're very petite. I want to show you the arm move I used on Glen, and there's a similar one with the leg. You can use them on someone larger and stronger because it's not a matter of force. You just need to be precise." The entire time I explained, my gaze kept being drawn to look down her shirt. It was less a function of my immaturity and more a function of being a virile male faced with a set of perky breasts on a beautiful woman. I was powerless to resist. I put effort into keeping my dick in his restful state.

Wheels turned behind Alaina's eyes, and I realized that she was very book smart, but she seemed to lack common sense when it came to self-defense. I resolved to make sure she participated in the self-defense class from now on.

Then she glanced down, and she noted that her shirt had come open. "Oh, crap. I didn't mean to flash you." She sat up, resting her ass on my abdomen, and retied the bow. "Sorry about that."

"My pleasure." Oh, fuck. Why did I say that?

She laughed. "I'm sure you've seen better."

I sat up, catching her and resetting her onto my lap. I kept my hands on her hips because they really liked being there. "Don't put yourself down."

"It was more that I was trying to defuse an awkward situation." She seemed to realize she was straddling my lap and her chest was inches from mine. If she leaned forward two inches, our lips would meet. "I'm really not sure what to say to defuse this, but I think if we both laugh as we get up, it'll do the trick."

The air between us grew thick with tension. Electricity arced between us, connecting our lips with the tingle of anticipation. I forgot everything except the burning desire I had to kiss her. Her eyes widened, and her gaze flipped between my eyes and my mouth. Mostly, she watched my mouth. Her lips parted as she sucked in a breath, but she didn't move to close the distance.

Her thighs tensed, a prelude to lifting off me, and my grip tightened on her hips. "Or you could stay right where you are."

"I think we've established that this wasn't the move you had in mind."

My lips were suddenly dry, and I licked them when I really wanted to lick her. Kiss her. Taste her. Run my hands all over her sexy body.

"Daniel?" She set a hand on my shoulder. "I think you should let go of me so I can get up."

"But do you really want me to?"

Indecision had her subtly licking her lips as her free hand hovered between us. "I'm a lot older than you."

"Not that much older."

"I took self-defense twenty years ago in college, when you were probably in kindergarten. I'm sure you have no shortage of willing partners your own age."

I slid a hand to her thigh and played my thumb along the exposed flesh at her hem line. "I have sexy librarian fantasies about you."

One thing about me—when I made a mistake that I really wanted to make, I committed to it.

At my admission, she inhaled sharply, and her breasts came so close to grazing my chest. "Daniel, the work I do here—I'm conducting a study, and if we did things we shouldn't, we could ruin months of research and over a year of planning."

"You're conducting a study?" It explained why the grant had netted us such an awesome and highly qualified counselor. I shook away the question because it didn't matter. "This doesn't have anything to do with that."

She pursed her lips, a shrewd light in her honey-brown eyes. "You're talking about a one-night stand?" Then she smacked her hand against my shoulder and visibly relaxed. "Of *course* you are. Sophia told me how you're committed to living a bachelor's life. A one-night stand. Why not?"

Before I could kiss her, she pressed a finger to my lips.

"I insist you wear a condom. Do you have any?"

"Yes." I always kept condoms around. "I always use protection." Because she hadn't moved her finger, I opened my mouth and sucked on it.

"That's good." She made a sound that showed she was impressed by my finger-sucking skill. "Sexy librarian. Hmmm. I'm not sure how sexy I am, but did you have anything more specific to your fantasy? Like, did you want me to punish you for returning books late?"

I got to my feet, lifting her with me to show off how strong I was. "I'm not into spanking and punishment stuff. I was thinking you would seduce me." Setting her on her feet, I spread my hands wide. "Are you up for some role playing?"

Chapter 2—Alaina

I realized part of my skirt was still stuck around my hips. Thankfully it was long enough to still cover me to mid-thigh. I smoothed my skirt back into place and disguised how I used that move to wipe off my palms.

They were sweaty because I was nervous.

Daniel DiMarco wanted to have sex with me.

Sex.

With *me*.

Handsome didn't begin to describe him. Tall, built, sexy—these words were too plain to capture the charm and charisma oozing from him. Dark needed to be in there, too. From his dark brown hair to his deep brown eyes and his dark olive skin, everything about him dripped sex and sin.

Most of the women I counseled there spent part of every session swooning over him. Add to all those physical attributes the fact that he genuinely cared about the women and men who'd been victims of domestic violence, and you had a man who had his pick of sex partners.

He could be a cover model, and yet he didn't seem at all vain about his looks. He took time with his appearance, sure, but it wasn't excessive. He lacked artifice. Tonight, he'd taken down a man who was on the verge of threatening me so he could find and terrorize another woman. Then he'd fed me wine and the best chocolate mousse cake I'd ever eaten. Right now, he had a smudge of chocolate near the corner of his mouth.

And he wanted to role play that I was a sexy librarian who was going to seduce him. I convinced myself not to squeal like someone half my age and jump on him.

Well, I'd already jumped on him. Thinking back, I realized I'd made a fool of myself. Rather than judge me, he'd turned it into a fun experience.

And then he'd propositioned me.

Since my divorce eight years ago, I'd had three quasi-serious relationships, several casual affairs, and a handful of one-nighters. I'd gone on too many bad dates to count. The one last Friday night had—

I lived inside my own head too much. I needed to stop thinking and start seducing.

"Sexy librarian?" Part of me didn't think this was real. I didn't think it was a joke because Daniel wasn't the kind of man who would do something callous or cruel.

His gaze roved my figure. I had a well-shaped body for someone who was pushing forty and had a kid. I didn't think I was anything to write home about, but his eyes had a heavy-lidded look that indicated desire, and the pulse in his neck ticked faster than when he physically exerted himself.

"Sexy librarian," he repeated. "Very, very sexy librarian. Or did you want to do a hot-for-teacher thing? I could call you Professor Miles or Doctor Miles."

Too many people called me by those titles for it to have any kind of sexual connotation. "I prefer the librarian thing."

I glanced around his loft again, searching for any kind of reading material, and that's when I noticed a decent-sized bookcase against the wall that faced his bed. The simple lines of metal came up to my shoulder, and I couldn't keep from skimming the spines to see what kinds of things he liked to read.

Or keep around. Some people had lots of books, but they didn't read them.

Many of Daniel's had cracked spines and seemed worse for the wear.

"Looking for anything specific?"

I felt his magnetic presence behind me, and I struggled not to lean toward him. "I think you stole my line. I was thinking you could start off on the sofa with a book, and I could distract you." I drummed my fingertips against my thigh. "But maybe you should be the one looking, and I'll ask if you want help?"

With a sensual smile that made his lips look extra inviting, he switched places with me. He parked his hands on his hips, and he put a thoughtful expression on his face. Okay—go time.

I checked him out, noting the way his shirt draped over his strong shoulders. Short sleeves stretched over big biceps. The shirt clung to his torso, hugging well-defined muscles. His sweats were looser. They hung low on his hips, but they didn't cling to his ass or thighs. I'd seen the power in his legs before when he helped Sophia with the self-defense class, and I knew his bottom half was just as delectable as his top half.

As I visually stripped him naked, he lifted the hem of his shirt and made a big show of scratching his stomach. Really, he was showcasing what he had to offer.

I approached. "Hey, there. I'm Lainie. Can I help you find anything?"

He glanced up, surprised, probably by the way I shortened my name. Nobody had ever done that, but I thought it would be good for our role play, and it would differentiate the woman who was about to seduce him from the woman who counseled victims of violence and abuse at his studio.

"Hi, Lainie." He held out a hand. "I'm Daniel. It's nice to meet you."

I hated touching hands. I hated when people touched my hands, and I disliked touching their hands. It was one of my less endearing quirks. Having a young child, I'd managed to combat my aversion for him, but I did not derive pleasure from that kind of physical contact, and I generally avoided touching others in this way.

Rather than take his hand, I moved in for a closer look at the bookshelves, and I made sure his hand brushed against my boob. I liked hands touching me in other places. "Let's see what interests you, Daniel."

I bent forward to bring his attention to my backside. Clara, my best friend, thought my caboose was my best feature, so I led with that.

"Do you prefer fiction or nonfiction?" Judging from his selection, he liked anything having to do with crime. He had true stories of crime, well-known crime fiction novels, and books about history, politics, and criminal justice. Reading was sexy. My attraction to Daniel shot up dramatically just from checking out the heavy hitters on his bookshelves.

"I like both."

Glancing over my shoulder, I saw that he was checking out my ass, and I realized it wasn't the first time he'd done it. Only this time, he didn't look away suddenly or pretend his attention was on something else.

"Do you see anything interesting?"

He ripped his gaze from my ass and focused on the books. "Yes." He snagged a random title from the shelf and held it up. "Maybe this one?"

I eased it from his grip and read the title. "The People Speak. Oh, it comes with a DVD. It must be about famous speeches."

He turned it over to read the back, and I scooted closer so that my back was against his front.

"It's about what gets left out of history books. It has writings and speeches from people history ignores." He was explaining without reading the blurb.

That sounded interesting, but it wasn't why I was there. I loosened the knot on the wide strings that held the top of my shirt together and created a big, red bow that dwarfed my breasts. Holding my shirt open, I fanned myself. "Is it me, or is it suddenly hot in here?"

It occurred to me that hot flashes weren't sexy. There was no way my awkward attempts were turning Daniel on. He should have been the librarian. I was sure he had the suave, sexy talk down pat.

I twisted to look up at him, and I found his gaze glued to the exposed skin in the V of my shirt's neckline.

"Hot," he echoed. "So hot."

Never having been the femme fatale before, I decided to go for broke—since he seemed to be responding to my bad acting. I undid my blouse, and then I ran my fingertips over my exposed skin. "Are you hot, Daniel?"

"Yeah, Lainie, I am." He gripped my hips and pressed his cock against my ass. "Are librarians equipped to help patrons cool down?"

I turned around and wiggled my front against his. I was so short that my mons met up with the thickest part of his thigh. "We could take off some of our clothes and see if that helps."

He tossed the book onto the top of the shelves and pushed my blouse off my shoulders. The silky garment fluttered to the ground, but his gaze only fell to my chest. "Damn. That only made me feel warmer."

"Oh, let me help." I lifted his shirt as high as I could reach, and he bent his knees so I could get it over his head.

I was about to thank him when his hands landed on my ribs, and his thumbs brushed over my nipples. I wasn't too sensitive there, but what he was doing felt really nice. I sucked in a breath. He passed his thumbs over them a few more times. Though the lace of my bra was in the way, it was enough to get them to stand up and harden.

I parked my hand on his cock. "You should kiss a girl before you feel her up."

With that pronouncement, I stroked him through the thin cotton of his sweatpants.

He thrust against my hand. "I've never done any of this before."

16

I wasn't sure exactly what he meant, so I reached up, threaded my fingers through his silky, dark hair, and yanked his face to mine. "Kiss me, Daniel."

His lips brushed against mine, soft and inviting. I let him play for a bit, and then I ran my tongue along his lower lip. He opened, and our tongues tangled in an erotic duet.

The kiss was much better than I'd imagined it would be, and I'd fantasized about it being hot. I'd seen him kiss a woman before, a tall blonde who'd come into the studio, presumably to pick him up for a date. Or maybe she'd just come for the sex. At any rate, the kiss had showcased his skill, and just watching it had left me weak-kneed.

Daniel had strong lips, and he knew exactly how to massage them against me to make liquid heat shoot through my body. I threw my arms around his neck and rose to my tiptoes.

He grabbed my ass with both hands and lifted me so I could wrap my legs around his waist.

Well, I tried to. My skirt was too tight around my thighs to get my legs apart.

With a low rumble of laughter in his chest, he unzipped my skirt and pushed it down my hips. It joined my blouse on the floor. His kisses moved to my neck, and he found a spot that made me moan loudly.

He nipped my ear. "Like that, Lainie?"

"Yes. Do it again." I meant it to sound like an order, but it came out as a plea. I was not at all authoritative when it came to sex.

He raked his teeth over the spot, sending shivers in all directions. His hands moved over my back, caressing from shoulder to thigh, pausing to squeeze my ass in passing. Then he tugged at my hair, and my bun came loose. He ran his fingers through my hair, which felt good, but I was sure made it look like a disheveled mess.

I broke away from his amazing kisses and wiggled down his body.

"Where are you going?"

I knelt on the floor and tugged his sweats down to his thighs. "In sexy librarian porn films, there's always a blowjob."

His eyes lit with amusement, and he laughed. "There's also anal. Do you want me to fuck your ass, Lainie?"

I slid his briefs down, and his cock bobbed in my face. Taking it in hand, I swirled my tongue around the crown to get it wet, a feline smile on my face the whole time. "I'm up for it if you are."

My ex-husband had introduced me to the joys of anal sex. I'd found it very easy to orgasm that way. I figured Daniel had enough experience to know what he was doing, and if it turned out he didn't, then I could always teach him a better method.

Daniel touched my hair, smoothing it back so he could watch me suck his cock. "Fuck, Lainie. Yes. I never expected you to be such a dirty-minded hot librarian. I like it."

I wrapped both hands around his cock, masturbating it while I sucked as much as I could into my mouth—which was maybe half. Daniel was well-endowed. He worked with me, thrusting his hips in time to the pace I set. He moaned, but when he really started enjoying it, he eased my head back.

"Let's get you naked, Lainie. It's entirely too hot for you to be wearing so many clothes."

Because I was only wearing a bra and panties, I laughed. Daniel pulled me to my feet, and he undressed me the rest of the way while also kicking away his sweats and briefs. He palmed my breast, playing with the nipple, and then he bent to take it into his mouth.

He lifted me, and we came down on the bed with him on top. In the bedroom, I loved being lifted and moved, positioned by my lover. It was a huge aphrodisiac for me, which was strange because I wasn't keen on being touched or manhandled outside the bedroom.

He touched me, firm caresses with his hands, and hot, wet kisses from his mouth. He urged my legs apart, kissing a path down my belly, and he settled between my legs.

He started slowly, alternating flicks of his tongue with longer licks. Molten heat rushed to my core, and by the time he locked his lips around the tip of my clit, I was primed. I thrust against his face, crying out as I approached that cliff. When I was almost there, he penetrated me with a finger, and that sent me over the edge.

"Oh, yes, Daniel. Fuck, yes!" My chest heaved from the effort, and my body writhed, unable to stay still.

I heard foil ripping. Daniel grasped my ankles and dragged me to the edge of the bed. Then he flipped me over so that my bottom half dangled, and my breasts pressed against the covers.

"Are you ready, Lainie, my hot librarian?"

"Yes," I breathed. "More. I want more."

He lifted my hips and positioned my knees under me with my legs spread wide. I was too weak to support my head and keep my face from mashing into the comforter, but Daniel didn't seem to notice. He fed his cock into my quivering channel and fucked me like a champion porn star. His pace varied. He started out slow and gentle, and then he jackhammered into me for a few thrusts. Then he went back to slow, with a twist of his hips before he slammed into me for those last inches.

When he used force, my body scooted farther onto the mattress. He moved me back a few times, and I realized he was playing with me, toying with my body to draw out the experience.

No wonder his lovers begged for a repeat performance.

I wouldn't, though. He was already out of my league. I intended to ride him until we both broke because I wanted to replay this memory when I was alone with my vibrator.

The tight coil inside me sprang loose, and I came again, harder this time, bowing my back and screaming into the covers.

Just when I thought he'd follow me into orgasm, he flipped me over again. One thing about having a lover who could lift and move me however he wanted—it was fucking hot. He spread me out on the center of the bed, and he held himself over me. He captured my lips for another kiss as he fed his cock back into me.

This time, he fucked in earnest. His hands roamed over my body while he licked, kissed, and sucked. I did the same, raking my nails over his skin, kissing the spots on his neck that made his whole body shudder, and then I reached between us to fondle his balls.

With a hiss, he pressed his forehead to mine. "Pull a little harder, Lainie. Yes, like that. Oh, fuck, yes."

I squeezed as well, alternating that with the pulling. With the skillful way he fucked, I was close to coming again. My manual dexterity faltered, and I let go of his balls. I gripped his shoulders, my nails digging into his incredible muscles, and I lost control.

Daniel cried out as well. He held me closer and surged one last time, his body shuddering as he climaxed.

Then he collapsed on top of me.

I was too spent to care that I couldn't breathe.

After a few moments, he rolled to the side, spreading out next to me. His chest heaved, and his olive skin had a sexy glow to it.

"Damn, Lainie. That was fucking amazing."

I agreed, but I was still too rubbery to do more than nod.

His head lifted, and he studied me with a frown. "Lainie, are you okay?"

"Peachy." My lips would barely move, slurring my answer. I closed my eyes, and I felt him flop back down. Minutes passed, and my wits returned. I inhaled deeply, finally remembering how to breathe. "Daniel?"

"Yeah?" He rubbed a hand down his face.

"You've tuckered me out. It's been a long day for me." I rolled toward him because I felt eye contact was expected so he could see my sincerity. "Can we do a rain check on the anal stuff?"

He'd lifted his head again, and I watched wheels spinning in his mind, not finding traction.

"You don't have to. I know it was a one-night stand, so I'm not sure you can technically do a rain check. But I promised anal, and I feel bad for not following through."

He sat up, and I did as well.

"Lainie, you don't owe me sex—of any kind. I gave you three orgasms, and you rocked my world. You have no reason to feel guilty for anything. I had fun." He waggled his eyebrows. "And I know you did as well. That's what's important."

Relief rushed through me. I squeezed his wrist. "I did. Thank you." Then I got up and gathered my clothes.

Daniel slid into his sweatpants as I took my things into the bathroom so I could freshen up and get dressed. When I emerged, he was still bare-chested, which was a mouth-watering visual, and he was cleaning up the dishes. I paused for a second because I'd never seen a man do the dishes without being asked. One day, I hoped my son would be the kind of person who just did what needed doing without making it into an end-of-days event.

He shut off the water and dried his hands. "I never taught you the moves I wanted you to learn. How about you participate in class next time?"

I wrinkled my nose. "I don't want to get sweaty before a counseling session. I'll get itchy, and I won't focus on the therapy."

"Lainie—"

"Daniel, it's fine." I cut him off, but I was also smiling because he was still calling me by the hot librarian nickname. "Look, if you want to cash in on that rain check, let me know by the Sunday after next if you're free after the session."

He frowned. "Why Sunday?"

"Because I'll need time to clear my schedule."

"I thought you didn't have plans tonight."

I'd never said that. "I'm writing a book. I had plans to outline a chapter. I have a deadline, and I've divided the work into manageable sessions, which I put into my daily schedule." I tried to run my life on a schedule. Not a week passed that I didn't have to revise the schedule, but it was better than leaving everything up to chance. If I did that, I'd fixate on the few things I wanted to do, and the things I needed to do would be pushed to a vague or nonexistent 'later' date.

"How about you clear it so I can show you self-defense moves?"

I wasn't keen on that plan, but I could tell from the set of his jaw that Daniel was committed to making sure I could defend myself. Since he was a huge proponent of that kind of thing, I knew it was important to him. "Okay. I'll have to bring a change of clothes. I don't want to get sweaty and gross in my work clothes."

"Whatever works for you." He slid his feet into sandals. "I'll walk you to your car."

At the car, I had no idea what to say to the guy who'd given me a night I'd never forget, but who I'd keep seeing every other week. So I said the only thing that came to mind. "Thank you for the cake."

He laughed. "My pleasure."

I got into the car, but he held onto the door, so I waited for him to continue.

"You know, we don't have to wait two weeks for that rain check."

I wanted to put on my seat belt, but I needed for the door to be closed first. It was yet another of my quirks. I had to do certain things in order. I mentally rearranged my writing schedule, and I kept in mind the hours his studio was open for business. "What about next Thursday?"

"Tomorrow?" He grinned.

"No. A week from tomorrow." Tomorrow, I was going to be very busy catching up on the work I hadn't completed tonight. "I can come by at closing time, but I can only stay for an hour-and-a-half."

He didn't look all that thrilled about the idea.

I began to think I'd made a horrible mistake tonight. Getting involved with Daniel, even temporarily, couldn't be anything but a bad idea. I stopped pushing. "Look, why don't you take some time to think about it, and text me with your decision by Sunday at eight."

He tilted his head and studied me. "You're kind of eccentric."

I shrugged. Of all the labels I'd been given in my life, that one wasn't bad. "Yeah, but I do butt stuff, which gives you incentive to overlook my quirks."

Again, he laughed. "I'll text you."

Two days later, I met Clara for lunch. Clara had designated herself my best friend when we'd met at a support group for new mothers. I'd misjudged the time it would take me to get Zack and myself to the meeting location, and I'd arrived early. I sat alone in the empty room, holding my sleeping infant.

As people came in, they ignored me. I was used to being overlooked or rejected. As Daniel had observed, I was a bit of an oddball. When I was feeling confident, I was better at blending in. But unexpected situations made me uncomfortable, which made it far more likely I'd say or do something out of the ordinary.

The support group was full of mothers who had partners at home, while I had nothing. I'd taken a pregnancy test at work, and I'd rushed home to share the good news with my husband. We'd been trying for a year, and he was working from home that day. I'd wanted to tell him the news in person, and I couldn't wait to share the joy. Unfortunately, he'd been otherwise occupied with sucking my brother's dick.

My life had imploded.

I'd divorced Adam, who'd subsequently married my brother. My parents argued their side, insisting that I was being selfish and overreacting. They'd said that of course Adam had fallen for Cameron. He was charming and attractive, where I was awkward and not as pretty as I'd once been.

I'd cut them all out of my life.

Well, not Adam. We shared custody of Zack. I'd written it into the terms of the divorce that they could only refer to Cameron as an uncle, not as a parent, and so Zack called my brother Uncle Cameron.

I'd ended up being a bundle of nerves at that first meeting. My divorce had been finalized months before, but I was still mourning the loss of the life I'd expected. I was off-kilter and taking care of a newborn. Later, Clara would tell me I had been giving off manic vibes. I'd worn two different shoes, and the different height on the heels made me walk funny. Worse than that, I had high-pitched hiccups, and I had gas, the squeaky kind you couldn't hide or blame on the baby.

Clara had parked herself next to me and said I looked like I needed a friend. She patted my hand, which freaked me out. I'd passed gas and cried, which made the hiccups louder.

Rather than abandon me, she'd laughed and farted louder. "Oh, good," she'd said. "I found my people."

Her husband had passed away suddenly when she was pregnant, so she'd been alone as well, though her extended family was supportive, so at least she had them. Eight years later, we were still best friends, and so were our boys.

Clara sailed inside the diner, her hair floofed out in a cloud of black curls, and she docked on the bench across from me. She wore a blue sundress with a skirt that billowed around her long legs. "You'd better start by explaining the text you sent Wednesday night."

I'd sent her an eggplant and a peach emoji, which I thought covered the topic sufficiently. She'd called me first thing in the morning, demanding details, but I'd overslept, and I'd been running late for work.

"I had a one-night stand with a handsome, younger man."

She adjusted her skirt, smoothing it under her legs, and digested what I'd said.

I moved to the next topic. "You're wearing a new dress, and you look very pretty. Do you have a date?"

Clara was the opposite of me in every way. She was eight inches taller, and she liked to wear heels that put her above most people. She had a voluptuous figure that drew attention everywhere she went, and she had an outgoing, vivacious personality.

If I didn't have her in my life, I'd sit home all the time. Clara made me go out and do things. She was gregarious and charming, and she made me say yes to new experiences.

She'd booked a zip-lining expedition for next month. I wasn't sure how I felt about that. Zack was a lot more adventurous than I, and he was thrilled at the idea. I recognized the ways Clara made me a better person, and I prized our friendship.

In return, I was straightforward, honest, and loyal. When she needed me, I dropped everything to be there. Her mother had battled cancer three years ago, and I'd helped with caring for Deon so Clara could be with her mom. Deon referred to me as his bonus mom. On a more regular basis, I consulted on every event in her life. You know—regular best-friend stuff.

Normally, if I was going to have a one-night stand with someone, I would run it past Clara first. She was great at reading people, and I trusted her assessment. I sucked at reading people, and I had a streak of impulsivity that had led me astray many times.

"Uh-uh." She wagged a finger at me. "You, first. Tell me about the guy. Where did you meet him?"

"It was Daniel, the man who sponsors the support group I facilitate every other Wednesday."

Her mouth opened, freezing as she selected an appropriate response.

I knew she required more information. "After the session, I was cleaning up, and a man came in. He threatened one of the women in the group, and he threatened me. Daniel saw the last part, so he did some martial arts move. Then he said I must be shaken up. He took me upstairs to his loft, and he fed me chocolate mousse cake and two glasses of wine. Then we had sex. I had three orgasms. He intended a second round, I think, but it was late, and I was tired, so I offered a rain check, and then I went home."

Her mouth closed, a sure sign she'd arrived at a decision for what to say. "Alaina, you've been going there for a year. You've known him for a *year*. That's not a one-night stand."

"We agreed it would be."

"Of course you did."

The server set salads in front of us both. We always ate the same thing when we went to that restaurant, so I'd ordered a Greek salad for her before she'd arrived. I always got the Thai with sesame dressing. I

23

liked the extra crunch to go with all the soft textures of the rest of the salad.

Clara poured dressing from the small cup onto her salad. "You make it sound so clinical. I want details. Describe him."

"About six feet tall. He has a larger frame and a build to match. He works out, so his muscles are very strong and quite large. Ethnically, he's Italian. His ancestors probably came from the southern region of Italy and mixed with groups in northern Africa. Thick brown hair that isn't thinning or receding. Dark brown eyes with long, dark eyelashes. Aquiline nose. Square jaw line. He's twenty-six or seven, and his sexual stamina was quite impressive."

Clara fished in her purse and pulled out her phone. "What is his last name?"

"DiMarco. His studio is called DiMarco Martial Arts."

She punched in the information. "He's on social media. Oh, *hello* handsome!"

"I said he was handsome."

"You didn't say he was drop-dead gorgeous. Damn, Alaina. He's a work of art." She showed me the image she'd found on social media. "I'd flick my bean to a picture of him."

He was at some sort of outdoor function. In one hand he held a plate of foods one would find at a barbeque. The grin on his face hinted at mischief.

"Yes, that's him," I confirmed. "He gives great oral, and he flicked my bean for me."

Laughter roared from Clara. She slid her phone back into her purse. "He had his arm around a woman in the picture. He seems like the kind of man who gets around."

"That was his sister, Sophia. She is the main self-defense instructor for our group. Daniel helps out most days." I chewed and swallowed, and then I addressed Clara's other point. "Sophia calls him a slut, and he doesn't deny it. He goes through a lot of lovers."

"I'll bet. That smile just oozes charm and sex appeal."

"I made him wear a condom." I was kind of put off by Clara's impression of Daniel. "But that's not all there is to him. He's a huge proponent of this self-defense program. He applied for the initial grant, and he's procured a few others over the past year to provide child care for the women who need it. He's really nice to me."

"Three times," Clara quipped. "That *is* nice."

"Anyway, we agreed it was a one-night stand, and we agreed it wouldn't interfere with the counseling and self-defense program." Belatedly, I recalled the offer I'd made. "There might be an addendum. The rain check I offered was for anal sex."

A coughing fit seized Clara. Her eyes watered, and she spit food into her napkin.

"Are you okay?"

"Geez, Alaina. I didn't know you went for back door action." She looked at her phone again. "Though, if I hooked up with a guy that hot, he might be able to convince me to go there."

I hadn't offered it on the basis of his looks. Being blessed genetically didn't make one predisposed to being good at sex. "As long as he's good at it, I don't really care if he's handsome or unprepossessing."

She leaned forward and lowered her volume. "It just seems dirty and gross."

I shrugged. "It can be. I mean, you have to understand what you're getting yourself into and not be bothered by it. It's definitely something I prefer to schedule so I can prepare. I will only do it in the evening, though, and never when I'm constipated."

Clara shook her head. "Okay, no. I can't." She shivered in revulsion. "Not my cup of tea."

"That's okay." I dove back into my salad. "You and I have very different tastes."

She thought for a moment, and then she shook her head and speared salad pieces.

I wasn't used to her holding back. "What?"

She shook her head. "No. It's—no." She lifted her fork and put it down twice. "Alaina, he's hot and more than a decade younger than you. He could have his pick of willing sex partners."

I understood her question. "I told him I was too old for him, and he said he found me attractive, and he had hot librarian fantasies. Now he has hot librarian memories. It's one night, not a relationship."

She exhaled. "Okay, as long as you're not getting gooey feelings for him. I know you, Alaina. You've been burned by life, but you're a romantic at heart."

I disagreed, but I knew better than to have that argument with Clara again. She was a woman of strong convictions, and she only changed them if life proved her wrong. As she'd nursed me through a shattered heart, she had decided I was afraid to love again, but that I could fall in love easily if I met the right person.

As for my opinion, I'd pretty much given up on finding a life partner. I was content with the way my life had turned out, and that was huge for me.

"Plus, he doesn't look like a Dom, and you need a Dom in your life."

Clara and I had discussed this before. While Adam didn't identify as a Dom, he was the take-charge type. I'd liked that about him more than anything else, and when he'd cheated on me, I'd been devastated. It was difficult to conceive of letting myself trust someone enough to submit to them on a regular basis, though I did engage in BDSM play on an occasional basis with casual partners.

"He manhandled me quite well," I scoffed. "He doesn't need to be a Dom to be what I need sexually. He just needs to be aggressive, which he was."

Clara didn't appear at all convinced. "Good thing it was a one-nighter with a possible rain check."

"Yeah." Something occurred to me. "Clara, you don't think that night should go on my 'Shouldn't've' list, do you?"

I suffered from making impulsive decisions. At the time, they always seem like the right course of action. I felt good about it, right up until it blew up in my face. I had many things on my 'Shouldn't've' list, and falling in love with Adam topped it.

The list was named for the Buzzcocks' song, *Ever Fallen In Love (With Someone You Shouldn't've.)* I'd fallen for the double use of apostrophe, and I'd adopted it as the title for my list. Over the years, I'd added to it—impulsivity was the bane of my existence, while its twin, procrastination, was the other thing I worked to combat—and it had grown very long.

You'd think someone like me, who scheduled my whole week on Sunday night, wouldn't have that problem. But I had a bad habit of not sticking to my schedule. The moment something else came up—like an invitation to a one-night stand with a handsome younger man, or if Zack asked to stop to get an ice cream cone on the way home from school—my schedule went out the window. I still made one because it helped me prioritize important tasks and appointments, but I didn't stress over changes.

"I honestly don't know," she said. "It's either going to blow over, and neither of you will mention it again, or it's going to blow up, and you're going to be devastated. I'm hoping for the former."

The sweetness and loyalty of my friend made me feel warm inside, though I mostly dismissed the dire part of her prediction. "Well, if the addendum happens, I'll text you a pointing finger and a circled finger emoji. Those mean anal sex. And, if it's good, I'll put an excited face at the end. Now, tell me about your date. Did it already happen, or is it coming up tonight? Did you need me to watch Deon? I don't have Zack, but Dee can hang out while I work on my book."

She waved away my offer. "It's tomorrow for lunch. I'm taking the dress for a test drive today, and my dad is taking Deon to a baseball game."

Chapter 3—Evan

Running a fledgling construction company wasn't easy, but I'd gone into this venture knowing full well what I was in for. My best friend's father owned a successful landscaping business that he'd created from nothing, and he was a supportive mentor. Though I had a good relationship with my own parents, I still called Anna and David DiMarco by "Mom" and "Dad" rather than their given names. From the first time Daniel had brought me home with him my sophomore year of high school, the DiMarco family had wholeheartedly embraced me.

At home, I was the seventh of nine total kids. My parents were great, and I loved my family, but sometimes I got lost in the shuffle. I was a lettuce kid—often overlooked because the cheese was zesty or the tomato popped or the turkey was glazed with honey. Stuck in the middle and surrounded by louder and more demanding siblings, it was nice to have the DiMarcos looking out for me.

Not a day went by that I didn't talk to Daniel, either in person or over the phone, and when we weren't together, we texted a lot. I'd had a couple guys dump me because they thought I was too close with Daniel. Women didn't mind so much, but men did.

One thing I'd never told anyone was the fact that Dan and I hooked up whenever we weren't seeing anyone else. We weren't ashamed of it, but if his parents ever found out, they'd start planning a wedding. While I would have been okay with it, Daniel wouldn't. He was still searching for something intangible, and he couldn't be hurried on his journey. Since neither of us were into cheating or dishonesty, we stayed friends with frequent—and very satisfying—benefits.

Also, I was a Dom, and Daniel viewed the whole BDSM lifestyle with mild amusement. As long as I approached him playfully, he responded. If I got too serious and gruff, he lost interest.

It was yet another reason we kept it casual.

Right now, neither of us were in a relationship. Work had been grueling today, and I wanted to blow off steam with my best friend, so I headed to his martial arts studio at a time when his classes should be ending. It was Thursday, and he was open until nine.

I found him in the small arena, teaching advanced moves to a group of six teenagers and four adults. Two students faced off. Daniel called praise and corrections as they sparred. I watched until there was a break in the action.

He glanced up and saw me.

I smiled and pointed upstairs, indicating that I'd wait for him there. We hadn't formally made plans, but we were the kind of guys who dropped in on each other all the time. I didn't expect sex, but I was definitely going to make a move.

In his loft, I grabbed a beer and looked through the stack of mail on the edge of the counter. I sorted out the junk and put it in the recycling. Then I poked around in the fridge. Daniel was an excellent cook, and he often had great leftovers. I found some lasagna and heated it up. Most nights, I was too spent to cook, and I wasn't great at it anyway. I'd eaten half a bag of chips, and then I'd munched an apple because the healthy evened out the unhealthy, or some shit like that.

When he came up, he found me finishing off his lasagna and paging through a sports magazine.

His gaze fell to the remnants of food on my plate. "Did you notice I used ground turkey instead of beef?"

I hadn't noticed a difference. My palate was the opposite of discerning. "It was good. Your mother's tomato sauce makes anything taste amazing."

"It was my sauce," he said drily. "We all put our own twist on it. Now, my mom's chocolate mousse cake recipe, I don't mess with. That's perfection."

"Yes," I agreed as I rinsed my empty plate and set it in the sink. "I didn't see any in there." He'd posted a picture of it online two days ago. I'd been hoping for a slice.

"We finished it last night." He snagged a beer from the fridge. "Are you going to put that in the dishwasher?"

I caged him against the refrigerator. My hands rested on either side of his head, but my elbows weren't bent, so there was distance between us. "It needs to soak first. Who is we?"

"Alaina. You know—the therapist who does counseling here for Sophia's self-defense class?"

Daniel liked to pretend the class was Sophia's—that she'd thought of it and done the work to get it up and running—but it wasn't. She did most of the teaching, but he'd been the one to research grants and

29

work with local community groups to keep it going. It meant the world to him, but he routinely downplayed its significance.

He also had a voracious sweet tooth, and sharing his dessert wasn't a default setting. I fingered a lock of his silky brown hair. "It was nice of you to share your cake."

"Some dickhead came here, looking for one of the women, and he tried to attack Alaina. She was shaken up, so I brought her up and gave her cake and a glass of wine." His gaze alternated between my lips and my eyes, and I understood the game he was playing. Daniel was—at best—a reluctant submissive, and if I tried to put a label on him, he'd dig his heels in.

I leaned closer, until only inches separated our lips. His breathing rate increased, but he didn't move. "Did you fuck her as well? That'd calm her nerves."

I expected him to say he hadn't. Not only was the therapist somewhat older than us, but I knew Daniel wouldn't do anything to jeopardize the program. He bit his lower lip and didn't say anything.

"Daniel?" I used my Dom voice, which always affected him, though he'd never admit it.

"We had sex."

"She's not your usual type."

"She did a hot librarian thing."

I'd never seen the woman, but the image I had in my head wasn't one of a hot librarian. From the way Sophia and Daniel had talked about her, I'd pictured someone matronly. "Is she attractive?"

A sultry, playful light entered his eyes. He set his beer on the counter, and then he slid his cold hand along my neck until he had it on my nape. Daniel could take me down in a heartbeat, but it would take a lot to make him actually do it.

"You know what's hot?" His breath, which smelled like my favorite lager, washed over my lips. "You are."

Subject changed. That was okay. I didn't really want to talk about a piece of ass he'd scored when I was busy seducing him.

"I'm going to bind your wrists and blindfold you while I do things to your body." With a gentle glide of my fingertips, I tickled across the erogenous spot under his ear and on his neck. "Things that are going to make you quiver and thrash, moan and groan."

Daniel wasn't into this stuff the way I was, so there was a fifty percent chance he'd veto the idea. Sixty percent because he'd fucked a hot librarian the night before.

"You're going to need to be more specific."

I claimed his strong, sensual lips with my kiss. His hand, still on the back of my neck, tightened its grip, and he groaned into my mouth. When I had us both panting, I broke away.

"Trust me. I've never let you down."

"Evan, you know I don't like being tied up."

I disagreed with his interpretation. He loved what I did to him when he was bound. Even now, his cock swelled in his loose pants, pressing against the front with a visible erection.

"Just your wrists." I touched his wrists lightly. "Blindfold." A light caress to his temple. "And your thighs." I traced lines across his legs. "Cock ring." I cupped his erection. "You're going to come so hard that you won't remember the hot librarian."

"She was funny," he said. "I see her twice a month, and I might see her again. She gave me a rain check on anal."

Abruptly, I released him and stepped back. "Is that where you want to be tonight—with her?"

His jaw worked as he watched me. Then he picked up his beer and downed the rest of it. The whole time, he kept his gaze on me.

"Answer me, Daniel." I leaned against the island counter, folding my arms over my chest.

He set the empty bottle down, and then he took two steps, erasing the space between us. A whole inch taller, he drew himself up to try to tower over me. "I'll let you tie me up and do whatever you want to me, but once you untie me, I'm going to have my way with you."

I gripped his hips and pulled him to me. "When I'm done with you, you're going to pass out from having a good time."

He loved a challenge. A smile played around his lips. "We'll see."

I kissed him again, taking control of our interaction with one, simple act. He submitted to me, as he always did, his body relaxing against mine, and his arms wrapped around my neck.

Then I broke away. "Let's get you naked and bound."

He slid out of his clothes in seconds, tossing them toward the closet where he kept his hamper and washer-dryer set.

I followed, tossing my shirt onto the back of his sofa. Daniel liked my body, and this would give him one last pleasing visual before I blindfolded him.

I'd already stowed the bag with my BDSM gear on the other side of his bed. I'd also removed his comforter, folding it at the top of the bed to provide a cushion between his head and the headboard, and also to elevate his upper body a bit. I tended to get rough when I was in the throes of passion.

He centered himself on the bed, his hand lazily sliding along the shaft of his cock.

I buckled a leather cuff around the wrist on his free hand, and then I connected the D-ring on the cuff to a short length of rope that I tied to the post on the headboard. Then I did the same with his other hand, forcing a stop to his masturbation attempt.

He watched me through heavy-lidded eyes. I kissed him, trailing sucking kisses and nibbling bites down his neck and along his collar bone. I ran my palms over his chest and up his arms. Limited to the places he could reach, he kissed me back. His arms jerked as he tested the bonds, trying to break free so he could touch me the way I touched him.

I kissed my way down his magnificent body, letting him watch me work. By the time I got to his cock, it was rigid, and a pearly drop leaked from the tip.

"Awww—does somebody liked being tied up?"

He snorted. "Somebody likes having his cock sucked."

I had been about to give him some attention there, but when I was told to do something, my contrary nature made me not want to do it. With a sly grin, I reached into my bag of tricks and pulled out a small strip of leather.

Daniel shook his head. "No fucking way. The last time you put that thing on me, I thought my dick would explode."

I pinched the tip of his cock, picking up the drop of pre-come, and then I licked it from my fingers. "It did, and you loved it."

From the way he shifted his legs, I could tell a struggle was imminent, so I got the spreader bar from my bag. He didn't protest as I secured cuffs around his thighs and attached the spreader bar.

I knelt between his spread legs and held the cock ring up for him to see. If he really didn't want it on, he could use his safeword. I waited several heartbeats, watching the subtleties of his expression as he waged an internal battle. When he pressed his lips together, I knew he'd decided to submit to my desire.

More importantly, his erection had softened to half-mast. Daniel leaned his head back and closed his eyes.

The purpose of the blindfold was to take away his sense of sight. I didn't want him to stop using it until I decided he couldn't. "Open your eyes, Daniel. Watch what I'm doing."

He opened his eyes and lifted his head, regarding me with a wrinkle of distaste on his nose. "Why? Do you want me to put one on you?"

"Maybe next time." I laughed, mostly because he thought I wouldn't wear one. "I didn't bring mine."

"Can't you just tie a rope around it like you do mine?"

Mine was metal and custom-sized. I would buy one for Daniel, but we both avoided anything that might put the fucking side of our relationship on more permanent footing. With a grin, I gathered his cock and balls, and I wound the thick string of leather around them before securing them with a knot that could be undone with a tug.

Daniel watched, and before I finished, his full erection was back.

Then I slipped the blindfold over his eyes.

Setting up my violet wand took a few minutes. I kept an eye on Daniel. As I moved around, making small noises, he became increasingly tense. Daniel was the kind of person who fought giving up control for as long as he could. We didn't always scene, but when we did, I relished forcing him to give up control. It was good for him.

I attached a ball tip electrode and turned it to a low setting. It glowed red. I started at his thigh. He jumped, scooting his leg away. Inching up the power, I tried again.

This time, he growled. "What the hell are you doing?"

I knew better than to react to his apparent displeasure. He was going to love what I was doing to him, but I'd have to drag him, kicking and screaming, which was why I'd tied him up. "What does it feel like?"

"It kind of tickles, but not in a ticklish way. More like in a flick-that-bug-off-me way."

Turning it up even more, I dragged it down the side of his thigh.

His growl turned to a reluctant moan.

"How's that?"

"That better not be a knife."

I knew he drew the line at anything that would cut or burn his skin. He didn't mind bruises or abrasions from restraints, though he didn't love when those happened.

"Evan? Please tell me it's not a knife."

"It's not a knife." Tracing the line down his thigh, I kept going.

"For real, it's not?"

I pressed it harder so he could better feel the blunt tip. "For real, it's not."

Down his calf I went.

"It feels really fucking good. Sharp, but in a good way because you're not using a knife."

Reversing direction, I dragged it up, retracing the places I'd already been. His body writhed as he gasped and moaned. He looked so fucking sexy, bound and blindfolded—and utterly at my mercy.

Changing things up, I put the electrode away and got out my body contact cable. This thing would electrify my whole body, and my fingers, or anything metallic I touched, would become an electrode.

I'd assured him I wasn't using a knife, but I hadn't said anything about a fork. A quick trip to the kitchen later, I held a fork in my hand. I started out using my fingertips. I held them over the sensitive skin on the side of his abdomen, about a quarter inch away, and I experimented with moving closer and farther.

Daniel shivered.

"Do you like that?"

"Yes."

This method let me touch him, and I really liked touching him. He'd always responded to my caresses, but now I drove him out of his mind. He writhed as much as he could in his restrained position. Moans fell from his sensual lips, and he begged me to fuck him.

I went for the fork instead. The electricity coursing through my body went through the fork. Four tines scratched over his stomach, and he cried out. I scattered short scratches over his body, stimulating an inch here and three inches there.

"Fuck, Evan. What are you doing to me? It's too much. I can't—I can't—"

The point of sensory overload was approaching. I pushed him, forcing him to endure a pleasure so good, it bordered on pain. By the time I stopped, redness suffused his skin, he was covered in sweat, his chest heaved, and he'd scooted so far away from the headboard that his arms were stretched out tautly.

Relenting, I put the fork down.

"You're doing very well, Daniel. You suffer beautifully."

"Something wrong with you," he murmured.

"You're my best friend, so that means there's also something wrong with you." I brushed a kiss across his lips. Because I was still using the contact cable, electricity tingled on his lips.

He flinched. "I didn't think it was that dry in here."

"It's not." Careful not to touch his skin, I removed his blindfold.

Those deep brown eyes blinked at me as his pupils adjusted to the light.

Before he could begin with the questions I knew he had, I licked his cock.

He shouted, and his hips lifted from the bed. "The fuck is wrong with you?"

Wrapping my hand around his shaft, I continued licking. He bucked and bellowed, but I moved with him. Then I closed my mouth around his cock.

With a shout and a lot of swearing, he climaxed in my mouth. I didn't even have to remove the cock ring.

Limp and spent, he didn't move while I disconnected my electrical equipment. Then I attended to his cock ring.

He watched me disconnect the spreader bar and remove the cuffs from his wrists and thighs. He cooperated as I rolled him over and drizzled lube on his anus. He sighed with pleasure as I sank into his body.

Seated deep inside him, I took a moment to savor what it felt like to have complete control over Daniel. I rested my full weight on him, and I nuzzled the back of his neck. With my whole heart and soul, I loved my best friend. I knew he loved me back, but the two of us would never admit it out loud.

I threaded my fingers through his, and I fucked him like a madman. Beneath me, Daniel sighed and moaned contentedly.

Chapter 4—Daniel

"Sophia, do you have Alaina's cell phone number?" I'd called my sister because it turned out I only had a landline and email contact for Alaina, and the landline led to her office phone.

"I think so. Why do you need it? Are you canceling a session?" The sounds of a bustling kitchen faded as Sophia went to a different room.

I'd texted her for the contact information, but she hadn't responded. "No. She asked me to find out something and text her, and I realized I don't have her number."

"What did she want to know?"

Normally I'd tell Sophie whatever she wanted to know. From the day she was born, a whole ten months after me, we'd been close. I had few secrets from my little sister, but if I told her I'd slept with Alaina, she'd cut off my nuts and feed them to squirrels.

"Fuck, Sophie. Never mind. I'll email her." It was her University email and office phone number, which was another reason why I wanted to send a text. Alaina was the kind of person who wouldn't want a personal email on her work account.

"You'd better not be hitting on her." Sophie picked up on my evasion, and she came back with suspicion.

"Yeah, because hitting on someone by text works."

"You could send her a dick pic."

"When has that ever worked to pick up a woman?" There was no way in hell I'd send anyone a picture of my junk. With my luck, it would end up on social media as a split-screen meme. The first image would show a baby carrot and say, "That's not a dick." The second would show my family jewels and say, "THAT'S a dick."

No fucking way I was going to take a chance.

"If Drew sent one to me, I'd respond." She giggled. Drew was her submissive boyfriend. He was a chef, and she managed his business, and they lived in a gigantic house in a gated community. I'd once

36

asked Drew if he was going to ask my sister to marry him, and he'd said it was her job to do the asking because she was the Domme.

"You're already together. If a guy you barely know sends you one out of the blue, you're probably going to block him. I'm not sending a dick pic to the very capable therapist who runs the free counseling sessions at my studio. If you want to get up close and personal with her, send a picture of your private parts, but if she quits because of you, I'm never going to let you forget it."

Now that I'd suitably turned the conversation around, Sophia made a doubtful noise. "Good point. How is Evan?"

Sophia—and by extension, Drew—were the only people who knew Evan and I hooked up. I knew she was asking along those lines. "He got a violet wand machine, and he used it on me. It was fun. I bet Drew would like it."

"He does," she said. "He bought a kit, and we've played with it a few times. I need more practice before I can do some of the advanced techniques."

"You should get the thing that makes your whole body an electrode, and then you should give him a blowjob."

She made a thoughtful noise, and I knew she was already planning her next scene with Drew. "I'll send you Alaina's information, but don't think I've forgotten you haven't told me why you want it. I will find out, big brother."

The fact that she sent the information meant she didn't think anything untoward was going on, and that was a good thing. Lainie and I both knew we needed to keep what happened between us from anyone involved with the program.

Evan didn't count. I told Evan about all my sex partners, and he disclosed his to me.

I texted Lainie that Thursday wouldn't work for me. Kendra was gearing up for a major tournament Friday and Saturday, and she had begged me for a longer practice session Thursday. But Lainie didn't care about any of that. She only wanted to know my decision so she could modify her writing schedule.

She texted back, "Okay, thanks for letting me know." There was no request to reschedule or questions asking for an explanation. She didn't flirt, hint, or otherwise refer to our one-night stand.

I'd never had a woman do that before. Lainie—Alaina—was the opposite of clingy. I couldn't figure out if I liked that or not. I'd ended budding relationships before when I felt the woman had become clingy. Right now, I wanted to text again, to ask if she had another night free, but I didn't want to come off as clingy or needy.

It took me two weeks—until the day before I'd see her again—to realize that perhaps she hadn't texted back for the same reason. Technically, the ball was in my court. She'd offered me a follow-up session, so it was up to me to reschedule. I should have texted her back, and now it was too late.

When she came in Wednesday, I was irritated with myself.

Students for Sophia's self-defense class were trickling in, but the child-care worker I'd hired hadn't yet arrived, so I was minding four children of toddler age. I liked kids because they were fun to play with. I was trying to get them to sing a song identifying body parts that also made them move around, but I was having limited success. Two were with me. One was trying, but he didn't quite know the difference between his knees and toes, and the fourth had her hands thrown in the air and was belting out key words at the top of her lungs.

Alaina came in. The students gravitated in her direction, and even I felt the pull of a need to connect with her. I wanted her to smile at me, to put her hand on my wrist or shoulder as she said my name and asked how I was doing.

Her blouse was blush-colored today. It was sleeveless and had a scooped neck that would gape open if she tried to pin me down. I could make out the straps of her bra through it in the back, and I wanted to know if it was satin and lace like the last one had been.

And did her panties match?

Her skirt was different than what she usually wore. This one was longer, hanging all the way down to her ankles, but the stretchy fabric was slit to mid-thigh on both sides. It was looser, not quite hugging her curves, and yet it left nothing to the imagination—possibly because I didn't have to imagine what was underneath.

Her hair was twisted up in a bun. She didn't have reading glasses anywhere, but she still looked like a hot librarian.

"Daniel?"

I tore my attention from Alaina to respond to the quiet voice. The child-minder had arrived. She was a teenager who took an intermediate class that met on Tuesdays and Saturdays. "Hi, Charlynn. We're up to four. Tyrese texted and said he was going to be fifteen minutes late. Come get me if he isn't here, and more kids show up, okay?"

She took over, shooing me away.

I headed toward my sister. Sophia was the calm in this storm, and she was a safe companion. Not only did I try to keep my distance from the students—some of the women tended to flirt with me, which was counterproductive to our goals with the program—but I didn't want to be alone with Alaina.

Because I really did want to be alone with Alaina. Alone, and naked.

Sophia looked at me strangely. "What's wrong with you?"

"Nothing." I frowned at her.

"Are you in a mood for a reason? Are you and Evan fighting?"

"Evan and I never fight." We argued, but we never generated ill will or hurt feelings, even when we agreed to disagree.

"Does he have a boyfriend? I know he's been going through a bit of a dry spell, and so have you." She slipped her hand into mine. "I can hang around tonight, and we can talk."

"I'm fine, Sophie. Evan and I are fine. He texted me about an open mic night he and Bryn are doing tonight. I was going to stop by later."

"I know when something is bothering you, and I'm not going to drop it." She smiled as she assured me that she'd meddle in my life. "But I'll table it for now."

Alaina made her way to us, a friendly smile on her face. "Hello, Sophia. Daniel. It looks like a good turnout tonight."

"It does," Sophia said. "Hey, Alaina, are you free tonight after your session?"

From the way Alaina froze, I knew she was thinking of her writing schedule. "Daniel wanted to teach me some self-defense moves afterward."

Sophia glanced at me, a question in her eyes.

Even though I had slept with Alaina, I resented Sophia's question. "Some guy threatened her last time after everybody had left. I suggested she stay after for a private lesson."

"Oh, you don't have to do that," Sophia said. "Just join the class. It'll be good for everyone to see you practicing the techniques alongside them. It'll deepen those connections you've worked so hard to build."

Alaina considered Sophia's reasoning. "Okay. I brought workout clothes. Is there a dressing room where I can change?"

While I knew that joining the class was a viable option, I didn't want her to. I wanted to give her a private lesson because maybe it would lead to more. It was the primary reason I hadn't fully committed to attending Evan's open mic performance. I'd mentioned it to Sophia to throw her off the scent. Right or wrong, I wanted some time alone with Alaina.

But Sophia was onto another topic. "And then afterward, you can come to open mic night with Danny and me. His best friend, Evan, and Evan's sister, Bryn, are going to sing something they wrote."

I'd expected Alaina to turn Sophia down flat. Open mic nights were notorious for awful poetry, songs, and monologues meant to be funny or ironic but weren't. It was the primary reason everybody drank while they were there. I didn't mind going to support Evan and Bryn, but I didn't feel the need to subject anyone else to that torture. It was the reason I hadn't even asked Sophia to go.

But Alaina's eyes lit, and she clasped her hands in front of her heart. "I love open mic nights. A few times a year, I drag my friend, Clara, to them. We always have a great time."

Sophia nodded. "We can drink alcohol and hang out. It'll be nice to get to know you outside of this place. You can leave your car here. Danny will be our designated driver."

I wasn't opposed to Sophia or anyone else staying the night. I had two sofas, one of which folded out into a sleeper, but the first image that popped into my head had Alaina in my bed. That could be awkward if Sophia was sacked out on my couch.

The class had assembled. I resisted the urge to grasp Alaina's upper arm and steer her where I wanted her to go. "Sophie, go ahead and start. I'll show Alaina where she can get changed."

Alaina didn't say a word as I led her down the hallway. I meant to show her to the bathroom, but it was occupied, so I took her to my office. We went inside, and I turned on the lights.

She looked around. "There are no blinds on the windows."

My office overlooked the parking lot in front, and it did not have blinds. Back when it had been my grandfather's office, there had been blinds, but they hadn't worked. I'd taken them down a couple years ago, and I hadn't replaced them. The front of the building faced west, and since I usually did my paperwork in the morning, the sun didn't bother me. If it did, I just moved my chair to the opposite side of the desk. The whole idea of window coverings had slipped my mind.

"Good point."

Poking my head back into the hallway, I found a line at the bathroom. Tyrese was supervising the kids standing in line. He grinned. "With kids, when one has to go, they all have to go."

I'd witnessed the phenomenon in the classes with my younger students as well.

"Come upstairs. Use my bathroom." My voice came out gruffer than I'd intended.

I unlocked the door separating my loft from the studio, and I held it open for her. Once again, I followed Alaina up the stairs. Once again, I was unsuccessful in not watching her luscious ass wiggle as she climbed.

Inside my loft, I closed the door. "You know where the bathroom is."

Alaina set her bag on the counter and faced me. "This got awkward, didn't it?"

"What?"

She wagged her finger between the two of us. "This. You and me. It's awkward. You won't look at me or talk to me. Daniel, I understand the concept of a one-off. Things are supposed to go back to normal now."

I waved away her concern. "It's fine. We're fine."

"Then you're upset that Sophia invited me out with you two tonight?"

My sister had few friends. She had a generous heart, but she'd been hurt by life, and she'd closed herself off for many years. She was just now starting to widen her circle. I liked that she was making overtures of friendship to Alaina.

"It's fine," I repeated. "Why don't you go get changed?" I'd stay where I was and picture her naked. I'd remember what it felt like to drown in her kiss, to taste her essence, and to feel the warmth of her body sucking my cock deeper.

She came to me, trapping me between the closed door at my back and her delectable body, and she crossed her arms over her chest. "Let's get it all out in the open. Otherwise we'll never be able to move on productively."

"Get what out in the open?"

"You're regretting sleeping with me. It was fun, but now you're thinking it was wrong to have sex with me for a lot of reasons. You've put it on your list of things you shouldn't have done."

I couldn't stop thinking about her. Thoughts of her popped into my head at weird moments throughout the day. I'd even thought of her when I'd been with Evan, which had never happened before.

"I'm a lot older than you. I'm the therapist for your program. I'm definitely not your usual fare." She ticked off reasons on her fingers, but they were ones that didn't matter to me.

Well, the therapist thing mattered. The program wouldn't be nearly as successful without her. But the other things weren't important to me.

"Stop." I sandwiched her hands between mine to make her stop listing all the reasons we might not be compatible. "I don't regret anything that happened."

She pulled her hands away from my hold. "But things haven't returned to normal. You're upset, Daniel, and it's aimed at me."

Dragging a hand through my hair, I exhaled hard. "I'm not upset with you, Lainie, but you're right. I'm struggling to get back to normal."

Silence hummed loudly in my ears as she stared at me. Her gaze didn't roam my body. It concentrated on my face, though not necessarily on my eyes. Finally, she nodded. "I'll participate in the class so that you don't have to be alone with me afterward, and I'll tell Sophia that something has come up, and I can't go with her tonight. None of those things is what we normally do. That should help you."

She picked up her bag and disappeared into the bathroom to change.

I sat down heavily on one of the chairs at my table.

Seconds later, the door to the bathroom opened, and Alaina came out. She hadn't changed.

"What's wrong?" I rose, facing her with my hands spread wide.

"It's also not normal for me to participate in the class."

She tried to move past me, but I snagged the strap of her bag and used it to haul her back to face me.

"Alaina, it's important for you to take the class. If nothing else, last time proved that you need to be prepared to defend yourself."

Her mouth had a stubborn set to it, and her gaze burned holes in my chest. "I'll take a class at the University. The new term starts in six weeks."

It was a reasonable solution, but it was stupid for her to do that when I was offering her a better class. I'd taken over DiMarco Martial Arts five years ago when my grandfather had retired, and I'd made a lot of changes. In the past two years, my programs had been nominated for state and national awards, and my training sessions at conferences always sold out. I was in the midst of looking for qualified instructors to expand my program offerings.

Maybe I was a bit of a control freak, but I wanted the people I cared about to learn from the best, and that was me.

"I can't stop thinking about having sex with you," I confessed. Mortified, I plopped back onto my chair and stared at the floor. "It's not your fault, Lainie. It's nothing you did. You're right—things should be back to normal. They are for you, and they should be for me. I'm frustrated with myself, not with you. I apologize for my gruffness. You should not let that deter you from participating in the class."

She touched my chin, urging me to face her. "If it makes you feel better, I have similar thoughts. I just have more experience with lusting after you without making it obvious."

I didn't know what to do with that information. I wanted to act on it, but we had a class waiting for us downstairs. I definitely wanted both of us to beg off going to open mic night so I could spend the evening rocking her world.

Laughing, she tugged at my wrist. "If you're up for a quickie, we can still make it back in a reasonable time."

"Quickies are not my best work." I trailed after her as she led me toward my bed.

"You're an artist—I know. But I'm sure you'll rise to the occasion." She lifted her shirt over her head as she shimmied out of her skirt and panties.

Satin and lace—both her bra and panties. My dick saluted. I snatched her to me and devoured her lips. My hands roamed her body, the tactile sensation feeding a need for the woman in my arms. I kissed her neck and palmed her breasts through the pale lace of her bra.

She pushed at my workout sweats, her hands hooking the elastic waist, while her feet pushed them down. Somewhere along the way, I'd picked her up, and she'd wrapped her limbs around me. I ducked into the bathroom to snag a condom. I meant to take us to the bed, but Alaina snatched it from me and tore it open.

"You're very impatient," I noted.

"Do you want to take me from the front or back?" She nipped a path down my neck. Neither of us had removed my shirt, so she didn't have access to much more. "We don't have time for anal—I know you haven't cashed your rain check yet—but you can bend me over the counter and get rough."

While she talked, her hand slipped between us to work her clit. It was one of the hottest things I'd ever seen. Very few of the women I'd been with had been active in seeing to their own pleasure. I didn't mind doing the work, but I needed more time than we had, and I loved how she stepped up.

"Which would you prefer?"

She considered for all of two seconds. "I can get there faster if I'm on top."

"Then you'll be on top." I rolled the condom over my dick. Almost before I was finished, she guided me toward her pussy. It was warm and wet, and I sank into her easily. Remembering her preference, I carried her to the sofa and sat us down.

She lifted up onto her knees, and she rode me with abandon. I kissed her mouth and neck. I massaged her breasts. And I helped her masturbate her clit. Watching her bounce on my lap was erotic as all hell. Tension and heat built too quickly. I was going to blow any second now.

"Fuck, Lainie. I'm close."

Her body stiffened, arching off me, and she gasped quietly. I wrapped my hands around her hips and pulled her down one last time, and her pulsing pussy milked a climax from me. She collapsed forward, and I held her against me as her body quivered and trembled.

"That was intense," she said. "Let me know when you want to cash that rain check."

"Soon." I kissed her neck. "What are you doing Friday night?"

"Dinner with the University president and Board of Regents." She got up and went into the bathroom. Water ran, and when she came out, she was wearing a form-fitting shirt and tight, moisture-wicking leggings. The whole outfit was black and pink, and it left nothing but licentious thoughts in my brain.

I'd seen plenty of women wear similar outfits to work out, and I'd never felt such an acute physical reaction before.

She finished stuffing her day clothes back into her bag. "It usually goes until ten. I don't have any classes Friday. I plan to write until noon, and I have a meeting scheduled at one. Do you have maybe an hour free between two and four in the afternoon?"

Friday classes didn't start until four. I grinned because I'd be seeing her in two days. "I'm free between two and four."

On the landing at the bottom of the stairs, she turned to me, a plea in her honeyed eyes. "Will there be chocolate mousse cake?"

I was going to eat it off her naked body.

Chapter 5—Alaina

When we joined the class downstairs, nobody seemed concerned that we'd been gone for nearly fifteen minutes. My coloring had returned to normal. The orgasm had been small, and most of my mental foreplay had come from memories of what happened last time in Daniel's loft.

Daniel had some redness on his neck where I'd bitten him perhaps too hard, but everyone was too busy paying attention to the technique Sophia was demonstrating to notice.

Sleeping with Daniel had been inadvisable, another line item on my 'Shouldn't've' list, but it was a mistake I couldn't seem to stop making. When he'd texted to let me know he wouldn't be cashing the rain check, I'd assumed he'd come to his senses. It was irresponsible of me to make him be the one to make that decision, but I didn't have the willpower to stay away from him. Daniel DiMarco was catnip. One sniff, and I lost my mind.

I'd been both relieved and disappointed. Clara had said it was for the best, and she'd dragged me out to see a movie and have dinner with her.

Tonight, I'd resolved to behave as if nothing had happened. I might have been successful if Daniel had been able to do the same.

Though I shouldn't have done it, I didn't regret fucking him on his sofa when I was supposed to be changing my clothes. On Friday, I'd show up on time and use him like there was no tomorrow because I knew it would be our last liaison. Sophia had joked that Daniel lost interest in women after he'd slept with them three times. I was still surprised he'd been interested in me for even one time.

Sophia and Daniel disappeared once the self-defense class was over. The group counseling session went very well. Sophia had been correct that participating in the class helped the women connect with me. Two women who usually didn't speak in the sessions opened up, sharing some truly horrific experiences. We had productive talk around them, and I'd scheduled a follow-up with one of them.

For my study, I needed genetic samples to look for stress markers on the chromosomes. People also filled out a questionnaire and consent paperwork, and they signed disclosure forms stating University policy on how their privacy would be protected.

Afterward, the ritual of folding the chairs and hanging them on the portable rack always helped clear my mind from the sad and disturbing things I heard during group therapy.

It made me glad Adam had only cheated on me. Though, in all reality, I couldn't imagine him being mentally or physically abusive. In all the years we'd been together—even during and after the divorce—he'd never lost his temper or raised his voice. I'd certainly done those things, but he had not.

"You don't have to do that." Daniel chuckled as he said the same thing he said to me every time when he came to help me set the room to rights. He folded four chairs, picked them up in two hands, and headed to the rack. "Why don't you head on up to my loft? Sophia hung your clothes up in the bathroom while she showered so the wrinkles would steam out of them. You can freshen up and get dressed."

My gaze immediately went to where I'd left my bag. I hadn't noticed it was gone. My purse hadn't moved. "Daniel, I don't have to go tonight." I'd sweated a little, and I definitely needed to freshen up.

He stopped folding a chair and looked at me.

Looking people in the eye wasn't in my comfort zone, though I'd learned to do it anyway because it was expected in most social interactions. I went to my purse and fished for my lip balm.

"Well, I'm not going to lie. Evan and Bryn aren't bad singers, but some of the acts are truly horrible. It's a fun group, though. Sophie is very different when she's not here. You'll see her relax and smile, even laugh. And she'll get to see a different side of you." He chuckled. "Don't cancel on account of me, Lainie. I think we'll all have a good time."

I decided to go. After all, Sophia had invited me, and so I was her guest, not Daniel's.

The café with the open mic night wasn't far away. Daniel's studio was just outside of town, and the café was on Main Street. Streetlights and store windows lent tons of light to the area. It was a warm summer night, and many businesses had tables and chairs set up on the sidewalk.

Daniel parked in the community lot, and we followed the sidewalk through several extended restaurant spaces. The sidewalk was crowded, and it narrowed even more when businesses claimed huge swaths of it. Daniel led the way, while Sophia and I trailed behind.

Sophia DiMarco looked a lot like her brother. They both had deep sable hair and dark brown eyes. They shared the shapes of their faces and noses. The geneticist in me noted the stunning similarities in their physical appearances. They were both very attractive, and they drew the attention of many people we passed.

For tonight, Sophia had changed into a flowing, summery dress with a black-and-white orchid pattern. It was sleeveless and fell to mid-thigh. My blouse was also sleeveless, and my long skirt had enough movement so that we looked like we'd coordinated our outfits.

Of course, Sophia looked a lot better. She was beautiful from head to toe. I liked to think I'd been as smashing as her when I was twenty-five, but I was most likely wrong. Back then, I'd been blind to fashion and completely convinced I was unattractive. That's when I'd met Adam. He was the first man who'd looked at me and saw someone worthwhile.

Or maybe he'd been looking at my brother, and I was the consolation prize because neither of them had been out of the closet—not even to themselves.

I knew why I was thinking of Adam. New mistakes always brought to mind old ones. Shaking away the ancient warnings in my brain, I focused on Sophia.

"Do you go to open mic night a lot?"

She laughed, a musical giggle that didn't seem like it would come from her. "No. Evan and Bryn do this every now and again. Daniel usually goes because he's a supportive best friend. I go when I can."

"Are you friends with Evan and Bryn?"

"I'm close with Evan. He and Daniel are joined at the hip most of the time, and I've always been close with Danny. Evan is like having a second brother. I've known Bryn for years, but I'm not as close with her. She's younger than us by a few years. I think she's still in college. Anyway, I only see her maybe a handful of times in a year." She slung her arm around my shoulders, a casual gesture that established her control of the situation and somehow promised shelter. "Don't worry, Alaina. I wouldn't have asked you to come if anyone there wasn't a nice person. Daniel is really the worst of the group, and you get along with him just fine."

"I heard that." Daniel walked backwards for a few steps so he could glare at Sophia. "I'm plenty nice."

She play-punched him in the arm while laughing. "You're judgmental. Evan is more accepting and understanding. He gives people the benefit of the doubt."

Daniel stopped and planted his hands on his hips. "I'm not unreasonable. You're making me out to be a bad person, Sophie. Be nice to me, or else Alaina is going to get the wrong impression." He faced me. "When I first met Drew, I didn't like some things about him and their relationship. But we're fine now."

I tilted my head. "Drew?"

"My fiancé," Sophia said.

My association with the DiMarcos didn't require me to know anything about their personal lives, and I hadn't known Sophia was in a relationship at all. "Congratulations. I didn't know you were engaged."

Daniel pressed his lips together, though he appeared happy and surprised rather than upset. "Neither did I." He hugged Sophia, picking her up and whirling her around. "Congratulations, little sister."

"Thanks," she said when he put her down. "It happened this morning. Don't tell Mom and Dad. We're going to surprise them this weekend. Plus, I don't have an engagement ring yet."

He opened the door of the establishment where he'd stopped, and he clapped her on the back. "First round is on you."

She went inside, and his warm, happy expression landed on me. His gaze roved up and down my body, and a hint of desire flared in his eyes, temporarily pinning me in place. I disliked looking people in the eye, but I found it difficult to rip my gaze from his.

"Don't do that," I whispered. "It's not normal."

He sighed. "I'll give it my best effort."

The inside was crowded, dark, and loud. Sophia waited just inside the door, her gaze sweeping the place for their friends. As I acclimated to the noise level, I noted the small, round stage set up along the far wall. Behind the counter, the workers rushed about in a flurry of activity. Small baskets of greasy food came through the window at the far end of the bar. Groups of people surrounded tables, some sitting, and some standing.

"There they are." Daniel set his hand on my lower back, guiding me through the throng. He scooted me right or left, depending on what was coming at us, but on the whole, he kept me out of harm's way.

Sophia brought up the rear.

One fun thing about being short that tall people don't understand—we can get through crowds faster without them. Give us a destination, and we're quite adept at weaving, ducking, and finding small openings in a shifting morass of human bodies.

But this wasn't about speed. This was about staying with the group and letting Daniel feel like he was protecting me.

48

We stopped at a high-top table where two people fended off wolves intent on attacking them for the three empty chairs they were guarding.

The first thing I noticed about the woman was that she touched people. Her hand began on her brother's shoulder and it slid down to squeeze his hand. Then it petted Sophia's hair before patting her on the back and running down her arms to hold her hands. She cupped Daniel's cheeks, and squeezed his shoulders before making a big deal out of feeling up his arms. She ended by holding his hands as well.

While all this was going on, she exclaimed over how much she'd missed them and how wonderful it was to see them again and how beautiful they both were.

I didn't care that she was handsy with Daniel. I cared that she might try to touch me. Some people were tactile by nature. They used their hands to explore their environment and make personal connections. These people were often highly regarded in society. People liked them. People wanted to be around them.

Not me. I wasn't people. I didn't care to be touched by people I didn't know. If I had to endure her pawing, I wanted it to end before she got to my hands. Unfortunately, since I was new to her, she was most likely to start with my hands.

It was good manners, I told myself. She was obviously a nice person. Daniel and Sophia both liked her, and she seemed very happy to see them.

When was the last time she'd washed her hands?

My anxiety level skyrocketed, and I felt myself freezing. My breaths came faster. I tapped against my leg, counting by sevens.

The man at the table came around to hug Sophia. He clapped Daniel on his shoulder. Then he gave me a big, welcoming smile. "You must be Alaina. I've heard so many great things about you." He offered his hand in a way that demanded I shake it. "I'm Evan Carrico. I'm sure you've heard absolutely nothing about me."

Sweat broke out on my upper lip and pricked the back of my neck under my hair. I'd worn it down, so I looked less like a hot librarian and more like someone who was there to enjoy herself.

He took my hand, his grip strong and firm, and he kept the contact brief. It was over before I could work up to freaking out. Relief flowed through me. My smile came out timid because that's how I felt. "I've heard good things about you, like you're understanding and positive."

Evan glanced at Daniel briefly before his attention returned to me. "Sophie must have said that. It doesn't sound like Daniel."

Daniel slid onto the stool next to him. "I said you weren't a bad singer, but she was definitely going to hear worse tonight."

"It's true." Evan laughed. "Alaina, this is my little sister, Bryn. She'll be the one doing the singing. I join in on harmonies, but mostly I play guitar."

Bryn framed my face with her hands. "I know I'm not supposed to comment on your looks since this is the first time we've met, but I have to say—you have the most amazing eyes I've ever seen. I'm so jealous." She leaned in closer. "I bet you flutter those pretty lashes and the boys come running."

I stared at her for a tense ten seconds. "Oh. *That's* what it takes to get their attention? I'll try it tonight, and I'll let you know how it goes."

Sophia and Bryn laughed as we all sat down at the table. Well, I had to climb up on the high stool. My feet didn't hit the rungs, but I could hook the tips of my shoes on them if I perched on the edge of the seat.

Evan waved to the server to come over. I'd ended up between him and Sophia. He leaned closer to me. "You're planning to flirt tonight? How is it that a beautiful woman like you isn't married?"

I hated when men said stupid things like that. It was obnoxious and disingenuous. Was I supposed to reply that I'd been married, but he'd cheated on me and was now married to my brother? Maybe I was supposed to say I was married to my work and didn't need a man.

Well, technically I didn't need a man. I needed sex. While I liked my electronic companions, I find it lacked that personal connection I sometimes craved. But that didn't mean I needed a man in my life for more than ten minutes at a time. Unless the man was like Daniel in bed. In that case, I'd need to clear an hour.

I mimicked his domineering pose. "Apparently, I haven't perfected the art of fluttering my lashes." I followed up by batting them at him in a fairly ridiculous, exaggerated manner.

Under the table, Daniel kicked Evan. I saw it because I'd glanced down. I looked up in time to see Daniel flash Evan a warning look. I had flashbacks to time spent in school where the one or two friends I had kept the others from teasing me too badly.

Part of me wanted to leave, but the part of me that wanted to make Evan pay for being nasty to me was stronger. I might identify as submissive, but I was no pushover, and I elevated holding a grudge to an art form.

Evan slung an arm along the low back to my chair. He was one of those guys with a trim, athletic build that probably looked good at the beach. He seemed like his favorite pastimes were jogging and lifting weights. "I meant no disrespect Doctor Miles. I just meant that you're smart and captivating. I have half a mind to snatch you up right now."

Given everything Sophia had said about Evan and the fact he was Daniel's best friend, I decided to put my grudge plans on hold.

My cutting sarcasm was another thing entirely. With my best condescending smile, I leaned closer and said, "When you double down on a bad pick-up line, it doesn't make it better."

A genuine smile spread over his face slowly. It started with his mouth, where I noticed the sensuality of his lips, how they seemed primed for hours of kissing. A dimple appeared in one cheek, ramping up the charming nature of his expression. It ended in his eyes, which I noted were blue. They sparkled with a hint of devilry and admiration.

At long last, he nodded once. "I think this is the start of something beautiful, Doctor. I'd like if you saved me a dance tonight."

I regarded him with a mixture of curiosity and amusement. "You're going to have to try harder than that."

Under the table, Sophia tapped my knee, so I turned my attention to her. She leaned closer. "That one is a heartbreaker, Alaina. Watch out."

The bar was sufficiently loud that I didn't think she'd heard anything Evan said to me. For that matter, Daniel had probably been guessing as well.

I studied Sophia, trying to figure out what she meant. Then I realized what Evan and I were doing, from a visual standpoint, could be construed as flirting. While I found him attractive, I wasn't sure I considered him likeable. Right now, he was cruising along in neutral territory because people I liked—Sophia and Daniel—had recommended him.

Finally I said, "You mean Evan?"

She nodded.

"He's about half my age, and I'm not sure if he's being hostile or if he's just socially awkward." I knew *I* was socially awkward, which was why I tended to avoid unstructured social situations like this. I questioned my sanity in agreeing to go in the first place.

She laughed. "Okay. I just wanted to make sure you're not getting ideas."

"Well, I'd hoped to get ideas here tonight. I've hit a wall with writing my book, and I need something to shake me out of the thought pattern I seem to be stuck in."

Her eyes widened, and she grabbed my arm. "You're writing a book? What's it about?"

"Ethical issues in advanced genetics research." Recalling how I'd bored Daniel with details, I opted for a short overview. "It's meant to be a textbook for graduate students."

Rather than her eyes glazing over, they lit. "What are you thinking would happen tonight to help you get ideas for that?"

"I only know that going home and staring at my research notes and computer screen aren't getting me anywhere."

"So you're looking to blow off steam?"

"Yes. I love open mic nights. Clara, my best friend, hates them, so she will only let me drag her to one a couple times a year. I write cringe-worthy poetry, and I like to share it." I ended with a grin because my poetry was horrible from a literary standpoint, and yet people tended to clap for me. I didn't quite know why, and I didn't care. It was a rush to be up there, and people were generally nice about being supportive of my right to suck.

"You want to get up there?"

I extracted my notebook from my bag. "Let me see if I have anything ready to read."

Sophia leaned in to look at my writer's notebook. It had lots of things in it—poetry, ideas for my writing, notes for teaching and research, quotes from articles or social media that I found interesting, and lists. I made lists for everything. Bryn came over to join us, and soon the three of us were cringing and laughing over some of the things I'd written.

Finally, we came to a grocery list where I'd annotated the reasons for each item. It wasn't poetry. It had come about because Zack kept asking me why we needed the things on the list. Some of my reasons for buying toilet paper were practical—to wipe our hineys—and others were whimsical—to always have a mummy costume handy. Carrots were for me to take out my frustrations on when I felt the need to destroy something in a productive manner. In the winter, they doubled as snowperson noses.

"That is fabulous," Bryn said. "It's funny and poetic."

I looked closer. Zack hadn't been impressed with my wit, but he was eight, and I was his mother. He'd felt I'd missed an opportunity with the toilet paper to make poop jokes. He'd decided to show me who was the better writer by penning his list, so I counted it as a parenting win. "It's not a poem. It's my grocery list."

As I said that, my brain went to work rearranging items, deleting the less funny ones, and adding more content to the better ones. I grabbed the pencil from where I'd stuck it in the spirals, and it flew over the paper, making liberal revisions.

Behind me, Bryn clapped.

"I love it even more," Sophia said. "Let's get you on the schedule."

"I'll do it." Bryn disappeared.

I finished off my revisions, and then Sophia read it over. She pointed out some places that needed further attention.

When Bryn returned, she slapped a number down on top of my page. "Number eight."

Evan and Daniel had been deep in conversation about sports and food and other things to which I didn't pay close attention.

At Bryn's pronouncement, Evan's head whipped around. "Eight? We're twenty, and we were here first."

Bryn lifted a shoulder. "They had a cancellation, and since she's not singing, they slotted her between two musical acts."

He seemed to accept that I was jumping in line ahead of them.

Daniel frowned. "I must have missed something. Lainie, you're going to perform? Is that what you guys were doing over there?"

"Yes. I have a truly horrible piece of poetry that will make you sorry you appeared in public with me." I lifted my glass of wine—someone had ordered it for me—and toasted my imminent public failure. "Here's to shared misery and low expectations."

"Just flutter your eyelashes," Evan said. "You'll do fine."

Chapter 6—Evan

I used to be suave with my flirting. Yesterday, I'd charmed a barista into throwing in a free banana nut muffin with my coffee. She'd smiled and twirled her hair.

The moment Daniel had come into the bar with the short brunette, I'd known she was different. First, there was the way Daniel treated her. She wasn't arm candy or a temporary amusement. From the way he talked about her and the way he paid attention to her, I knew he liked and respected her.

She wasn't his usual type. He liked tall, blonde women who commanded attention and adoration. Alaina was the exact opposite. The top of her head didn't reach his shoulder. She exuded confidence even though she was visibly nervous. One look at her, and you could tell she was intelligent, the kind of person who was going to make a real difference in the world and probably already had to a lot of people.

Even her appearance was a study in contradiction. Her curly hair went in all directions. Wild and out of control, it was a marked contrast to her outfit. Daniel had been right—she was the perfect fantasy woman to play the hot librarian.

But the thing that had irritated me most was that Daniel hadn't mentioned me to her. She knew almost nothing about me.

It wasn't new that Daniel didn't talk me up to a woman he'd fucked. They weren't usually around long enough to become part of his life. But he'd known Alaina for a year. A *year*. In a whole twelve months, my name hadn't come up once.

By contrast, he talked about her to me all the time. He was always saying how great she was, how wonderful and thoughtful and generous. Two weeks ago, he'd been almost enamored of her when he'd described the way she'd fulfilled his hot librarian fantasy.

Meeting her, I'd wanted to find her flaws. I wanted to unmask her as shallow and catty. But I'd been the asshole, and she'd responded by very nicely putting me in my place. In minutes, she'd settled into the group as if she'd always been there. Sophia and Bryn seemed to really like her.

"What's wrong?" Daniel sipped his flavored water and kept his voice so that only I heard it. "Why were you rude to Lainie?"

"Lainie? Now you've got a cute nickname for her?"

He frowned. "Evan, I know when you're not happy about something. What is it? What happened?"

Daniel and I had started our casual affair when I was sixteen and he was seventeen. We'd been together—without being *together*—for nine years. We were best friends. We talked several times every day, and we shared everything, big or small.

And he hadn't mentioned me to Alaina.

I mean, he hadn't mentioned how attractive he found her. He hadn't mentioned how he treated her like a prized possession or how in awe he was of her.

For years, we'd resisted caving to the pressure to date each other because it didn't feel right for just the two of us to be in a relationship. I was a Dom, and he wasn't a sub. Sure, he was willing to play with me, but that was more out of a sense of fun and adventure. He didn't feel a need to submit.

And yet, it didn't feel right to be in a relationship without him. I'd dated, and been in relationships, but none of them had felt like the real thing. I enjoyed them, but I felt like I'd been biding my time—and I hadn't known what for.

Now I knew.

This was jealousy. For the first time, he'd met someone who could come between us, and I wanted to hate her.

But I couldn't.

I found her utterly captivating.

When she laughed or smiled, I found it impossible not to look in her direction. When she spoke, I fought the urge to soak up every word. I basked in her attention. Daniel did the same.

We were both starstruck, and she seemed completely unaware.

Her turn for the open mic came quickly. With a hopeful sigh, she asked us to wish her luck. Bryn and Sophia cheered for her, hooting and hollering raucously. Daniel and I clapped, both of us trying to look like we weren't panting after crumbs of her attention.

I glanced at Daniel, and he didn't appear to be nearly as affected as I felt. I was trying to hide it—generally I was good at playing my emotions close to the chest—and my insides felt like they were about to explode. Daniel wore his heart on his sleeve, and he didn't seem to be in turmoil at all.

But I knew she hadn't been just a one-night stand for him. Maybe it started out that way, but I knew my best friend. I knew he wanted to see her again.

Or was I wrong? Was I projecting the complicated mess of my feelings on him?

She adjusted the microphone stand down. "Short person problems," she joked. "Thank you for coming out tonight to support your friends and family, and the family and friends of perfect strangers."

Once she had the microphone where she wanted it, she waved to the audience. "Hello, Bell's Tavern! I hope you all had a lot to drink already. You're going to need it. My name is Alaina, and I'm going to read you my shopping list. I'd call it poetry, but that's really stretching the definition of poetry. Drink up."

She had them eating out of the palm of her hand. Okay, maybe it was just the people at our table. There were some audible groans.

"Toilet paper is where it starts and ends. It wipes away some of the shit life throws at you, like when your cat pukes on the rug or your kid misses the toilet even though they were sitting on it."

A few people laughed. As she went through her list, fewer people talked, and more people listened. She had a way of relating her list to everyday problems.

"Carrots are for venting my frustrations. Whenever life gets overwhelming, I julienne a few of those suckers. The carrot becomes my problems, and by the time I'm done, they're harmless little splinters." She paused, leaning forward as if confiding a secret. "For three years after my divorce, I ate a lot of carrots. It's amazing how cathartic it feels to slice and dice your ex's penis and then sprinkle them over a salad."

People whistled and cheered.

Alaina ended with a shy smile. "You guys have been fantastic tonight. Thank you."

Bryn and Sophia hugged her when she returned, gushing over how well it had gone.

From his perch next to me, Daniel grinned. "Lainie, I didn't know you were such a ham. You seem so shy and demure all the time."

"She's not demure," Sophia said. "I've seen her be assertive when the situation warranted it."

I'd seen it as well. Alaina gave as good as she got, and it was another reason I was drawn to her.

56

"And not shy," Daniel agreed. "You had the audience eating out of your hand."

I traced a finger though the condensation on my glass. "I'm a little disturbed by the carrot part."

"Yeah," Daniel said. "I didn't know you were divorced."

"Did he cheat?" I heard myself asking. "I mean, why else would you target his penis?"

Alaina scrunched up her nose. She didn't want to discuss her ex.

"Sorry," I said. "It's none of my business."

Most people would rush to assure me that it was okay to pry, and they'd spill all the dirty details.

Not Alaina. She let the topic drop. Conversation picked up, and a half hour later, Bryn and I were close to our performance time.

Sophia looked at her phone. "Oh, shit. Daniel, Mom's been trying to get hold of us for twenty minutes. Grandma Russo is in the hospital."

Daniel froze.

"Do you need me to come?" I asked. Open mic night wasn't a priority if my best friend or his family needed me. I knew how close Daniel and Sophia were to their extended family. "I can drive."

Sophia listened to a voice mail. "She took a nasty fall and is in surgery. Mom's freaking out. She wants us there." To me, she said, "That's okay, Evan. I'm sorry about missing your set tonight."

"Don't worry about it," Bryn said. I echoed her sentiment.

Sophia pulled Daniel to his feet and snagged his keys from his pocket.

I set a hand on his arm and leaned closer. "If you need me, just call, and I'm there." To Sophia, who handled things like this much better than Daniel, I said, "Seriously—whatever you need. Call me."

Sophia kissed my cheek. "Thanks. Alaina, come on. I'll drop you back at Danny's studio."

"I'll take care of her. You two get going." I didn't care if Alaina was on board with that plan or not. She was stuck with me. "Text me when you know more."

Alaina watched them go, apprehension darkening her honeyed eyes. "I feel like I should do more, but logically there isn't anything I can do."

Her hand rested on the clasp of her purse, as if she could find answers in there. I closed mine over hers, offering comfort. "The DiMarco family is pretty tight-knit. They'll have plenty of support, and I'm on standby. They know I'll come whenever any of them calls."

Frozen in indecision, she stared at me. After a long time, she patted my hand, and then she withdrew both of them from my grasp.

"I know. I just feel for them. It's never easy when someone you love is in danger."

I didn't get the feeling she was rejecting me, but it stung that she pulled away from my touch. I knew I had no right to expect her to welcome attention or physical contact from me, and I struggled to try to not read something into it that wasn't actually there.

Bryn and I went on and did our thing. I did passably well, which was good considering my mind was divided between worrying for Daniel and Sophia, and wondering what the fuck I was doing by having naughty thoughts about Alaina.

When we finished, Alaina congratulated Bryn. "You have a very pleasing voice." To me, she said, "Nobody texted you while you were onstage."

I'd left my phone with her in case Daniel texted or called.

"Thanks. We can get going now." I hoisted my guitar case and followed the ladies outside. I walked Bryn to her car before loading Alaina in mine. Her car was back at Daniel's place, so I didn't need directions.

I pulled into the empty parking lot and stopped in the spot next to hers. Daniel's SUV wasn't anywhere around, so I knew he was still at the hospital. I planned to call him as soon as I left there.

Alaina opened the door. "Thank you for the ride. I hope everything works out with Daniel and Sophia's grandmother." She left, the door closing with stunning finality.

Before I knew what I was doing or why, I hopped out of my truck. "I think we got off on the wrong foot," I called from the other side of the bed.

Hand on the latch of her car door, she paused and looked over at me.

I hurried around my truck because I didn't want that barrier between us.

She watched me, her eyebrows pinched with indecision.

"I know—you're trying to figure out whether you should say my behavior was okay or that everything is fine because I stopped behaving like a jerk."

The pinched lines went away, and her lips parted. "I didn't think you liked me or cared whether I liked you. If you're doing this because you don't want to upset Daniel, then please don't. It's unlikely we'll run into each other again."

My reasons for mending fences were purely selfish. I stuck a hand in a pocket and danced around a bit. I couldn't remember the last time I'd been this nervous around someone I found attractive. "That would be unfortunate. I very much would like to run into you again. I'd love to go back in time and redo the night. My brain scrambled or short-circuited or something, and I said some things I shouldn't've. I'm sorry."

Her eyes widened, and she pressed a hand to her chest. "You're attracted to *me*?"

I was glad I didn't have to explain further. "Yeah. I was surprised. I don't usually go for older women." As I said it, I wanted to kick myself. "That didn't come out right. Alaina, can we pretend like we're meeting just now?"

She seemed to stare at my lips.

They tingled, just from that bit of visual contact. Before she could get too far in her thinking, I caved to a base impulse. I parked a hand on her waist, and I slid the other around to cup the back of her neck. Then I kissed her. My lips massaged an erotic letter, begging my lady fair for another chance.

At first, she didn't move, not even to push me away. Then the hand she'd pressed to her chest turned around and slid up mine. It stopped at my shoulder, her fingers flexing as if she wanted to dig in, but wasn't sure if she should. She tilted her head, giving me better access, and when she kissed me back, my heart and mind celebrated.

I closed the distance between us, pressing her to the sedan and trapping her with my body. Electricity sparked inside me, sending a thousand signals to my nerve endings. She felt so good against me. I wanted to lift her so I didn't have to bend so much and so our parts lined up better, but I didn't want to break the spell we'd woven.

She sighed, and I urged her mouth open so I could deepen the kiss. Her bag dropped to our feet, and she wrapped her arms around my neck. She rose to the tips of her toes and played with the short hair on the back of my head.

I broke away to kiss a path down her neck and let us both catch our breath, and that's when she pushed against my chest.

I stopped kissing. "Are you okay?"

"I slept with Daniel."

"What?" I knew she'd slept with him. I knew she'd rocked his world. It was the reason I'd been jealous.

Was it the reason I found myself so attracted to her?

No. I'd never cared for a woman just because Daniel had taken a fancy to one.

"I slept with Daniel," she repeated. "It was casual, a one-night stand sort of thing. He's your best friend. I thought you should know."

"He told me." I resolved not to play games with her. "We tell each other everything."

"Is that what you're looking for? Casual sex?"

Her question threw me for a loop, and my mind went blank.

"It's okay if you are," she continued. "But maybe you want to discuss it with Daniel first? I wouldn't want to cause a rift between you, especially not for something that doesn't mean anything."

Did I want this to be casual? I didn't know what I wanted. I'd known her for a few hours. "Lainie, I just know I want to see you again."

She glanced away, her eyes moving over the scenery which included my truck and Daniel's building. The frown wrinkling her brows returned. "You're in construction?"

"Yes. I recently started my own company."

"Do you do roofs?"

"Yes." In a million years, I wouldn't have predicted the conversation would head in this direction.

"I need my roof replaced. Maybe you can come over and give me an estimate?"

Stepping back, I put some space between us. "I wasn't angling for a job."

"I know." She smoothed her hand down her skirt. "You want sex."

"If you're not interested in me, you should say so."

She bit her lip and looked toward my truck again. Finally, she sighed. "I find you attractive, and you kiss really well."

I heard the *but* dangling at the end of her sentence, but she'd stopped talking. I rubbed the back of my neck. Being nervous was not something I did well. Anxiety and jealousy were unfamiliar to me, and she made me feel both.

After a completely awkward amount of time, I prompted her. "But?"

As if I'd pulled her from a trance, she nodded. "But you should talk to Daniel first, and I really do need an estimate on my roof. I had two companies come out today, but I didn't like the first man, and the second didn't seem to understand what I was asking for. He wanted to put shingles over what's already up there, and I want a new roof."

A roofing job wasn't what I'd wanted out of this, but she'd been clear about wanting me to talk to Daniel first. I inhaled sharply.

"I meant today." She spoke almost too softly for me to hear. "I had sex with Daniel today, and we have plans to get together one more time. It was meant to be a one-night stand, but it was late, and I got tired, so we rescheduled some of it."

Daniel and I had never slept with the same woman before. We had wildly different tastes in partners. I'd never encountered this situation, and so Alaina was right—I needed to talk to Daniel first. From the way he'd talked about her before, I wasn't comfortable saying whether he'd care if I pursued Alaina.

"I'll talk to Daniel."

She peeked up at me, her gaze lingering on my lips. "And also give me an estimate?"

I left with her phone number and address, and an appointment to see her the next afternoon. While I didn't give a rip about her roof, it was the only way I was going to see her again without intervention from Daniel.

I called Daniel to ask about his Grandma Russo.

He picked up on the first ring. "She's out of surgery and in recovery. My mom and aunt are fighting over who gets to go into the recovery room to see her when the nurse comes back."

"Okay, so you don't know anything?"

"She had an emergency bypass. The doctor said it went well."

I thought Sophia had said she'd fallen? Maybe the heart attack had caused the fall? "That's great to hear. Do you need anything?" Part of me wanted to go to the hospital even if he turned me down, just to be there for him.

"Nah. Sophie and I won't be allowed to see her tonight anyway. We're here mostly to provide moral support and go on coffee runs. She's out of danger, so we'll probably head out soon. How did it go tonight?"

I bristled because I didn't want to tell him everything, but I knew I had to. I didn't keep secrets from my best friend. Alaina had said their association was casual. Danny had said the same thing. I wasn't trying to steal her from him; I just wanted to spend more time with her. Preferably naked.

"Bryn was great. I hit the wrong note a couple times, but I don't think anyone noticed. People seemed to enjoy our song."

"I'm sorry I missed it."

"It's fine. You'll be there next time. We'll probably do it again next month."

"I'll let Lainie know so she can prepare another shopping list." He chuckled. "I did not expect her sense of humor, maybe because I usually see her under such serious circumstances."

"Yeah." Squeezing my eyes shut, I braced myself for the spilling of my guts. "She's amazing. I mean, you said she was beautiful and smart, but I wasn't prepared for the real thing."

"You were kind of a dick at the start of the night." He exhaled hard. I could envision him washing his hand down his face, exhausted after a long day and the stress of worrying about a loved one. "Did she get back to her car okay?"

"You mean, once I got her alone, did I revert to a nervous teenager who keeps sticking his foot in his mouth and saying stupid and offensive things? No, I didn't. I was nice. She was nice. I apologized for our rough start, and then I kissed her."

Silence from the other end.

"Daniel?"

"I'm here."

"Are you pissed?"

Background noises disappeared, and I knew he'd left the waiting room in search of privacy. "I'm surprised. You seemed really dismissive of her when I told you we'd slept together."

"I hadn't met her." I cleared my throat. "You put her up on such a high pedestal that I figured there was something wrong with your perspective. Anyhow, she told me that she had sex with you today, and that you plan to meet up again on Friday."

"That's true." He quieted for a moment. I knew him so well that I had no trouble picturing him chewing on that utterly kissable bottom lip. "Sophia invited her tonight. She wasn't there with me, if that's what has you worried. We're not dating or romantically involved."

Until he said it, I hadn't realized it mattered. It had never been an issue before. I hadn't planned to steal her from him, but I already knew I wanted more than casual sex from her. I preferred to have an emotional connection to my sex partners, while Daniel didn't seem to care if he did. "I asked if I could see her again, and she said that I should talk to you first because she didn't want casual sex with you or me to come between us. I don't want that to happen either. You're my best friend."

"You want my permission to sleep with her?"

"It seems stupid, but yes, I do."

"If it's what she wants, then I don't see a reason you shouldn't go for it. But just be warned that I'm not sure I'm finished with her. And then there's the fact that she and I need to remain on amicable terms because of her work at my studio. We need her, Evan. She's not replaceable. So just be careful, okay? She's not someone you can use and throw away. The success of our program is at least half due to her."

I choked because if anybody was into using women and throwing them away, it wasn't me. I tended to try for a long-term relationship with a fair number of people I'd dated. But I guess she wasn't under the impression I wanted to go out with her. She thought I wanted to tango between the sheets and call it a day.

"I'll turn on the charm. She'll come away with a smile on her face, and I won't end up on the carrot part of her shopping list."

"Let's hope not. Do you need me to send her number to you?"

"No. She gave me her phone number and address. She wants me to give her an estimate to replace her roof." I delivered that news in an appropriately dry tone.

Daniel laughed. "She's terribly practical, Evan. It's okay if you don't want to give her a roof replacement estimate. She'll understand. Or you can draw clear lines between what you do on top of her house and what you do on top of her. She's good with boundaries."

I wanted to make a joke about Daniel assuming I'd be on top, but we both knew I usually preferred pinning my lovers down. With Danny, it was impossible to pin him down because he was the martial arts expert, not me. That was one reason I liked to use restraints with him. The other reason was that I liked the way he looked in them.

The next afternoon, I parked in front of Alaina's house. It was a classic Georgian house in a neighborhood full of Georgian and Tudor style homes. I could see where Alaina would prefer Georgian to Tudor. She was the kind of woman who liked clean cut lines and to have everything organized. I'd bet she knew by Sunday night what clothes she was wearing each day of the week. She'd know which shoes and jewelry would go along with them as well. Her house was probably neat and tidy—everything in its place.

The driveway continued past the house to an unattached garage with the same Georgian architecture as the house. It was designed to look as if it had been a carriage house, but it wasn't tall enough to ever have been used for that purpose.

The neighborhood was older, and it featured wide streets lined with trees and well-groomed yards. I lived in a townhouse-style condo in a neighborhood that had been designed to pack in the maximum number of people per square foot. We had patches of grass between the buildings and the parking lot, but most of it was a concrete jungle. Out back, we had tiny patios that looked out onto other people's tiny patios. I could hang out with my neighbors without ever leaving my yard.

I parked in the street in front of the house. My truck, outfitted with toolboxes and a frame to hold ladders and other equipment, stuck out like a sore thumb. It was a vehicle destined to be out of sight by five o'clock.

As I headed up the walk, Alaina's car pulled into the driveway. Rather than continue into the garage, she stopped next to the house. I approached as she gathered her purse and a couple of tote bags, and I opened the door for her.

"How was work?"

Halfway out of the vehicle, she paused for a second to look at me. Interestingly, I noted that she didn't look at my eyes, though her gaze swept over my face. Since I hadn't said anything off-putting or inappropriate, I filed this observation away for later consideration.

"Work was productive, which is always a good thing." She slung one bag over her shoulder, and I took the other. "Sorry I'm late."

"Not a problem. My job ran long today, so I just got here."

She unlocked the side door and held it open, inviting me inside.

Being the chivalrous soul I am, I took over the job of holding the door. My bag, where I kept a tablet, as well as the documents and forms I needed to create an estimate, wasn't large or heavy. Her bag easily weighed three times what mine did. Judging from the books and papers I spied in the bag she still had, that one was even heavier.

She led me down a hallway. We passed a huge living room that was mostly empty on my left and a library filled with books and comfortable furniture on the right. Midway through the house, we came to the kitchen. She set her bags on the table and motioned for me to do the same.

"How long have you lived here?"

"Five weeks. I had it inspected before I bought it, and I knew it needed some work. The roof is the most pressing problem, so it's first on my list. It's worse than what I was led to expect. When we had those rainstorms last week, I had drips and a wet ceiling upstairs." She smoothed her hair back, checking the tidy bun with her hands. "What do you need from me?"

I wanted to start out with a kiss. I'd gone home after work to shower away the stench of the day and change into clothes that weren't soiled. I had coveralls in my truck in case I had to do something that would leave me dirty. I wasn't sure if this was more than an estimate or less than a date or what.

"Nothing right now. I'm going to get up on the roof and see what's going on. Then I want to get into your attic to check out the situation on the underside."

"Alright." She smoothed her hand along her skirt, a gesture I was coming to read as a nervous affect. "That's a strange way to flirt."

So far, I hadn't figured out how to flirt with her. "What do you mean?"

"You want to get into my attic and check out the situation from the underside? Evan, please don't take this the wrong way, but as someone who sucks at flirting, even I have better pick-up lines." She followed up with a half-smile, and excitement lit her eyes.

Okay, we were flirting. I was on board for this. I chuckled to let her know I wasn't offended. "For example?"

"Hello." She drew it out and dropped her voice a couple octaves, and her gaze raked up and down my body. Then she smiled. "Simple. Cheesy. Awkward. I'd rather just come out and say I find you attractive and would like to have sex with you."

"That's direct," I allowed.

"But it's not flirting. Flirting is, by definition, indirect. But I'm not good at reading body language, and I always end up doing or saying something wrong in unstructured social situations. I prefer being direct, though many people find it uncomfortable." She smoothed her hand down her skirt again, and her gaze dropped as well.

The Dom in me loved her penchant for lowering her gaze, though I recognized that it didn't imply submission. "I can be direct."

"Thank you. Did you want to do the estimate first, or did you want to tell me about your conversation with Daniel?"

Anticipation was a potent aphrodisiac. "I'll check out your roof first."

"Okay." A question simmered in her eyes, but she didn't ask it.

I really liked having the upper hand. I went outside and secured my ladder. Her roof didn't have a sharp pitch, so I was comfortable walking around up there. I took measurements and checked out the damage. This roof should've been replaced five years ago. Where an oak tree stretched out above the house on the back corner, it was rotted through. That was most likely the source of the leaking.

Following the problem down, I found issues with four windows. Water was a steady and destructive force, and it had done a number on the house. The siding was new, and I figured the previous owners had updated it to hide some of the damage.

I put my coveralls on, and then I went inside, knocking loudly and announcing myself as I did so.

"In the kitchen." Alaina's voice carried down the hall to me.

I followed it, and I found her wearing different clothes. The hot librarian garb—which I found very sexy—had been swapped out for jeans and a black shirt with cartoon chromosomes dancing on it. The jeans hugged her backside, showing off those delicately rounded cheeks.

She whisked something in a bowl perched on her hip. When she saw me, she pursed her lips as she took in my coveralls.

"Yes, they're dirty. Don't worry—I won't touch anything that isn't already dirty."

"You still want to get into the attic? The others didn't."

That explained why she'd thought it was a pick-up line. "Yes."

"Okay." She set the bowl down. "The opening is on the landing upstairs. It has steps that fold down."

Good. I didn't have to haul in one of my ladders. I checked out the situation there to find more damage than appeared on the outside, which was what I'd expected.

I stowed my coveralls in my truck, and then I used the main floor washroom to tidy up. This might or might not be a date, and I was going to be ready for either eventuality.

Alaina was still in the kitchen. She'd set out an array of vegetables and was in the process of scrubbing them.

"What's for dinner?"

She jumped and whirled around. "I didn't hear you come down."

"I didn't mean to startle you." I'd always been light on my feet, but I hadn't been purposely quiet while moving around the house. I set my clipboard on the counter away from where she was working.

"Is that the estimate?"

"Measurements. I need to check some prices and run some numbers. But I can tell you what I found."

She nodded and turned off the flow of water from the faucet. "Okay."

I had her undivided attention, and I liked it. Though she faced me, and she sort of looked at me, she did not meet my eyes. I didn't get the feeling she was being untruthful or avoiding something, so I gave her a direct assessment. "You need a new roof. You're going to need a lot of the plywood replaced, and a few joists in the attic need to be shored up. The leak has been going on for a number of years, so there's damage to the two windows on the south wall and two on the west wall. The windows need to be replaced, and once I get the wall opened up, I'm predicting the headers will need to be replaced, as well as some of the two-by-fours in the frame."

She blinked rapidly three times, and then she seemed to dismiss my presence. Returning to the task I'd interrupted, she finished cleaning lettuce and red peppers, and then she peeled carrots.

As she moved to the cutting board, I stopped her by setting a hand on her arm. "Alaina? That's maybe more damage than you anticipated, but it's stuff that needs to be fixed as soon as possible. It's only going to get worse the longer you wait."

Briefly, she glanced at my face. "I'm making salad and salmon with yogurt sauce."

"Okay." I drew out the word because I was really puzzled by her reaction.

She went to the chopping board and started in on the carrots. I thought about her poem and what she'd said about carrots. They symbolized a chaotic or emotionally upset mind.

Pieces began to fall into place. I thought about her reluctance to look people in the eyes, and the way she'd frozen when I'd touched her hand. Daniel had mentioned how she scheduled her week on Sunday nights. She was incredibly smart and driven.

I opened her cupboards and found everything inside jumbled. There was no discernible organization to her food storage. I wandered into her library to find her books arranged by author, though they weren't alphabetized. Her appearance was meticulously neat, and I knew she was writing a book. Nothing I found fit neatly into a box I could label, but I had my suspicions.

Back in the kitchen, I found her where I'd left her, the knife moving with purpose and precision. She wasn't ignoring me. She'd done this before—focused on another topic or task—when I'd said or done something she needed time to process.

I had a niece with a lot of the same attributes. She displayed elements of OCD, and when things didn't happen as she expected them to, she ignored the person delivering the news she hadn't expected to hear or the problem she hadn't anticipated. It was part of her coping mechanism. She sometimes did things she found calming, but she did them excessively.

Like julienning carrots.

But that didn't mean Alaina got a free pass. She needed to deal with the situation.

Alaina was an adult, so she was most likely aware of what she was doing. Based on this notion, I stood behind her and planted my hands on the edge of the counter on either side of her body. I knew she was aware of me because she stiffened slightly, though she kept chopping the shit out of those carrots. They were beyond julienned and approaching slivers.

"Stop." I spoke calmly and gently, though authority infused my words.

Her hands stopped moving.

"Put the knife down."

She set it on the cutting board.

"You're freaking out right now, aren't you?"

One stiff nod was her only movement.

"Tell me why."

Her fingers twitched, seeking the knife.

I wrapped a hand around her wrist. "I'd rather you weren't holding a knife while I'm pushing you out of your comfort zone."

"I'm not prone to violence," she said.

"Not unless I'm a carrot. Got it. Let's agree the carrots are cut small enough, and whatever is bothering you isn't going to go away through the abuse of vegetables."

A strangled laugh was her response, so at least she wasn't mad. I was taking a real chance dominating her without her permission and requiring her to follow my orders. Because, make no mistake, I was issuing orders, and I expected her to comply.

"Tell me one thing that bothers you right now." It was a wide-open order, and she might very well tell me to get out of her personal space.

"The windows were supposed to last another three-to-five years. I have them on the schedule to be evaluated in three years."

"If the roof was fixed, you might be able to put off replacing the windows for a few months, but they'll need to be replaced as soon as possible. There's rot, and if there isn't already, you're going to have mold. I'm not sure the structure of the house is going to survive much more damage." She needed facts, and I aimed to give them to her.

"It messes up my timeline."

"You didn't have all the information when you made that timeline. I can look over your other projects and let you know a little better where they fit. Life is sometimes messy, and you have to adapt to new knowledge."

She angled her head, scowling over her shoulder at me. "I understand how life works." She didn't bother to hide her irritation, but now it was directed at me.

"Good." I wasn't there to argue. I was there to support and encourage.

"I know what you're doing." The scowl didn't ease.

As I was doing several things, I needed more information. "What am I doing?"

"You're topping me. From the way you behaved last night, I suspected you had a dominant personality. This confirms it."

Excitement rushed to my cock. Smart women were so sexy. I chuckled. "I do identify as a Dom."

I hadn't been pinning her in place, and she turned to face me. My arms were still on either side of her. I wanted to touch her, but I kept my hands where they were. I wasn't sure she was ready to experience all that I was.

"What did Daniel say when you talked to him?"

I wasn't going to let her take the lead, but the fact she tried made me smile. "We're not finished discussing the windows."

"You said they could wait a few months, and you said you needed some time to run the numbers and give me an estimate on the roof. I have a budget. When you give me the estimate, I will compare it with the other estimates and make a decision. I feel we're finished discussing repairs on the house." She pushed at my chest, though only the tips of her fingers touched me.

I took a step back. "Alaina, the windows can't wait very long. I'll give you an estimate for those as well."

She considered this. "I know what replacement windows cost. I can't afford to do all the windows yet. I'll have to redo my budget, and it'll take some time to save up. I just want an estimate on the roof."

"I'm talking about replacing framing as well, and you don't need them all replaced."

"Oh, yes I do." Her tone warned that arguing would do no good. "If you only replace one window, it will be noticeable and ruin the aesthetic of the house."

I realized her problem ran deeper than merely an unexpected expense. Visualizing the outside of the house, I counted nine windows on the front and nine on the back. Each side had four more. The doors in the front and rear were centered. I wondered if the lone side door, which ruined the symmetry of the house, bothered her.

"They won't stand out."

"Evan—" Her patience had run out. Nostrils flared, and danger muddied her eyes. She crossed her arms over her chest, protecting herself from emotional unpleasantness.

"Alaina, I know what I'm doing. From the outside, the only difference will be if another window needs repair, in which case, it already stands out."

"But from the inside, it'll be horribly different." Shoving aside my arm, she stormed out, and she invited me to follow her with a curt wave of her hand.

She led me down the hall to a room on the end. The elegant door with an artful glass design was open, and she stalked through it, coming to a halt in the center of the room. A curved desk sat in front of a pair of windows. Boxes were neatly stacked against one wall, and a sofa sat against another. The totes she'd brought in from the car were on the floor in front of the desk, and the top of it had papers, books, and office supplies scattered all over. An open box was there as well, and it looked as if she'd unpacked half of it before stopping.

I would've thought Alaina's work space would be meticulous. She sure was a study in contradictions, which only made her more intriguing.

She gestured wildly to the windows. "You want to replace one of those and not the other. Maybe you can make it blend in from the outside—I'm not sure that's possible—but you can't make it look right in here. The stain will never match."

The room had three windows. Two were on the back wall, and one occupied space on the side wall. I'd proposed replacing one on the back and one on the side. She was right. New stain wasn't going to match old, faded stain.

She shook her hands toward the ceiling. "My bedroom is above this. I cannot get up every morning and look at windows that don't match."

Technically, she could, but I wasn't going to call her out on it. She wanted solutions.

"I can stain the third window to match the new ones, or I can replace the third window as well."

She made an X with her hands, and then uncrossed them to push away the information. "No. Just the roof, Evan. If you don't want to do it, then don't, but that's all I'm willing to discuss right now."

"You're a very stubborn woman," I observed.

"I'm aware. I'm also difficult to deal with for long periods of time, and I don't intend to change." She was about to say more, but I moved in and set my hands on her shoulders.

"I think you're fine just the way you are, and I'd never ask you to change. You told me what you want, and now I'm going to tell you what I'm going to do." I studied her face, noting the firm press of her lips and the fact that she preferred to look at my mouth rather than my eyes. "I'm going to write up an estimate for your roof. I'm going to do a separate one for the windows. I'll have them to you by the weekend, and you can take whatever actions you deem appropriate."

She huffed out her disapproval, which I'd expected.

"And now, I'm going to tell you that Daniel said if it was okay with you, then it was okay with him."

"Okay." She didn't show much of a reaction. Maybe she was still pissed about the windows, which was a distinct possibility because now she was glaring at them as if they'd betrayed her.

"So, what do you want, Alaina?" My hands were still on her shoulders, and we were fast approaching that moment when it would either be romantic or the chemistry would fizzle out.

She faced me, and she looked me in the eyes, which I hadn't expected. "I want to know why you haven't thrown in the towel and made a run for the exit by now."

"What do you mean?" I scrambled to figure out why she'd think that.

"I know it appears I'm being unreasonable. I'm not doing it on purpose, but most people would have lost patience by now."

My answer was going to blow things up no matter what I said, so I opted for the direct approach because I knew she would appreciate it. "I've realized you're possibly neuroatypical, and you need time to process the unexpected. And perhaps some re-explaining or different reasoning when you hear things you don't want to hear—because you're stubborn."

She frowned and her gaze once again fell to the region of my mouth. I figured that was all the eye contact she could handle for now.

"What are you thinking?"

"I'm wondering what you think 'neuroatypical' means and trying to figure out how you're applying it to me." She worried her bottom lip with her teeth for a moment. "I'm also trying to figure out if I like that you're touching me more than the weight of your hands is annoying."

Yeah, the awkward moment had come. I moved my hands away from her shoulders and let them dangle by my sides. Then I stuck one partially in my jeans' pocket and gestured with the other. "I think you're somewhere on the ASD spectrum. I have a niece who has autism, and you have some similar behaviors. It looks different in women than in men. Women tend to mask it better. And you, Alaina, are very intelligent. I bet most people just think you're quirky because you're a genius."

I'd called her smart, but her frown didn't go away.

"It doesn't bother me that you're neuroatypical. It's part of who you are. But it helps me understand why you reacted the way you did. I noticed some stuff last night, and some more stuff today."

She rolled her shoulders, and then she folded her arms. "What behaviors?"

"You don't like your hands touched. You tend to look at mouths rather than eyes during conversation. You like to know what's coming at you, and you prefer when someone is direct. You make a schedule every Sunday night, and you don't like when life deviates from it. I'm sure it happens all the time, and you deal with it. And you're really, really smart. I'm sure there's more, but I've known you for less than twenty-four hours."

Her mouth opened and closed a few times, and she shuffled her feet without unfolding her arms. "You're very observant."

"I like you, so I've been paying attention."

She looked at me again, her gaze meeting mine, and I recognized an edge of hostility or defiance. "You're much younger than I am. You're very handsome, confident, and charming. I don't understand why you like me. Unless this has to do with Daniel? Do you guys like to have sex with the same women?" Her gaze drifted toward the window, and she continued. "It's normal for close friends to have similar tastes. It's what bonds people together in the first place."

Without hesitation, I burst that bubble. "Daniel and I have never been attracted to or slept with the same woman before. Until you, he's been partial to tall blondes. You're more my type than his."

"He's not dominant." She was in front of the window now, peering outside, though I'm not sure if she was seeing anything except her thoughts.

"No. That's my thing."

A bell went off in the kitchen. She startled, and then she rushed from the room.

Chapter 7—Alaina

Dinner was going to burn while I was in the study trying to figure out how two younger, smoking hot men had come to be interested in having sex with me. I knew I was pretty—most people thought I possessed a cuteness because I had a small stature and symmetrical features—but I was under no illusion I was a prize. I came with a whole set of quirks, and not all of them were as cute as I was.

I slid oven mitts over my hands, and then I pulled the sheet pan from the oven. The salmon looked and smelled perfect. I'd meant to have the yogurt sauce mixed by now, but Evan's news about the windows had derailed me. He was right that I didn't do well when the unexpected happened. I was useless in an emergency. Adam used to get so exasperated with me. Now, it was just another bullet he'd dodged when we'd divorced.

"Alaina? Are you upset with me for any reason other than the windows?"

I wasn't upset with him about the windows. I was pissed at the inspector I'd hired only two short months ago to find all the issues with the house. I'd lusted after this house since I was seven years old and we'd driven by it during the holidays. It had been lit up for the season, and I'd fallen in love with the graceful symmetry. When it had come on the market last spring, I hadn't been looking to move from the cozy bungalow near the University. I didn't need a six-bedroom house for Zack and me or a half-hour drive to work. I didn't even have furniture for half the rooms.

But how often does a woman get to fulfill her little girl dreams?

Nothing was going to deter me from buying it, but I might not have moved in until after I'd fixed it up if I'd known the extent of the problems. The plumbing was proving problematic, and I was sure it needed an overhaul of the electrical system. I was sorely tempted to learn the building trades myself, but I lacked the time and patience.

I steadfastly refused to mention any of these issues in front of Adam, who'd toured the house after I'd bought it and who came inside for a cup of coffee most times he dropped off or picked up Zack so we could communicate about our son. I was also doing my best to minimize them in front of Zack. I loved my son, but he told his father everything going on in my life. He also told me everything going on in Adam's life, even though I never asked anything except how he'd been during the days I didn't see him.

"Alaina?" Those heavy hands landed on my shoulders, pulling me from my thoughts.

Atypical. Though I'd never been formally tested—women with autism were overlooked because the current models were based on the male brain, and autism looked very different in women—I was well aware of how I was different from everybody else. I didn't care about labels, though I knew autism and ADD both applied to me. It was harder for me to function in society than it was for the average person. I knew my mind flew at a million miles an hour and had problems settling on one topic. I knew I had personal habits and preferences that seemed obsessive or exacting for those living with me. I knew people found me strange or unusual, and that they attributed it as a side effect of my intelligence.

I worked very hard to be relatable in a professional capacity—the practice of behaving in a way that made sense to society but not to me was called masking—but I didn't often apply that effort to my personal life. I felt I should be able to be myself once I was home from work. I didn't care if that meant I'd be single forever. Of course, I still worked to be flexible with Zack because my issues weren't his issues. He was the opposite of me in so many ways, and I didn't want to stifle his brand of wonderfulness.

I was comfortable with myself, and I wasn't willing to let anybody cause me to second-guess my personal happiness.

I didn't mind Evan's hands. They were lighter now, less burdensome and more reassuring. "I'm not mad at you, Evan. I'm angry with the inspector I hired, and I'm wondering what else is falling apart in this place that I didn't budget for."

I needed to get the ingredients for the yogurt sauce, but I didn't want to move out of his hold.

Before he could start talking and offering to look around, I faced him. I set my fingertips on his chest—it was my palms that were extra-sensitive, not my fingers—and I said, "What kind of Dom are you? My ex was authoritative, though he didn't necessarily identify as a Dom, and I know I'm submissive when I'm comfortable with someone. I have played around with this dynamic before, and I know everybody has different kinks."

Whatever he'd been about to say died on his lips. Neurotypical people put a lot of stock into looking people in the eye, which was a cultural norm denoting respect. It meant you were paying attention. For me, it was easier for my mind to wander when I looked at people's eyes.

I found I could glean a lot more information by studying people's mouths. Even when the eyes were remote, every emotion manifested in and around the mouth. I found them infinitely easier to read, and they rarely overloaded my senses.

A small smile started, a tell-tale sign of amusement, quirking the corners of his mouth. Evan was an excellent kisser, which was a good indication of his ability to eat pussy. The thought brought a smile to my face.

His hands slid off my shoulders, down my arms, and they stopped at my hips. It was a very dominant move, and a little thrill ran through me. As I'd told him, I'd played BDSM games before, but something about the slant of Evan's mouth told me he didn't play games. He took being Dominant very seriously, and I found the submissive parts of myself taking over. It calmed me considerably.

"How about we have dinner, and we can discuss what kinks we both like?" Rather than let me go, he tugged me closer. My pelvis bumped against his thighs, which was another sensation I quite liked. Then that expressive mouth was on mine.

Hot and insistent, it staked a claim. I opened on a sigh, and his tongue danced with mine. Warm, delicious feelings sluiced through me, a series of chemical reactions releasing an addictive product.

When the kiss ended, he moved away a few inches, but his hands lingered on my hips until I turned away to gather the ingredients for my yogurt sauce.

He set the table without being asked. I didn't know if he did it because he wanted to get into my pants or because he was thoughtful, but I appreciated the way he jumped in and helped.

When he tasted the salmon, his mouth widened with appreciation. Little lines appeared beside his smile, and I thought those lines were the sexiest thing a face could boast. They indicated a person who found joy in life, especially when they appeared on someone so young.

Not that I was over-the-hill. I was in my sexual prime, though, biologically, there was a good chance Evan had passed his peak. No matter. I had an impressive collection of vibrators. Adam had never been able to quite get me there on his own. I think it was due to the fact he liked to hold hands during sex, which many people found sweet and romantic, even when used as a form of restraint, but it only distracted me from completion.

Not that I was comparing Evan to Adam on purpose. It was just that Adam had been the last man who was twenty-six when we had sex. Except for Daniel, but Daniel hadn't brought to mind thoughts of Adam.

I needed to stop thinking of Adam. Just because Evan had an authority about him didn't mean they had anything else in common. Already Evan had discerned more about me than Adam ever had.

"You're twenty-six?" I didn't care about his precise age. Evan's news about my house had thrown me off, and now I was nervous and making small talk, probably badly. Awkward was my hashtag.

"Twenty-five. Daniel's a year older than me."

"Ah. So I'm robbing an even younger cradle. Go, me." I pumped my fist in celebration.

He laughed. "It's safe to say that I pursued you. Let's call you a cougar instead of a cradle-robber. It has a better connotation." He took another bite of salmon. "Damn, Alaina. You're a fantastic cook."

I hadn't made any sides, only a salad. I wasn't sure if he'd stay, and cooking for one meant I skimped on side dishes. I would have opted for a baked potato for just myself, but I figured if he stayed, he'd want something more substantial, thus the salmon.

"I'm competent."

"That's a humble assessment."

"It's a recipe I memorized. Competent cooks can replicate what others make. Fantastic cooks can change things around to make them better or different. I don't change recipes. I just follow them."

He shook his head. "Agree to disagree. If I followed this recipe, it wouldn't turn out nearly as well."

"Then you wouldn't have followed the recipe." I didn't want to discuss food or cooking. This was fuel for a better event. "What kinks are you thinking you'd like to use this evening?"

"Bondage." He lifted a brow, which I noted, but he frowned ever so slightly, asking for consent.

"For restraint," I conceded. "I don't have patience for Shibari, and I find Kinbaku too painful. I like rough play, but not tight bindings."

That sexy corner of his mouth curved again. "Rough play? Tell me about that?"

It took a moment for my brain to process his question because I was too focused on kissing him again. He had a very sexy, expressive mouth and strong, lush lips. In the midst of fantasizing about kissing him, I realized he was still waiting for me to answer. I tore my gaze from the beauty of his face and looked at the food on my plate. "I like to be manhandled. Picked up, tossed around, positioned, groped, pinned, wrists held down."

From the way his mouth went slack, I think he hadn't expected my description. "You're certainly petite enough for me to toss around like a sack of potatoes."

"I'm not delicate." I hated how people who were larger tended to treat me as if I was going to break. "And, in the bedroom, I really don't care to be treated that way."

Accepting my terms, he stabbed at his salad. "What about rough play on your nipples?"

"Yes, please. They are not at all sensitive." Breast feeding ruined me for light sensory play in that region. "Rough sex, hair pulling—all the rough stuff is on the approved list."

"Spanking?"

I looked at his mouth again. The few times I'd played, the spanking aspect had been very disappointing. But the set of his jaw promised he'd be different. "I'm not against it, but I've never seen a benefit to it, so I'm not enthusiastic about it. Do you like impact play, Evan? Are you a sadist?"

"I'm more of a control freak. I like impact play, but it isn't my favorite way to torture a sex partner. I didn't bring my floggers. I brought some restraints and clamps." He thought for a moment. "I have my violet wand case in the truck, but only because I forgot to take it out."

From the brief flash of a frown, I knew he was telling the truth, and I deduced that he wasn't sure he wanted to mention it to me. I tried to make light of it. "Maybe we can save it for next time."

I meant it as a joke, but as soon as the words were out of my mouth, I realized it seemed like I was fishing for more than one night. I wasn't.

He absorbed my suggestion in thoughtful silence while he chewed. After he swallowed, he nodded thoughtfully. "Maybe."

"With the manhandling thing, I didn't mean to imply that I would like that all the time. It's more of an erotic foreplay thing for me."

"Makes sense." He stared at me.

I felt the power of his gaze move over me like an indirect caress. I didn't look up to meet his gaze. I liked that he understood I was listening and paying attention even when I wasn't observing annoying societal norms.

"We should have a signal, a clear line between play time and the rest of the time."

I liked his idea, so I nodded.

"I'll call you 'Lainie,' and that will signal the start of play. When I use that nickname, you'll recognize me as your Dom. You'll refer to me as 'Sir,' and you'll follow my orders."

The nickname I'd tossed out for fun at Daniel was one he'd used last night. It looked like his best friend had picked up on it. My chest felt tight, and my bra was suddenly three sizes too small. "Would I have to kneel?"

"Would you like to?"

"No."

"But you would if I ordered you to."

Would I? It seemed like a token of respect he hadn't earned, not for a one-night stand. "I'm not sure. I wouldn't today, so you shouldn't ask me to."

"Perhaps next time?" Lines of amusement peeked out around his sensual mouth.

Realizing he was accepting my position, I relaxed. "Perhaps next time."

"Lainie, let's get the dishes cleaned up." He rose and collected our plates.

So absorbed in our negotiation and his mouth, I hadn't realized they were empty. "There's more, if you're still hungry."

He chuckled. "I'm hungry, *Lainie*, but not for food. What's your safeword tonight?"

"Stop." I joined him at the counter. I put away the leftovers while he rinsed dishes and loaded the dishwasher. Someone had trained him well.

He paused and looked over at me. "Stop? You don't want to play protest games?"

"Not until we know each other better."

"Fair enough." He wore a huge smile while he finished up. "I'm going to run to my truck to get the restraints."

I wiped down the counter, and then I went to the table. This was going so much faster with two people, and I loved that I didn't have to direct his actions and look over his work. That alone was making me hot.

My erotic triggers had definitely changed over the years.

While I was bent over, I felt him behind me. Then his arms came down on either side of me, landing on the wet table. His package—the cock one, not some mysterious gift—pressed into my backside. I felt his chest leaning over me, but it didn't touch my back.

He's used the nickname, I realized, signaling the start of play time. I finished wiping the table.

A dry cloth landed in front of me. Now I was close to swooning. I dried the table. Evan lifted his hands so I could get the spots he touched.

"I wonder if you understand exactly how hot it is that you do dishes?"

He chuckled, a soft sound that was more of a rumble than a noise. One hand lifted, and I felt a tug where my hair was coiled into a bun. A second tug, and the strands sprang free, tumbling over my shoulders and probably shooting spiral fireworks in all directions. He set two hair pins on the freshly washed table.

Then his fingers threaded through the mess, massaging my scalp without pulling too hard on the tangles. I found myself straightening up and leaning back against his powerful chest. His hands left my head and traveled down the front of my shirt, stopping when they landed on my breasts. He kissed my neck as he kneaded my breasts over my clothes.

"Take your pants off." The authority in his voice left no doubt he expected me to comply. "I prefer you in skirts."

"Do you want me to put a skirt on?" I had dozens of them. My clothing preferences went in cycles, and right now, I was on a skirt kick. I'd put jeans on in case he needed to take me up on the ladder or into the attic to show me something. But I'd opted for lace panties in case the jeans came off.

"No. But next time, I want to see you in a skirt."

"Yes, Sir." I undid the button on my jeans and unknitted the zipper. He gave me space to lower my jeans and step out of the legs.

He took them from me, folded them, and set them on the table next to my hair pins. Then he whirled me around, picked me up, and tossed me over his shoulder. A thrill shot through me. I knew I'd asked for this, but Evan was the first man who'd ever taken me at my word. That was also sexy.

One arm held me secure, and his other hand squeezed and patted my ass. "You have a very sexy ass, Lainie. I'm going to enjoy spanking it."

"Here's hoping I do as well." It was not as easy to speak with his shoulder digging into my stomach as I'd envisioned.

"You might. You might not. But I'll enjoy it whether you do or not."

He took the steps smoothly, which I appreciated, and he found my bedroom without a problem. The door was open, and he paused inside the threshold.

I knew what he was looking at. The master bedroom was huge. It swallowed up a quarter of the upstairs. Across from it were two good-sized bedrooms, both empty. Zack had chosen the second-largest room, which was on the other side of the house. I hadn't bought furniture for this new house yet, so a bed and chair were the only items in my room. I had a chest of drawers, but it was inside the cavernous closet with my clothes.

Pictures waiting to be hung leaned against the wall underneath where I wanted to put them. I'd misplaced my stud finder and some of my other tools in the move. A small table sat next to my bed. It supported a lamp and an alarm clock.

He approached the bed and slid his travel bag from his shoulder. It hit the carpet with a dull thud.

I expected him to put me down next, but his free hand only widened the scope of its caresses to include my thighs as well as my ass.

"This is a perfect bed for bondage, Lainie. The headboard has slats, and the footboard has tall posts. Please tell me it's not an antique."

"I hope not. I bought it new nine years ago." I'd let Adam take most of the furniture in the divorce because I didn't want anything that reminded me of him—besides Zack, but Zack usually only reminded me of himself.

"Good. If we break it, you won't be too upset." He set me on my feet.

Before I could tell him that I would mind if we broke my bed frame, his lips were on mine. They claimed me with an unmistakable authority, dominating my thoughts and driving them away.

It was really nice not to be able to think.

His tongue plunged inside, stabbing and swiping and keeping me off-kilter. I threw my arms around his neck and ground my front against his. His big hands roamed my body, bringing heat with them and sending flares straight to my pussy.

He lifted my shirt, breaking the kiss to pull it over my head. I was poised to go back to kissing, and he obliged, but he pinned my wrists behind my back. I grumped a protest because I very much enjoyed touching him, and so I tried to break free.

The strength of his hold only increased, and my pussy approved.

He trailed wet kisses across my cheek and bit my earlobe. Electricity raced from there to my nipples. I moaned and tilted my head, inviting him to stay in that region.

The kisses alternated with nips as he made his way down my neck to my shoulder. Sensations ran riot in my systems, overriding everything else. This was the blissful side of sensory overload, and I almost never got here without panicking. Something about Evan inspired trust in me, and I gave myself over to him.

He stepped back, releasing his hold on my wrists.

Suddenly aware I hadn't been breathing much, I inhaled deeply as his gaze roved greedily over my body.

"Do that again." The order was quiet, and it did not invite discussion.

I inhaled again, my breasts lifting with the action. Then I made a request. "Can I take off your shirt?"

"Yes."

He stood still as I unbuttoned the three buttons at the top of his shirt, and he bent so I could pull it over his head. It was a nice shirt, something he'd wear on a date, not something he'd wear to give an estimate.

"You dressed up for me."

Half that sensual mouth lifted in a smirky smile.

I felt bad. "I didn't dress up for you."

The arrogant grin didn't abate, and his gaze zeroed in on my lace bra. "I like this outfit a lot. You're very sexy, Lainie, and you look so good in lace that I'm not sure whether I'm going to take if off of you, or have you keep it on."

My guilt eased, and I studied the chiseled perfection of his bare chest. Ropes of delineated muscles attested to an active lifestyle. He had dark peach nipples and a smattering of freckles across his shoulders and down his arms. He was tan all over, though his arms were darker than his shoulders and chest.

I didn't know if he had rules about what I could and couldn't touch, but since he hadn't said anything, I touched. I traced my fingertips over his smooth skin. My brain screamed at me to use a firmer pressure, but I didn't want to chance this being unpleasant for him. Gooseflesh rose in the places I'd touched, and my hand trembled.

"You can press harder, Lainie. Do what feels good for you. If it's too much for me, I'll tell you."

I'd never had a lover who acknowledged my quirks or made allowances for them. Or who even noticed when I was holding back. I increased the pressure of my caress so that it felt good for me, and I was careful to follow the lines of his muscles because what I was doing probably felt more like a massage. He let me explore for a bit, and then he caught my wrists.

"Too much?"

"Yes. If you keep doing that, I'm going to start humping your leg."

The visual that leaped to mind caused me to laugh.

Evan smiled, too. "Go grab your vibrator and some lube."

"I have six. Was there a specific kind you wanted? Also, I have heated lube and regular."

"Select two vibes, and bring both kinds of lube." He squatted down and opened the heavy-duty nylon bag. When I returned, he held a set of padded leather restraints.

I set the vibrators and lube on the table, and then I held out my wrists. He secured the restraints in place, frowning because the smallest notch in the buckle was still loose on me.

"Are those maybe for ankles?"

"No. They're for men, but you still have insanely small wrists." He encircled one with his hand, touching his thumb and index finger together. There was plenty of room for me to slip my hand free.

However, that wasn't what my brain fixated on. "Men?"

"Yeah." He glanced up, the frown still marring his chin. "But that usually doesn't matter."

"Do you usually sleep with men?" It really was none of my business. It wasn't like we were married or even dating. This was casual sex, and either of us could have casual sex with anybody we wanted. After all, I'd slept with Daniel the day before, and I planned to see him tomorrow.

Now he stopped, and he studied my face. "I'm bisexual. Does that bother you?"

"No." It didn't, not in the slightest. At least he was open about his sexual preferences. I'd told Daniel that sexuality was a spectrum, and I knew that younger generations were more open about embracing that facet of our natures. But I couldn't stop thinking about Adam and how he'd betrayed me. I took a deep breath to release the negativity because Evan wasn't my ex. He wasn't even my current. He hadn't lied to me or betrayed me. He didn't deserve to be on the receiving end of the distress I was combating.

I wanted my brain to stop thinking altogether, like it had when he'd kissed me. Daniel came to mind.

"Alaina?"

"It's fine, Evan. I'm sorry if I sounded like I had a problem with it. I don't, and it's none of my business anyway." I pictured a shirtless Daniel next to Evan, and I wondered what it would be like to see them going at it—two attractive men kissing and wrestling each other out of their clothes.

"You've developed a frown line between your eyes that says otherwise."

"It says my brain won't stop thinking about you naked with other hot guys, and I can't get it to shut off." I licked my lips. "It stops when you kiss me. Maybe you should kiss me again?"

He leaned closer, until his lips were an inch from mine. "Which hot guys were you picturing me with?"

I sincerely didn't want to say, so I leaned forward and pressed my lips to his.

Not only did he fail to take the bait, but he straightened up, which put him out of reach. He regarded me with a firm set to his mouth. "Lainie, I asked you a question. When I ask you a question, you must answer."

I needed the reminder that I'd turned over control to him. My hand smoothed down a skirt I wasn't wearing, so it looked like I was feeling up my thigh. Touching my skin wasn't as calming as the fabric of a skirt would be, so I abandoned the effort to self-soothe. "Sir, I didn't think you'd like my answer."

He lifted a brow. "If I didn't want to know the answer, I wouldn't ask the question. Who did you picture me with? Is it an actor who plays a superhero?"

Oh, that would have been safer. "No, but now I am. Oh, my panties are getting very wet."

"You were warned, and now you've earned a punishment."

He turned me around, and he clipped the restraints together behind my back. Then he pushed my front half down to bend me over the side of the bed. He pushed my panties down to my knees.

Before I could process what he meant to do, I felt the impact of his hand on my butt cheek. The sound of flesh hitting flesh echoed through the room, and a sting bloomed where he'd struck me.

My first instinct was to use my hands to push against the bed so I could escape the spanking, but the restraints did their job. My elbows moved, but that wasn't helpful.

Evan's hand came down on my arms anyway, pushing down to hold my body still. "Since this is your first time being disciplined by me, let's go over the rules. Every time I spank you, you'll count it out and thank me for it, and you'll use my title."

He spanked me as he explained the rules, and he wasn't fooling around with those hits. He was wholly unlike the two other Doms I'd played around with—he didn't treat me as if I was breakable.

"Six, Sir."

"Nope. They don't count if you don't. Start at one." While giving that instruction, he added two more.

I hated miscounting. "One and nine, Sir. Thank you."

He chuckled, a low sound that betrayed amusement, but he didn't correct the way I counted. He paused, his palm moving over my flesh. "You're already turning red, Lainie. How does it feel?"

"It hurts. It burns a little, but my pussy is even wetter."

He hit again.

"Two and ten, Sir. Thank you."

He took me to twelve and twenty, and then he jerked me to my feet. His hand fisted in my hair while the other squeezed and scratched at the tender flesh of my ass. The sensations of pain and pleasure left me baffled, though I understood the science behind the chemical and psychological effects of why I felt the way I did.

"How do you feel now?"

I was breathing hard. My wrists were bound behind me. Evan was manhandling me with precision and ease, and I'd just had my first really satisfying spanking. More than all that—my brain was not hosting a thousand simultaneous thoughts.

I smiled. "Fantastic, though I expect you wanted me to feel chastened for not answering your question directly."

"Or at all."

"Sir, I did—and am—picturing you with hot superhero actors. I'm even envisioning you and Ironman double-teaming me."

"But that's not what you were thinking at first."

With a sigh, I gave in and admitted what I'd been thinking. "I was picturing you and Daniel together. But he's your best friend, so I didn't want to make it weird."

Rather than be upset, he merely appeared thoughtful. "Was that so bad?"

"Not for me, Sir, but your hand might be sore."

The slow smile should have warned me he was up to no good. "A little. Perhaps some wet heat will make it feel better."

He turned me back to face the bed, but he pulled me against his front. One arm banded across my shoulders, and the hand he'd used to spank me headed for a warmer, moister destination. Due to how wet I was, his fingers parted my lips and slid along my well-lubricated clit. They didn't stop to play. Instead, he slid two fingers deep inside my pussy.

Having not quite expected the intrusion—it wasn't violent, but it was sudden—I inhaled sharply.

He didn't check in with me to see if I was okay, which I kind of liked. His fingers swirled, feeling me up from the inside. He added a third, and then he pumped them into me. I gasped at the way he stretched my vaginal tissues, and I leaned my head against his chest.

"Shh," he whispered. "Don't make a sound, Lainie, and don't you dare have an orgasm. This is therapy for my sore hand."

Drenched with my juices, his hand rubbed against my pussy, stimulating all parts of my clit. The fingers inside me curved to hit my sweet spot.

A moan escaped.

Evan clamped a hand over my mouth, and he fucked his fingers into me—deeper, faster, harder. The thrust lifted me to my tiptoes. I struggled against his hold, but he had a firm grasp. My arms had been immobilized, and he held me prisoner with an arm pressing to my chest and a hand over my mouth. The edge of his hand covered most of my nostrils, leaving me unable to draw enough oxygen.

Given the angle of his view, I had no doubt he knew full well what he was doing.

Being helpless was a new feeling for me. Though it was disturbing, and I wasn't sure I liked it, I found it fucking erotic as all get-out. Nothing about this situation was under my control. Evan determined my position and condition, and I could only relax and subsume my will to his.

Without warning, a climax slammed into me. My body convulsed, and my eyes rolled back into my head. I collapsed against him, my body pulsating on the inside and limp on the outside. The hand over my mouth now kept me from becoming a pool of gelatin on the floor.

He pressed his lips to my temple, and he held me against his body. "You naughty, naughty woman."

"Yes, Sir," I managed. "I'm so very bad."

"Spanking you didn't do anything but make you wetter. Rough fingering and breath play made you come so hard you almost passed out in my arms."

I could only smile. "It's nice to learn new things about one's self."

He heaved a dramatic sigh. "Looks like I'm going to have to kick things up a notch." With that, he hooked an arm under my knees, lifted me up, and tossed me onto the bed.

I landed on my elbows with my bound arms pinned under my back, which thrust my breasts into the air.

Evan straddled my thighs, and he leaned forward, resting his weight on his hands. He lowered his head, and the heat of his mouth closed around my nipple. He nipped at them with his lips, laved them with his tongue, and sucked with soft pulls. It felt pleasant, but that region had ceased being sensitive long ago. Also, I was still wearing a bra.

"I can handle it harder."

He lifted his face, and his gaze met mine.

I struggled not to look at his lips instead.

Rather than say anything, he kissed me. The soft massage gave way to a thorough ravaging that left me breathless. Pleasure thrummed and throbbed through me. When he leaned up again to look at me, he wore that arrogant smile that said he knew exactly what he was doing.

"You like to start gently, and then build up to see how much I can take."

He brushed another kiss across my lips. "I love that you're so fucking intelligent, Lainie. It's sexy."

I was book smart, and I'd used books to study social interaction. I was used to meeting people at their expectation. I wasn't used to people trying to understand mine. He'd stopped just to make sure I understood the method behind his dominance. The fact that Evan was trying made a part of my heart come alive, a part not even Adam had activated. It had hidden from him, peeking out and wanting to be found by someone who cared enough to look.

It was disconcerting.

"I'm going to get rough, Lainie. I'm going to tie you to the bed and do things to you that are going to make you moan and beg, shout and cry. Before I do any of that, I need to get some things set up."

"So, all this was just foreplay?"

His grin grew. "Yes, with more to come. I like to play, Lainie." He leaned up, resting his weight on his heels while still straddling me. He ran his hands over my body, touching me everywhere he wasn't sitting, even reaching under me to caress my back and squeeze my ass.

Then he flipped me over and unclasped the restraints. They were still around my wrists, a surprisingly heavy weight, but now I could move my arms.

"Take off the rest of your clothes. Lay in the center of the bed with your arms stretched out and up." He hopped off the bed and went to his bag. I watched him tie lengths of rope to the bed posts on my headboard. Then he threaded them through the metal rings on my restraints. When he had my arms bound in place, he stood back and surveyed his work.

While he did that, I watched him. Evan was a study in masculine beauty. His muscles were hard and honed. Substantial, yet not bulky. He didn't have a six-pack, which actually denoted dehydration, but he was trim and fit. I liked a healthy body. I'd love to see more of it.

"You might be more comfortable if you took your jeans off." I flashed the cutest smile I could summon to further my cause.

He shook his head, and he didn't try to disguise his amusement. "Topping from the bottom will get your bottom smacked."

"I was just being a good hostess. I like for my guests to feel at home."

Evan climbed onto the bed and straddled my midsection. "You're not a hostess right now, Lainie. You're mine—my submissive.

Manipulation—which is what you were doing—will not be tolerated." As he spoke, his hands stroked from my ribs upward, all the way to my wrists. The restraints seemed to serve as a stopping line, and I appreciated that limit.

He was a hundred percent right that I was trying to manipulate him. I wanted him to undress so I could see all the sexy parts of his body. Just from the way his jeans hung on his hips and hugged his ass, I knew good things were waiting behind that denim.

"Is it topping from the bottom if I tell you that I'm eagerly anticipating seeing you take off your pants?"

"Expressing wants and needs isn't topping from the bottom. Attempting to get me to do what you want through flattery or suggestion is."

He scooted down until he was over my thighs, and then he leaned down and took my nipple between his lips. He played for a bit before sucking it inside and searing it with the heat of his mouth. His teeth scraped, and his tongue laved, increasing the pressure and the riot of sensation.

My breath caught, and I inadvertently tugged on the restraints because instinct had me wanting to hold his head in place. "Oh, Sir, that feels so good."

With a hard pull, he abandoned that nipple to pay attention to the other one. Before long, I writhed and canted my hips, inviting him to investigate my pussy. But Evan was singularly focused on my breasts. Back and forth, he sucked, pulled, and nipped with his mouth, while my other breast enjoyed the way his fingers twisted and pulled.

After a time, he sat up and looked down at them. I glanced down as well to find them deep red and swollen, and more erect than I'd ever seen them before.

"You weren't kidding about liking rough nipple play." Pleased creases lined his mouth as that one, sexy corner lifted. He rose onto his knees to fish in his pocket. "Let's see how you like these."

He held up clover clamps connected by a delicate chain.

"I've never used those before," I said. I glanced at the more benign alligator clamp he'd abandoned on the bedside table. "They seem like an advanced tool."

"They are, but given what I've already done to you and how you've reacted, you're not going to be impressed with regular clamps." He pinched a nipple a few more times, and then he attached the clamp.

Fire. Hot, burning pain raced through my breast and radiated up through my arm. A smaller trail of flames blazed a path to my pussy.

The sensation was too overwhelming for me to have the coordination for a verbal reaction.

"Breathe, Lainie. Inhale."

It took all my strength to drag in a ragged breath.

"Good girl. Now let it out slowly. Breathe through the pain. Accept it. Embrace it as my will."

Tears blurred my vision, and my body trembled.

"It's okay to scream."

"I don't want to scream." A strange, strangled voice squeaked out of my throat.

"That's okay. Let's see how you feel when I do the other one." With that, he plumped and plucked, and then the teeth of the clover clamp bit into my tender flesh.

The pain didn't just double. It was exponentially more than I could accept.

I screamed.

My torso arched, trying to push away the pain. My nipples felt like they were no longer part of my body. They were just conduits for searing agony.

Evan's thumb stroked between my legs, petting the hard point of my clit. It was too much, a torture I couldn't abide combined with one I couldn't escape.

I tried to buck, to get away from the pain in my nipples and the overstimulation of my clit, but Evan's restraints kept my hands from being useful, and his weight on my thighs prevented me from gaining meaningful distance.

"You're so fucking beautiful, Lainie. Your suffering is a graceful dance that makes my dick rock hard." His lips brushed against mine, but my mouth wasn't on the same page, and I didn't kiss him back. He didn't seem to notice or care. His lips moved gently over my face, worshipping my cheeks, my eyelids, and my temples before traveling down my neck.

He licked my nipples where they swelled around the clamps, and then he kissed his way down. He wrenched my legs apart, pressing my thighs open and holding them with his large, strong hands. Then his kiss was on my pussy. His tongue swiped long paths, and his lips grazed softly against my sensitive parts.

As he played, I acclimated to the pain. The intensity of the fire waned, a manageable flicker instead of a consuming blaze. My screams quieted.

I looked down, noting that the inferno had moved to Evan's eyes. He lazily licked my pussy, but his gaze drank in the sight of my restrained and tortured body with utter glee and no small amount of possessiveness. His goal was to tease me while he watched me come undone.

He lifted his head away, but his finger penetrated my vagina. "How are you doing, Lainie?"

"I ache, Sir." I whimpered, begging for relief.

He climbed off the bed, his gaze holding mine for precious seconds before roaming my body. I watched him, looking for any sign he might relent, but the satisfied slant to his mouth didn't inspire hope.

"Please." My whispered plea only increased his satisfaction. I was considering begging some more when his hands went to the waist of his jeans.

Slowly he opened the fly, taunting me with his unhurried pace as he revealed zebra patterned briefs. It seemed to take forever for him to peel out of his pants. His erection strained against the thin fabric, trying to get to me as badly as I wanted it to succeed.

But Evan wasn't ready to cede his will to easy pleasure. He picked up my vibrator and climbed back on the bed, sitting with his hip next to my thigh. He turned the dial at the base to familiarize himself with the settings. I liked to start slow and dial it up as I got closer, but telling him that would be construed as topping from the bottom. This wasn't about what I liked or I wanted; this was about the pleasure he derived from torturing me.

He played, running it up and down my slit before pressing it to the tip of my clit. He teased gasps and moans from me, and he used that data to figure out the spots and angles that drove me wild. And then he slid it inside.

My whole body was on edge, already quaking from the pleasure and pain he'd dealt. It took all of thirty seconds for the tight coils to spring loose. Arching, I cried out and lifted my ass clear off the bed. He followed, holding the vibrator inside me, and he turned up the rate of vibrations. My orgasm came harder. I cried out as my body convulsed. My brain shut off as the throbbing tsunami washed through my system.

When my mind regained the ability to pay attention to my surroundings, Evan sat in the same spot, a soft smile on his face. "That was beautiful, Lainie. Ready for more?"

I wasn't sure more existed. I licked my lips. "I'm sure you mean that rhetorically."

He laughed. "Yes." Then he pressed the tip of the vibrator to my clit.

It was too much. I groaned a protest and tried to move my ass away. My wrists were tied, which left a lot of movement for the rest of me. Evan used his forearm to push my hips back down, and he leaned on me to pin me in place.

"Evan, please. It's too much."

He kept the vibrator on my poor, over-stimulated clit and tilted his head. "Lainie, you forgot to use my title."

"Sir," I shouted. "I'm sorry, Sir. I won't forget again."

"We'll see about that." The press of the vibe on my clit eased. He knelt up and shed his briefs.

The visual confirmed my suspicion that he was magnificent. He knelt between my legs and rolled a condom over his cock. My whole body quivered, half in anticipation of having him inside me, and half afraid I was too spent to accommodate him.

I whimpered as he entered my sopping channel. Evan hovered above me, his weight resting on his hands, and the strain of holding back showed in the way he pressed his lips together.

"God, Lainie. You feel so good." He pushed inside farther, until he was balls-deep, and then he paused to capture my mouth with another of his drugging kisses. Then he pressed his forehead to mine. "I'm going to make you come until you pass out."

"That'll be a first," I said. I hadn't meant it as a challenge, only a comment that I hadn't ever orgasmed to the point of exhaustion, but Evan grinned as if I'd thrown down a gauntlet.

He fucked me with slow, skillful thrusts that rubbed my sweet spot. His forehead was still against mine, though his weight rested on his elbows. Then he lifted, shifting his center of gravity and swiveling his hips in a way that stole my breath. The beginnings of another orgasm pulsed inside me, a precursor to something I couldn't hope to control.

One hand came between us, a fingertip tracing designs on my chest and breasts. Then it twisted in the chain connecting my nipples together. How in the world had I forgotten about the clamps? Searing pain startled the throbbing right out of me, and I cried out.

It began a vicious cycle that only made him fuck me faster. He pulled, and I shouted, and soon he hit a frenzied pace. My pussy acclimated to the pain, welcoming the heat and sublimating it to feed the ticking bomb low in my abdomen.

All of a sudden, he removed the first clamp, and the second followed immediately. The feel of freedom was a double-edged sword because every nerve ending in my body screamed, and so did I.

His mouth clamped over mine, gagging and muffling the sound, but I was too out of control to do anything but feel. His moans and grunts showed that my pain was a powerful lover's caress. He pushed my thighs open wider and pounded his cock into my body. I thought he would come at any moment, but he held out, driving me to a dizzying height. My orgasm detonated, and my consciousness took flight. Through the roar of the engines, I heard Evan's shout.

When I opened my eyes, the lamp on my bedside table was on, and my vibrators were still there with the unused lube. The sheet covered me. I stirred, lifting my head to see the clock.

"Welcome back, Lainie." Evan's voice, hoarse from yelling or because he'd been asleep, came from behind me.

I turned, rolling to see him lying next to me. "I fell asleep?"

He grinned and sat up. "I told you I'd make you pass out."

"Yes, you did." My grin matched his. "You passed out, too." I was guessing, but I was reasonably sure I was right.

"Yes. I collapsed on top of you, but you were insensible and didn't notice."

The whole night, I'd been restrained. I itched to touch him, to memorize those hard planes and dips of his chest and arms. I did so now, running my fingertips over terrain I'd explored earlier.

He settled back against the pillow, allowing me the access I wanted.

"You enjoyed the scene." The deep rumble of his voice was like a purr, complementing the way I caressed his skin.

"Yes. I'm so glad you used clover clamps instead of alligator. I can't really feel the alligator ones."

One brow lifted, and a brief line appeared on his chin. "You've played around with clamps before?"

"Yes. I have an alligator pair somewhere, I think in a box of kitchen stuff I haven't unpacked yet."

He brushed a strand of hair away from my eyes and tucked it behind my ear, probably to see my face better. "You seem like the kind of person who would be a highly organized packer, and who would unpack everything within the first week."

I snorted. Many people thought I was highly organized. While I wasn't disorganized, I wasn't over-the-top. "Clara helped me pack for the move, and she labeled the boxes with the room where they were supposed to go. The movers put boxes in the rooms they were supposed to. I've unpacked a lot, probably eighty percent. Mostly I have clothes and books left."

"You liked being tied up." He brought the topic back to the scene.

I knew he wanted to debrief about it, but I wondered why he'd ask for feedback about a one-night stand. "Yes, Evan. You crafted a magnificent scene. Pain and pleasure are definitely your forte."

My hands had wandered down to caress his thighs. He had an incredible body, and I wanted to be able to recreate it in my memory when I masturbated. After the past couple of weeks, my brain had ample material for new fantasies.

"I thought tonight was amazing as well." He sat up, capturing my hand briefly, and kissing it before letting it go. "Alaina, I want to see you again."

For once during a conversation, my mind went blank.

"Alaina?" Evan cupped my cheek in his hand. "What are you thinking?"

I shook my head and responded truthfully. "Nothing."

The tiny, happy lines around his mouth faded. "Do you want to see me again?"

"You mean, for sex? Or to work on my roof?"

My whole life, I had a knack for saying the wrong thing at the wrong time. As much as I studied how to read a social situation, I inevitably fucked up.

Evan snatched his hand away. He threw back the sheet and got out of bed. I watched as he gathered his things. "You know what? You're right. It was stupid for me to think this could be more than one night."

I scrambled for something to say, but my mind was too muddled and confused to process the situation. I didn't understand what I'd done or said that was wrong, and I didn't know how to make him not mad at me. I watched him dress and throw his things into his bag.

"Evan? I don't understand what just happened."

"Nothing," he mumbled. "Nothing happened. We had dinner. We had sex. It was good, and now it's over."

"You're mad at me."

He looked at me, his gaze roaming my face before dropping away. "I'm not mad."

I got out of bed and stood before him. I touched a finger to his bottom lip. "Your words say one thing, but your lips say another. I'm sorry, Evan. I didn't mean to upset you."

He closed his eyes, and he pulled me to him, tucking my head under his chin and wrapping his arms around me. "It's okay, Alaina. I'm okay. I just—sometimes I move too fast. Sometimes I assume things that aren't true. You didn't do anything. You were wonderful." He pressed a kiss to the top of my head. "I'll email you the estimate by Saturday, okay?"

"Okay."

It seemed like everything was resolved, but after he left, the house felt strangely empty, and I felt unsettled inside. Had I been wrong about his reason for sleeping with me? Did it have less to do with his attraction to me—which I believed was real—and more to do with some kind of rivalry between him and Daniel?

"Fuck me," I muttered to my empty house. "I guess this is yet another item for my 'Shouldn't've' list."

One day soon, I was going to have to stop adding to that list.

Chapter 8—Daniel

The bell over my door tinkled. Instinct had me on alert. I couldn't see the door from my position in the back of the large studio, so I worked my way to the front of the room. Fridays were short days, with classes running from 4-7 pm during the summer. During the school year, I opened at three and closed at eight. It sounded counter-intuitive, but people liked to pack more activity in during the school year. In the summer, I also opened up two weekday mornings.

The other half of my building was rented out to a sandwich shop that did pretty good business. The owners were looking to retire, and they'd opted not to renew their lease when it ran out at the end of summer. Instead of looking for new tenants, I was slowly saving up money to turn it into a gym. I wanted to have workout equipment, but I also wanted to have a permanent kickboxing ring. The class I'd introduced two years ago was now my most popular offering. Originally a single night class, kickboxing now took place four times a week, twice during the day, and it had expanded into beginner, intermediate, and advanced sections. Additionally, I'd taken on one student to coach for competition, and I was looking to expand that enterprise as well. Through Kendra, I'd found out I had the makings of a pretty decent coach.

Once the lease was up, it would need to be remodeled. I'd already talked to Evan about it. He wanted me to get other estimates—in case his fledgling company couldn't handle the job—and I refused. Evan was a good, steady person, and when he set his mind to something, it was inevitably successful. I knew his company would do well because he was at the helm.

Looking into the lobby to see why the bell on the front door had gone off, I spotted Evan.

He jerked his chin up, indicating he'd wait for me upstairs. I nodded and went back to leading students through cool-down exercises, but my mind was on my best friend. He didn't look at all happy, and I worried about what had happened to bring him down.

After the place cleared out, I locked the studio doors, and I went upstairs.

Evan stood in front of the shelf unit under where I'd mounted a huge television. Beer in hand, he sipped while he perused my selection of DVDs. He glanced over as I came in. "Are you going to shower?"

"Nah. Summer session. I had two beginner and an intermediate class. I didn't break a sweat." My serious students made time during the week and on the weekend. Tomorrow I'd be gross, but today I was fine. Plus, I'd showered a few hours ago after Alaina had left. We'd worked up quite a sweat.

He nodded. "You want to stay in or go out tonight?"

"Whatever you feel like." He was the one out of sorts. I was going to get him to tell me whatever he was upset about by the end of the night, but I might have to get him drunk first. Noting the empty bottle of the beer he'd already finished on the counter, I crossed the loft and stopped near him.

He took a long pull from his beer, draining it halfway. "Stay in. I don't feel like dealing with the whole meat market aspect of a bar tonight."

"Okay. You want to drink beer and watch a movie?"

He poked at the spine of a movie where everything got blown up in the end. I liked action flicks, so most of my movies were in that vein. "Yeah."

Despite his answer in the affirmative, he didn't sound sure. I took a step back and watched him. Evan Carrico was a handsome specimen of manhood. He'd let his light brown hair grow in the past few months, and the gentle waves nearly reached his chin. Since he worked outdoors a lot, the sun had kissed blond streaks into it. The length wasn't enough for a ponytail—I told him I'd beat him senseless if he ever put it in a man-bun—but it was enough to get in his eyes.

Evan had stunning eyes. Sparkling light blue, they were his best feature. Looking into them, I could discern his every emotion and most of his thoughts.

Right now, I couldn't figure out what he was thinking. I only knew he was disturbed about something.

"How is Grandma Russo?" He leaned an elbow on top of the shelf unit and regarded me with his lips pressed together. "You didn't say if she came home yet?"

I hadn't talked to him since yesterday morning, but I'd texted him. "She's fine. Still in the hospital, but we're pretty sure she's coming home tomorrow. Sophia and I are going over tomorrow night with our parents."

"Is Drew going?"

"If he's not working, I'm sure he'll be there." Drew was my sister's fiancé, which she'd disclosed to everyone at the hospital. My parents had been thrilled, and it had taken my mom's mind away from worrying about her mother for a little while. Drew and I had a rocky start when he first came into Sophia's life, but now we were friends. I liked the way he made my sister happy, and I'd come to appreciate him as a person.

Evan nodded. "Did you want me to go?"

I took Evan to most family events, so nobody would think twice, but I shook my head. "It's going to be one of those boring nights where we all sit around trying not to get in anybody's way but also be there in case my mom or aunt or grandma need help."

Normally Evan would be fine with my answer, but tonight, he scowled and turned his attention back to the movie selection.

"Ev, what's wrong?"

He pursed his lips, and his eyes glittered with all kinds of problems, but he didn't look at me.

"Don't say *nothing*, because I can tell that's not true."

Lifting his face, he nailed me with a glare that didn't seem fully directed at me. "I'll bottom for you, you know. All you have to do is ask."

Evan was a Dom. While he occasionally bottomed for me—only for me—it rarely lasted long. Usually he'd use his considerable charm to turn the tables because I didn't care if I was on top or the bottom. I just cared that we were together.

I searched his face for a sign that he just needed to bottom for me to make him feel better, but I came up empty. I didn't think it would solve his problem, but I figured it would help him work through whatever was weighing on his mind.

Keeping my gaze locked to his, I liberated the bottle of beer from him. Then I pushed him against the wall next to the shelving unit. It was naked brick, which warmed up the aesthetic of the place, but it was rough and hard. I kind of thought he needed me to be rough.

I took a sip of the beer, and then I planted a hand on the brick next to his head. Leaning closer, I breathed on his face. "You want to bottom for me?"

His nostrils flared, and his eyes hardened, glittering like blue diamonds.

Fuck. This was not my forte. I wasn't a Dom, and I didn't generally care to force my lovers to do anything. But this was my best friend, and he was hurting. I didn't know why, but I wasn't going to leave him to twist in the wind when he needed my strength and the certainty of our friendship.

Understanding that he needed to submit more than he needed to bottom, I set the bottle on a DVD case lying on top of the shelves, and I put my other hand on the brick, caging him between the harshness of the brick and my body.

Evan was strong, but I was stronger, and I was skilled at subduing an opponent—or a friend who needed to be overpowered.

Leaning in closer, I stopped with my lips an inch from his. "What do you want, Evan?"

The diamonds began to crack. "You know what I want."

"Say it," I demanded. "Ask for what you want, or you're getting nothing."

"Use me." His lips barely moved, and a hint of desperation darkened his eyes. "Choke me with your dick. Don't let me come."

I could tell this wasn't going to be at all romantic or playful, which was my favorite kind of sex. Evan wanted me to hurt him, and he trusted me to do right by him. But I had to make sure.

"Take your shirt off."

He grasped it behind his neck and pulled the cotton shirt over his head, and then he let it drop to the floor.

Very deliberately, I pinched his nipple, squeezing it hard enough to flatten it between my finger and thumb.

He gasped, but he didn't call his safeword. The hardness in his eyes didn't disappear, but the desperation diminished a bit.

I pinched the other one. Evan had sensitive nipples. I could get him going with a flick or a lick, and I used them now to bring him down from his state of agitation.

"Say it again," I said. "Beg."

"You're a dick," he said.

"Best dick you've ever had." I smirked as I rolled his pinched nipple.

A groan squeaked from him. "Please, Danny. Fuck me. Use me. Be selfish and mean."

Being selfish didn't come naturally. I was a generous lover who got off on watching how my lovers fell apart in my arms.

Evan was going to fucking explode, but I was strong enough to hold together the pieces. I handed him the mostly empty bottle. "Finish it. Rinse it out. Take off your clothes, and kneel next to the bed."

While he did that, I tore the covers off the bed and threw them on the sofa. Then I rummaged around in my chest of drawers for his cock ring. After he'd teased me last week, I'd gone out and bought one for him as a joke. It looked like I was going to get some real mileage out of this joke.

I turned to find him standing behind me. He hadn't undressed, and he wasn't kneeling. For someone who could be an exacting Dom, he sure was a shitty submissive.

Rolling my eyes at his insolence, I closed the drawer and went to him. He was wearing jeans, but they were soft and loose the way he liked them. I grabbed his privates, crushing his cock and balls in my hand. Color left his face, and he dropped to his knees—slowly, because I was still squeezing his boys.

Air whooshed out of him as I eased my grip. As he recovered, I slapped his cheeks a few times, light taps that were jarring because he wasn't used to being hit at all, much less in the face.

Then I stood up and shoved my foot against his dick. "Naked. Now."

Without getting up, he divested himself of his jeans and briefs. Once he was back on his knees, I put the cock ring around his junk. It was thick and heavy, and it pulled down on his entire package. I knew it was uncomfortable, but I also knew he needed that right now.

Evan on his knees didn't make me hard, but I did respond to the undisguised lust that had shattered the hardness of his eyes. I stroked my cock through my workout sweats, and he licked his lips.

Yep. That did it. Evan, hungry for my cock, always heated my blood. I pulled off my shirt and stripped out of my sweats and briefs, dropping them to the floor. Approaching him, I stroked my dick, teasing him with what he wanted.

He moaned, and despite the heavy cock ring, his member lengthened. At his sides, his fists clenched.

I smacked my dick against his cheek—lightly, because I wasn't into pain—and grabbed a handful of his hair. "Ask for it."

"Please," he breathed. "Fuck my face."

Slapping him a few more times, with both my cock and then my hand, I said, "You can beg better than that, you dirty whore."

Yeah, I didn't know where that came from. Oh—yes, I did. I'd heard my sister call Drew a whore and a slut before, and he'd really liked it.

It had a similar effect on Evan. His eyes dilated, and his whole body shuddered. "Please," he whined. "Use me, Danny. Fuck my face and my ass. Choke me, punish me—use me as your bitch."

Okay, so we were doing this. It was kind of fun, more like role playing, which helped me enjoy calling Evan nasty names. I liked role playing more than I liked the D/s stuff Evan preferred. The violet wand, though...

I was getting off track. I stuck my fingers in his mouth, fucking them into that orifice to get his saliva going. Then I traced his lips with my cock. He whined for more. I teased him for a while, making him whimper with wanting me. When I though he had enough, I eased past his lips, wetting my dick with his saliva.

He closed his mouth around my cock, sucking it deeper and deeper with each thrust. His tongue cradled it, flicking against the underside the way I liked.

But this blowjob wasn't to get me off; it was to tame the frantic wildness of Evan's emotions. In that spirit, I snagged a handful of hair, and I surged forward, shoving my cock down his throat until his lips met my pubic hair. His face turned beet red, and the veins in his neck stood out. His eyes watered from the effort it took not to gag. I counted three beats, and then I eased back, letting him breathe.

I did it again and again, pulling his hair and choking him with my dick until tears ran down his cheeks. I'm not gonna lie—it felt really good. I would have kept doing it, except I wanted to see his face twisted with bliss, not agony, when we came together.

To let him know we were done with this part of the scene, I shoved him away, not tempering my strength so that he fell backward. Sprawled on the floor, he coughed and his chest heaved as he recovered.

"Get up," I commanded. "Bend your slutty ass over the back of the couch."

He crawled to the sofa and heaved himself up until he was bent over the top. The comforter and sheet I'd put there provided a lot of padding.

I kicked his feet apart and squeezed a handful of his sexy ass. The rounded globes were the result of a lot of heavy lifting, and one of them filled my hand perfectly. It would be too easy to fuck him like this. Evan wanted to be used, and I aimed to give him what he wanted. So I let him stew for a bit while I looked for where I'd hidden the glass anal beads he'd left here a few months ago. I'd liked them quite a bit, and I was sure Evan would as well. I found them in the back of my bottom drawer wrapped in an old towel.

I took them to the kitchen to wash them. To spice things up, I mixed a bit of hot sauce in with the lube I spread over the beads. They weren't small beads. He was going to feel each and every one.

First, I squirted lube on my fingers. Evan lifted up to look over his shoulder, so I shoved him back down with my clean hand. I held him in place by the back of his neck as I fingered his anus.

He let out a little moan.

"Do you like that, anal slut?" I inserted another finger, sawing them in and out. "How about that?"

"Yes," he murmured. "Use me. Fuck me. Make me yours."

I fucked him that way, massaging his prostate, for a bit longer, and then I inserted the first bead. Once the hot sauce hit, he howled. His back bowed.

"What the fuck did you do, you sick fucker?"

Since I had a solid hold on his neck, he didn't move much. However, I needed better leverage, so I twisted his arm behind his back and held him down that way. I inserted another bead, and he shouted, but he didn't call his safeword.

"Do you like that, whore?"

"No! What the fuck did you do? How do you know that's safe?"

I laughed at that one. "Drew sometimes over-shares stories about his sex life." I didn't care to hear his stories because they involved my sister, but that didn't stop him. He seemed to take pleasure in traumatizing me. "Don't worry, Ev. It's going to sting you like the bitch you are."

No idea what that meant, but it mollified him. He settled down, and I fucked the hot beads in and out of his ass. He stopped struggling, but his shouts of protest and moans of pleasure only got louder.

"Fuck, Danny! Fuck—I'm close. I'm so close."

That was my cue to back off. Note to self: Evan liked hot sauce.

I removed the beads slowly, his sphincter expanding as each one popped out. His moans turned to whimpers. I smacked his dick a few times and pulled on his ball sac. I liked when he did it to me—or when Alaina did it. She was the first woman who'd ever done that to me, and I hadn't even had to ask for it or show her how to do it.

I tossed the used beads onto the heap of my clothes. Then I pushed him over the end of the sofa, rolling him as he went so that he landed on his back with his ass in the air and his knees near his head. It was an ignominious position, but the shame seemed to make him feel better. It was also making me really horny to watch him enjoy everything I was dishing out.

Stroking my cock, I went around the sofa. When I got to Evan, I lowered down and put my balls in his face. "Lick and suck, bitch."

His hot tongue flicked out, licking his way around my balls before he sucked one into his mouth. The heat and pressure caused waves of pleasure to wash through me. I loved when he played with my balls, though most of the time when he did that, he had me tied up. He had a talent for finding the spots that made me gasp and writhe, and this time was no different. I stroked my cock as he tongued my balls.

In the spirit of fairness, I reached out and stroked his cock as well. It was hard as a rock and purpled with passion. I played with it, lifting it and bending it back toward his anus. He groaned and whimpered, and a pearl of semen leaked from the tip.

I leaned down and licked it away. He tasted so good. I wanted more, but I denied myself for now.

"Get up on your knees. Face the back of the sofa."

He scrambled into position. I'd planned to fuck him, but I was seized by the desire to spank him for not telling me what was bothering him. I smacked his ass. He looked over his shoulder, surprise written on his features.

"You've been a bad slut, and you need to be punished." I spanked him five or six times. My handprints marked his pale ass, and I traced a fingertip over the redness.

"Thank you, Danny."

Evan only shortened my name when he was feeling particularly emotional. I took it as a sign he was closer to dealing with whatever was wrong. "Get on the floor and crawl to the bed."

I watched his dick sway as his sexy ass crawled to my bed. He knelt next to it.

"Get on the bed. Lay on your stomach."

He did as I asked, even spreading his legs so that I had unrestricted access to that sexy ass. I climbed on top and fed my slick cock into his back entrance. His body tensed, and he braced his hands against the bed to fight me.

I'd expected this. Evan could push all he wanted, and he wouldn't dislodge me. I forced his arms flat against the mattress, and I pinned his wrists as I hammered into his body. I fucked him without mercy or restraint. My body pummeled his, and we moved across the mattress from the force of my thrusts.

When we got to the other side of the bed, I turned us both on our sides. I twisted him so that his top half was facing up and his bottom half was on his side, and then I used one arm to pin his arm and shoulder. My hand clamped over his mouth.

"You're mine," I said. "Mine to use. I'm going to fuck you hard, and I'm going to come inside your ass."

Under my hand, he shouted a muffled and enthusiastic consent.

I was gentle.

I knew he'd asked for it hard and dirty, but I could only do that for so long. It was a fun role, but it wasn't what did it for me. I held him against me as I made love to him. I eased my hand away from his mouth and gagged him with my kiss as I masturbated him. We came together, the way I wanted—and the way I knew he wanted.

And I held Evan's quaking body in my arms as he came down from the high of submission.

He removed the cock ring from his soft dick. "What the fuck was that stuff you put in my ass?"

I chuckled and released him, rolling to my back so I could sprawl out and relax. Evan was officially not in submissive headspace anymore. "Hot sauce."

"I'm going to get you back for that." His lips barely moved.

"Not a chance. You try that, and I'll tie you up and make you my bitch."

He didn't say anything to that.

"Ev?"

"Yeah?"

"What's wrong?"

"Something has to be wrong?"

"For you to offer to bottom, yes. That's not something you ask for." I didn't mean to make out like he was always the top, but unless I asked, that was how it worked out.

"Did you see Alaina today?"

I was thrown by his change in subject. Throwing a scowl in his direction, I noted the tense set to his shoulders. My scowl melted. "You're jealous that I had sex with Alaina? You had sex with her last night. She told me."

"You said it was fine." He propped himself on an elbow to look down at me. "You said I could scene with her if it was what she wanted."

"I know." There was no way I was going to let him go all alpha-Dom on me. On any given day, I was pretty alpha. I just wasn't a Dom. I sat up and faced him. "I'm not the one who's jealous."

He sat up and rubbed his jaw. "I know." Seconds passed. "We've never had sex with the same woman before."

No, we hadn't. "So? It was bound to happen."

"No, Daniel, it wasn't. You like tall, skinny blondes. I steer clear of them."

This was the first time he'd said he purposely avoided women who looked like the ones I tended toward. "I thought they just weren't your type."

He ran a hand through his hair. "I should go."

I wasn't about to let him leave before I knew what was wrong, especially not when he'd practically admitted to being jealous. I set a hand on his wrist before he could move. "Evan, are you jealous of her being with me, or of me being with her?"

He shook his head, which was an evasion, not an answer.

"Evan, you're my best friend. You can tell me anything."

"Both." He sighed and stared off into the distance. "I was jealous a couple weeks ago when you said you'd slept with her. Normally I wouldn't care who you slut it up with, but you talked about her differently. You like her. You respect her."

"I respect most women," I countered. I adored women in general, and so did he. It was the primary reason Evan and I still dated other people. "Especially the ones I have sex with."

"She's different." His crystal gaze met mine, and those diamonds were back. "She's special."

My hand slipped off his arm. "You have a crush on her?"

"Don't fucking even think about telling me that you don't."

I hadn't thought about it. I liked pretty much everything about her, from her generous spirit to her sense of humor to her incredible smarts. Thoughts of her crossed my mind frequently, especially since I'd come to know her in a different way than before.

I ran a hand through my hair, and I considered his assertion. Did I have a crush on Alaina? Only a fool wouldn't. "She's older than us. And really freaking brainy. I've never met anyone so smart, and she has a quirky sense of humor."

Earlier, when she'd come over, she'd shown up a half hour late, apologies flying out of her mouth as she stripped down and set out the lube and condoms. Then she'd surveyed the setup and asked if she should apologize for making the afternoon too hedonistic.

I'd laughed my ass off, and then I'd taken her in my arms to show her a good time.

"Daniel." Evan's warning came through, loud and clear. He was coming to the end of his rope.

I sighed. He had a crush on Alaina, my sexy librarian. It explained why he'd offered to bottom, and also why he'd wanted to be tortured and punished. "You feel guilty because I knew her first. You want to ask her out, and you think you'd be stealing her from me."

He gaped, but from the way his mouth worked, I knew he was trying to figure out a way to come out on top. "So, I have your permission?"

"I didn't say that." I scratched my stomach and regarded him somberly. "You were right that I like her. I'm just leery about making a move because she's central to the success of Sophia's program. If I fuck up, I could blow up the whole thing." I met his gaze again. "And so could you."

He chewed on that for all of ten seconds. "Where does that leave us?"

The question took me by surprise. I blinked. "Us? Evan, no matter what, you're my best friend. That's never going to change."

"I meant sexually." He spread his hands wide, an appeal for me to understand what he was saying. "Daniel, we've been together for nine years. You're the only constant in my love life, and I'm the only constant in yours."

His love life? We had a sex life in common. Love? He was my best friend. Of course I loved him. But was I in love with him? Because I was completely certain that's what he meant. Breaking his gaze, I got off the bed. In a daze, I picked up the anal beads. I threw my clothes into the laundry, and then I went to the sink to wash the beads.

Evan followed me. "Daniel."

"We always said it was casual." I scrubbed, probably harder than I needed to. "We see other people all the time. You even have relationships."

I fucking hated when he was in a relationship. I strove to be polite to whomever he was seeing, but inside, I was waiting for them to break up so he'd come back to me.

"I've tried. Every single one of them blew up because once they found out I'd slept with you, they wanted me to stop being friends with you." He put his hand on my shoulder and spun me around to face him. "Daniel, I've chosen you over everyone I've ever been attracted to, and you've chosen me as well."

"I don't do relationships." Yeah, it sounded lame to me, too.

"Because you've been in one with me since we were teenagers."

He'd been my first and favorite sexual experience. My mouth opened and closed. I shut the water off and went into the bathroom.

He followed. "Don't tell me I'm wrong."

I started the shower. He wasn't wrong. He was never wrong. He knew me better than anyone, and I knew him just as well.

Wrapping an arm around his waist, I picked him up and took him into the shower with me. Pressing him against the tile, I immobilized him as I held him at arm's length. "So, where does that leave us?"

Water sluiced over us, washing sweat and lube down the drain, but it left our problems—all the things we'd never acknowledged that weren't going to stay buried any longer.

He shook his head. "I don't know, Daniel. I don't fucking know. It was never a problem until Alaina."

"It's not her fault. Don't bring her into this." My grip tightened on his shoulders as the water threatened to set him free.

"She's already in this, Daniel. Do you think we'd be having this discussion if we hadn't both fallen for her?" He squirmed out of my grasp and closed the distance between us. "Daniel, I want her, and I want you. You want her, and you want me. That's never happened before."

He kissed me, his lips capturing mine in a harsh clash of wills that both of us were destined to lose. His hand wrapped around my cock, and mine found his. We stroked each other, slick fists pumping in rhythm as our kiss went on and on. After a long time, I broke the kiss and set my forehead against his.

"She likes a gentle lover with a sense of humor and imagination. That's me."

"She likes roughness, kink, and bondage," Evan countered. "And I have quite an imagination."

"You and I are so different, Ev. That's why we never got together permanently."

He snorted. "We *are* together permanently. Nobody has been able to come between us. Your lovers leave because you're emotionally unavailable. You're emotionally unavailable because you're in love with me. Same thing on my end, but I've tried harder to move on."

I hadn't put effort into being with anyone for more than a couple of weeks, and even that was only whenever Evan had a boyfriend or girlfriend. He was right, and I was finally ready to admit it. "Fine. I love you, and you love me. We're officially together. Now what? I'm not going to be your sub. Can you really give that up?"

When he'd first started on his path to becoming a Dom, I'd thought it was a phase. As I got to know the kink better, I realized it was who he'd always been.

He shook his head. "Alaina. We both have crushes on her, and I'm pretty sure she likes us back." He groaned because I was using hand moves on his cock that he really liked. "She likes both of us in bed, and I'm fairly certain she likes us out of bed as well," he added, as if his groan had made me forget what we were talking about.

"You want to ask her to be with us? Like a threesome situation?"

"Why not? It could work."

"What if she says no?"

"She won't say no." He increased the pace of how he masturbated me. "But she probably won't say yes right away."

We fell silent as our orgasms washed over us. We stayed that way as we finished showering and got dressed.

He helped me make the bed, and then we settled on the sofa to watch a movie. Evan slung his arm around me and pulled me closer to snuggle. We'd never done that before. It felt right, so I stayed where he put me.

"I asked to see her again." His confession came during a quiet scene. "She misunderstood. Today, I emailed her an estimate to replace her roof, and she hired me. I start the Monday after next."

I hadn't asked to see her again. She'd rushed in and out, apologizing for scheduling her day so tightly. "I won't see her until the week after next."

"That's too far away," he said. "We need a plan."

"Yeah," I agreed. "A plan to convince an incredibly sexy woman with two doctoral degrees that she should fall for two guys who are a lot younger."

"Two charming, hot guys," he amended. "Don't sell us short. When have we ever failed when we work together?"

Never. I was nervous that this would be the first time. Perhaps she would like her men the way she liked her doctorate degrees—in a pair. But there was an even greater chance she would laugh at us before politely refusing. "If she refuses, are we still staying together?"

"Yes. That's permanent. We're a packaged deal now."

I felt really good about that.

"I'm going to call her." He reached for his cell on the coffee table.

"What?" I hadn't expected him to want to rush right out and tell Alaina we were together. "You can't tell her we're together over the phone. We have to do that in person."

He shot me a sardonic glance. "I know that, Daniel. I'm calling her because we left things in a bad place, and I haven't been in the right head space to be able to talk to her. I want to get us on back on a positive track."

I thought about her hesitation when she'd told me about sleeping with Evan. I'd taken it for reticence to hurt my feelings while staying true to her need for honesty, but with this new information, I saw her actions in a different light. It also gave me a different perspective on Evan's strife.

"Alaina. How are you doing?" The timbre of Evan's voice deepened as he went into Dom mode, and he said her name like a caress. I wasn't sure how it affected her, but it did a number on me. Even though he wasn't talking to me, I felt myself calming and melting toward him.

I heard her voice, but she spoke too softly for me to make out every word. I caught enough to know she was working on her book.

"Can you take a break for a few minutes?" He phrased the question as an order, and he smiled at her positive response. "I wanted to talk about last night."

Silence came from her end.

Evan's confidence faltered. The hand on my shoulder squeezed, but he kept his voice strong. "Lainie?"

I tilted my head to better hear her response.

"I'm here. I'm sorry, Evan. I know I upset you, but I'm not sure what I did wrong."

Every muscle in my body tensed, and I sat up straight, breaking from his snuggling embrace. He caught the question in my eyes and shook his head. "You didn't do anything wrong. I realized I didn't make myself clear. I was hinting instead of being direct. You prefer for me to speak plainly, and I didn't."

"You were clear." Her voice came through much louder because he'd put her on speaker. "You want to see me again. I was surprised."

"Why? We have chemistry, and we're very compatible."

She exhaled, and I felt her relief. "I understand now. You want to continue having a D/s association."

"Yes. What are your thoughts on the issue?"

Confusion had me staring at Evan. I was under the impression he wanted to pursue a romantic relationship with her, but that wasn't what he'd said.

Alaina made a thoughtful sound. "I'd be okay with exploring that idea."

Evan opened his mouth to say something, but she kept talking.

"You're a very good Dom, which is a rare thing."

"Thank you."

Flattery was going to get her everywhere with Evan. I rolled my eyes.

He didn't notice. "I'd like to see you again. Soon."

"Well, my schedule is packed for the next week, and then I'm going on vacation to the Outer Banks. There isn't anywhere I can slot you into my schedule until I get back. I'm sorry, Evan. I have so much work to do before I leave. I barely have time to pack."

He frowned.

"Please don't think I'm blowing you off. I'm not."

His scowl eased. "Where are you right now?"

"In my office." She was quiet for a beat. "Want to have phone sex?"

From the way his lips parted, I knew he was surprised by her offer. The more I knew Lainie, the less surprised I was by her strange mix of planning and impulsivity. It was like she was engaged in a constant battle against a tendency toward chaos.

She laughed, a sexy sound that was huskier than her regular laugh. "Should I call you *Sir*?"

"Yes." A huge smile broke out over his features. Evan loved titles, and I never used one. "Lainie, I want you to go upstairs to your bedroom and get the vibrator I used on you last night."

"Yes, Sir." Papers shuffled, and a click announced the closing of her laptop.

I smacked his arm and whispered, "What the fuck are you doing?"

He lifted a brow to indicate the answer was obvious. "What are you wearing right now?"

She chuckled softly. "Do you want the real answer?"

Evan kept his steady gaze on me. I thought he was moving too quickly and in the wrong direction, but it seemed like Lainie was on board with this plan, and so I nodded. If this was what she wanted, then we'd have to take a different route to her heart than I'd considered. He twined his fingers with mine, making a silent promise to me. I wasn't sure what he was promising, but I knew he wouldn't move forward if I objected.

"Of course. I always want you to be honest."

"Striped pajama pants on the bottom, and an old shirt on top."

"What color are the stripes?"

"Um, brown and magenta. The shirt is faded blue. It doesn't match. I'm not wearing a bra, and my panties are black satin with white and pink flowers."

The description of her outfit made me smile. I loved that she was wearing clothing that didn't match. It showed another side to her personality, one that let go of pesky details and strove for comfort. I motioned for Evan to order her to take off her pants. I loved the curves of her hips and the sight of her luscious ass.

He merely smiled and set his hand on my cock. The light pressure through the thin fabric of my sweats was enough to stir my desire yet again tonight.

"Okay. I have the vibrator, and now I'm getting the lube."

"Get the heated one."

"Yes, Sir. Anything else?"

"Grab a second vibrator, just in case."

"Good idea, Sir. I'm not sure about the batteries in this one."

I marveled at how relaxed and happy she sounded, and I immersed myself in getting to know this different side of her. And also Evan's hand moved lazily over my budding erection.

"You should tell her that I'm here, listening," I whispered.

He shook his head and mouthed that it would create too many questions that needed face-to-face answers.

"What movie are you watching?" Alaina inserted that casual question as something exploded onscreen and random people screamed.

"One where D.C. gets blown up. I forget the name."

I turned down the volume.

"I'm sitting up on my bed. I have the vibrators and lube." She seemed to have dismissed the movie and the noise it made in the background.

"Good. Now lick your finger. Get it nice and wet."

"Yes, Sir."

Licking and sucking had never sounded so sexy before. Evan's fingers traced the hard outline of my cock through my sweats.

"Play with your clit, baby."

"Should I take my pants off?"

His gaze met mine, and I read the ruthlessness of the Dom he was. "No. Put your hand down your pants. Just touch the tip of your clit—nothing else."

"Yes, Sir. It feels good, not as good as when you do it, though."

"Lainie, those fingers are a proxy for mine."

She made a delicious noise, and then she sighed. "Sir, your hands are a lot bigger. Two of my fingers cover as much surface area as one of yours."

"Use two fingers."

"Ohh, that's better. Mmmm, Sir, you have a magic touch."

His hand slid into my sweats, and he traced a path around the sensitive crown of my dick with the tip of his finger. "I know, baby. Are you feeling good yet?"

"Yes."

"Now put your fingers in your mouth and suck on your juices."

"Yes, Sir." Faint sucking noises came over the speaker, and my erection throbbed. Imagining what she was doing while Evan teased was nearly enough for me.

"Did you put me on speaker?"

"Yes," she said. "The phone is resting on my chest."

"Pull your shirt up. I want you to play with your breasts. Talk to me, Lainie. Describe what you're doing."

"I've got one in each hand, and I'm kneading them."

His hand encircled my erection, and he pumped up and down. His touch was too light to be anything other than teasing. "Pinch them until it hurts. Harder, baby."

She yelped.

"That's it. Keep that pressure. Breathe through it."

"Yes, Sir," she whimpered. "I'm imagining the clover clamps."

"Lainie, do you remember when you were picturing me with men?"

"Mmm-hmmm." She half-moaned, and half-mewled.

"Picture me with one right now, but don't tell me who."

"Oh, Sir, that's so hot."

With a mischievous smile, he jerked the waist of my sweats down, and he sucked hard on the crown of my cock. Then he abandoned me. "Lainie, in your imagination, what is my lover doing? Keep rolling and pinching your nipples as you describe the scene."

"You're sitting in a black leather chair. He's kneeling on the floor between your legs."

That puckish grin grew as Evan gestured to the floor at his feet.

I responded with a glare.

"He's naked. Oh, Sir—he's so handsome. I love looking at his sexy body as much as I like looking at yours." She gasped. "Can I touch my pussy again?"

"Let go of your nipples very slowly, Lainie. That's my girl. Now put the warming lube on the vibrator with the best batteries."

We engaged in a staring contest while Alaina did her thing. Evan pointed to the floor once again, and I shook my head while mouthing, "No fucking way."

"You've done it before."

I'd given him dozens of blowjobs, several of them while kneeling on the floor just as Alaina described, but I didn't like doing it when he told me to. "Ask nicely," I insisted.

"Sir?"

Evan cleared his throat. "Ask nicely if you can put it in your pussy."

"Oh, please, Sir? Please let me put the vibrator in my pussy."

"Tell me what my naked lover is doing kneeling on the floor between my knees while you slowly slide the vibrator into your hot little body." Evan unzipped his jeans and eased them down to his knees. Then he stroked his cock lightly, exactly as he'd teased me moments ago.

"He's sucking your cock. You're playing with his hair, but you're letting him suck you the way he wants to."

It was like she knew what I wanted, how I needed for it to be on my terms.

"Turn it on, baby. Lowest setting." He rested his head back, closed his eyes, and masturbated as he walked her through increasing the rate of vibration.

Her moans and squeaks, those cute sex noises she made when she was really enjoying herself, came through with increasing volume.

I slid to my knees and pushed Evan's hands away. He played with my hair as I teased and tormented with my lips, teeth, and tongue. I knew all his sweet spots.

"Press the other vibe to your clit as you fuck yourself, Lainie. I want to hear you come."

"Yes, Sir. Oh, it feels so good." She tried to speak, but short words and random sounds poured out with increasing abandon.

Evan's moans came louder and closer together as well. He was so close, but he was resisting having an orgasm. I left off sucking his cock long enough to wet my finger with a liberal amount of saliva. Then I pulled him down toward the edge of the sofa, and I eased my finger into his ass.

Alaina shouted her release at that moment, and Evan was powerless to resist the way I sucked his cock and massaged his prostate.

I sat back on my heels as I waited for him and Alaina to recover.

"That was so hot, Lainie," he mumbled. "I don't want to wait two weeks to see you."

"I'm sorry," she said. "I wish I could squeeze you in. I'll make sure to put you in for the week after, though. I promise."

"You'd better. I'm going to spank your ass for every day you make me wait."

"That sounds lovely, Sir. I'm counting the days." She laughed, but it was a tired sound.

"Sweet dreams, Lainie. I'll talk to you soon, okay? Get some sleep."

"I will, Sir. You, too, okay?"

When the call was over, I straddled Evan. He hadn't moved from semi-reclined position I'd put him in, and he opened his mouth as I guided my cock inside.

"She thinks you just want to have Dominant sex with her." I grasped the sides of his head to keep him from trying to respond. "She has no idea you want to have a relationship. You have to talk to her about topics other than sex, or that's the only connection she's ever going to make."

Evan used the same trick on me that I'd used on him, and he had me rocketing over that cliff in no time.

Spent and sprawled on the sofa next to him, I thought about how I wanted to go about winning Alaina's heart, and how Evan's strategy needed to change.

Chapter 9—Alaina

Our time in the Outer Banks had been perfect. The weather had cooperated, and hanging out with Clara and Deon was always relaxing and fun. Getting away was exactly what I'd needed, and Zack had a blast with his best friend.

The plane got in later than scheduled, which caused me some anxiety. The moment they'd announced a delay in the flight time, I'd texted Adam to let him know what was going on. While he wasn't inflexible with our custody schedule, we both preferred to keep things as normal as possible for Zack's sake.

As we waited for our luggage, I called Adam to tell him we'd landed, and that I'd be heading directly to his house once we collected our things.

I noted messages from both Daniel and Evan. For the past ten days, they'd taken turns calling and texting me. Most of the time, they asked me about my day and talked about benign topics. They told me how things were going with them.

While I enjoyed talking with Daniel and Evan—they were both friendly and likeable, and I was finding out we had a lot in common—I found the entire situation confusing, and I resolved to sit down and talk with both of them—together. I had no idea what they were doing, but we needed to get this all out in the open. I'd had phone sex with each of them twice before I'd realized their calls weren't alternating by chance.

Zack stood right up next to the baggage carousel, keeping a sharp lookout for our suitcases. I'd packed most of our essential items in my carry-on bag, but I still hoped our bags had made it to the same destination as us.

My son had inherited my eyes, and my anxiety-driven penchant for completing tasks. From Adam, he'd inherited a calm acceptance for how problems changed his plans and a habit of second-guessing himself. The blond hair came from both sides, as my father and brother were blonds, as was Adam and his mother.

I remained several feet behind him so that he wouldn't look to me for confirmation of which bag was ours. I wanted him to learn to take the initiative, to realize that he was in control of his choices and his actions, and that it was okay to make a decision on his own.

He looked over his shoulder at me, the small smile on his face telling me that he was both nervous and excited. "Are Dad and Uncle Cam waiting for me?"

"Dad is. I think Uncle Cam had to work late."

Our vacation was entirely due to Clara. She'd invited us to go to the Outer Banks for the week with her and Deon. Her parents had a place there where we could stay. We went every summer. It was nice to relax with people I adored.

Taking time off work right now wasn't difficult. I had plenty of personal time saved up, and I'd worked ahead on my book so that I'd be on schedule when I returned. So Zack and I had flown down Saturday evening, and I'd scheduled our return to get us back in time for him to be with Adam.

I'd left the key to my house in an envelope, and I'd entrusted a neighbor to keep it for Evan. Perhaps I hadn't known him long, but I felt safe letting him have a key to my house while I was out of town, and of course, through our regular conversations, I was getting to know him better.

And Daniel... *le sigh*. He was on my mind. I liked him. He was fun and funny. He didn't take himself too seriously, and I noticed when I was with him or just talking to him, it was easier to relax. He was a natural leader and comfortable in his own skin, and that rubbed off on the people around him.

And I really liked rubbing against him. In my fantasies, I was going to relive the Three Glorious Nights and Two Orgasmic Phone Calls with him for many years to come.

Then there was Evan. Don't get me started on him. Just thinking about him, recalling the masterful way he kissed, was making me feel as if I was about to swoon.

Despite adding so much to my 'Shouldn't've" list—or perhaps because of it?—I was one lucky woman. I just needed to get to the bottom of the mystery of why either man was interested in me.

The older I got, the more I was thankful I'd divorced Adam. His life with Cam was boring and predictable. While I liked—and needed— a schedule, I wasn't a stickler for just having boring events on it. I hadn't minded one bit moving things around to have a wild time with two younger studs, and Clara had learned to cajole me into going with her or doing things outside of my comfort zone. I didn't resist too hard.

"Mom?"

I looked down to see that, while I'd been daydreaming, Zack had retrieved our suitcases. He wore a huge grin. I ran my fingertips through his hair in the back, ruffling it without mussing it because my son was now very much into his appearance. He'd even begun using products to shape it into what I referred to as a tidal wave moving across his head.

"Good job, honey. Let's get moving so you can have dinner with your Dad. He said to tell you that he's making your favorite."

Zack's favorites changed on a regular basis, so I had no idea what Adam was making.

Zack's mouth puckered thoughtfully. "I hope that means chicken quesadillas. He thinks my favorite is still chicken nuggets with a side of macaroni and cheese."

Well, I'd been under that impression as well, but I refused to serve highly processed foods to my son. I smiled because I'd made chicken and vegetable quesadillas twice for Zack and Deon in the past few days, and they'd been well-received both times.

We made good time from the airport to Adam's house. Adam came outside as we pulled up, and he met us at the car. My ex-husband was a moderately handsome man. He was average height by statistical measures, though he towered over me, and he had an average build. Overall, he was the epitome of what you'd expect a nice, unassuming guy to look like.

Zack rocketed out and hugged his father, which brought a smile to my face. I loved that they had a good relationship. It was important for both of them.

I turned the car off and pushed the button to open the trunk.

"How was your trip?" Adam kept an arm slung around Zack, and I noted how they also shared a nose and the shape of their chin. "Alaina, what did you feed him? I swear, he's grown an inch in four days."

Laughing, I shook my head. "I hope his feet are the same size." Adam had bought Zack limited-edition sneakers with a basketball team's logo on the side.

"So do I." He looked at Zack expectantly.

"We had fun. I'll tell you the details over dinner." Zack—with a little assistance from Adam—extracted his bag from the trunk. "I'm going to go unpack, okay?"

Zack liked to unpack first thing when he arrived at one of our houses. It was his way of making sure he was truly at home.

"I'm right behind you," Adam called to Zack's fading figure. "I want to talk to your mom for a minute."

Not for a second did I think he wanted to talk to me about being late. But I did consider that he'd want to keep Zack longer to make up for it. We were only three hours late, so I thought it would be petty for him to ask.

I looked at Adam's mouth, and I found it set hard, though it wasn't firm. He was consciously trying to mitigate what he was about to say. An edge of a future worry bumped against my mind.

Adam stared at my shoes.

"Did somebody die?" One of the things Adam did not like about me was the way weird or blunt questions flew out of my mouth the second my brain thought of them. It was yet another reason I liked to be single—I could just be myself and not have to censor my thoughts. I stopped talking in case someone had actually died.

"Not that I'm aware of." He pushed his hair back from where it had flopped over his eye. "Look, Alaina, your parents are having people over this coming Sunday to celebrate their fortieth wedding anniversary."

Sunday was my day with Zack. I got him Saturday at four until Wednesday at two. Sometimes we swapped days or let one or the other take him for a few hours for a special event. But for this, I was not going to offer to let him take Zack.

I pressed my lips together to keep all the vitriol inside. I hadn't spoken to my parents, or anyone in my family, for nine years. Well, except for Cameron, but it was hard to avoid the "other" parent living with my son. Due to Adam's relationship with Cam, Zack saw my parents on a regular basis.

"They would really like if you came."

The invitation took a moment to process. Once it did, I let loose with my fury dialed up to eleven. "They asked *you* to extend an invitation to me?"

"Yes."

Shaking my head, I rolled my eyes to let some of the steam out. "I don't believe it."

My parents were the kind of people who were all about the show. For this landmark anniversary, they would have sent out invitations months ago. I would be shocked if they hadn't rented a garden or conservatory—probably the one where they'd exchanged their original vows—and had the whole affair catered. If they'd wanted me there, they would have sent an invitation.

"I may have brought it up." Adam had switched to staring at his feet, as he was barefoot.

"Why would you do that?" During our divorce, my parents had sided with Cameron. They'd been nice to Adam and horrible to me. When my mother suggested I give Zack up and let Cam adopt him— because two men couldn't have a baby of their own, but I could always have another—that was the last time I'd talked to her. I gave them to Adam in the divorce, and I cut them all out of my life. I'd even changed my last name to Miles to symbolize the distance I wanted to keep between us.

"Alaina, your parents are getting older, and you have a son. Don't you think it's time—for his sake—to bury the hatchet?"

I stared at him as if he'd grown horns, devil ones, not a unicorn one.

He scoffed at my horror. "I'd be there with you."

"And Zack?" This was a strange way to ask for extra time with Zack.

He shrugged. "Maybe Zack can spend the afternoon with Deon? I'm not sure he should witness what you might say if you lose your temper."

His request made less sense to me. "Let me get this straight. You want me to go to a party for your in-laws with you and Cameron?"

"Cam will go separately."

"Have you been in an accident? Adam, did you hit your head? I've heard concussions are nothing to mess around with. You really should see a doctor, maybe get a CT scan."

He inhaled and exhaled, and he shoved his hands in the pockets of his cargo shorts. "I just think it would be good for you, and for them, if you were on speaking terms. I'm not saying you'll ever be friends with them or even that you'd see them for more than holidays or major events—like you used to do. But, Alaina, they're your family."

I studied the lines around his mouth, and I noted guilt. I set a hand on his arm. "Adam, we were always headed in this direction. They were a toxic relationship I cut out of my life. You never liked how they treated me. For fuck's sake, the whole time we were getting divorced, you were the only person who was nice to me."

When I got my second doctorate, Zack was three. Adam had come to the ceremony. He'd brought Zack to witness my accomplishment. He'd done that for a dozen things over the years. I remembered when I was in labor, I'd been alone and scared out of my mind. I'd called my mother, and she'd said she would come be with me if I agreed to give the baby to Adam and Cameron.

My anxiety had shot through the roof. I'd called Adam, sobbing so badly that he'd thought the baby had died. He'd come to the hospital, and he'd stayed with me the whole time. He even drove me home afterward. I know that sounded like the least he could have done, but I had barely spoken to him since I'd moved out of the house eight months before. He'd been outraged when he'd found out what my mother had said, and I'd overheard him on the phone, telling her to leave me alone.

Even after the divorce, he'd been there for me when my family had not.

On the strength of those horrible memories, Adam wrapped his arms around me. He rested his chin on my head, like he used to do when we were married.

"I'm divorcing Cam. Zack doesn't know yet. I'm going to tell him tonight that Cam moved out."

I jerked away from Adam because I connected the way he was holding me with his confession. Though I hadn't been involved in their relationship, I knew a lot about it from Zack. He never mentioned Adam and Cameron fighting or anything tense happening at that house.

"What happened?"

Adam shook his head, a wry twist to his lips. "He cheated on me. Karma's a bitch. I guess I deserved it."

This development didn't surprise me. From the time he was born, my younger brother ruled the roost. Cameron Weppler was the prized son, and in our parents' eyes, he could do no wrong. Cameron had grown up expecting to be the center of attention. He resented and belittled all of my accomplishments, and he'd pulled our parents away from celebrating anything about me. They hadn't even attended my college graduation. Adam's family had been there to support me.

I'd never understood what Adam saw in Cam. When he'd first met him, he'd disliked my brother. Over time, they'd become friends, but it used to annoy Adam that Cam was so self-centered. Until, I guess, it didn't. My brother could be very charming when he wanted.

I wasn't a jerk like my brother, and I felt bad for Adam because he was hurting. "Nobody deserves it. I didn't, and you don't either."

"Thank you for saying that, but it's okay if you don't really think it." Adam sighed. "Though it's not like you to say something you don't mean."

"I do mean it. I also meant it when I said I was finished with that toxic relationship. I'm sorry Zack won't see Cameron or his parents anymore, but he'll get over it. He has you, and he has me. Besides, he likes your parents a lot more."

Where my parents liked to have Zack visit for an hour or two once a month, Adam's parents liked to spend time with him. They took him camping and out to dinner, and they talked to him on the phone.

Adam's dad liked to putter around and build things from wood, and he was teaching Zack to build bird houses. They even showed up for events that happened at my house, and they were unfailingly kind to me.

He ran a hand through his hair, messing it up briefly before the blond strands fell back into place. "Well, I tried."

"You did." I chucked him on the arm. "Even though you knew there was no way on Earth I was going to change my mind."

"Yeah. Well. You know me—an eternal optimist."

I'd never once thought of Adam as an optimist, but I kept that to myself. "I'm sorry, Adam. Really, I am. If you need help with Zack on your days, you can call me. My schedule is sometimes open when yours isn't, and Clara works from home, so we can always call her."

"Thanks, Alaina." He smiled tremulously. "I knew I could count on you."

Chapter 10—Alaina

Leaving was awkward. I mean, yeah—I was sorry that he was hurting, but I also felt that he knew what he was getting into. He'd known my brother for five years before he'd slept with him. It wasn't like Cameron had hidden his selfish diva side. It was his most defining personality trait.

On the way home, I envisioned taking off my bra and putting on sweatpants. I'd start a load of laundry, pop some popcorn, pour some wine. Tonight was for me to chill out, be bad, and cackle evilly every time I thought about my brother being dumped. Maybe I'd work on my book a little. Despite all the ways my plans had changed in the last month, I was on schedule and looking to pull ahead.

Then I remembered I had counseling at DiMarco Martial Arts Studio, so I slid the timeline back to later. Since I didn't have to work tomorrow, I wasn't worried about how late I stayed up. I also mentally identified likely times I could wrangle Daniel and Evan into meeting me together.

But when I got home, I found my driveway occupied by a huge, metal trash bin, the kind that was delivered and picked up by a truck. Cars lined the street. I parked as close as I could get to my house. I got my suitcase from the trunk and wheeled it toward the front door. Somehow, I'd thought Evan would be finished with the roof by now. Even if he hadn't been, it was after five. Most crews I'd seen working in the neighborhood knocked off around four.

The front door was locked, so I went in through the side entrance, which was the door I normally used. Fragments of roofing tiles and nails littered the driveway around the bin. I noted that with a frown. I'd ask Evan if he had a plan for cleaning that up. Zack liked to play outside, and I didn't want him to get hurt on a rusty, old nail.

Inside I found a strange man in my kitchen. He was average height and blond, like Adam, but he was far better looking. Not that Adam was ugly. He wasn't. He was a regular guy. But the man in my kitchen looked like he'd stepped off a magazine cover.

And he was cooking. He moved around my kitchen with ease and familiarity, though most of the pans and some of the implements he used did not belong to me. Also, he was cooking up more food than I had left in my pantry.

He glanced up, noticing me, and a sinful smile curved his lips. "Hi. You must be Alaina." He wiped his hand on a towel and offered it to me to shake.

I did, and I was thankful he kept it brief. "Who are you?"

"Drew. I'm Sophia's fiancé."

"Oh, okay. She's mentioned you before." She hadn't mentioned that he'd be cooking in my kitchen on this, or any other, day.

He laughed. "I hope so. She's told me a ton about you. Daniel has as well. Dinner will be ready in fifteen minutes. Can you let them know?"

I heard construction noises outside, but it wasn't the pounding of nails I'd expected would happen with a roof replacement. It was the whirr of a power drill, and it was coming from the direction of my office.

I headed down the hall, wondering what they could possibly be doing. My roof was above the second floor, not the first. And it was outside.

Hovering in the doorway, I noted that my office was devoid of furniture. The desk and boxes were gone. The pictures I hadn't yet hung were gone. The windows were all there, but the drywall that had surrounded them was gone. Evan and one of his workers held a window in place while somehow also drilling into the wood around it. They finished and stepped back to admire their handiwork. Outside, I spied Daniel and another worker doing the same from the outside. Behind them, I recognized Sophia and an older woman, but I couldn't see what they were doing.

"Evan?"

At the sound of his name, he turned, a huge smile lighting his face. "Lainie, welcome home."

His use of my sub name tamped down some of the fury rising in my gut, but it didn't distract me. I gestured to the mess in the room. "What are you doing?" My tone came out pissed because I'd figured out what was going on, and I wasn't pleased. I'd hired him to do the roof—only the roof—and not the windows. I distinctly remember saying in the email that I was budgeting to have the windows replaced next summer.

We'd talked every other day, and he hadn't once mentioned anything about my windows.

His smile didn't dim. "Surprise!"

I sincerely didn't know how to respond. In general, I was a fan of surprises. They usually brought good things like cake or a friend I hadn't seen in a long time. Or, if Zack was involved, it was breakfast in bed for Mother's Day or a card he'd made for me or a gift Adam had bought for him to give to me.

Just as he'd done when I'd frozen in the kitchen when he'd delivered the bad news about the state of my windows, Evan closed in on me. He stood less than a foot away, his authoritative presence calming the worst of my anxiety. However, it did nothing to ease my anger.

I looked up at him, meeting his gaze so he could see how much I seethed. "I hired you to do only the roof."

Rather than bow to the powerful force of my ire, he set his large paws on my shoulders. "The roof is mostly done. Tomorrow is the final inspection, and we'll get the cleanup completed."

My glare didn't abate.

"It's a gift." He jerked his head back to indicate the other man in the room. "This is my brother, Alec. You saw Daniel outside with Isaac, another one of my brothers. Sophia and her parents are both here, and you probably saw Drew in the kitchen. He said he's not much for construction, so he's been feeding us. Dinner should be ready soon."

"Fifteen minutes," I muttered.

"Cool." He let go of one shoulder and slid his arm around behind me. He steered me a few steps toward the far window.

Sophia and an older man came inside, carrying a sheet of drywall. They fitted it to one side of the window. It was already cut to fit around the window and electrical outlets. They held it up, and Alec went to work with his power tool.

"We're all donating our time and expertise, and Sophia donated the windows."

Never in my life had anyone been this generous, much less a whole group of people, most of whom I'd never met. Tears stung my eyes. "But—why?"

Sophia glanced over, a proud smile widening her mouth. "You do so much for so many, and you don't ask anything in return. Think of this as a way for Daniel and me to thank you for your incredible generosity."

The older man had been watching her proudly, and he nodded to me. "Hi, Alaina. I'm David DiMarco. I've listened to the kids rave about you for a year, and when Evan told us about your situation, I knew exactly how we were going to solve your problem."

"It's a good thing, too." Alec said. I noted how much he resembled Evan—a my-age Evan—in the structure of his face and the way he was built. "The rot extended farther than Evan thought. We had to replace all of the headers, put in supports, and replace some of the frame for the wall and ceiling. You couldn't have left this for another winter."

He finished screwing in the drywall and came over to shake my hand.

I girded myself for unpleasant contact and thanked Alec for his time.

Alec nodded as if it wasn't a big deal. "We'll get the first layer of mud on it tonight, and then we'll be over Friday to finish it off."

"Dinner," Drew bellowed from the kitchen.

"Oh, good," Sophia said. "I'm starving. Let's get washed up. Drew brought paper plates, and my mom set up for a picnic outside."

They left the room, and I was alone with Evan. His arm was still slung around my shoulders, and he watched me carefully.

"Still mad?"

"No. I'm overwhelmed. I can see where Daniel and Sophia would be here, though not really, because I get paid for my time through the grant, and I'm also conducting a genetic study on the participants who gave consent. So, I'm getting something out of the counseling sessions. I'm not donating my time." I looked up at him, meeting those crystal blue eyes even though I'd be more comfortable looking at his mouth.

He shook his head. "What you do for those people extends far beyond what you're getting out of it. You're helping people get their lives back. You're helping them deal with serious trauma and learn to stand on their own two feet. You can't put a price tag on that. You might get a small stipend, and maybe you'll find something with your study, but that's nothing compared to what you give so selflessly."

"I really don't think it's a big deal."

He let go of my shoulders and faced me. "And that's why you're such an incredible person. That's why we're all here."

"Oh." My shoulders sagged, and my gaze dropped to his mouth. He had such luscious lips. "I kind of thought you were doing this because you planned to sleep with me again."

His jaw dropped.

Yeah. I hadn't thought that through very well. "Sorry. I shouldn't be so blunt." I bit my lip in an effort to force my brain to slow down and think before I said more.

"That's okay. I find your directness refreshing and weirdly charming."

I coughed out a laugh. "Nobody has ever said that before."

"You might be hanging with the wrong crowd." He followed with a cheeky smile, which was also sexy.

I pressed my hands together so that the outlines touched, but my palms were free of pressure, and I took a deep breath. "Evan, you didn't have to do all this just to sleep with me."

His gaze roamed my face. I felt the weight of it on my skin.

"We need to talk." I blurted again, and I took comfort that at least I'd said something I'd already thought through.

"I agree, and it won't be a short conversation. It's one I'd like to sit down and have with you when there aren't a bunch of people expecting us for dinner, and I know you have to jet out of here afterward. Can we talk tomorrow? I'll be here, working with my crew. Maybe you'll ask me to stay for dinner again? Or we can order takeout?"

I loved that I would have the processing time I needed. "I'd like that."

He grinned. "It's a date."

Leaning down, he brushed his lips against mine. The brush became a massage, one that weakened my bones as I melted from the inside. Before I knew it, our tongues tangled, wrapping around one another in a preview of what we both wanted to happen to our bodies.

It ended way too soon, and he eased away. His lips were a little swollen, and a glance up showed me the blue of his eyes had darkened to sapphire. He grinned. "More of that later, Lainie, but right now, there are a few people waiting to meet you."

Peeking through the brand-new window, I observed a fair number of people bearing DiMarco or Carrico traits. "You have how many siblings?"

"I'm seventh of nine. Six boys, three girls." The way he recited the numbers told me it was a question he was asked often. "There's a twenty-three year span between the oldest and the youngest."

I'd met two of his siblings, and in my back yard, I met Kellen, though he was more interested in seeing his brother.

Evan engaged in a hearty handshake with Kellen, hugging his brother to him. "When did you get back in town?"

"Just now. I dropped Amelia off at Alec's house, and Allie said you were here, so I came over to help out." He glanced around. "Or eat. You know me—always on the lookout for a good meal."

As the two caught up, Sophia tugged on my wrist. "Alaina, come meet my parents. They've been looking forward to this all day."

Sophia's mom, Anna, engulfed me in a big, maternal hug. It was warm and comfortable, the kind of affection I'd always craved from my own mother. But where my mother limited displays to an air kiss on the cheek and a hug that didn't muss her clothes, Anna didn't seem to understand the concept of rationing affection or reigning in her feelings.

After hugging me, where she gushed about how wonderful it was to finally meet me, she pushed me away and held me at arm's length with both hands on my shoulders. "Aren't you just a pretty little thing!"

Sophia huffed. "Mom, she's not a thing. She's a woman."

Anna waved away her daughter's correction. "Oh, she knows what I mean. Don't you, Alaina? Or should I call you Doctor Miles?"

I breathed a laugh. "Alaina is fine, and I'm not offended. People who know me by my accomplishments are usually surprised by my physical appearance." The opposite was also true—people who knew me by sight were often surprised at what I'd accomplished. Genetically, there was no link between physical size and brain capacity or work ethic, but people tended to judge based on appearances.

"I wasn't." Daniel appeared on my other side, a cheeky grin curving those intensely kissable lips and giving me flashbacks to what they felt like on my skin. "I knew the moment I walked into your office to interview you that you were a force to be reckoned with."

Anna nodded. "That's a good thing. If you're going to deal with my two, you need a strong personality."

Sophia and Daniel engaged in mutual eye-rolling, but mirth remained around their mouths.

"Let's get you fed." Anna steered me toward a portable table where food had been arranged. "Drew puts out a good spread."

Drew, the blond man I'd met in my kitchen, stood behind the table. Hands on hips, he looked at Anna with a cocky smile. "Almost as good as yours, Anna."

"Close enough." She laughed.

It must have been a joke between the two of them. I watched this development with interest. My own parents had always been solicitous toward Adam, but they'd never joked or developed a deeper connection. Adam's parents had always been nice to me, but they were put off by my social awkwardness. Anna had bonded with her daughter's fiancé, and the two genuinely liked one another.

Then I reflected that if she treated him half as warmly as she'd treated me, it would be easy to grow real feelings. I'd only known her for a few minutes, and I already felt a strong connection to the woman.

Zack would absolutely love her.

As Anna piled my plate with more food than I could possibly eat, she introduced me, or reintroduced me to everyone there. Each introduction included a vignette to help me remember them, which I appreciated.

Alec was the oldest Carrico. He and his wife, Allie, had three children. Alec had once met the President while he'd worked on her campaign.

Isaac was the third oldest Carrico. He liked to juggle knives, but he said he wouldn't do it today because Anna said it would give her a heart attack from the worry.

Kellen was the middle child of the Carrico clan. He'd met his wife, Amelia, when she'd crashed her car into the front window of his apartment. That was why Anna had come to believe one should never live on the ground floor of an apartment in a busy city.

David, Anna's husband, owned a landscaping business that he was thinking of selling so he could retire. Anna thought he was much too young to retire, and no husband of hers was going to sit around the house all day and do nothing. He'd laughed in response.

Looking at him, I could see Daniel in thirty years. He'd fill out a little more, but he'd still be active and sinfully handsome. He smacked a kiss on Anna's cheek. "I'll retire when I have a grandkid to spoil."

Sophia poured dressing over a heap of salad. "See, Mom? Nothing to worry about. Daniel and I are years away from even thinking about kids."

Anna glared at Drew. "Don't you want kids?"

"Eventually." He set a roll on Anna's plate. "You have to try this, Anna. It's a new recipe, and I want your opinion."

She beamed, and she led me to where the group had gathered to sit on the timbers edging flower beds along one side of the yard.

"You need a patio, dear," Anna said. "A big house like this needs outdoor entertaining space."

"I'd put on a deck." Alec chimed in from the other side of me. He pointed along the back, where the door that led to the kitchen was located. "Put a slider in the kitchen. There's plenty of space along that back wall. Come out onto a deck." He spread his hands to indicate where the deck would be located.

"Hot tub, right there." Isaac drew a circle in the air behind my office. "Another slider. The deck could wrap around it."

"Yeah." Alec's smile grew as the duo redesigned the back of my house in a way that would ruin the symmetry but improve the function.

If I had a large family, or even a lot of friends I needed to entertain, they'd come up with the perfect plan. I thought about what it would be like to have warm, supportive, affectionate parents like Sophia and Daniel's, and a large family like Evan's. Though there were a lot of them, they seemed close. Evan and his sister liked to write songs and sing them together. Three brothers had shown up to help out at my house even though they'd never met me.

As I listened to Alec talk about his children, the oldest of whom was Zack's age, my heart ached for what my son was missing out on by having such a small family—and it was about to shrink even more once Adam got a divorce. Adam had a younger sister, but she didn't have kids. Even if that changed, they'd be so much younger than Zack. He would love them—he adored babies—but he wouldn't be able to be friends with them.

From the start, I'd loved how close Daniel and Sophia were. I'd wanted Zack to have siblings close to his age. I'd wanted him to have a bond with them that I'd craved with my own brother.

I'd wanted half a dozen kids. Adam had only wanted one. I had felt I could talk him into a second and third without too much effort, but I might have had to beg for additional children.

I sighed.

Sophia, who'd parked herself between her mother and me, leaned closer. "What are you thinking?"

"That Zack would love this."

Sophia glanced around. "Construction? That's great. He could help Mom and me stain all that molding."

"He'd learn a lot from being here," I agreed. "But I meant having a large family. I've always wished he had at least one sibling." I heaved a sigh again. "But it's too late for that now."

"Zack is your son?" Alec interjected.

"Yes. He's eight."

"Is he with his dad?" Sophia asked.

"Yes. I dropped him off before coming home."

Alec snorted. "My mom was fifty when she had my youngest sister. Allie had our third last year, and she's forty-six. You're what? Thirty?"

"I'll be thirty-nine in two months."

He waved away my dire response. "Plenty of time. Life doesn't even really start until you're forty. Allie was your age when she got pregnant with our oldest."

I liked Alec a lot, probably because I saw so much of Evan in him. Though, if I were being objective, I'd known Evan for two weeks, and this was the third time I'd seen him in person.

I knew there was plenty of time for me to still have a couple of kids or even adopt, but I had no desire to do that alone, and I was vehemently against having another permanent relationship.

"At any rate, he's happy and healthy. It's enough."

Lots of talking and laughing happened during the meal, and some of it was mine. The Carrico and DiMarco families got along as if they were all close cousins, and they seemed to have adopted me. Alec extended an invitation for me to bring Zack over to meet his wife and children. I loved how conversation ebbed and flowed, how people moved around, joining different groups to chat.

Everyone appeared happy, and the joy was contagious.

Sophia stayed by my side throughout the hour of eating and talking. At one point, I looked over at her to find her staring across the yard, Drew firmly in her crosshairs. He was intently listening to Evan describe something that involved a lot of hand movements. "You don't have to stay here to take care of me. I'm fine. It's okay to go see Drew."

A feline smile curved her lips, though she didn't stop staring at Drew. "Sometimes I just like to look."

"He is very handsome." I couldn't seem to stop my gaze from landing on Evan, and then going on a hunt for Daniel.

Someone sat down beside me, in the place Alec had vacated. I looked over to find Daniel regarding me with a friendly smile. "Hey, Lainie."

"Hi, Daniel. I haven't had a chance to thank you for everything you've done here today." Every time I'd planned to seek him out, someone else stopped by to talk with me.

He waved away my gratitude. "It's nothing."

"I disagree. You, Sophia, and Evan convinced all these people to give up their time to come here and do all this work. It's a big deal."

"I didn't help," Sophia said. "It was mostly Evan. He was incensed that you weren't listening to his warning about how seriously the work needed to be done. It's a good thing you aren't his sub. He would have paddled your ass."

I knew Sophia was a Domme, and she had to know that Evan was as well, but I hadn't expected her to comment about it to me. While I struggled to pick my jaw up off the ground, she continued.

"Of course, if you *were* his sub, discipline might still be forthcoming." She tore her gaze from Drew and nailed me with a firm, knowing look.

I wondered what she thought she might know. Surely Evan hadn't told everyone he'd slept with me or that he'd been very bossy during phone sex. I knew he'd told Daniel. *I'd* told Daniel. Perhaps Daniel had told Sophia? But then, he'd have to confess that he had also slept with me.

While I didn't think either of them was ashamed or embarrassed by having spent some quality horizontal time with me, I also didn't think they'd disclose that information carelessly.

Of course, I didn't know Sophia well enough to know whether she would judge me or even care about my sexual exploits.

She smiled at me the same way she'd smiled at Drew. I felt like prey.

Daniel cleared his throat, breaking me out of my thoughts. "Lainie, I was wondering if you could give me a ride to the studio when you go?"

Fleeing to the safety of Daniel's friendly smile, I turned my attention to him. "Yes, of course. What time is it?"

"Almost time to go."

I realized Sophia must have come with Drew. I braved her predatory air once again. "You're welcome to join us."

"Sure. That'll give Drew a chance to clean up, and then he can come get me."

The DiMarcos, Alec, and Kellen left when we did, leaving Isaac to help Evan finish taping drywall joints and whatever else people needed to do to make drywall paintable.

In the car, Sophia called shotgun. My SUV had plenty of leg room in the back, so Daniel wouldn't be cramped.

She bounced in the seat, more animated than I'd ever seen her. "Hey, Danny, did you notice Kellen showed up in time for food and left right afterward?"

He laughed, a deep, musical note that played pleasantly along the back of my neck. "As always. If there's a way to avoid working and still get paid, Kellen will find it."

"I thought he'd just come in from out of town?"

"He got here last night," Daniel supplied. "He could have come when Evan picked up Alec this morning. He went over to see his parents, and then he was supposed to be at your place five hours ago."

I thought it was wonderful that he'd made visiting his parents a priority. "I'm sure he didn't come all the way home to put windows in my house. He came to visit with his family. That's understandable."

In the rearview mirror, Daniel blew me a kiss.

I was so shocked, I nearly missed turning onto the street where his studio was located. Slamming on the brakes, I slowed enough to make the turn.

Sophia grabbed the armrest for stability. "Holy shit, Alaina. I'm glad this thing comes with seat belts."

Heat burned my cheeks and neck. "Sorry. I forgot where I was going for a moment."

Unable to stop myself, I glanced in the rearview mirror again to find Daniel wearing an expression that was entirely too cocky.

I had so much to tell Clara when she came home from the Outer Banks this weekend. This much juicy gossip demanded a face-to-face exchange and a lot of wine.

Inside the lobby, Sophia excused herself to go upstairs and change. I'd put on yoga pants and a cotton shirt at home because I'd remembered that Daniel and Sophia wanted me to participate in the classes instead of just run therapy sessions afterward.

In the larger practice room, one of Daniel's employees ran a group of children about Zack's age through a series of karate moves. I stepped to the side for a better peek. I'd wanted to enroll Zack in classes, but Adam wasn't sure about it, and the classes I'd seen spanned both our custody days. If Adam wasn't on board with the plan, then he wouldn't take Zack to his classes.

"It's a beginning Muay Thai class."

"I have never heard of that discipline."

He stood next to me, but his gaze was on me and not the class. "It utilizes eight points of contact instead of four. It flows well into the mixed-martial arts classes."

Looking up, I met his gaze briefly before letting it drop to his mouth. I knew four points of contact were two hands and two feet, but people didn't have more limbs. "Eight?"

"Elbows and knees."

"Oh. That makes sense."

He tilted his head. "If you're interested, I hold adult classes on Tuesday and Thursday evenings, and every other Saturday. I have Taekwando, MMA, and kickboxing."

I shook my head. "Thanks, but Tuesdays are busy enough, and I teach a class on Saturday morning."

"You could come on Thursdays, but I wouldn't be leading the class. I'm coaching a competitive student for the first time, and I'm committed to working with her on Thursday evenings. But, if you came to class, I'd let you use my shower afterward." He lifted a brow.

I wasn't sure if this new familiarity was because we had come to know each other better in the past few weeks or if he was flirting with me. "Is that a proposition?"

"Yes."

Okay. Flirting. I wasn't sure I should reciprocate. I figured this whole road I was traveling with him was already on my 'Shouldn't've' list, so anything I added was just a subsection of the original mistake. I capitulated to the urge to flirt. "What if I didn't come for class, but I just came for the shower?"

His smile grew. "How about tonight, you stick around? I don't have any chocolate mousse cake, but I do have a can of whipped cream."

Daniel's offer had my pussy throbbing with anticipation. "What kind of librarian has whipped cream in a can?" I glanced down. "Oh, I didn't bring the right outfit."

His gaze roved down my form. "I disagree."

Warm feelings swirled inside me, but guilt was also there. "Evan also asked to see me again. We have dinner plans for tomorrow."

That sensual grin didn't change. "I know."

"Does he know you're propositioning me?"

His smile grew. "Evan and I have no secrets." With that, he kissed my cheek. "I have to go change. I'll see you in a few."

He left, and people started filing in for our session, and I found myself swept up in other people's problems.

At the end, Sophia pulled me aside. She'd stayed for the therapy session, which she sometimes did, thought she hadn't shared anything with the group.

Away from the others, she whispered, "I saw you kissing Evan at your house." She bit her lip, as if she had rehearsed more to say, but she wasn't sure she had the courage to go through with it.

I knew she was afraid things would go south, and I'd quit coming. Daniel was worried about his own behavior causing the same thing, and yet he still wanted me to come upstairs after the session so we could recreate the awesome sex from the last few times.

I touched her arm. "We scened, and I think he plans to ask me to scene again because it went well the first time."

Her eyes widened in alarm. "Alaina, Evan is..." There went the lip-biting again.

"Far too young for me. I know. But we're both consenting adults, and we had fun, so I don't see the harm. We both made sure the other understood it was a casual affair."

She noticeably relaxed, exhaling a long stream of air. "Good. I'm certain Evan is in love with someone already, but he's being stubborn about committing."

As I put away the chairs after everybody had gone, I thought about what she'd said and how I might be interfering with Evan finding love and happiness. I didn't want to do that to him.

Chapter 11—Daniel

Later that night, Evan came in through the side door, next to the stairs leading directly to my loft. We still hadn't decided where to live. He was right that my loft wasn't good for more than one person because it lacked any semblance of privacy. But I disliked his condo. It was small. There was no way my furniture would fit inside his place. We'd have to put my grandparents' elegant dining table into storage.

So we'd been alternating where we slept, all the while quibbling over whether we should rent or buy, and what, exactly, we should rent or buy. That was the original reason I'd moved into the space above my studio—I preferred to spend my time doing things that were more physically and mentally rewarding than looking for real estate.

He sniffed the air when he got upstairs. "Did you bake cookies?"

"It's a candle."

"You lit a cookie-scented candle for a romantic evening?"

I shrugged. "Who doesn't melt in the face of chocolate-chip cookies?"

"Someone who is expecting cookies, only to find it's a fucking candle teasing them with the scent, and they have no hope of tasting one."

By the time he got to the end of his diatribe, I was laughing. "Are you hungry, Ev? I have leftover pecan pie in the fridge. My mom made it."

"You're a monster. I want a cookie."

I kissed him instead, which shut him up. "How did it go at Alaina's?"

"Fine. Isaac and I got the rest of the drywall up. We taped the joints and got a layer of mud on it. I'll check it tomorrow, but with the weather as humid as it's been, we're looking at Friday before it can be sanded. I'll have her pick out some paint tomorrow. I was thinking we'd head over Sunday to paint the two rooms and get her furniture moved back."

"Did you tell her you were coming tonight?"

He grinned. "No. She thinks we'll be talking tomorrow over dinner, and perhaps we will. This'll be a surprise."

I'd heard from Alec and Drew that she hadn't reacted well to the surprise. Evan had to talk her into not being pissed at him for doing more than she'd asked. "The group therapy session is over. I'm going to head down to help Alaina put away the chairs. Do you want to come with me?"

"I'd like to come *on* you." He had that look, the Dom one that I responded to about half of the time because it was all kinds of cute and sexy, but sometimes it annoyed me.

If so much hadn't been on the line tonight, I might have taken him up on that offer. "Maybe later. We'll see what she's open to before we go making plans like that."

We had no way of knowing if she was open to having both of us together, or if she'd want to continue seeing us separately. Then later, we could ease into the three of us being together.

Downstairs, I found Alaina so deep in thought that she'd frozen in place with her hand on the back of a folding chair. She didn't notice that I'd entered the room.

"Lainie?" I tried to speak quietly so I didn't startle her.

She blinked a couple times, looked around, and then folded the chair in her hand. "Sorry. I didn't hear you come in."

"Something on your mind?"

"Always." She laughed. "I wish it had an off switch."

I thought everything she said was interesting. I could listen to her ramble on about genetics or psychology for hours, though I might have to cave to the urge to kiss her a lot while she was talking. I couldn't imagine what it must be like to have all that brilliance bouncing around in my brain all the time.

Glancing around, I looked for signs my sister was still in the building. "Did Sophia leave?"

"Yes. Drew picked her up a few minutes ago." Alaina and I stored the last few chairs.

Holding out a hand, I lifted my chin. "You still want to come upstairs?"

A shy smile curved the corners of her mouth, and she dropped her gaze. "If you still want me to."

"I do." Because she hadn't put her hand in mine, I shifted strategy, and I tugged at her elbow.

Before we could get anywhere, she turned away to grab the handle of her purse.

"Alaina? Are you sure about this?"

"I'm sure. Did you have something particular in mind for tonight? Maybe a yoga instructor? I'm dressed for that scenario."

Laughing, I put my arm around her, resting my hand on her hip. She relaxed into the embrace, which quashed the bit of doubt I'd felt due to the bombshell we were about to drop on her. "I thought we'd maybe have some wine, talk for a bit, kind of ease into things?"

"Okay. That sounds good."

I locked the front door, armed my security system, and led her upstairs to my loft. I held doors for her because that was how my father had raised me—to hold the door for whomever I was with and enter after them.

Alaina made it two steps into my loft before she froze. "Evan?"

He'd been leaning against the island counter separating the kitchen and dining areas. He stood up straight, flashing his sexiest, most alluring smile. Now that I was free to not bury my attraction to Evan, his smile even caused an insistent stir inside me.

He closed the distance, parking his hands on her hips, and he pressed a short kiss to her lips.

I closed the door to my loft, and I took her bags. As I set them on the counter, I noted how stiff and uncomfortable she appeared. "Lainie? Are you okay?"

"This is weird."

Evan gave her some space, and he spread his hands wide. "Is it really?"

"Yes." She sounded resolute. "And unexpected." Her gaze found mine, lingered for a brief moment, and then dropped a bit. "Did you know he was here?"

"I did." Three glasses of wine waited on the counter. I handed one to Evan, and I brought another to Alaina. "Evan and I wanted to talk to you."

Suspicion cast her eyes a darker shade of brown. "You do?"

Rather than respond, I kissed Evan. I meant it to be short, a little token of affection to get the point across, but it morphed into something deeper. By the time I drew back, we were both breathing heavily. A huge part of me wanted to skip the conversation and get right to having two sexy people in my bed, but I knew the talking part was too important to omit.

I slid an arm around Evan's waist, and we both faced the woman we wanted to join our relationship club.

She studied us, her shrewd eyes dissecting our faces and the way we stood close to one another. Then she downed the entire glass of wine. Without saying a word, she took a deep breath, set the glass on the counter, and picked up her bags.

Before she could leave, I closed my hand over hers to stop her. I took the bags and put them back. "We want to talk to you."

She motioned to Evan. "It seems like you got your point across."

Evan tilted his head. "Did we?"

I shook mine. "I think you misunderstood the point we were trying to make."

"The two of you are a couple," she said. "It was very apparent in the familiar way you touched each other and the ease you have in each other's presence. I just don't understand why you propositioned me if you and Evan are together."

"Because I like you. Evan likes you." I guided her deeper into the loft, and I settled her on the sofa. "We're seeing each other, yes, but we both want to keep seeing you. Together."

I sat on one side of her, and Evan sat on the other.

She popped up like a piece of toast fleeing the heat and paced away a few steps, but she didn't go toward the door, so I felt we were making progress.

"We didn't mean to freak you out," Evan said. "We kind of thought you'd be okay with us being together."

Her eyes widened. "I don't care who you see, Evan. We were together one time for a casual roll in the sheets." She nailed me with those wide eyes next. "And maybe we were together more than once, but it was still a casual thing. You made sure to clarify that condition before we slept together. I didn't expect to sleep with either of you ever again. We should have left well enough alone. I shouldn't be here tonight."

I tried to stand, but Evan pulled me back down. He was all about body language, and I knew he didn't want me to intimidate Alaina by looming over her. I scooted to the edge of the sofa because I didn't like the distance between us.

"Alaina, we both like you. A lot." Evan rested an ankle on his knee, his relaxed pose in exact opposition to my open anxiety. He leaned back and took a sip of wine. "You and I are compatible. You and Daniel are compatible. We were thinking the three of us could be compatible together."

If I thought she was in shock before, that was nothing compared to now. Her mouth moved, and she sputtered several unrelated syllables before turning and pacing away.

Now I really wanted to go to her, to take her in my arms and soothe her upset.

Evan sprang up and blocked my path. I hadn't even realized I was on my feet.

"Move." I knew he liked to be in charge, but I wasn't about to let him stop me from consoling Alaina. I could move him out of my way with no problem. He knew this, and he knew I'd halted out of respect for his wishes.

He set his hands on my shoulders and smoothed a caress down my arms. "Give her time to process."

I stared, my gut telling me that he knew something I didn't. "What's going on?"

"She just needs time to process. If you rush her, she's going to leave."

Her back was to me, but I could see the way she pressed her fingertips to her forehead.

"There's no reason for her to get upset about this." I motioned to her petite form. "She needs to know we're serious."

"I know you're serious." Her voice floated over her shoulder. "That's why I'm trying to understand."

"Understand what?" Talking was a good sign, and I aimed to keep her going. "Ask anything, Lainie. We'll tell you anything you want to know."

Her hands fell to her sides, and she turned to face us. "How long have you been together?"

Evan moved so that we both faced her from across the living room space. He answered. "It happened after the last time you were with Daniel. I came over that evening, and we decided to take the plunge."

A curt nod was her only movement. "But you've been sleeping together for a lot longer. How long have you really been together?"

I understood what she was really asking. "Nine years. We started a casual sexual relationship in high school. It only stopped whenever Evan was seeing someone seriously."

Her gaze roamed Evan before returning to me. "What about your relationships?"

I shrugged. "I've never been on more than a handful of dates with a woman."

"Have you had relationships with other men?"

Evan answered in the positive, and I responded in the negative.

"Why haven't you entered into a committed relationship with each other before twelve days ago?" Her arms crossed, and I couldn't tell if she was consoling herself or steeling herself for our answer.

I shrugged. "It just didn't seem right."

Evan appealed to her on a different level. "I'm a Dom, and Daniel isn't a sub. He bottoms for me, but he doesn't submit, and sometimes I bottom for him. More importantly, we're both still attracted to women."

Her nose wrinkled. "I would imagine you're both also still attracted to men. Attraction doesn't go away just because you're committed to someone."

I couldn't help but grin because she nailed our reasoning perfectly. "That's true. We're both very attracted to you."

"Or you're just afraid that if you fully commit to one another, you'll be missing out on something. Or maybe you're afraid of having a mature, adult relationship with someone who really matters." She swept her hand toward us. "Now that I can see what's in front of my face, I'm not sure how I missed it before. Except, of course, that I'm clueless when it comes to interpersonal relations. But even I can see how much you two love each other."

Goofy feelings suffused my chest, and I grinned at Evan. "We do, and maybe we were too immature to commit before, but we're there now."

"Good." She pressed her lips together, rolling them in as she thought.

"So you're willing to entertain the idea of dating us both together?" Evan dialed the charm up to eleven. His blue eyes sparkled, and he used the crooked smile that made me want to kiss him senseless.

Reigning in my impulses, I crossed the space and stopped in front of her. I dragged a fingertip lightly down her cheek and along her jaw. "Alaina, we're both crazy about you. I can't get you out of my head, and Evan can't either."

As I leaned down to kiss her, she slapped a hand over my mouth. "I'll get out of your head a lot faster if we go back to being colleagues and nothing more."

Disengaging her hold, I kissed her knuckles. "I don't want you to get out of my head. I like you there."

"No. It's a distraction, a diversion that's going to keep you from being fully present in your relationship with Evan." She peered around me. "I know you think it's going to be a problem that you're a Dom and Daniel isn't a sub, but I think you've been working around that issue the whole time you've been together. Given your willingness to commit to Daniel, you're obviously willing to accept whatever compromises you've been using this whole time."

Evan's brows drew together. "Alaina, Daniel and I have talked about this a lot. We both want you, and we both want to continue to see you—together."

Her head snapped back, a sign of shock. "Like a threesome?"

"Yes." I grinned to alleviate the worst of her alarm. I thought we'd been clear, but it was evident she hadn't been traveling on our wavelength. Our efforts at communicating definitely needed to improve. "You have a great sense of humor, which I think we need if the three of us are going to try this. Evan and I have never done anything like this before. Have you?"

"No, and I'm not doing it now." She closed her eyes, and I recognized her struggle to put her thoughts in order. Then they popped open, and she put distance between us by standing behind the other sofa. It was a physical barrier to mimic the emotional one she was busily reinforcing. "Look, the two of you belong together, and I'm not getting between you."

"You're right," Evan said. "You're not. I love Daniel, and he loves me. That's separate from what we feel for you."

She barked a laugh. "Don't start spewing romantic sentiments to me. We had a good time, but emotions weren't involved."

I frowned. "They weren't meant to be. That's true. But it doesn't mean they weren't."

"Alaina, please give it a chance." Evan wore that sexy smile again, the one that claimed to know the secrets locked deep in a person's heart.

Alaina didn't melt. "My ex-husband cheated on me with my brother. They've been married for eight years."

I hadn't known that about her. A glance at Evan found him equally flabbergasted.

Evan recovered first. He pointed, circling his finger gun among the three of us. "Nobody is cheating. Not only did Daniel and I tell each other what was going on, but you were very honest and up-front about everything. You even told Daniel that I'd asked you to dinner tomorrow."

Unmoved, Alaina shook her head, the slow back-and-forth motion sealing a fate I didn't want to face. "Dinner is not happening. Nothing is happening. Evan, I appreciate your offer, but I'm declining. Daniel, same thing. We will return to having just a professional association. I wish you both nothing but the best. You're very compatible, and you have a terrific chance for a successful, lifelong relationship."

"But... We like you." I felt like an idiot because that was all I could think to say, something that sounded whiny and immature, and I hated that I didn't have a better argument.

Her smile turned regretful. "I had fun with both of you, but that needs to stay in the past. I advise you to stop looking for completion outside of your relationship. It can only damage the special bond you have spent the past decade forging."

Nine years wasn't quite a decade, but I understood she was rounding up.

"Lainie, please reconsider." Yep, I still sounded like a whiny, clingy moron.

Evan shot me a desperate look. He was great with his hands, but words weren't his thing. I was excellent with words, arguments in particular, but in this instance, I could think of nothing to convince her to change her mind. I hadn't thought she would turn down, or even question, our offer, and so I hadn't thought through rebuttals to her reasons.

A hint of sympathy lightened her eyes, and she came out from behind the sofa. She took my hand, something she'd rarely done before. Then she slipped her other hand into Evan's. She mostly held them with her fingers, which felt strange, but this small amount of physical contact was far better than having her freaking out with a piece of furniture as a barrier.

"I can see that you're both afraid. Statistically, you have an excellent chance for a successful, long-term relationship. You grew up together. You come from similar backgrounds and have similar life experiences. Your families are welcoming and supportive. You'll do fine. You don't need a crutch, and keeping me around is nothing more than a crutch." She released our hands, a sense of finality in the gesture that I hated.

Evan wasn't ready to give up, either. "Alaina, we both want this. You're not a crutch. You're incredible, and we want you in our lives."

"You *think* you want this, but it's a product of fear. There's a lot at stake with what you're doing. If it doesn't work out, you'd lose so much more than a lover. You'd lose your best friend and the extended family that you both love. It's hard, but you'll be fine."

I glanced at Evan. "We're not afraid. We wouldn't have taken this step if we didn't know it would work out."

"Daniel, I'm twelve years older than you. I'm closer to forty than you are to thirty. I've been married and divorced. I might look like I have my shit together, but I'm carrying around a lot of emotional baggage. I haven't spoken to my family in more than eight years. I was in a great mood earlier because my ex-husband told me he was getting divorced, and I felt like the universe had delivered retribution. Except for a physical attraction, we have very little in common. For some reason, you both have me up on some sort of pedestal. I've

139

enjoyed it, but it's not real, and it only underscores how little you actually know about me. I like you both, and I'm turning you down because I want you both to have a happy life. That won't happen with me, especially not once you dig deeper and see the mess I keep under wraps."

She took a breath, her gaze lifting to the ceiling. "I'd be lying if I said I haven't enjoyed being on your pedestals. You're both excellent lovers and good people. Thank you for everything you've given me. I will always remember our time together fondly. And whenever I see the two of you together, I'm going to feel nothing but joy that you've found lasting love and happiness."

With that, she touched her fingertips to my cheek. Then she touched Evan.

And then she was gone.

Evan and I stared at the closed door, both of us too stunned to move, for a long time.

Chapter 12—Alaina

Fortunately when I arrived home, it wasn't too late to call Clara, and I knew Deon would be in bed. Armed with a sharp wit and a glass of Chardonnay, she acted as my sounding board and a bolster to my conscience. I related everything that had happened since I'd left her only twelve short hours before.

"You wanted to say yes," she observed.

"To the proposal of a threesome with two younger men who are both excellent lovers, I wanted to say yes. But you know how I feel about relationships."

"They're emotionally messy and not something you want complicating your life." She laughed. "Yes, I am aware of your aversion to getting your heart broken again."

Clara disagreed with me on that topic. Deon's father had passed away suddenly when she was pregnant. She'd mourned him, and when she was ready, she'd started dating again. She'd recently ended a five-year relationship with a man who had teenaged children. Though she was taking a break right now, she was already planning to put herself back out there. She was the optimist, not me.

"I'm perfectly happy with my life the way it is. I do not need a partner to make my life complete."

She snorted. "Maybe you need two partners. They could keep each other occupied when you need a break."

That was a selfish way to view a relationship, and most of the time, I wasn't a selfish person. "They're so in love with each other. The affection was noticeable the first time I saw them together. I thought perhaps they were just very close friends, but now I know they were always more."

"Alaina, I can't fault your judgment, but I'm questioning whether you stepped away too soon."

"Too soon?" I picked at my cuticle. Though I had an inkling about what she was going to say, I was curious to know if I was right or wrong.

"Maybe they do need you right now to help them get settled. Or maybe they just need one night with you together to prove to each other that you were a catalyst and not the glue? I don't know. I'm just thinking out loud. Also, I'm trying to justify you having the threesome you very clearly want."

I did want it, but not at the cost of their future happiness. Then it hit me that I was being extraordinarily narcissistic to think my pussy was powerful enough to either bring them together or pull them apart. Laughter at my idiocy burst forth, and I shared my realization with my best friend.

Clara and I talked a while longer, our conversation meandering over a variety of topics. I went to sleep very late, but I slept with a clear conscience. And I slept in Zack's bed because mine was in an unused room where I didn't feel comfortable sleeping. Evan had moved my bed to the room across the hall, probably because it was the nearest empty room, but the room just didn't feel right.

Zack's room was on the other end of the house. The stairs split the upper floor, with three bedrooms on either side. Zack had chosen to have his room on the other side of the staircase because it opened to a neutral area where we'd put a sofa, bookshelves, and his gaming equipment. It was his own, open-air living room. I didn't like having him on the other end of the house, but I adapted by checking on him frequently. I wanted to hide a baby monitor in his room, but I felt that was perhaps a little too smothering.

Being a parent was definitely the hardest challenge I'd ever taken on.

I'd taken the week off, figuring I'd need to relax after being away from home. Since the day before had been full of stress and the shock of unexpected happenings, I slept in.

At least, I tried to.

I awoke at eight to the sound of men's voices outside my house, the clunks and thunks of heavy metals, and the high-pitched beeps of construction vehicles backing up. I peered out the window to see five men picking through the flower beds lining the front of my house.

Dressing in record time, I rushed down the stairs and flung open the front door. "Who are you, and what are you doing?"

The three men closest to me halted their actions and stared. I'd startled them. The two others were not in sight. One wore a hat with an embroidered "D" on it to indicate our area's baseball team. He looked toward the driveway, and then back at me.

"Good morning, ma'am. We're with Carrico Construction. We're just cleaning up after replacing your roof." He indicated the large tool he'd shoved into a bush I disliked. "This is a heavy-duty magnet that'll find stray nails and such."

Carrico Construction. Of course. The large waste receptacle bisecting my driveway was a clue that Evan would return to complete the job.

I visibly relaxed. "Oh. Is Evan here?"

He shook his head. "He'll be along soon. He said he had some things to do before he came to the work site."

"Thank you. I'm sorry I startled you."

He grinned. "That's okay, ma'am. Do you want me to tell Evan to come see you when he gets here?"

Did I want to see Evan? I supposed it was inevitable. My smile felt stiff and false. "There's no rush."

I felt a rush of adrenaline. I wanted to see him every bit as badly as I dreaded it. Last night had been difficult for him. The disbelief and misery blazing from his eyes and inscribed in the set of his mouth had tugged at my heart last night. I fervently hoped he and Daniel had found appropriate solace in each other's arms, but I wasn't sure it would be enough.

Both men were ambitious and successful, which meant they weren't the kind who gave up easily when there was something they wanted. And they were so very challenging to resist.

I showered quickly. Then I spent extra time choosing my clothes and fixing my hair, and I even dabbed on a little makeup, something I didn't normally do when my plans included staying home in comfortable clothes and parking my ass in my office to get some writing done. That was not an occasion worthy of even a shower.

The expected knock came from the front door a lot later than I'd anticipated. I'd spread my research and print resources out in the room where Evan had moved my office furniture, and I was completely absorbed in my task. The sounds of the men working outside had faded from notice.

The first thing I noted was the absence of sound from outside, and I figured the workers had finished clearing out loose nails and whatnot, and they wanted to let me know they were leaving.

But the outline on the other side of the wavy glass design was taller than the workers had seemed. It showcased broad shoulders and a sexy outline I knew I was going to fantasize about for the rest of my life. I took a deep breath before opening it up, and I pasted on the politest smile I owned.

His gaze roamed my face, the last, indistinct echo of a caress. "Good afternoon, Alaina. We're finished with the job, and everything passed inspection. Did you want to see the roof?"

Did I want to climb up onto my roof? I'd never considered doing such a thing before. I lifted a shoulder. "Sure."

His lips parted, but I couldn't tell if my response had surprised him, or if he was anticipating spending some quality ladder-climbing time with me.

I chose to believe that few of his clients wanted to stand on their roofs.

Or maybe he thought I didn't trust his work?

"You're going to need to put on some pants."

The way he said that had me looking down to see if I was half naked. I smoothed a hand down the side of my skirt. I'd chosen it because it emphasized my shape in a rather flattering way. Plus, he'd mentioned that he liked me in skirts. I might have turned him down, but it made me feel good to be the recipient of his admiring gaze.

Though, right now, his gaze was just regular. Which, I guess, was progress.

"Really? You mean climbing a ladder in a skirt could be unsafe?" I infused my voice with a hint of irony in the hopes that my comment would come off as funny, but I went a little overboard, and it sounded highly sarcastic. I walked it back as soon as it sprang loose. "Sorry. That sounded funny in my head. I'll go change."

As I turned away, I caught a glimmer of amusement in his features as he muttered, "Jeans, not leggings."

Because I preferred to wear skirts or leggings, I owned exactly two pairs of jeans, and the clean ones were not in great shape. However, they looked okay on me, so I didn't worry about the worn spots or the ragged tears where the ends of the legs dragged on the ground because nobody made pants for short people. I slid them on, and I changed my top to one I didn't mind getting dirty. So much for my attempt to dress my casual best for a guy I wasn't dating.

I found Evan outside, securing an extension ladder against the side of the house. His side was to me, and I noted the way his jeans outlined his ass and hugged his thighs. Just looking at his delicious figure made my knees weak. Daniel was a lucky man.

He motioned to the ladder. "Do you want me to go up first so I can help you get onto the roof, or second?"

I envisioned the ways he might stabilize me if I misstepped or catch me if I fell, and I realized my need to shake my ass in his face was nothing more than selfish vanity. "I'm not likely to fall, and if I do, I don't want to take you out with me. You go first."

His expression communicated doubt that my fall could cause him to lose his footing. "If that's what you want."

The double meaning wasn't lost on me, not with the sharp edge that had crept into his tone.

He helped me steady myself as I transitioned from the ladder to the roof, and I was grateful for his assistance. The old shingles had been brown and red, and the new ones were not.

"You went with black?" It sparkled in the brightness of the midday sun.

"You said to keep it authentic. A white, Georgian-style house typically has a black roof."

I hadn't noted the difference from the ground, but I had noticed the house looked more striking from the road. "I like it."

Evan chuckled. "Good, because it's not going anywhere for fifteen-to-twenty years. Closer to twenty if you trim that oak back or take it down altogether."

I looked toward the offending tree, its canopy spread wide to protect us lesser mortals beneath. "I'll call an arborist."

"Daniel's dad owns a landscaping company. He's not an arborist, but he does a decent job trimming trees."

I needed to have less to do with the DiMarcos and Carricos, not more. "Thanks. I'll keep him in mind."

Evan didn't push the issue. He pointed out features and techniques that would preserve my roof and stop the elements from ravaging my dream house.

I didn't ask questions because I realized my knowledge of home repair was woefully inadequate. Once we were back on *terra firma*, I thanked him for his effort, and I promised to leave a good review on websites where people went to look for reputable contractors.

He flashed a lopsided smile. "I need to check the drywall in your office and bedroom."

"Sure." I hadn't been in those rooms, so I didn't have an opinion to offer. I knew a little about drywall. Adam and I had replaced the drywall in the house we'd bought together, where he now lived with my brother.

Well, I guess my brother didn't live there anymore. I needed to text Zack to check in with him, and I probably needed to call Adam to see how Zack had taken the news.

"You're going to need to choose paint colors," Evan continued as he strode down the hall toward the office. "Depending on the state of the mud, we may be able to paint Sunday. No, not Sunday. We're busy Sunday."

"I can paint," I said. "Don't worry about that part." I'd painted the entire house before I'd moved in. I wasn't looking forward to doing it again, but I'd live. Clara would help. She always came through when I needed her.

He examined the mud, lightly touching several places. "It's almost ready. Most places are dry. I'll be back tomorrow to give it a final sanding. Will you be home after five?"

I had plans to meet some of my colleagues for drinks, but we got together regularly, so canceling wouldn't be the end of the world. "I can be."

"Great. We'll swing by after work and finish up your drywall. We can move your furniture back as well."

I waved away the offer. "I can do it."

He paused his caressing of the walls and looked at me, his shrewd gaze assessing the likelihood I was full of shit.

"Really, I can."

Evan came closer. "Alaina, I don't trust you to call me if you need help."

I didn't see why I would call him. Despite all the phone calls and texts that made it seem like we'd been building a friendship, we weren't friends. We were people who'd slept together, and then I hired him to replace my roof. "I have friends. Clara will be back by then, and in the unlikely event everyone I know is too busy to help, then I can call Adam. He'll grumble, but he'll do it."

"Adam?" Evan frowned.

"My ex."

"Not many people stay in touch with their exes."

I really didn't understand his observation, but I felt we were losing the point of the conversation, so I didn't ask why he'd think I wouldn't talk to the father of my child. Even when I'd been heartbroken and livid, I'd maintained a somewhat neutral association with Adam. Over time, things had grown cordial.

"The point is that you don't have to worry about me, Evan. I'm not alone in this world."

Rather than set his mind at ease, my assurance seemed to upset him further.

"Look, Evan, I don't think running to you is the best way to step back and give you and Daniel the space you need."

His lips pressed together, and his nostrils flared. I didn't want to look at his eyes to see the anger there, but I forced myself to face his icy glare. "We didn't ask for space."

Fuck. I didn't want to argue with him, so I cut to the inevitable end. "You know what I meant."

146

"Yeah. I know what you meant." The blue steel in his eyes hit me with an almost physical force.

I took a step back. "Go ahead and do what you need to do. I'll be across the hall."

Ten minutes later, I struggled to focus on my writing task, and Evan appeared in the doorway. "We'll be back tomorrow, probably around five-thirty or six."

He'd continually used a plural pronoun when describing who would be coming tomorrow, but I was too chicken to ask which of his brothers would accompany him or if he'd decided against asking any of them to help. Not that it mattered. Evan had left without waiting for my reply.

The next evening, I toned down my vanity. I didn't bother with makeup or a skirt. I wore leggings and a loose-fit dress. It was comfortable, and it disguised my curves.

A text let me know Evan was running late. I baked tiny potatoes in butter, rosemary, and coriander, and I sautéed scallops for myself. Zack hated seafood—he would only eat chicken—so I tended to eat the things I liked that he didn't when he wasn't home.

The knock on my front door came at six-thirty, long after I'd finished eating and cleaning up the kitchen. I'd been catching up on a show I'd discovered that already had five seasons under its belt, and I'd painted my nails. So I waddled to the door, walking on my heels so I wouldn't ruin the metallic blue on my toes.

Unlocking the door took long enough to make the wait awkward for Evan and whichever brother was built like Daniel.

Once I got it open, I stepped back.

Evan and Daniel flooded into the house, their combined presence taking up much more space than should have been possible.

Daniel looked at my hands and feet. "I thought you'd be reading a book or conducting an online symposium or something."

I couldn't tell if he was making a joke or if he was still upset with me for declining his passionate appeal. So I attempted something witty in response. "I did that last night."

They were carrying equipment like toolboxes and a shop vacuum. They'd cleared out my furniture and put up plastic sheeting over doors so the dust wouldn't travel.

"I left everything the way you had it."'

"Good," Evan said. He pushed forward, and I backed up to get out of his way.

Daniel shot me a mournful look before he followed Evan upstairs.

I went back to watching my show, but I found it even harder to keep my mind on it with Daniel and Evan in the house. There was too

147

much tension between us now. We hadn't even observed simple pleasantries.

When I was upset about an emotional problem, I always turned to cleaning. I attacked Zack's bathroom first, and when Daniel and Evan moved downstairs to work on my office, I went after my bathroom with a vengeance.

"Alaina?"

In the midst of scrubbing the cupboards under the sink, I hadn't seen or heard Daniel come in. My whole body jumped, jamming my elbow against the edge of the cabinet, and my heart hammered hard from the extra burst of adrenaline.

"Sorry. I didn't mean to startle you." Daniel squatted down next to where I now sat on the floor. His gaze traveled over me, landing on where I held my elbow. "Are you okay?"

"I'm fine."

"You hit it pretty hard. Let's get some ice on it."

Before I could assure him that a little bruise wouldn't kill me, he'd hauled me to my feet. My knees were weak from being near him and from the way he manhandled me. Also his hands lingered on my waist, defining it even though my dress was supposed to be a disguise.

He took the scrub pad from my hand and set it on the clean bathroom counter. "Can you extend your arm?"

"Yes." I didn't try, not with him so close to me. Also, I didn't want to encourage him to continue to be so hands-on nice to me. His scent, the solidity of his physical presence inches away, the feel of his hands on me, and the way the memory of his kiss tingled on my lips—all of that combined to make me freeze. If I didn't poke the bear, he wouldn't poke back.

"Show me."

"Daniel, I'm fine."

"This isn't open for discussion."

My stubborn streak responded to his order. "You're right—it's not. I said I was fine. Are you and Evan finished sanding the drywall?" I jerked out of his hold as I spoke, putting necessary distance between us.

Daniel crossed his arms and leaned against the wall behind him. "Yes. It's ready to be painted."

"That's great. I bought some primer. I'll get a coat on tomorrow." I examined my throbbing elbow, but it was hard to see anything, so I turned toward the mirror.

"It's swollen," he said. "I'll get you some ice."

He left.

I washed my hands, and then I followed him down the stairs. I found him in the kitchen, pushing the button on the refrigerator to make ice come out. He could push all day, and the thing would only make a whirring sound.

"It's not hooked up to a water line."

"Why not?"

"The house is old, and there isn't one. Having a line run is on the list of repairs, but it's way down at the bottom."

He opened the freezer drawer. "You don't have any ice."

"I know." I fished a boo-boo bunny from the door of the freezer, and I held it to my elbow. "But I'm prepared for small owwie incidents."

He grinned. "Did you just say *owwie*?"

Evan came into the kitchen. "Daniel, are you ready to go? The truck's packed up." He focused on Daniel, completely ignoring my existence.

His attitude bothered me, so I faced him. "Evan, are you sincerely pouting because I turned you down? Isn't that a bit much?"

He spared me the briefest of glances. "I'm giving you space."

"Yes, well, you didn't have to launch yourself into orbit."

Daniel looked away. With his hands on his hips, he looked like he was angry, but I caught the silent laugh he tried to hide.

"Alaina, I don't want to fight with you."

"Your hostility says otherwise." Perhaps I didn't want to poke Daniel—he poked back so nicely—but I didn't mind poking Evan. It looked like we were back to the passive-aggressiveness of our initial meeting.

"Alaina." That one word warning came from Daniel. "Give Evan a break. We're both still dealing with Wednesday night."

"You seem fine."

"I've known you for a year. I know how to talk to you through a veneer of professionalism. Evan doesn't have that to fall back on."

I'd found comfort in the reliability of a professional association. People were polite and reasonable because emotions weren't involved. Nothing was personal. Since I'd hired Evan to do work on my house, we did have a situation on which to base neutral civility, and so I disagreed with Daniel's assessment.

"Nonsense." I turned to Evan. "You're here in a professional capacity. This is part of what you do for a living. I don't see the problem."

His lips curled with distaste. "I'm not here in a professional capacity. Daniel and I came over to finish a project we did for you as a favor."

The reminder hit me like a slap to the face. "Then bill me for the cost of the project. I didn't ask for a favor, and I wasn't looking for charity." Paying for windows wasn't in my budget, but I would somehow make it work, even if I had to take out a second mortgage.

"Don't be stupid," Evan retorted. "You needed those windows and supports replaced."

I hated when people called me stupid or clueless, something that had been a regular occurrence throughout my formative years. My parents were the worst offenders, but my classmates had been just as bad, and many of my teachers had referred to me as a brilliant mess. Nothing triggered me like those words. I also hated being labeled "rude," but I was more understanding about that one.

Rage boiled my blood and roared in my ears. "Or you just wanted a reason for me to be beholden to you because you're a control freak."

Those icy eyes bored into me, stabbing vitriolic frost crystals into my flesh.

Daniel slid between us, his hands lifted in case he needed to do more than provide a barrier. "Hey, you two. Let's not do this."

"She started it," Evan spat.

"And you kept it going." Daniel looked from me to Evan and back again. "Alaina, Evan doesn't react well to being called out on his behavior. Though I admire your backbone, the two of you are being driven more by obstinacy than reason."

"Reason?" Evan cocked his head and stroked his chin. I noted that he needed a shave, and also that the light brown stubble made him look extra handsome. "I don't see a need to always be cold and calculating. There's nothing wrong with showing honest emotion."

My chest lifted as I inhaled deeply. "Of course an overgrown child would say that."

In a flash, he'd bypassed Daniel, and his hands banded around my upper arms like steel manacles. He hauled me to him, lifting me a little so that I was forced to the tips of my toes. The boo-boo bunny fell to the floor with a soft splat. I ventured a look at his eyes, and I failed to comprehend the complexity of what I saw there. Looking at the hard press of his lips clued me into the depth of his fury. They were under so much pressure, they'd thinned out and turned white.

In a completely inappropriate display of biology, a flood of moisture made my pussy so slick it was almost uncomfortable. The last time he'd manhandled me, things had gone well. I could do nothing but gasp and hope he kissed me. And also, I hoped he didn't kiss me, as I'd made it clear I was no longer open to having that kind of association with him.

"Evan." Daniel's hand clamped on Evan's shoulder, and iron lined the threads of his warning. "Let her go."

At Daniel's order, Evan let me go so abruptly I stumbled backward and fell on my ass.

Daniel shoved Evan away, and then he picked me up. "Perhaps it's best if the two of you don't see each other for a while."

"He—He wouldn't hurt me."

Daniel made sure I had my feet firmly under me, and still his touch lingered.

"You don't know that." Evan's back was to me, muffling his growled statement. "You barely know me at all."

I knew he was thoughtful and kind. I knew he'd taken the time to understand me in a way nobody else in my life ever had. I also knew that if I continued arguing with him, he would continue arguing with me until Daniel dragged him out of there.

"Were you feeling an urge to hurt me?" His hold on my arms had been firm, but not restrictive or painful.

A desperate, disgusted noise came out of him. "No."

"Really?" Daniel's disbelief filled the room, and he pulled me inches closer to him, possibly to protect me. "Because it looked like you were seconds from beating the crap out of her."

The mosaic of emotions I noted glittering in Evan's eyes for the brief moment I'd looked began to make sense. My conscious brain identified what my subconscious already knew. "He was going to kiss me."

With my pronouncement, Evan whirled back to face me. Wonder and bafflement competed to wrinkle his very expressive chin. "You don't know that."

Arguing with him felt good, but Daniel was right that it wasn't productive. "Am I wrong?"

Silently, he shook his head.

"Arguing is like foreplay for you."

A reluctant chuckle fell from Daniel as he shook his head. "It seems she knows more about you than you thought."

"I don't understand," Evan said. "Is it a sensory thing? Does the idea of being with the both of us seem overwhelming to you?"

I thought I'd made my reasoning clear. "I never considered it, not after you told me that you guys were together."

"But if you *did* consider it?"

"But I wouldn't. You guys have some crazy notion that you need to keep me around in order to make sure you have a happy life together, but it's simply not true. I have nothing to do with the bond you share."

"You're the only woman we've both been attracted to." Daniel traced his fingertips in a circle on the back of my shoulder. "That's significant."

I faced him fully, forcing him to stop drawing erotic images on my back, and I spread my hands wide. "Is it, though?"

"It is," Evan responded.

Even though I disagreed, I could see that they both were convinced they needed to be with me. So when Daniel leaned down to kiss me, I didn't stop him. I'd be lying if I said I hadn't thought a lot about this in the past two days, imagining what it would be like to be the spicy meatball in their stud sandwich. I just hadn't considered the possibility it might happen.

And, not stopping him? That was pure selfishness on my part. But if life had taught me anything, it was that sometimes selfishness was a good thing. They wanted me, and I wanted them. One night would be enough to prove to them that I wasn't a necessary component to their happily-ever-after. It would be a heavenly memory for me, and if it wasn't a 'Shouldn't've' for them, then it would be a 'Shouldn't Do Again.'

Clara was going to flip her lid when I told her about this.

Daniel's lips landed on mine. Soft and inviting, they teased and asked, seeking permission to linger there or to tread deeper. I let myself get lost in his kiss for precious moments before I kissed him back. His mouth opened on a groan, and he pressed his body against mine, somehow tangling all my limbs with his while also keeping us on our feet.

Chapter 13—Evan

My first reaction when Daniel kissed Alaina was pure lust. It was one of the most unexpectedly erotic things I'd ever witnessed. My second reaction was jealousy—not because they were kissing, but because I'd wanted very badly to kiss her, and I hadn't followed through. I wanted her to ask for it—or, at the very least, consent.

She froze for all of ten seconds, not pushing him away or pulling him closer, and then she tilted her head to improve the angle. Her lips parted, and her tongue clashed with his. Blood rushed to my dick, and my jeans were suddenly too tight.

Daniel wasn't one to wait once he felt he had permission. Whether it was food or sex, he was the kind of man who gorged himself until he was sated and licked his fingers afterward. He wrapped his arms around her, pressing her body to his as his hands roamed her back and grabbed handfuls of her ass.

Soft squeaks and moans of enjoyment sounded from her side of the kiss. Daniel's noises were fewer, but correspondingly louder. With a heartfelt groan, he ripped his lips from hers and trailed kisses down her neck.

She opened her eyes and peered at me over his shoulder, and I picked up on the worry bubbling up through her passion.

I'd been upset with a woman who wanted nothing more than to make sure I had a happy, successful relationship with my best friend. Whether or not she admitted it, she cared deeply for both of us. I was just now realizing I'd been a consummate idiot. Daniel had advised me that we should wait and try again, but I'd been too selfish to see the wisdom of his approach.

Alaina had been right to call me out on my immature behavior. I really needed her in my life.

And she needed someone like me to push her out of her comfort zone and to provide a safe and understanding place for her to be herself. And also to argue with her. I had the sense she'd found our disagreement stimulating.

I moved closer to my precious duo of lovers, assuming a position behind Alaina. I set one hand on her hip, and I cupped the back of Daniel's neck with the other. He responded to my invitation, lifting his head to face me. Skipping the slow build, I captured his mouth for a searing kiss. Daniel wasn't one to acquiesce when he wasn't in the mood, and he definitely wasn't in the mood right now. He fought for control, our tongues dueling in a masterful clash that robbed me of breath and reason.

The hand on Alaina's hip slid between her and Daniel, stopping when I had her breast firmly in hand. Through her dress, I plumped and kneaded. She leaned back against me, and her hand grasped my wrist, urging me to keep doing what I was doing.

Just before my lungs burst, I broke away from Daniel. As we gulped air, our gazes locked, and we celebrated a silent victory as we resolved to show her what it meant to be ours.

Our gazes fell, and I found Alaina watching us, her eyes wide, and her cheeks flushed with pleasure.

I affected my laziest Dom smile, and I said, "Would you like a kiss, Lainie?"

She inhaled deeply, her torso pushing against mine and Daniel's. Indecision wavered in her eyes, but passion was clouding the issue, so I took a leaf from Daniel's book and kissed her. It took but a second for her to turn her body to face mine. She lifted to her toes and wrapped her arms around my neck. Kissing her right after kissing Daniel felt incredibly right. Being with Daniel had always felt like coming home, but now I felt complete.

And I absolutely loved the feel of all three of us together.

Ending the kiss, I drew back. Her gaze was on my mouth, but I knew that meant she was paying attention. It was her equivalent to gazing into my eyes.

"What do you say we take this upstairs to the guest room where my bed is currently located?" Her shy smile accompanied the brief lift of her gaze, and she turned to include Daniel in the sweetness of her invitation.

The pained look in Daniel's eye belied his struggle. He had more at stake than just his heart. He exhaled a long breath. "Are you sure, Lainie? Five minutes ago, you were saying this would never happen."

She bobbed her head, a brief acknowledgment of her changed mind. "If you're sure, then I'm sure."

He scooped her up, his long strides heading in the direction of the stairs. I followed, turning off lights and locking the front door as we

154

passed it. Daniel went straight to the room where we'd moved her things so they wouldn't get dusty from construction, and he sat her on the edge of the bed.

She shimmied out of her leggings, kicking them aside. "I want to see you guys make out. That was so hot." She jumped to her feet and clapped her hands together.

I laughed in response to her enthusiasm, and Daniel laid an open-mouthed kiss on me that liquefied my knees and had me grasping at his shirt. He went for my shirt, pushing it up, and somehow grabbing my ass.

Wait. That was Alaina pushing at my shirt. Daniel broke the kiss and helped Alaina with my shirt. Before he had it over my head, she'd attacked my jeans. They slid down my legs. The Dom part of me objected to being double-teamed and not in control. Also, in my fantasy, we undressed her first, and we teased her to the edge before any of our clothing came off.

While Daniel tried to get my jeans off my legs, I snagged his shirt and tossed it in the growing pile of clothes. Then I went after Alaina's dress. In seconds, I was wearing only my boxers, Alaina had been stripped to a rose-colored bra and panties, and Daniel had lost his shirt.

She exchanged a glance with me, conspiring with devilish intent. I kissed Daniel, and she rid him of his pants. Then my boxers slid down my thighs. I felt her hand close around my cock, and then the warmth of her mouth wet the tip.

Daniel jerked away from our kiss, his attention on the vixen kneeling at our feet.

Alaina's wet kiss alternated between his dick and mine, her mouth closing around one smooth head for a brief, sucking tease before doing the same thing to the one in her other hand. Back and forth she went, sucking each cock deeper with each pass. Then she tugged, bringing us closer together until our cocks touched. She tongued both at the same time, and then she tried to fit them both into her mouth. She didn't get far, but it felt really fucking good.

Daniel gasped. "This is so much better than the horny librarian."

She stopped to give Daniel a death glare.

I elbowed him playfully. "Dude, it sounded like you didn't love the horny librarian, when I know for a fact you did. Talking about it is how I got you in restraints the next day." To Alaina, I motioned for her to keep going. "He just means you're blowing his mind. Again. It's a thing you do to both of us."

A frown pinched between her eyes, and she got lost in thought.

I touched her hair. "Lainie? Whatcha thinking about?"

"Bad puns. If I remember, I'll tell you later." She dropped our cocks and got to her feet, her hands sliding up our chests. Her gaze darted back and forth. "I need to go get condoms and lube from the master bathroom. Is there anything else you want?"

Daniel's brows lifted. "Anything else? Like what?"

"Vibrators," I supplied. "She has quite a collection."

He shook his head. "I think we have all the phalluses we need for now."

I wanted to play with both of them until we all passed out, and vibrators or dildos would make for kinky fun, but I understood that Daniel wanted this to be a vanilla experience.

She left the room, and I kissed Daniel. "You're sure about this?"

"Yeah." He nibbled on my lower lip. "You?"

"Yes. I want her to ride you while I fuck you."

He considered this. We'd never had sex in front of someone else before, and I knew he was nervous about bottoming for me.

"That would be so hot." Alaina had returned. She set a box of condoms and three bottles of lube on the small, round table next to the bed. Then she placed a small trash bin underneath. Next, she set out wet wipes, tissues, and several hand towels.

For the first time, I wondered how many lovers she currently had. For some reason, I thought that because she'd slept with both Daniel and me, she wasn't seeing anybody else. It was a stupid assumption. Someone as beautiful and smart as Alaina would have dozens of men after her.

Was that why she'd turned us down? What self-absorbed fuckheads we were.

"The black one is a warming lube, so avoid it for anal unless you like a bit of spice there. I don't mind it, but sometimes it's annoying. I keep saying I'm going to get a bigger bedside table, but I never do." She finished arranging the items, and then she looked up. Her frown returned. "What?"

Daniel eyed the box. "I thought you said you haven't done this before?"

"I haven't, but I'd rather be prepared than have to run across the hall in the middle of the deed." She stared for a moment longer, then she looked down at the pharmacy of items. "Did I forget something? You said no to the vibrators, so I didn't bring any."

I drew her into my arms and hugged her to me. "You're very thoughtful. We didn't even bring condoms."

"Well, you didn't expect to end up in my bedroom."

Daniel planted kisses along her shoulder. "We hoped." When he got to her neck, she shivered and gripped my arms harder.

"You like that, Lainie? Daniel's a great kisser."

"Yes," she agreed. "You're both very talented."

I captured her mouth, claiming her whether she wanted to be claimed or not. Daniel and I finished undressing her, and we lifted her onto the bed. We flanked her, and the three of us spent time kissing and touching one another. With two of them, it was almost impossible to give them each the attention I wanted. Since Alaina was in the middle, we focused mostly on her. I played with her nipples, roughing them up to elicit squeaks and moans. I felt Daniel's hand, wet with her juices, on my cock.

After a while, Alaina climbed over me, and Daniel moved closer, putting me in the middle. They both focused on me, kissing, touching, and licking. The sensations evoked by two sets of hands was exquisite. Daniel's caresses were softer and larger, and Alaina's were harder because she liked to use more pressure, but her hands were much smaller than his. The dichotomy proved highly erotic.

Daniel's hand moved up and down my cock in a lazy stroke. Alaina kissed a path down my chest, her teeth leaving behind sharp stings she laved with her tongue. It seemed my little vixen had a sadistic side, and I found I quite liked it.

She met Daniel at my cock. The two of them played around, licking it and kissing each other. The sensations and the visual were driving me crazy, and I couldn't modulate the volume of my moans. Then Daniel started sucking my cock in earnest, and Alaina went for my balls. First, she tugged gently, and then she sucked a sac into her mouth.

Heat brought the riot of feelings to a boil. I shouted, arching my back and grasping handfuls of bedding.

Alaina left off her sweet torture and sat up, studying me as her hand expertly fondled my boys. "Daniel, do you ever tie Evan up?"

With a wet slurp, Daniel released my cock. "No. He's not into subbing, and I'm not the kinky fucker in this relationship."

I'd been so close to coming, and they both brought me down a notch, extending the tease. I didn't mind because I knew, the longer the journey, the sweeter the reward. "You like what I do to you when I tie you up."

"True." Daniel's slow, sensual smile stole my breath, as did his admission. "I definitely look forward to being at your mercy."

Alaina snorted. "Daniel, you're plenty kinky. You like role playing, and it seems like you enjoy bondage."

"He's also a fan of some kinds of cock-and-ball-torture, light impact play, and the violet wand." I added fuel to Alaina's argument, and then I turned the tables. "Alaina, you also like bondage and light impact play."

Her eyes lit. "Role playing, nipple torture, hair pulling, spanking, and alien abduction." She dropped my balls and walked her fingers along my thigh, digging her nails in as she went.

It hurt, and it felt good. Maybe I was a bit of a masochist? I'd certainly enjoyed the small ways she was violent with me.

Daniel cocked his head. "Alien abduction?"

She waved away his question. "Conversation for another time."

Sitting up, I snagged her around the waist and rolled as I pulled her so that she ended up underneath me. Then I kissed her breathless. Daniel's fingertips traced sensual patterns up and down my body as I worked my way down Alaina's.

She spread her legs, making room for me even as Daniel occupied her mouth with kisses that ranged from tender to savage. I licked her pussy as I watched him move to her breasts. He sucked gently.

"Harder," she said. "They're not at all sensitive. It's okay to bite."

His gaze found mine, and I grinned. I flicked the tip of her clit with my tongue before moving down that long muscle and fucking my tongue into her vagina.

Daniel must have found a pressure she liked because her fist tightened in his hair and arched into what he was doing.

"Fuck," she said. "Daniel—yes. Oh, yes. Evan, I'm so close. Please don't stop."

As she warned us, fluids wet my face, and her vagina pulsed around my tongue. It was a small orgasm, but she was no longer able to hold up her bent knees. They flopped to the side, and I surged up to share the taste of her pussy with Daniel.

We kissed, our tongues dueling, tasting Alaina's orgasm and each other. Kissing Daniel had always been different—better—but this was even sweeter. Without breaking our point of contact, I maneuvered him down onto his back. Only then did I trail kisses and sucking bites down his neck. I sank my teeth into the fleshy part of his chest, moving ever lower.

Alaina stirred. At first, she watched us, but before long, she joined in. Once I abandoned Daniel's lips, she took over. She found the places on his neck and behind his ears that made his body shudder and shiver.

I watched them as I lubed up his ass and positioned myself between his legs.

Alaina straddled his head and lowered her pussy to his face. Then she bent forward and licked his cock. She bobbed on his dick as she watched me breach his opening, her hips fucking his face faster and faster.

I knew Daniel was in heaven. We'd talked at length about how we both loved eating pussy, especially Alaina's, and I knew he could lift her with no problem if he needed to reposition her. But I wanted my fantasy.

Grabbing a good handful of Alaina's hair, I yanked her mouth away from his dick, and I handed her a condom. "Put it on him, Lainie, and ride him as hard as you want."

Excitement sparkled in her eyes, which were trained on my lips.

I couldn't help it—I kissed her, and she kissed me with so much passion, I thought my heart would burst.

She had him sheathed in no time, and she straddled his abdomen. Due to the way I'd lifted his legs, she was going to have to shimmy her ass back to get his cock where we all wanted it to be. I helped by tugging her hips into place and guiding his cock into her dripping pussy.

She leaned forward, resting her weight on her hands on either side of his torso, and moved her hips. We both fucked Daniel, Alaina on his cock, and me in his ass. Daniel thrashed and moaned, his motions increasingly erratic. He was going to come soon if we kept up this pace.

I slowed down, and I pulled Alaina up until her back was against my chest. I peppered kisses along her neck and shoulder. I ran my hand over her front side, kneading her breasts and tweaking her nipples before rubbing on her clit.

Daniel watched, his chest heaving from the effort and his eyes bright with desire. He liked what he was seeing.

Alaina had slowed her ride, and the way I stimulated her made her moan. She rested her head back against my chest, and I bit her shoulder.

She cried out, but she didn't jerk away. Her hips moved faster, snapping as she ground against him. Daniel took over stimulating her clit, and I played with her breasts. They were silky soft, and I loved the way they felt in my hands. Her cry grew louder, and then it cut off abruptly, her entire body going stiff. Daniel's groan, the one that said he was having an orgasm, followed.

I fucked Daniel with quick strokes, and I came inside him.

Alaina collapsed on top of Daniel, and I flopped onto the bed beside them.

After a few minutes, she reached out and set her hand on my arm. "You bit me." Her words were a bit slurred from the aftereffects of her climax.

"He bites," Daniel confirmed. "He has an intense oral fixation, which is definitely a plus when it comes to sex."

I could only grin at her. "You bit me as well."

"Yes," she said, her eyes drifting closed while a huge smile remained. "Biting...good."

The happy hormones in my system faded, replaced with sleepy ones. My eyelids grew heavy. The day had been long. I'd risen at six to go to work, and I'd spent the day remodeling a bathroom.

"She's asleep." Daniel's whisper jerked me awake. "And I need to take this condom off. Help me move her."

We got her situated under the covers. Daniel took care of the condom, and I fell asleep next to Alaina.

I regained consciousness enough to note half my body hung off the bed, and no covers were anywhere near me. But Alaina's boob was pressed against my arm, so I wasn't upset.

"Evan. Wake up."

Peeling my eyes open, I blinked at the unfamiliar surroundings, and I washed my hand down my face. "What time is it?"

"Seven. I have a half hour to shower and get out of the house. You and Daniel need to get going." She shoved at me again, but when I didn't move, she climbed over me, grumbling. "Daniel hogs the bed and the covers."

I looked over, and sure enough, Daniel occupied more than half of the bed. One arm was under the pillow, and the other was flung out across the pillow Alaina and I had shared. The sheet and comforter were tangled around his legs. Judging from the placement of his knee, Alaina must have spent part of the night with it pressed into her kidney.

With a groan, I sat up. From experience, I knew I could shout, and there was only a thirty percent chance he'd wake up. So I leaned over and touched his face lightly.

His whole body jerked, and he opened his eyes. "What?"

I decided to spare him the knowledge that Alaina wasn't happy with him. "Alaina has to leave, and she's kicking us out."

"What? Where is she going?"

"She didn't say."

"You didn't ask?"

"I just woke up. Fuck off until I get some coffee in me."

"Was she mad?"

"She wasn't happy."

"Where did she go?"

"Shower."

"Let's surprise her." He was up and gone before I could tell him that was probably a bad idea. We hadn't progressed to the point with Alaina where bathroom matters were activities we did in front of each other.

Reluctantly, I followed. I found him in the master bathroom, scowling at the closed shower curtain.

"Why not, Lainie?"

"Daniel, I didn't set an alarm last night. I slept like a rock, and I slept later than I meant to. I need to be out of the house no later than seven-thirty if I'm going to make it to work on time."

Daniel had to be home by eight-thirty, so we had to leave soon anyway. Saturday classes were popular with smaller children and busy adults, and he'd never missed opening his studio.

The scowl on his face abated. "Sorry. I'll make breakfast."

"You don't have to do that. I'm going to a breakfast for doctoral candidates. It's the start of a day of orientation activities." The shower curtain opened, and she grabbed a towel from the hook on the wall.

She didn't seem to mind us being there at all. She stepped out of the shower and patted the towel on her skin without trying to cover up.

"If you want a quick shower, go ahead and hop in. I'm sorry I can't offer breakfast or a second round."

"Next time." I was dedicated to looking on the bright side. She'd never said this was more than one night, and I wanted to press for assurances we were on the path to something more.

"Sure." She squeezed water from her hair and opened a cupboard full of lotions and hair products.

I glanced at Daniel. He shrugged, and the two of us got into the shower. I threw a wink in Alaina's direction so she understood she was invited.

A tight smile was her only reaction.

We showered quickly. When we finished, we found she'd set out fresh towels on the vanity. True to her word, she had us all out the door thirty minutes after she woke me up.

"Can I call you?" I opened the door to her car so she could get inside.

She tossed her purse inside, and then she faced Daniel and me. "How about you take a couple days to think about this first? Talk to each other. I'm still not convinced this is the right path forward."

"It seems like we need to talk with you," Daniel said. "Evan and I have already decided what we want."

She touched his cheek, the caress of her fingertips communicating affection. "You're a sweet, sweet man."

"Who hogs the bed." I threw that out because I figured her next word was 'but,' and I didn't want to hear what came next.

At that, she laughed. "Yes, well. That problem is not high up on the list. Look, I have to go. How about we talk next week? Wednesday or Thursday evening?"

Before either of us could answer, she got into her car and drove away.

Daniel and I walked to my truck, which was parked in the street. He stuck his hands in the pocket of his wrinkled jeans and said, "I don't think she was asking."

"Neither do I, but I sure as hell am not going to wait almost a whole week until I see her again."

"Nope. I'm going to make that chocolate mousse cake she loves. We can bring it over tonight."

I grinned at his plan. "I like that idea."

Chapter 14—Daniel

We might end up painting a couple rooms, but I was determined to make an offer Lainie couldn't resist.

One thing I loved about pursuing this woman had absolutely nothing to do with her. Having Evan by my side made wooing her so much more fun and interesting. We were in it together. I had my best friend by my side and in my bed.

When I got home, I found Sophia waiting for me in my loft. The coffeemaker bubbled and hissed, and the tempting aroma wafted around the big space. Sophia wore workout clothes, and she stood at the counter, pouring mix into the waffle iron.

"Hey," I said. "When did you get here?"

She glanced at the clock on the stove. "About fifteen minutes ago. I texted you last night that I was coming over."

"Oh." Even before I felt my pocket, I knew my phone wasn't there.

Sophia pointed to it on my counter. "It's nice to know you can go out all night and not care where your phone is."

I wasn't sure if that was a shot at me or at society's dependence on a portable computer, so I changed the subject. "Are you joining the morning kickboxing class?"

"Yes. You kicked my ass the last six times we've sparred. I'm out of shape. I need to get back to where I can take you down with the flick of my wrist."

Chuckling, I poured myself a mug of coffee. Evan and I had stopped off to get him some on our way back from Alaina's because he was a grouchy bitch when he didn't get his fix. I'd indulged, so this was my second cup.

"The flick of your wrist? I think you're overestimating how good you used to be."

If glares could body-slam a person, Sophia's would have done the trick. "Danny, where did you spend the night?"

I opened my mouth to respond, but nothing came out. Though Evan and I were together, we hadn't told our families. Tomorrow was the last Sunday of the month, the day my family got together for dessert and dinner. We'd invited Evan's parents so we could share the news to the whole group. It was big news.

I'd wanted to have Alaina locked in as part of our threesome, but she was proving elusive. That was okay. I knew she'd present a challenge. It was one of the things I liked about her.

"Elsewhere."

She folded her arms. "At Evan's?"

That one was easier to evade. "No."

The timer on the waffle iron went off, and I went to change while she finished making breakfast.

"Are you hungry?" Her voice carried into the bathroom.

"Starving." Food was a safer topic. Plus, I liked waffles, and I saw that Sophia had already made a strawberry topping.

"So, whoever you spent the night with didn't feed you this morning."

"That would be true."

"Evan would never neglect you like that."

I emerged from the bathroom, and I stopped shouting to her. "Sophie, let it go, okay?"

"Sure. You spent a meaningless night with another hot blonde. Where was Evan?"

Next to Evan, my sister was my closest friend. We had few secrets. I knew, without a doubt, that Sophia had picked up on the fact Evan and I were together, and she was going to bait me until I came clean. And so I did the only thing I could—I glared at her.

"Danny, it's just that, the other night when we were over at Alaina's, I saw Evan kiss her. Then, when I asked her about it, she said they'd had a casual fling."

I stiffened. This was so much worse than the other conversation I'd been avoiding. "So?"

"So, doesn't it worry you?"

"Why would it?"

"Because Alaina is important to our self-defense program. What if she falls for Evan? She's so much older than him, and Evan isn't going to fall for her because he's already in love with you. I don't want her to get her heart broken and stop showing up here." Sophia was so upset that she wasn't watching the pan of strawberry syrup on the stove, which was close to turning into overcooked mush.

I moved it off the burner, and I got the next batch of waffles when the timer on the iron went off. "He won't break her heart. Evan isn't a jerk."

"I know he's not. He'll let her down gently, but that doesn't mean she won't get hurt." Sophia sighed, and she took a plate of strawberry-topped waffles to the table. "She's not like other people, you know."

"I know." I wasn't sure what I was agreeing about, but I wholeheartedly thought that Alaina was in a class all by herself.

"No, Daniel, I don't think you do. She's sometimes awkward, like she doesn't catch social cues or something. It's probably because she's so smart, she forgets to slow down for the rest of us mere mortals."

I happened to know that Alaina didn't consider herself any better or worse than anybody else, and I knew Sophia hadn't meant to sound critical of Alaina. "Or she's just neuroatypical."

Sophia stared at me. "I don't even know what that's supposed to mean."

Two days ago, I hadn't either. But after Alaina had turned down our offer for a threesome, I'd been confused by aspects of her reaction. Evan had explained a few things, and now Alaina made a lot more sense to me.

"She has autism. She doesn't like to look people in the eyes, and she doesn't like her palms touched. She misses social cues sometimes, but she's aware that it happens. She works really hard on masking, which is trying to meet social expectations even when they don't make sense to her or feel natural for her."

Dropping her fork, Sophia sat back in her seat. "Oh. I'm an ass. I completely missed that."

"It's fine. She's put a lot of time and effort into adapting to a world that doesn't understand her."

She started eating again. "You think Evan understands her?"

"Better than most people. He was the one who picked up on her quirks."

We fell silent as we ate. My sister was a fantastic cook. "Is that cinnamon in the batter?"

"Yes. It works with the honey in the strawberry topping. You like it?"

"Hell, yeah. Is this your recipe?" My sister was marrying an award-winning chef with his own television show, but she was no slouch in the kitchen. Thanks to our parents, we were both accomplished cooks.

"Ginny suggested cinnamon." Ginny was Drew's business partner and best friend, and she'd become close to my sister in the past year. "She was at Ellen's last night."

Ellen was a close friend of Sophia's, and she was her mentor for all her Domme crap. I liked Ellen, but I didn't see her all that often.

We finished breakfast, and I managed to keep the conversation topics away from Evan and Alaina. Sophia helped with the dishes, and then we went downstairs to open the studio.

I thought Sophia had dropped the idea of me with Evan or Evan with Alaina, but on her way out after working her ass off in the advanced kickboxing class, she said, "Danny, I worry about you."

I had a twenty-minute break between classes. I guzzled some water and frowned at her. I didn't want to ask a follow-up question, but she trapped me into doing it. "Why?"

"Because you and Evan seem to be spending a lot more time together, and then last night, you spent it apart."

Staring because I wanted her to give up the line of questioning, I silently dared her to continue.

At last, she sighed. "Just be careful. I love you, big brother."

"I love you, too. Give Drew my best, and I'll see you tomorrow."

My studio was only open for four hours on Saturday, so I closed at one. Evan showed up and helped me spray antifungals on the mats. I alerted him to my sister's fears.

"If anything, she's liable to break my heart." He laughed. "She has no idea that you made a move on Alaina before I did or that we're both seeing her?"

"None, and she only knows about your one night with Lainie. It's best to keep our families in the dark until we have something concrete to tell them."

He frowned. "I disagree. We should tell them we're together, and that we're seriously dating a possible third. We're looking to be a thruple."

"That's not a word."

"If you know what it means, then it's a word. That's how new words are made." He grinned, and we went back and forth, discussing the idea as he watched me make chocolate mousse cake.

I let him lick the beaters, and we did not arrive at an agreement before we got to Alaina's house. He wanted to be upfront about everything. I wanted Alaina's consent before I started announcing that the three of us were an item.

Evan took the lead so I could keep the cake behind my back. She was going to like this surprise. In my imagination, I could see delight shining from her eyes. We hadn't brought wine, but I'd seen a rack in her kitchen, so I knew she had plenty. She'd melt, kissing us both, and then she'd drag us upstairs to make sure we were thoroughly hungry before we devoured the cake.

He reached out to ring the buzzer, but it opened before he made contact, which meant she'd either seen us pull up or was heading out for the afternoon.

Except a man stood on the other side, demolishing my theory. He was a couple inches shorter than Evan, which put him firmly at medium height, and he had a nice enough build. He had blond hair and pleasant features. I didn't want to say the guy was good-looking, but he wasn't at all homely. He kind of looked like one of those stereotypical neighbor types who spent a lot of time on his lawn or cleaning his barbeque grill. Not that there was anything wrong with those pursuits. I think what bothered me most about the guy was that he looked like he belonged there, in that type of house with someone like Alaina.

Evan looked back at me, a question in his eyes that I answered with the lift of my shoulder. I had no clue who the guy was, why he was answering Alaina's door, or if he was involved with her. That last part was my number one concern.

He seemed surprised to see anyone on the other side of the door. His brows lifted, and he opened the door. "Sorry. I didn't see you there. Can I help you?"

Evan went into full Dom mode, where he squared his shoulders and somehow looked larger and more imposing.

Because this guy seemed like he was more Alaina's type than either Evan or me, I went full alpha as well. While Evan had an impressive, muscular body, mine was larger and even more muscular. Plus, I'd worn a short-sleeved shirt that pulled tight around my biceps, emphasizing my guns. I'd noticed Alaina checking me out before, and I knew she liked my body.

"We're looking for Alaina." Evan used his Dom voice, which was deeper than his regular voice and turned a simple statement into an order.

The guy didn't seem affected. "I'll get her."

It wasn't his place to invite us in or make us wait on the porch, so Evan opened the screen door, and we went inside.

Now the guy appeared mildly irritated. He looked closer at each of us. "Wait here." He turned and went down the main hall. "Alaina, you've got a couple of students at the door. At least, I think they're students." His voice faded as he no doubt maligned our character to the woman we'd set our sights on.

Evan frowned in my direction. "You think she has a date?"

I had no fucking clue.

Just then, footsteps pounded on the stairs. We looked up to see two little boys coming down, their hands full of plastic dinosaur toys.

The second boy also carried a yellow dump truck. They looked to be between seven and nine years old. The blond kid was a little taller than the black-haired kid. They stopped short when they saw us.

The blond kid gaped. "Who are you?"

I noted that his eyes had a feline slant to them, exactly like Alaina's.

"I'm Evan," Evan said. "This is Daniel."

The other kid didn't have Alaina's eyes. He narrowed his big, brown eyes at us. "Are you students? Alaina doesn't like students to come to her house. She says she gets enough of them at work."

Alaina came down the hall, the blond man following on her heels. She wore the same silk blouse and tweed skirt from earlier. It was very professional looking, and it shouldn't have made my pants tight, but it did.

She frowned at us, but she addressed the children. "Zack and Deon, dinner is on the table. Go wash your hands."

"Mo-om," the blond kid whined. "We were going to play dinosaurs outside."

"Eat first." She focused on the one that didn't have her eyes. "Deon, your mother said you're avoiding dairy. I didn't put parmesan cheese on your spaghetti."

He heaved a sigh. "No meat. No dairy. The woman is trying to kill me."

Alaina gave them both a look that shut them up and got them marching past her.

The blond kid, who, by default, must have been Zack, paused in front of me. "My mom skipped lunch and we're having an early dinner, so please don't keep her too long. She hates cold spaghetti and reheated noodles."

I nodded. "Noted. Thank you."

The children disappeared into the kitchen, and Alaina turned her attention to the man behind her. "Adam, I appreciate your effort, but the answer is still no. They made their choice years ago, and I've moved on."

He pressed his lips together. "We'll discuss it later."

"No, we won't." She didn't look happy, but I supposed it was par for the course when dealing with an ex-husband who'd cheated on her. I couldn't help but think of what she'd said about chopping carrots for three years after their divorce.

Adam inclined his head toward us. "Aren't you going to introduce us?"

She heaved a sigh. "Adam Mazurek, meet Daniel DiMarco and Evan Carrico. Daniel owns the martial arts studio where I do group therapy, and Evan is his boyfriend who replaced my roof."

Adam shook my hand first. "It's great to meet you, Daniel. Alaina has mentioned you and your sister to me. It's great what you're doing to help empower people."

He had a good grip. It was firm, but not overly so.

"Thanks," I said. I wasn't sure what to say to him because Alaina really hadn't said much about him, aside from the cheating and the carrot things.

Then he shook Evan's hand. "Hi, Evan."

Alaina motioned to the front door. "Adam, I'm not going to change my mind. You got them in the divorce, and I don't want them back."

With a long-suffering sigh, he left the house.

That meant Alaina gave us her full attention.

"What did he get in the divorce that he's trying to give back?" Evan asked.

"My parents."

So many questions zinged through my mind, but I was hyper-focused on one fact. "You never said you had a kid."

She looked at me like I was the biggest idiot in the world. Then she noticed the chocolate mousse cake in my hand. Gears turned behind her eyes. "You brought dessert over to sweeten me up and try to talk me into changing my mind."

Evan crossed his arms over his chest and widened his stance, settling in for a long discussion. "I thought we changed your mind last night."

She dropped her volume, hissing quietly to keep her voice from carrying. "That was one time to prove to you that I was right, and you were wrong. I have not changed my mind. You were supposed to change yours."

"We haven't." Even to my own ears, I didn't sound so sure.

Her eyes closed, and her lips moved as she counted. When they opened, she didn't seem less annoyed. "Look, I can't talk to you about this tonight. I told you the earliest available time I had was Wednesday after work."

"Because Zack will be with his dad?" I sounded like a complete asshole, but I couldn't seem to use any other tone.

Alaina didn't pick up on it. "Yes. He's with his father Wednesday afternoon through Saturday afternoon."

That explained why she never had time to see me at the start of the week.

Before I could say more and possibly piss her off, Evan jumped in. "It's a date." He took the cake from me and handed it over to her. "Think of us when you're savoring this."

Then he smacked a kiss on her cheek and tried to pull me toward the door, but nobody was moving me when I didn't want to be moved. I brushed a kiss across her lips, but she didn't return the gesture. "We're not going to change our minds."

In the car, I looked at Evan. "That did not go according to plan."

"No," he agreed. "But now we know why she's holding back."

"Because she has a kid."

"Yep. She's thinking about more than just herself. That means she does like us." He threaded his fingers through mine. "We'll just have to prove that we're worthy of being around her son. It'll take longer, but I have faith that we'll get there."

I wasn't so sure. Why had she never mentioned him to me? I'd known her for a year. You'd think the topic of her son would've come up at least once.

"I'm in love with her." The declaration burst out of my mouth without consulting my brain, but the moment I heard the words, I felt the truth of it to my core.

"I know," Evan said. "I've known since the first time you met her. It was in the way you talked about her. I used to get jealous because I wanted you to feel like that about me."

"I do love you." I took my eyes off the road to throw a meaningful glance at Evan. "I've always loved you."

"Yeah. That's clear now. You know, you put her on a pedestal because you didn't think you had a chance with her, which I could handle. But then you slept with her." He broke off, staring at his lap and shaking his head. "I'd never been jealous of your sexual conquests before. But this—this consumed me. I spent that whole night trying to drive her out of your head."

I hadn't known any of that. "Is that why you slept with her? Is that why you want us to be with her?"

"No." He lifted his gaze, and I felt it penetrate the side of my head, but we were in heavy traffic, and I couldn't take my eyes off the road. "When I met her, I understood what you saw in her because I saw it too."

"Are you in love with her?"

"I'm not sure. She knocks me on my ass in a way you never did, so I'm not sure if it's the kind of love that's going to last a lifetime, or the kind of attraction that's going to burn hot and fast. I understand why she doesn't want to rush into anything."

170

We'd arrived at his condo. I pulled into a parking spot and looked over at him. "I never knocked you on your ass?"

He interpreted my teasing grin correctly. "I'm not going to fight you. I'm too smart to think I can win against you. But, no, you never knocked me on my ass. The moment I met you, I knew you were going to be part of my life forever, and I found comfort in knowing that. I just wasn't sure if the attraction would mellow into a strong friendship or heat up into sexual love. For fuck's sake—I was fifteen when we met. I didn't know anything but what my hormones told me."

He got out of the car, and I followed him to the front door. While he went about unlocking it, I planted my hand on the door frame, caging him between the condo and my body. "What about now? Do I knock you on your ass now?"

One thing about caging a Dom—it only ramped up his alpha nature. With a casual lift of his brows, he opened the door and went inside. Once the door was closed, he framed my face with his hands. His lips hovered less than an inch from mine. Evan couldn't overpower me, but he was a master at teasing the fuck out of me.

"Is that what you want, Danny? Would you like me to tie you up and paddle your ass?"

When Evan got like this, my brain scrambled. Yet I recalled enough to say, "That's not even a little bit close to what I said."

"But is it what you want?"

I'd steadfastly maintained that impact play didn't appeal to me, but the truth was that I'd never tried it. Right now, I wanted to get out of my head because my mind wouldn't stop replaying what happened at Alaina's house.

"Evan, I need you to be honest with me. Is her having a kid an issue for you? Because it kind of is with me."

He shook his head. "You don't mind that she has a kid. You're upset because you've known her for a year, and you didn't know about him. I'm not upset because I've known her for a month, and our conversation hasn't exactly been about family."

I thought back over the things Alaina and I typically talked about, and I realized the topics usually had to do with the logistics of her job at my studio. There had been moments when our personal lives had come up, which should've opened the door for her to talk about her son. And for the last couple of weeks, I'd made a concerted effort to talk to her about everyday topics, and I always asked how her day was going. I would've thought his existence would have come up.

"I just want to get her out of my head for now. I want you to make me stop thinking."

His eyes blazed. "I can do that, but my idea of getting you out of your head and your idea of it might not be the same. Ask for what you want, Daniel."

I knew the kinds of kinks Evan tended toward. He'd either tried them on me or spent time trying to get me to consent to trying it on me. But what came to mind wasn't anything he'd ever suggested. "Hot and cold. Wax and ice."

The blaze stalled as the wheels in his brain kicked up five notches. "I'll need to run to the store."

I gestured in the direction of his bathroom. "I've seen candles under your sink." His mother liked to give them as gifts, but Evan wasn't the kind of person who burned them at any time except when the power was out.

He shook his head. "Those are the wrong kind. They have additives for color and scent that make them unsuitable for wax play, and most of them are made from beeswax, which burns too hot. I need paraffin or soy." He trailed off, mumbling something about sheets.

"So, that's a 'no' on the hot and cold?"

"I just need to run to the store." He spun his keys around his finger and caught them in his hand, the soft clash of metal comforting and familiar. "Want to come with me?"

"How about I start dinner instead?" We'd hoped to eat with—and on—Alaina.

"Sounds like a plan." He grinned. "We can talk through the particulars while we eat."

Chapter 15—Evan

One thing about being a Dom—everyone assumed you were well-versed in every kink. At twenty-five, I'd only identified as a Dom for a couple of years, and my kinks tended to be more mainstream. I used bondage, sensory deprivation, and light impact play on a regular basis. Even the sensory deprivation piece usually involved innocent things like a blindfold or the occasional hand over the mouth. I knew people who used noise-canceling headphones or blindfolds that showed they meant business. I'd been to play parties where a Domme used a bullwhip, but I'd never done any of that. My submissive partners tended to want bondage and sensory play. To that end, I only owned a deerskin flogger.

I guess I'd been holding out for Daniel. I'd wanted to tailor my kinky interests to things he enjoyed. Despite what he said and how he talked about it, I knew he liked being restrained. It was apparent in his heightened reactions to anything I did to him while he was tied up. He didn't go in for impact play, so I'd stopped at deerskin—a flogger that felt more like a massage than anything else. I'd thought he would like the violet wand—he had—and so I'd attended a workshop on how to use it, and then I'd invested in some basic equipment with him in mind.

But it was difficult to investigate kinks when the man you loved insisted he had none. In the past few months, I'd found out more about Daniel than I had the entire time we'd been together. He liked electronic stimulation. He entertained role-playing fantasies. And now he wanted to try wax and ice play. I'd had wax poured on me before, so I knew it stung a bit, much like being flogged, but without the impact.

Was that what turned him off about flogging? Did he want the sting in a more sensual way instead of a violent way? As I drove to the store, I considered that he spent his days teaching others to fight, and that involved taking hits. He probably wouldn't want to relax doing the same things he did all day at work.

With a sigh, I accepted that my life partner was going to lead me down paths I hadn't previously considered. I'd never, in a million years, thought I'd be pursuing a woman with Daniel. In the back of my head, I'd always thought the two of us would settle down together one day, and we'd look back on our dating days with fond memories, but no regrets. Having sex with women would be something we used to do. Now, we were looking to move forward with an incredible woman I'd never had the imagination to even fantasize about. But she was perfect for us.

We just needed to convince her that we were perfect for her.

In the meantime, I called Sophia. While she wasn't my mentor, she often hooked me up with people or places that helped me learn whatever I sought to learn. She'd been supportive of my journey the whole time, but she'd come out right at the start and told me that she wasn't comfortable mentoring anyone when she still looked to her mentors for advice and support.

"Hey, Soph. I have a question, which I hope will be quick. Do you have a few minutes?"

"Sure. Drew is catering an event, so I'm catching up on some business manager stuff right now, and then Drew's mom invited me and my mom over for dinner." Sophia managed Sensual Secrets, her fiancé's catering service and bakery. Lately it had grown to include managing Drew's budding career as a TV chef. She had her hands full, and I'd never seen her happier.

"A family bonding night. Sounds like fun. Have you invited his family to your Sunday thing yet?" My first invitation had come when I was nineteen. The DiMarcos were friendly, but they prized their family time, and they didn't often invite outsiders to their monthly gatherings.

"Not yet, but that's only because they're always busy. I've never met anybody who travels as much as his parents do. They're gone more than they're home." She cleared her throat. "But that's not why you called. What's up, buttercup?"

The way she treated me, you'd think she was a lot older, but we'd graduated from the same high school the same year. I let that go because I was used to the vagaries of sister-types. "Wax and ice. I've done ice play before, but not with wax. I've only seen a demo on wax, so anything you can tell me would be helpful."

She made a thoughtful noise, which told me she was thinking about hot wax and her submissive. "Well, the first thing you should do is let your partner know that this is your first time. That way they'll know to speak up right away if something goes wrong."

"Got it. I know the type of candle matters. I'm on my way to the store for paraffin or soy. I know you can't use scented or anything fancy because the additives increase the melting point and can scald or burn skin."

"Good. I'd get pillars instead of tapers. That way, you can let the wax pool a bit before you pour it, and you'll have more control over when and where drips happen. Okay—logistics. You need to clear the area of clutter. Have a fire extinguisher nearby, but also have a bucket of water. Sometimes you have a tiny fire, or you just need a smaller amount of water instead of the whole fire extinguisher."

"I have a fire extinguisher and a bucket, so that's not a problem."

"Put an old sheet or blanket down. No matter how careful you are, wax gets everywhere, and it doesn't come out of fabrics too well. It's a bitch with hair, so if you're with someone who has long hair, definitely put that up. Oh—and shave the areas where you're going to put the wax. Even women have those fine hairs on their arms or butts, and pulling wax off when it's stuck in hair is the opposite of fun for most people, especially at the end of a scene or during aftercare."

I thought about Daniel's face when I informed him that he'd have to shave body parts, and a hearty belly laugh rolled from me.

"So, it's a guy. Is it Daniel? Because I haven't seen his ass in years, but he has hair on his chest and legs, and he's going to throw a fit if you ask him to shave. He makes fun of Drew for waxing."

Daniel didn't have a ton of hair on his chest or legs, but I didn't think it mattered how much was there. Out of habit, my first impulse was to deny I was planning a scene with Daniel, but I stopped myself. While we were going to do our big reveal tomorrow, Sophia already knew we hooked up every now and again. I didn't have to lie or obfuscate.

"It's Daniel, and it was his idea."

"Okay, well, he has sensitive skin, so you should probably have him use a soothing lotion after he shaves." She spent the next twenty minutes walking me through the finer points of wax play, especially when juxtaposing it with ice.

By the time she finished, I'd planned a sensual experience that was going to take Daniel's mind away from our troubles and keep him firmly in a submissive headspace. I thanked Sophia, and I managed to end the call without promising juicy details the next time I saw her, which would be tomorrow.

When I got home, I found Daniel in the kitchen. He was bent over the oven, stirring something that smelled scrumptious. "Barefoot and in the kitchen—exactly how I like my men."

He glanced up for a second. His gaze roved over my body before settling back on the cubed potatoes in a glass pan. "I'm not sure if that's funny or sexist."

"It can't be sexist. We're both men."

Closing the oven, he straightened up. "Those need ten more minutes. I made a spicy dressing to go over the salad, and I sautéed some shrimp for the salad as well."

While it wasn't a meal I'd ever dream up, I knew it was going to be excellent. I slung my arms around his waist, pulling him closer to me. "I love that you're a great cook, and I appreciate that you're willing to cook for us."

He snorted. "It's that, or we eat what you make. I love you, Evan, but you shouldn't be allowed near a stove."

I heartily agreed with him. I pressed a brief kiss to his lips. "I need to shave you."

He reacted the way I thought he would—he pulled away and furrowed his dark brows. "What?"

"Wax will adhere to hair, even the little fine ones, and taking the wax off of you won't be nearly as fun as putting it on you."

His mouth opened and closed as he tried to figure out what to feel or how to respond.

"Your back is fine." In an effort to help him with his internal wrestling match, I kept talking. "But I'd like to shave your chest and thighs. I'll avoid your arms and lower legs, but I'm going to have to go over your ass cheeks just in case."

It was enough time for him to think of something to say. "But why do *you* have to shave me? I can shave myself."

At least he was willing to shave. I'd doubted he would want to go through with it after he heard about the shaving part. I looped a finger through the belt loops on his jeans and tugged him back to me. Cupping a hand around the back of his neck, I feathered a kiss over his luscious lips. "Because I'm your Dom, and I want to."

"You're my—" He stopped speaking, closed his eyes, and exhaled a long stream of frustration.

"Danny, tonight, I'm your Dom. I'm going to tie you up and make you forget everything but the fact that you belong to me. I won't make you call me by title, but I will accept and enjoy your submission."

"Yeah." Without opening his eyes, he pressed his forehead to mine. "I know. I just—the labels bother me."

"You think submission means you're weak." I knew where his macho, toxic masculinity thoughts were rooted.

"It seems weak. I know Drew isn't weak, but I couldn't imagine living the way he does."

"Sophia is a sadist, Danny. I don't mind being sadistic if I'm with a masochist, but I don't crave it. I want your submission in the bedroom only, and even with that, I'm up for switching or vanilla, if you're in the mood for that."

His eyes popped open. "I'm not afraid of pain. I just don't find it sexually stimulating."

"I know. You like sensory play. That's what we're going to do tonight, and shaving you is going to be part of the sensory experience." I brushed another kiss over his lips. "Trust me."

"I trust you." His answer came too quickly for him to have thought about what I was really asking.

"Trust me to see to your needs. Trust me to take control of you tonight."

This time, he took a moment to think. After a while, he nodded. "I trust you, Evan. Always, and with everything."

"Good. This is my first time playing with wax, so you're going to have to be vocal."

He stalled, freezing for several long moments. "You've never done this before?"

"No, but I've been to a demonstration, and I did my homework. I know what I'm doing, but it's all theoretical right now."

A huge grin sprouted on his handsome face. "So, this is just a thing between you and me?"

"Yeah, just like the violet wand, except to learn that, I participated in a training workshop."

If possible, his grin got even bigger. "That was just a you-and-me thing?"

Rather than respond, I studied him. Daniel was, by nature, a happy person. It wasn't difficult to get him excited or bring out his effervescent side. His good looks and positive personality went a long way toward rendering him consummately charming. But he was practically bursting right now, and I'd never seen him this eager about engaging in kink with me.

"Daniel, is the reason you're reluctant to be my sub due to the fact that I've dominated other people?"

His grin faltered. "Maybe. I hadn't thought about it."

I dragged a fingertip along the edge of his jaw, a light touch that made him melt toward me. "Being with you is everything I've ever wanted. From now on, everything we do is between you and me."

"What about Alaina?"

It seemed Alaina had a point when she decided to give us time to talk about what we really wanted. "How about we concentrate on us tonight, and tomorrow, we'll talk about how Alaina fits into our relationship?"

He nodded. "Okay. Dinner is ready now, so we should eat, and then we can do weird things in the shower together."

The food was amazing, as it was every time he cooked, but my mind was on the logistics of the upcoming scene.

We left the dishes to soak, which meant there was no way they were getting done tonight, and we went upstairs. The second floor of my condo had two bedrooms with a bathroom between them. I guided him toward that door.

"Get undressed."

He looked at me sourly. "There was a time when you'd kiss me, and we'd undress each other."

It looked like Daniel was going to take the Brat Path to submission. I was okay with that because I wanted him to do whatever made him feel comfortable enough to get there. Plus, I liked his sassy side. It was something he shared only with those close to him. However, I'd have to discourage him from topping from the bottom. It was a process, and we had the rest of our lives, so I could afford to be patient.

"Kissing happens when I say it happens."

Rather than wrap his arms around me and try to press his advantage, he went into the bathroom. He grumbled, but he did what I told him to do.

I liked watching Daniel undress. His body was a study in masculine perfection. Broad shoulders, narrow hips, and muscles cording him from head to toe. He exuded strength and power, and he was mine.

"Stand up in the tub."

This part probably wouldn't be erotic or romantic. I doused his body with water, and then I slathered shaving cream on his backside. He didn't have much hair on his ass, but I wanted to spend a lot of time playing with that luscious feature, and I didn't want either of us to regret it. I went over his back for the same reason. When I turned him around and attended to his chest and the fronts of his thighs, I found his cock halfway hard.

Smirking, I said, "I see you like having your body shaved."

"I like when you touch me." His simple statement was absent any kind of snark or attitude.

I pressed a kiss to his lips, and then I finished shaving him. Daniel had actual hair on his chest. It started just below his sternum and thickened as it moved down toward the nest of curls around his cock. I took my time with his chest, rubbing my hand along behind the razor's path. By the time I finished with his thighs, his cock was hard and ready for action.

I rinsed him and patted him dry, and then I led him into the bedroom.

He looked around, noting the changes I'd made before I'd joined him in the kitchen. "You put construction plastic over the bed?"

"To catch the wax."

I'd also put plastic over my oak veneer dresser. The top was clear of the items I normally kept on it. That was where I'd set out two candles and a bucket of water. The fire extinguisher was in the corner behind an upholstered chair. A cup filled with ice sat next to a small lunch cooler with more ice inside.

Lastly, I'd taken all the candles I threw in cabinets whenever someone gave me one, and I had spread them on the dresser, the chest of drawers, and the window ledge. While he waited, I fired up my butane lighter and lit the candles. Then I doused the lights.

"It's romantic." His smile was back, the dreamy one I'd spent countless hours trying to coax from him. "But can we put an old sheet on the plastic? That's going to suck to lay on."

He wasn't wrong, but I didn't have old sheets. I grabbed one from a set I liked less and spread it over the plastic. He helped smooth out the wrinkles.

"Thank you."

Rather than reply, I kissed him, plunging my tongue into his mouth. It was a masterful kiss, meant to knock him off balance. Electricity zinged between us, and he melted against me. He tugged at my shirt, lifting it slowly. His hands moved over my skin as he bared it, and he ensnared me in his erotic spell every bit as much as I had captured him.

With slow, languorous movements, I guided him to the bed. I kissed him until I had his magnificent body positioned where I wanted it. Then I broke away to trail sucking kisses and sharp nips down his neck and shoulders. I marked his body with my lips and hands, running my palms over his newly smooth chest and legs. Then I flipped him over to enjoy his backside the same way.

When I paused, he sighed.

"I'm going to bind your wrists now."

"You don't think I can stay still?" His tone held a hint of amusement.

I loved the way he looked in restraints. I loved when he strained against his bonds and found himself helpless and at my mercy. "Doesn't matter if you can. It's what I want."

"Okay." He pushed a pillow up, shoving it between the headboard and the mattress as he stretched out his arms.

I also loved when he was pliable and agreeable. The neoprene cuffs took but a moment to put on, and then I attached them to the headboard. The Velcro would hold, and it was a quick release if anything unexpected happened with the candles. Then I blindfolded him. For once, he didn't protest.

Now that he was exactly how I wanted him, I slid off the bed and stood to the side to drink in the sight of Daniel's gorgeous body. For a second, thoughts of Alaina intruded. I was sure she would like the visual. If she was there, I'd have her assist me. Then I'd untie Daniel. I'd toss her to the bed, and Daniel and I would both have our way with her.

Blinking, I willed that fantasy to the back burner.

"I know you're staring at me." Daniel laughed, further ridding me of mental distractions. "Do you like what you see?"

I didn't bother denying it. "You have a tight ass, and I'm going to wreck it."

"As long as you use plenty of lube."

Since he was game, I grabbed Daniel's toolbox from the closet. It was filled with toys I used on him, each cleaned and neatly stored. Snapping a latex glove onto my hand, I poured a liberal amount of lube on my fingers. "Spread your legs."

He did, eagerly tilting his hips to lift his ass up.

I rewarded him by massaging his sphincter with my gloved hand and tugging on his balls with my other one. He moaned, so I slipped a finger inside, playing around to loosen him up. He thrust against me, and he groaned louder.

"Fuck, Evan. If you keep that up, I'm going to blow my load before we really get started."

That earned him two fingers. I let his prostate mostly alone as I sawed in and out to open him wider. "D'you like this, Danny? Huh? Do you want more?"

"More, and harder."

"Beg for it."

"Please, Evan. I need to feel you inside me. Please fuck me."

Honestly, I was surprised he begged so easily. So much about being in a relationship with him was better than anything I'd imagined. He was mine—completely mine—and I absolutely loved it. The feeling of power inflated my head. I took a moment to enjoy it, and then I breathed through it. I needed to maintain focus to make sure Daniel had a great experience.

I withdrew my fingers and grabbed the anal beads. Making little circles over his buttocks with one hand, I fed the beads into his ass. Gasps and moans escaped from his lips, and he arched into the dual caress.

"Is this what you wanted?"

"Yes. No. Yes. Fuck, Evan. You're evil, and I love it."

Chuckling, I played a bit, pushing beads in and out until his gasps turned ragged. I left them sticking out of him while I retrieved a cup filled with the tiny ice cubes my refrigerator made.

Dragging one down his spine had him shivering, but it didn't raise gooseflesh. Daniel ran hot, and the ice cube melted faster than I'd anticipated. Rolling with it, I set out several cubes on his back, ass cheeks, and the backs of his thighs. Immediately, they began melting. Icy water spread over his skin. As each cube melted, rivulets formed. They sought lower elevation, and the dribbles left gooseflesh in their wake.

Daniel shivered. "That feels so good."

It was going to feel even better after I applied hot wax. I wiped away the water, sweeping it down his sides. It adhered to his skin and pooled underneath him, which gave me an idea.

I slid the remainder of the ice in the cup underneath him. Trapped between plastic sheeting and his body, it had nowhere to go. There was no getting away from the cold.

He groaned. "Fuck. That's harsh, Ev."

"Don't worry—I have plenty more ice in the cooler."

His entire body shuddered, which made me smile.

Body oil came next. I squirted a line down his spine, and then I massaged it into the muscles on his back, ass, and thighs.

"Are you putting baby oil on me? Is this a bodybuilder fantasy?"

While Daniel did have a body that rivaled any bodybuilder, I didn't nurse those kinds of fantasies about him. I ignored that question and addressed his concern. "The oil is so the wax comes off afterward. Plus, you do look really hot oiled up, tied up, and ready to be fucked."

A deep breath was his only response.

I lit a wax-play candle. My attention divided between drinking the erotic tableau spread before me and waiting for enough wax to pool around the wick. Wait time was crucial for a sub. Increased anticipation meant his senses were on high alert, and the fact he laid there without moving meant he'd surrendered to my Dominance.

The first drop hit his shoulder blade with no warning. I wanted an honest reaction to start us off.

A soft exhalation escaped him.

I dripped several drops, spreading them down his back and over the rounded globe of his ass.

He moaned and groaned, and when I got to his thigh, he hissed.

Leaving off for a second, I gave him a chance to safeword. "Color?"

"Green, but fuck, that stung."

I dropped a few more, the white wax splatting on his skin and drying quickly. Uncertain noises sounded from him, and I listened closely to see if he'd decided whether he liked the stinging sensation.

Then I gave him a break. I dripped wax down the other side, starting at his shoulder and moving down to his thigh. I let more wax coat his back and ass, and I only did a couple drips on his thighs.

From the noises he was making, I decided he liked the different sensations.

Next, I concentrated on his ass. I poured three drops, and then I spread the hot wax with my fingertips.

He swore.

"Problems?"

"My dick is so hard that it hurts to lay on it like this."

That was an acceptable pain. My own cock throbbed with need edging on pain. Chuckling, I kept up my ministrations. Thanks to the oil, the dried wax cleared away with the swipe of my hand. I examined his skin, and then I went over the area again. This time, I added ice back into the mixture, alternating hot and cold by placing an ice cube on his skin and pouring wax around it.

Beneath me, Daniel writhed. His mind was so far gone that he forgot the cuffs on his wrists and tugged against them.

He moved so much that he flipped over. Rather than draw him out of subspace by reprimanding him, I repeated the patterns on his front side, only I had to be careful not to get the wax in his pubic hair.

Driving him to this point was a power trip for me. This was the experience I'd craved with him for so long that I'd all but given up on it ever happening.

Though I'd stopped with the wax and ice, his body still thrashed and squirmed, seeking a climax he sorely needed.

I didn't want to move him or bring him out of his headspace, but I couldn't wait any longer. The anal beads were still inside him, but I couldn't reach them very well. Thankfully they were on a bendy silicone string, so they weren't hard to get out.

Tonight, I wanted to feel him inside me, but I didn't want to switch our dynamic. It was a fallacy that whoever was getting their ass fucked was the powerless one. Power was given, and it wasn't dependent on strength or position. I lubed myself up, spread more over his cock, and I straddled his body.

He calmed immediately. His chest rose and fell as if he'd just run a marathon, and he waited for my kiss.

I didn't disappoint. Our lips and tongues clashed. He sought to be subsumed by me, not to achieve dominance. I calmed his frenetic kiss by taking over. His body didn't relax, but it did melt toward mine.

Then I positioned his cock at my entrance. I sank down slowly, reveling in the feel of him inside me. Leaning forward, I removed his blindfold. He blinked as his eyes adjusted to the candlelight, and then his gaze locked onto mine. I read the depth of his love and submission in there, and my heart soared even higher.

I fucked him, slowly at first, and increasing my pace as I was able. His hips moved with me, and he tugged even harder on his restraints. Nothing compared to seeing him like this.

Leaning down, I brushed my lips against his. We were both too far gone for a proper kiss, but that wasn't my intention. "Come for me, Danny."

"Yes," he hissed, lifting his hips faster and drilling into me harder. Soon his eyes rolled back, and I felt the strength of his orgasm bursting inside me.

Easing off him, I planted a firmer kiss on his slack lips. Then I scooted forward until I straddled his chest. "Open your mouth."

He did, though he didn't have enough control to open wide. No matter. Whatever didn't make it into his mouth would end up on his face and neck, and I liked the way my orgasm looked dripping from his chin. Taking my cock in hand, it didn't take long to finish myself off. Ejaculate shot from the purpled tip of my cock. Some of it landed in his mouth, but most of the stream ended up on his face and neck.

His tongue darted out to lick away anything it could reach.

Utterly spent, I collapsed next to him.

"Evan?"

"Yeah?" I fought to keep my eyes open. I needed to undo the cuffs and administer aftercare.

"Thank you for this. It was incredible. I love you."

A billowing sense of love and pride chased away the sleep trying to steal over me. I turned on my side and dragged a caress down his chest. "I love you, too."

Chapter 16—Daniel

Sunday dinner with my parents was something we did at the end of every month, and we rotated between my loft, Sophia and Drew's house, and my parents' house. Sophia and Drew had the largest house, but it was my turn to host the gathering. Because my loft was too cozy for more than four people, I'd moved the location to Evan's condo. It was a better gathering place than my loft, but only because he had a small patio with an outdoor dining set and a yard where we could set up a folding table.

"We need a bigger entertaining space," Evan said as he locked the legs of the folding table into place. "And a bigger bed. What's the largest size bed?"

"California king, I think." I wiped down the table. "But let's hold off on that until we convince Alaina to join us."

He snorted. "I'm not waiting. You take up more space in a bed than is humanly possible. It's not easy to sleep next to you."

I was a deep sleeper, and I tended to spread out when I was unconscious. Grinning at his dry tone, I said, "But I'm worth the effort."

"Yeah, you are. But our next place needs to have a huge master bedroom so we can fit the bed."

"Maybe our next place will be Alaina's house. Her master bedroom is huge. It can fit a California king and still have room to do cartwheels." I thought about what it would be like to wake up between Evan and Alaina every morning, and I very much liked the idea. But if it was her house, and not mine or Evan's, would it feel like home?

I didn't have an answer.

"Odds are against it." Evan's dire pronouncement interrupted my doubtful thoughts with ones that were even less optimistic.

"Why?"

"She has a kid, and she's very analytical. If she agrees to date us, she's going to slow walk the relationship. You can't mess around when

184

your child is involved. She probably won't even let us meet him for a few months. Really meet him—yesterday doesn't count."

I frowned. "You think she won't want us around her son?"

"I think she's the kind of person who doesn't introduce her son to anyone she dates unless it's serious."

That stung, but I understood why she would do that. "Well, it's a good thing you and I are serious."

Later, I was in the kitchen with Sophia, discussing how to split a pie in a manner that was fair but also netted me the biggest piece. Sophia also wanted the biggest piece, so our objectives weren't quite aligned.

"Key lime is my favorite, not yours. Go drool over the apple-walnut pie." She pushed lightly at my chest.

While I liked the apple-walnut more, I couldn't just drop it and let her have her way. "It's tart and sweet, guaranteed to put hair on your chest. You don't want hair on your chest."

She poked at my abdomen. I flexed and tightened in time to prevent her from doing any damage, but from her expression, I knew her real shot would be verbal.

Her grin grew, curling mischievously as her eyes narrowed. "I heard you weren't into having chest hair anymore."

"Fuck you. Evan didn't tell you anything."

A sharp smack stung the back of my shoulder. It didn't hurt, but it communicated displeasure. I turned to see my mother scowling. She shook a finger at me. "Watch your language." With that, she finished passing through the kitchen and joined Evan's parents on the back patio.

Evan was out there, playing catch with his seven-year-old nephew and eight-year-old niece. In addition to his parents, his brother Alec had brought his family over for the day, his sister Elissa had brought her two over, and Bryn and Cora had joined us as well. Being one of nine meant lots of family was always around. Over the years, I'd grown used to this, but for the first time, it occurred to me that I wouldn't be able to leave when I wanted to be alone. I was going to host them all until they left.

I rubbed my back. "Mom isn't a hitter."

Sophia lifted a shoulder. "She's still mad at you for not giving her an accurate count of who would be here today."

"I had no idea this many people were going to show up. I thought it was going to be us and Evan's parents."

She leaned closer and lowered her volume. "How did the wax play go? Did you like it?"

By way of response, I glared.

Her smile grew. "I'll take that as a yes."

To throw her off the scent, and because the topic wouldn't leave my mind, I said, "Did you know Alaina has a kid?"

Sophia's brows drew together, and she looked at me like I was an idiot, much the same way Alaina had. "Yes, and you knew it, too."

"No, I didn't. She's never mentioned him before."

Sophia continued staring like I'd sprouted antlers.

"I'm being serious."

"I know you are, which is what's concerning."

"What's concerning?" Alec leaned between us, checking out the pies. "Those look so good. I love your mom's pies. You two better not be conspiring to hog them."

We were, but that was nothing new. It was a thing Sophia and I did. We were dessert junkies, and we'd fight to the death for our mama's pie.

I cleared my throat. "You met Alaina. You've been to her house. Did you know she had a son?"

"Alaina? That's the therapist whose house we put windows in?"

"Yeah."

"Yes. I forget what she said his name is, but she showed me a couple pictures on her phone. Cute little blond-headed boy who is just a little older than Ashton. He's eight, I think. Ashton won't turn eight for another three months."

She'd talked about her son with Alec, but not with me. My jaw dropped. "I wonder why she never said anything about him to me."

Alec considered this. "You have a professional relationship. You're younger, single, and you have no children, where she has more in common with me. The subject probably didn't come up."

His reasoning would make sense if Alaina and I didn't have a personal relationship, but we did. I had deep and abiding feelings for a woman it seemed I didn't know as well as I wanted to.

Sophia smacked the back of my shoulder in the same place my mom had targeted. "Daniel, she's talked about him in front of you before. Remember that poem she did at open mic night? She talked about the many uses of cereal, including using them to teach her son how to aim for the toilet instead of spraying all over the place like a territorial cat. Last month, you asked her if she had plans for the Fourth of July, and she said she was taking Zack to a street fair and to the park to watch fireworks. Apparently, you don't listen very well."

As Sophia spewed at me, I recalled hearing her talk about someone named Zack, but I'd thought he was a guy she was seeing. And I'd been under the impression she'd made up most of the stuff in her poem for effect.

I took offense at her accusation. "I pay attention. I thought the poem was theoretical. She didn't specifically say she was talking about her son. She spoke generally. And with the fireworks, I thought she had a date."

Sophia's eyes widened, but she waited until a little later, when we were relatively alone, to share what was wrong. "Daniel, is Evan bothered by her having a child? I know he's involved with her, and a kid is a pretty big deal. If he's going to stop seeing her, then he needs to let her down gently, and he needs to not offend her."

Rolling my eyes, I said, "Evan isn't shallow."

"I know, but—"

"Daniel!" Evan's call interrupted our hushed conversation.

I looked across the yard to find him motioning us over. Dinner was nearly over, and dessert was about to be served. With so many people there, we'd been forced to eat dinner first and have dessert second, which was not how we normally did things.

Evan and I had decided to announce our news during the changeover.

Every bit as attuned to sweets as I was, Sophia perked up. She squeezed my arm gently. "We'll continue this later."

She headed for dessert, and I headed over to Evan. The summer breeze ruffled his light brown hair, and sunlight glinted from the sparkle in his eyes. He smiled, and the dimple in his right cheek peeked out. He took my breath away.

"Ready?" He set a hand on my shoulder, and the surety of his touch chased away the worst of my butterflies.

"Yeah. You?"

"Yeah." He tapped a grilling fork against the stainless-steel ledge on the grill to get everyone's attention. Once they were quiet and turned toward us, he looked at me, checking on how I was doing.

Evan had been out to his family since his thirteenth birthday. They were used to him dating men and women. But I'd never been interested in any man except Evan. My family had urged me to come out of the closet, but I'd never felt like I was in one.

"Thank you for coming today. As you know, Daniel and I have been best friends since the day we met nine years ago during a summer workout session for our high school football team. You all like to joke about how we're joined at the hip."

My mother and his mother exchanged a glance, but I didn't have time to wonder about it.

Evan took my hands in his. "Daniel, whenever I've needed a friend, you've been there. If I needed to talk, you listened. When I wanted to start my own construction company, you cleared days to help me with the legal paperwork. If something went wrong—or even very right—you were the first person I called, and you always answered. You're my best friend, and I love you more than anything in the world. Will you marry me?"

Silence fell over the group. Though all eyes were on me, I felt the weight of none of them.

Stunned, I whispered. "I didn't know you were going to do this."

His smile only grew. The warm blue of his eyes glittered with the strength of everything he felt. "Surprise."

My head started bobbing before I could get the words out. "Yes. Yes, I'll marry you."

He wrapped his arms around me and laid an open-mouthed kiss on me that was positively indecent considering our parents and several children were present. But I didn't care. I melted into him, and I kissed him back with all the love I felt bursting from my core.

When it ended, my mother came toward us, her hands out. She cupped my face, bringing my head down so our foreheads touched. Tears streamed down her cheeks. "I'm so glad you stopped being stubborn. Congratulations."

She extended her hug to include Evan and his mother, who'd snagged him for a congratulatory hug.

They stepped back, hands to their hearts in a big show of being drama queens, and my mom said, "Lois, you called it. All those years ago, you said we were going to be family one day."

Lois flashed the same dimple Evan had. "It took them long enough, though. I thought they'd have sealed the deal long before now. I'll admit, I was getting worried."

Dessert wasn't forgotten, but it was delayed by a round of congratulatory hugs and handshakes.

The only dark spot in my happiness was Alaina's absence.

But there was time for that later.

Chapter 17—Alaina

The Monday back at work after taking a week off to spend time relaxing or working on my book was a weird sort of reality check. Not only was I confronted by a mountain of email—I refused to check my work email when I was on vacation—but my day was booked solid with meetings. While my mind was still whirling with images of sunsets on the Outer Banks, and I fought to keep away the feel of Evan and Daniel's kisses or the complete shock on both their faces when I shooed them out of my house on Saturday, my colleagues were prattling on about chromosomal complexities.

Normally I'd find much of what they said intriguing, but today it took a herculean effort to concentrate. By the time lunch rolled around, I'd turned down six offers for company. I retreated to my office for a much-needed sensory break.

As a geneticist, I often spent long hours in the lab alone. As a Dean, I had to balance my need for order and schedules and normalcy with lots of paperwork, socializing, and solving problems other people couldn't. Sometimes I fantasized about stepping down as Dean so I could concentrate on my research, but my position allowed me the influence and control to pursue my areas of interest, so I kept on with it.

Life was a constant series of trade-offs, and I'd come to terms with it. That didn't mean I was free from moments of resentment.

I sat behind my desk, rested my head back in my chair, closed my eyes, and breathed deeply.

"Hi."

The familiar, perky voice roused me quickly. Though it belonged to someone I liked, it was out of place here in my sanctuary. My eyes shot open to see Sophia standing in the open doorway.

I'd forgotten to close it.

The first thing I always noticed about Sophia was the confident way she held herself. It didn't matter that she was a stunning beauty or that the soft set of her mouth denoted friendliness and a generous spirit. You immediately knew not to mess with her. When I'd first met her, I'd been intimidated by her bearing, and as I came to know her, I realized she meant to come off as formidable.

But that didn't automatically mean she was aggressive or a bully. It was more like she was keeping her power contained nearby, but she could unleash it at any time.

I liked the way she embraced life and took charge. I rose to my feet. "Sophia. Hi. I wasn't expecting you, was I?" I knew I wasn't. Everything was written down in my schedule, and Sophia wasn't in my planner until next week, when the next group therapy session was scheduled.

"No. I was in the area, and I took a chance that you had a few minutes to talk."

"Sure." In the past few months, I'd come to realize she didn't need the group therapy sessions like she had when we'd started. Her life had become busy as well, and I knew it was a matter of time before she stopped teaching the self-defense classes. The contract we'd signed called for two years, and we'd made it sixteen months, which was longer than I'd expected. I would need to find another instructor if I was to keep the study going.

I motioned to the table in the opposite corner of my office. It was a friendlier setting, but it maintained distance between me and my companion. I liked Sophia, but I really needed a break from people to recharge my batteries.

She closed the door and sat down. "You can eat your lunch while we talk."

My PBJ sandwich and apple slices waited on my desk. I grabbed them and sat with her. "What's on your mind?"

"I can't stop by just to see a friend?"

I liked Sophia a lot, but I wouldn't call her a friend. As I pondered how to respond, she waved her hand.

"You're right. I know. We're not quite there yet. I'm here because I want to tell you something, and I think you should hear it from a friendly source."

"Okay." I had zero possible instructors lined up. Replacing Sophia would be nearly impossible. I suspected her authority and empathy went a long way toward convincing women to stay with the class for longer than a couple of sessions.

"Evan got engaged yesterday."

I'd just taken a bite of my sandwich, so the peanut butter stuck to the roof of my mouth kept me from responding. My first feeling was immense relief that she wasn't quitting.

Frowns creased her chin and between her eyes. "That wasn't quite the reaction I expected."

A long sip of cold water eased the stickiness in my mouth. I cleared out the food. "I thought you were going to tell me you were quitting the program. I'm so glad that's not the case."

"Oh. No. I'm not quitting. I was afraid you might when you heard the news."

She'd lost me. I put down my sandwich. "Why would you think I'd quit? I made a commitment, and I always honor my commitments."

"Yes, but you were involved with Evan, and he's Daniel's best friend. And there's more that I have to tell you." Her grimace pointed to an uncomfortable revelation. "Remember how I told you he was already in love with someone, but he wasn't acting on it?"

I was not yet uncomfortable. "Yes. I hope you're going to say he's engaged to Daniel."

Her lips parted, the tense lines around them easing in surprise. "You knew?"

"Yes. I had urged them to consider what they truly wanted from life. I'd hoped they chose to be together."

"When was this?"

"Saturday. And Friday. The three of us talked on Friday, and I pointed out that they should consider what they truly wanted in life. They returned unexpectedly on Saturday to talk some more, but I was terribly busy. Adam had just dropped off Zack, and he's getting divorced, so he wants to make some changes in our agreement, and I don't. We were finishing up a heated discussion when Daniel and Evan showed up, and I was making dinner for Zack and Deon. I didn't have time to phrase things nicely, so I told them to talk to each other and to be candid about what they really wanted."

She snagged an apple slice from the container I'd opened. "I didn't know you were friends with Daniel."

I wasn't under the impression I was either. "I'd say we're colleagues. We work together, so we talk a bit, and he's confided some personal things. He might view me as a sort of mentor."

A mentor he wanted to have sex with.

That went along thematically with his librarian fantasy. It occurred to me that perhaps Evan was incorrect in assuming Daniel wasn't submissive. He had a pattern of seeking out authority figures for meaningful relationships.

Okay, I needed to stop analyzing him. It was an avoidance behavior on my part.

"You're taking this a lot better than I thought you would. I'm so relieved this won't affect your decision to continue therapy."

I wasn't sure what she'd expected. And then it hit me. They'd chosen to be together. Bitterness rose in my throat. As much as I wanted to deny it, what I felt for Daniel and Evan was the product of more than animal attraction. I liked them both a lot. Individually and together, they were just incredible people.

Though they were different from each other, they somehow both set me at ease. I didn't feel like I had to be anyone other than myself. Evan understood me in a way nobody else ever had, and Daniel was a quick study. He'd liked my quirkiness even before he'd known that I identified as neuroatypical.

All this time, I'd thought I'd successfully avoided developing strong feelings for Daniel or Evan. Now I knew I'd been lying to myself.

Urging them to be together—without me—was the best thing for their relationship. I was okay with being single. Since my divorce, I'd found freedom in not having to take care of a spouse, not having to compromise what I wanted and how I wanted to live for the sake of someone else's sensibilities. Adam was mostly a good person, but it had been exhausting to have to consider my every word and move, to weigh how he would react against the thoughts in my head or the actions I wanted to take.

As sorry as I was that they'd moved forward without me, I was equally relieved that I didn't have to alter my life to accommodate two more people's wants and needs. Working with neurotypicals was exhausting enough. When I went home, I wanted to be able to relax and be myself. Besides Clara and Deon, Zack was the only person who accepted me for who I was, warts and all. Daniel and Evan meant well, but neither of them had a real understanding of what it would be like to have me in their lives as more than a sexual partner.

I spent the rest of the day in a fog of somber acceptance.

Wednesday after work, I slid into comfortable clothes—pajamas—got together a plate of snacks and a glass of wine, and I set myself up to finish writing a chapter of my book. My outline was fantastic, and I'd found new research to support some of the findings I planned to discuss in that chapter.

Clara called to chat, and I finished off the wine and snacks while talking to her. I was pouring a second glass when the doorbell rang.

She heard it as well. Her volume dropped, though there was no way someone standing on the other side of my front door could hear her. "Are you expecting company?"

"Not that I know of." I looked through the peephole to find Daniel and Evan on the other side. My heartbeat sped up. Back when we were first dating, this is what it used to feel like when Adam dropped by unexpectedly—excitement and anticipation mixed with a little bit of dread and anxiety to keep me on my toes. "What do they want?"

I was whispering as well.

"Who?" Her volume was even quieter. "Do you need me to come over? Call the police? Alaina?"

"It's Daniel and Evan."

She made a thoughtful noise. "They didn't cancel on you, did they?" The question sounded more like an accusation, but I could have been wrong. Interpreting tone of voice was not one of my many talents.

"No, but they're engaged, so I figured that meant they weren't coming."

"What are you wearing?"

"Pajamas." The pants were a little too loose, and they hung on me in a way that wasn't flattering. The shirt draped down to my thighs, covering most of the mess. "I am not prepared for company."

She was quiet for two seconds. "Hon, are you standing at the door, looking through the peephole, and whispering to me while they stand out there and wait for you to open the door?"

"Yes."

She laughed. "Call me later with details. I'm hanging up now."

I didn't want to end the call. Clara was my lifeline and my security blanket. I wanted her to come over and answer the door for me.

But the call had ended. With a reticent sigh, I opened the door.

From the other side of the glass storm door, they both looked at me. Two gazes checked out my very comfortable, very un-sexy attire.

Daniel opened the outer door, and they filed inside.

I stepped back to allow the big guys some room. "I wasn't expecting you."

Evan cocked his head, and his mouth turned down. "You said Wednesday at six. We're a few minutes late because Daniel had to make sure his hair was just right."

Daniel shot Evan a nasty glance.

Before this went on for much longer, I said, "I hear congratulations are in order. I'm glad you talked. I think you're going to be very happy together."

Shades of confusion marred Daniel's kissable mouth. Evan's frown deepened. "Who told you we were engaged?"

Even though identifying tone wasn't my strong suit, his displeasure pummeled against me. Automatically defensive, I stepped back. "Does it matter?"

"No," Daniel said. "What matters is why you think that means we would stand you up tonight?"

He was far less upset. I responded to the softness of his voice. "You're engaged. You've made your decision. I didn't see a need for you to keep your appointment. I'd made other plans."

Daniel's gaze roved up and down me, and curiosity kept his lips parted. "Other plans? You look like you're ready to curl up on the sofa and watch TV until you fall asleep."

"Close. I was going to work on my book until ten, and I like to be comfortable when I write."

He glanced around the foyer. "Is Zack with his dad?"

"Yes."

Evan stepped forward, negating the distance I'd put between us. "How about you invite us in? We can sit down and discuss this; give it the attention it deserves."

My eyes blinked rapidly, a nervous tic that hadn't manifested in years. I hated the way it made reality seem like a stop-motion animation, and it contributed to my oncoming panic attack.

Evan scooped me up, lifting me in his arms like I was a child. "It's okay, Lainie. Breathe with me, okay?"

Being in his arms calmed me a lot more than anything he said. I leaned against his chest and squeezed my eyes shut to stop the nauseating filmstrip. Rather than breathe, I turned my face into his solid warmth, and I set my fingertips against his chest.

He sat down on my sofa with me still in his lap, and he was quiet while I shamelessly indulged one last time in what it felt like to be in his arms.

Then I felt Daniel's fingers smoothing my hair away from my face. "Lainie? What happened? What set you off?"

With a resigned exhalation, I forced myself away from Evan. He didn't stop me from climbing off his lap, though I noted the way his fingers flexed, as if they itched to keep me from moving. Daniel sat next to him, and he reached for me.

Evading his attempt, I parked myself across from them in a chair that matched the sofa where they sat.

"I thought that since you were engaged, we wouldn't have to have this conversation."

Daniel's mouth set hard. I liked that he never tried to mask his feelings. "You don't want to hear what we have to say?"

"I don't." Nothing they said would change my mind. The fact that they'd showed up could be explained away by their moral belief that they should break the news to me in person. It showed their respect for me.

But the fact that they were still here meant they hadn't changed their minds. Though they'd decided to wed each other, they still wanted me to take part in a ménage relationship.

"That's not exactly fair," Evan noted.

"I'm aware." I forced myself to meet his gaze. The raw pain in his eyes manifested as a physical pain in my belly. "I'm happy for you both, but none of the arguments against me participating in your relationship have changed."

Daniel leaned forward. "Alaina, I'm in love with you. I think I have been from the first moment I met you, only I thought I didn't stand a chance. You're so intelligent and funny, driven and caring, and so very beautiful. Evan has some pretty steep feelings for you as well."

Ripping my gaze from Evan, I noted Daniel's anguish, and I hated that I'd caused it. I closed my eyes to stop the panic attack from returning. "If I explain all the reasons this won't work, will you even listen to me?"

"No." Evan's voice sounded flat, but that didn't disguise the jagged edge dangling over my neck like a circular saw blade. "You're going to cite our long friendship and our closeness as an excuse to not even try."

So many things could—and would—go wrong between one of them and me, and it would negatively impact their relationship with each other. What if Evan never fell in love with me? What if I found I preferred one man more than the other? Jealousy had so many ways into that mess, and I was reticent to try for so many other reasons.

I'd already had a failed marriage, and I'd found I liked being single.

I had a son to protect. In his whole life, he'd only met three men I'd dated. Two of those had been colleagues first, which was how Zack had come to meet them at all.

I was always busy, and I didn't see how I had the time to devote to growing and maintaining a relationship with one partner, much less two.

Forcing my brain to address the reason Evan had cited, I said, "It's a valid concern."

Daniel rubbed his jaw. "You're afraid you'd come between us. That won't happen."

"You can't know that."

"We're solid, Lainie," he continued. "As you requested, Evan and I have talked at length about what we want and what it would look like to live in a thruple."

The two exchanged a glance, and they both smiled.

Focusing on a point behind them both, I inhaled deeply and held it for a long moment before letting it out. "You barely know me, Daniel, and Evan, you don't really know me at all. We had sex, and it was good. Really good. Excellent, in fact."

Oh, lordy. There went my imagination, showing me a slideshow of all the ways they'd rocked my world so far.

Evan took advantage of my pause. "We're in the beginning stages of a relationship. I freely admit that we need to spend more time together. But if we're committed to making it work, then we can't fail. Relationships are about commitment and the work you put into them. We're prepared to do the work."

"I'm not." The denial burst from me. It painted me in a bad light, but they needed to stop looking at me through sex-covered glasses. "I'm not prepared to do the work. I'm not willing to gamble on a relationship with two men who are more than a decade younger than I am. I like not having to hide my reactions or watch my phrasing when I speak or evaluate my emotions before I express them. I like not having to apologize for not wanting to hold hands or flinching from unexpected touches. I like sleeping alone. It is exhausting to be around people who expect me to be like them when I'm just not."

A tear splashed down my cheek, and I swiped it away because it itched.

"You're both young and hopeful, and that's a great thing. But we're in different places in our lives. I like you both. I find you both attractive. But it's not enough. I wish you a lifetime of happiness, which I'm confident is very achievable without me."

Forcing myself to look at them, to face whatever negative reaction they were going to have, I lowered my gaze to meet Evan's and then Daniel's.

I found them both staring at me, their expressions inscrutable.

After a long time, Evan nodded. "I hear what you're saying."

Daniel glanced at him. "Seriously?"

"Yes," Evan maintained. "She expressed her wishes, and it's our job to respect them."

Daniel's frown pointed in my direction, though I was reasonably certain he wasn't happy with Evan. "You're giving up?"

I wasn't sure if he was addressing me or Evan, but I had a ready response. "It was just supposed to be a couple of fun nights, and it was. Let's not make it into something it's not."

He didn't like my response, but Daniel finally seemed resigned to accepting my refusal. "Are we still friends?"

I'd never considered Daniel a friend. We didn't talk much about our personal lives, but we did have polite and friendly conversations while we went over the logistics of the self-defense and therapy program. Even our text conversations were superficial. He called sometimes, but I'd been so busy, we hadn't been able to talk for more than a few minutes. I liked him as a person, and I looked forward to returning to our previous relationship. I smiled, the first genuine one that evening. "Yes. We're still friends."

He spread his palms. "Can we be the kind of friends who hook up every Friday for a threesome? Evan could plan scenes, or we could have unscripted, sexy fun."

Evan seemed as surprised by Daniel's proposal as I felt. He stared at his fiancé as he scratched below his ear. "Daniel, she just said no to all of that.'

"No, she said no to having a relationship with us. I'm not talking about having a relationship. I'm asking to be friends with benefits. And, since I know how much Alaina likes to schedule things, I was thinking that having a standing Friday night deal would work for her."

Gears turned in Evan's brain. His blue eyes took on a delighted sparkle. "That could work. If something comes up, any of us can cancel at any time for any reason. You wouldn't even have to give a reason. I could set up a group text, and you could just say whether the coming Friday would work for you or not."

This was progressing quickly and in a direction I hadn't predicted. Did I want to have regular sex with two insanely hot, younger men? Yes, but I had a one-track mind, and it was steadily beating a cadence of do-not-engage. Daniel, I was finding, was a master negotiator.

I shook my head. "That's not a good idea."

Seemingly unaffected by my refusal, Daniel rubbed his hands together. "Since we're still friends, and I'm starving, we should eat. Evan and I were going to take you out for a romantic dinner, but since that's off the table, how about you let us take you out to a regular dinner?"

I looked down at my clothes, and I thought about where a night like the one he was proposing could lead. "Thanks, but I already ate. Why don't the two of you go ahead and have that romantic dinner to celebrate your engagement?"

Chapter 18—Daniel

Too much, too fast.

That's the reason Evan had given for Alaina's refusal to date us. We'd asked for too much from her in too short of a time period. Alaina was a planner. She liked routine and when things happened as expected. The unknown was a dark, scary place she preferred to avoid. Staying away from her for an entire week sucked. At least I had a competition to attend Saturday, and I fielded congratulatory calls from relatives as word got around that I was getting married.

And being with Evan helped. We cleared my stuff out of the loft and started renovating it into practice space for classes. With the space from the sandwich shop that was closing down and the loft freed up, I was considering expanding class offerings to include yoga and pilates. Evan was working with an architect to reconfigure the small classroom downstairs into locker rooms with showers, and I also needed to install an elevator. The upper floor of the sandwich shop was already used for offices and storage, and I planned to use that for my office. If my business grew accordingly, I'd need to hire office help.

Alaina came into the studio Wednesday with her shoulders slumped, and the usual sparkle was missing from her honeyed eyes. Some of it returned as she greeted the class participants, but it died out when her gaze landed on me.

Sophia noticed immediately and shoved me into my office. Piss and vinegar spouted like steam from every pore of her body. Shutting the door cut off the chatter from the lobby and sealed my fate. She crossed her arms and glared at me. "What the fuck did you do?"

"Me?" I knew she was asking about why Alaina had dark circles under her eyes and a sudden frailty about her, but I didn't know why she thought it was my fault. "What are you talking about?"

"I told Alaina that you and Evan were engaged so she wouldn't be blindsided by anything the next time she saw you."

I seized upon the flaw in her plan to blame me for Alaina's appearance. "*You* told her, and you're blaming me? If she's upset about Evan and me, that's not my fault. I didn't do anything wrong."

Sophia inhaled, her lips pressed together and lava boiling in her eyes. "She was fine when I left, but Danny, she looks like someone died."

My mouth fell open. "What if someone did die? And you're in here, accusing me of I don't even know what, and she's out there, trying to put on a brave face when she lost someone close to her?"

Sitting abruptly and slumping down in a chair, Sophia washed a hand down her face. "I'm sorry, Daniel. You didn't do anything wrong, and Alaina wasn't at all upset when I told her that you and Evan were engaged. She was happy for you."

I fucking hated that Lainie looked so out of sorts. I wanted to wrap my arms around her and make all the bad parts better, but I didn't have that right.

With another sigh, Sophia straightened up. "I feel like there's something you're not telling me, Daniel. I don't like secrets between us. It hurts to think that you don't trust me with important things."

Crouching down, I took her hands in mind. "Soph, I may not tell you everything, but that's okay. You don't tell me everything that's between you and Drew, and I don't tell you everything that's between Evan and me. That doesn't mean I don't trust you."

I left Alaina out of it. I wasn't ready to confide to my sister that I was in love with her. She'd probably picked up on that, and that's why she was making wild accusations.

I tugged her to her feet. "How about I start class, and you ask Alaina about what's bothering her?"

Sophia studied me, her discerning gaze reading my face and possibly my mind. "I don't think she'll tell me anything."

"You can offer friendship and a sympathetic shoulder." Opening the door, I herded her out of my office. "Maybe she doesn't tell you anything, but that doesn't mean the gesture was pointless. Sometimes it's enough to know somebody cares about what you're going through."

I planned to wait until afterward, when I got to see Alaina alone, to talk to her.

As I ran the participants through warm-ups, I watched Sophia and Alaina talking in the lobby. As Sophia had thought, Alaina declined to pour out her woes. But I was right that the simple act of asking made a difference. Alaina squared her shoulders, and a real smile curved her mouth.

Sophia and Alaina joined the class for warm-ups. I was pleasantly surprised that Alaina was still participating in class. Judging from the welcoming smiles from the other members, it was the right move.

I helped out with one of the demonstrations, and then I left. Early on, I'd realized that my involvement could be counterproductive. This gave me time to pop in on an intermediate class being taught by one of my advanced students who'd turned out to be a pretty good teacher. Time passed quickly, and soon Alaina was the only one left downstairs.

I entered the small arena to find her cleaning up the way she normally did. The smile from earlier had faded, and she appeared exhausted. Taking a folded chair from her, I pushed her into one that was still open. "Sit, Lainie. Rest a bit. I'll clean up."

"Thanks." She got up and went to where she'd put her bag on the counter. "I'm going to leave."

Before she made it halfway to the door, I said, "Are you upset with me?"

She froze in place. "No. I told you I was happy for you, and I meant it."

"Then, what? Why do you look like you haven't slept in days?"

"Zack has been having panic attacks. Adam is getting divorced, and Zack somehow got it into his head that it's his fault." Tears filled her eyes.

Before the first one spilled out, I had my arms around her. I held her against me tightly, cradling her head as she cried. With all my being, I wished I could do more to help her than just hold her in my arms. My heart ached, a dim echo of what she must be feeling.

"We've both told him that he had nothing to do with it, but he thinks that if he'd behaved better, then Cameron wouldn't have left. Adam doesn't want to tell him that Cameron cheated and that Adam threw him out, which I support because little kids don't need to be part of adult drama, but Zack is smart. He knows he's not getting the full story, and he's internalized that doubt." She pulled back, sniffling and reaching into her bag for tissue. "It tears me up to watch him work himself into a panic attack. We're working on calming techniques, but he's my kid, so he doesn't want to listen to me. This morning, I found him punching a pile of pillows. I hadn't realized he'd internalized that much anger."

Here, she fell apart again. Sobs wracked her body, shaking her so hard that I scooped her up and sat down on the floor with her in my lap. I petted her hair in what I hoped was a soothing gesture, and I rocked her as she let out what was probably a week's worth of emotion. Once the storm began abating, I planted little kisses on her forehead and made soothing noises.

I had no idea how long I held her, but after a time, she realized she was on my lap and in my arms. Her whole body stiffened, and she scooted until her bottom was on the floor. "I'm sorry. I shouldn't have done that."

Perhaps because I hated being helpless when someone I cared about went through emotional Hell, but the apology rubbed me the wrong way. "Why? Because we're suddenly not friends? Because you think turning me down means I don't care about you or that I'd be happy in the face of your distress? I'm not an asshole, Lainie."

Her mouth opened into an O, a shape that matched the widening of her red-rimmed eyes. "I just meant that I wouldn't have burdened you before, so I shouldn't do it now. I should be trying to restore the association we had before we broke the rules."

The lawyer side of my brain wanted to seize on the idea of these fictional rules she thought we'd broken, but the rational side of me won out. Alaina's life revolved around rules and expectations, and railing against supposed rules wasn't going to do anything but make her feel attacked.

"Lainie, nothing's going to go back to the way it was before. I'm always going to care about you. The romantic aspects aside, I *like* you. I like your personality and your brains. I like talking with you. I love your offbeat sense of humor and the way you seem organized, but you're really not."

Her eyes sparkled like amber in the sunlight, though this was a trick of residual tears and florescent lighting, and she didn't bother to hide her shock. "You really do consider me a friend."

"I do."

She dabbed a tissue under her eyes to wipe away where they still leaked. "You're a good person, Daniel. I'm glad you were able to move on so quickly."

I hadn't moved on one bit. Evan and I had long-term plans that required we forge a solid friendship with Alaina, and I was in a prime spot to get that ball rolling. But she didn't need to know that now.

I got to my feet and helped her up. "I'd invite you upstairs to wash your face, but Evan tore out the loft and is in the middle of converting it to practice space."

"You're expanding?"

"I'm going to move classes upstairs and put in a gym and kickboxing ring down here."

She glanced around, possibly picturing what it might look like. "Daniel? Would it be weird if I signed Zack up for a class? I think he needs a physical outlet for his emotions, and I read that martial arts are a great way to help him with that."

"I think that's a fabulous idea."

Evan and I had agonized about how we were going to find ways to hang with Alaina, and she'd come up with a good solution. I reined in my urge to grin and strut out of the room, and I led her to the lobby.

Flyers for beginner classes were on the display table on the other side of the lobby. I handed one to her. "Beginner classes don't officially start until September, but you can bring him by next week, and I'll work him into the class."

"Oh, I wasn't looking for special treatment."

"Let it go, Lainie. You could have asked me this a year ago, and I would have given you the same answer."

She hugged me briefly, a quick squeeze that was over before I could return it. "Thank you, Daniel. I appreciate it."

The next couple months passed quickly. I didn't see Alaina nearly as often as I wanted. Evan made a habit of popping into the studio Monday afternoons, and he sat with Alaina while she waited for Zack. The pair progressed from stilting and awkward conversation to easy companionship. I took over teaching the beginner class that Zack was in, and the two of us formed a quick bond. Kids tended to like me anyway, and Zack came in with a positive attitude because Alaina had said nice things about me at home.

On Thursday evenings, Evan and I showed up at her place with a pie. Just like everything else, the first time was forced, but after that, it got easier. She'd invite us in, and the three of us would have pie while we talked about myriad topics. A few times, her friend Clara joined us. Evan got a kick out of the way Clara bossed Alaina around and took care of her. It seemed his little subbie looked for alpha characteristics even in her friends.

Alaina hadn't been kidding about Zack's panic attacks or how wrenching they were to witness. The first one I witnessed came at the end of a session during the second month of class. Adam picked him up on Wednesdays. The man was standoffish and a bit icy with me, but he was warm and encouraging with his son. And today, he was late, which was not a new thing. Sometimes Alaina showed up instead, and she took Zack out to dinner before handing him over to Adam.

At the end of class, the other students poured into the lobby. Zack stood in the back corner of the room, facing a wall. His chest heaved, and his face was beet red. The workout hadn't been strenuous. Some kids had worked up a sweat, but it wasn't anything that should lead to that kind of physical distress.

Concerned, I jogged over, and that's when I saw he was clutching at his chest.

"Zack? Buddy? What's going on?"

"My heart hurts," he gasped. "I can't breathe."

Since he was gulping large amounts of air and his lips weren't blue, I knew he was getting enough oxygen. Probably too much. I had him sit on the floor and lean back against the wall.

"Slow down your breathing, Zack. Watch me. Breathe with me." Sitting in front of him, I modeled deep, calm breaths, and he followed my lead. "Let your hands fall by your sides. That's it."

Slowly, I coached him through relaxation techniques I'd found online. I'd researched them after Alaina had told me Zack was having attacks. After ten or so minutes, his color returned to normal, as did his breathing.

He looked up at me with those discerning honey-colored eyes that were exactly like Alaina's, and he gave me a sad smile. "Thank you, Mr. Daniel. I feel better now."

I glanced around. The next class was getting set up, but I wasn't teaching it. Adam hadn't arrived yet. Since we were out of the way, I didn't suggest Zack move. "Do you want to tell me what set you off?"

Now Zack scanned the room. "I'm supposed to have dinner with my grandparents and Uncle Cameron tonight, and I don't want to go."

I knew that Cameron was Alaina's brother, and so I figured he referred to her parents. Keeping my tone neutral, I asked, "Why not?"

His gaze dropped, his face paled, and he looked like he was going to be sick.

Worry and dread prickled the back of my neck. "Zack, we're friends. You can tell me anything."

"Do you promise to keep it a secret?"

"If I can, I will." I didn't make a blanket promise because I knew better.

He sighed. "Uncle Cameron keeps saying mean things about my mom, and my grandma keeps telling me that I should tell my mom and dad to let Uncle Cameron have custody of me for part of the week."

I pressed my lips together. Alaina had told me the barest details about why she didn't have a relationship with her family, and this only further clarified what she'd escaped. "You don't like what they're saying, and you want them to stop."

"I told them to stop, and I got yelled at. Mr. Daniel, I really don't want to go to dinner with them tonight."

Glancing up, I spotted Adam in the doorway. He watched us with a frown furrowing his brow. "Zack, I know it's hard, but I think you should tell your dad that you don't want to go."

He looked over to where his dad was standing, and he slowly got to his feet. "If I do that, then he won't get back with Uncle Cam. He's so sad all the time since Uncle Cam left."

"I think he'll be even sadder if you don't tell him how you're feeling. You have valid concerns, Zack, and keeping them a secret from your dad isn't going to make anything better."

"But he'll tell my mom, and she's going to get mad. Really mad. She cries when she's mad. Then she'll get sad and cry even more. I can't stand it when she cries."

This kid was carrying too much baggage for someone so young. I tried to give him some perspective. "Zack, being happy or sad or anxious or angry are all normal, human emotions. It's okay to have them, and it's okay for other people to have them. If your mom gets mad or sad and cries, then just give her a hug until she stops. She'll still want to know what you're going through."

He took my hand and looked up at me as we skirted the perimeter of the room. "Mr. Daniel, my mom is going to be home all alone. There isn't anybody there to hug her."

I gave his hand a little squeeze. "Don't worry about your mom. She'll be here tonight, and I'll take care of her. Okay? So be honest, and trust that your mom will be among friends."

We'd made it to Adam. His questioning gaze slid from Zack to me and back again. "What's going on?"

I let go of Zack's hand and encouraged him to go to his father. "Zack had a bit of a panic attack tonight. He's doing better, but there's something he wants to talk to you about."

At the mention of the panic attack, Adam's eyes widened. He put his arm around Zack and pulled him closer. To me, he said, "Thank you. I appreciate you taking the time to help him calm down."

"No problem." I held up my fist, and Zack bumped his into mine. "I'll see you next week, Zack."

"Bye, Mr. Daniel."

I watched them leave the building, and I pinpointed the exact moment Zack revealed the cause of his upset to his father. Adam got on his knees in the parking lot, grasped Zack by the shoulders, said a few words, and then hugged him tightly.

That night when I came in to help put away chairs, I found Alaina on her cell phone. Her lips were compressed into a thin line as she listened. I couldn't make out what Adam was saying, but I heard enough to distinguish his voice.

I stowed chairs quietly, staying out of her way as her body vibrated with anger.

Evan appeared in the doorway. He'd been working on the remodel of my place several evenings each week and on the weekends. My dad and I were helping, and some of Evan's brothers stopped by every now and again to give us a hand. The upstairs was nearly ready to open as classroom space. Next weekend, I had a crew coming to add an elevator shaft at the other end of the building. I would lose my office space temporarily, but I'd make it up in the long run with increased profitability.

His jeans were dusty, and his shirt had sweat stains, and he looked fantastic. All he needed was a tool belt, and he'd be my construction worker fantasy come to life. The thought made me laugh because he *was* my construction worker fantasy come to life. I crossed to him, a smile on my face because just seeing him made me happy. He wrapped his arms around me. Our kiss started out innocently enough, but smoldering heat caught flame. He pressed me to the wall and deepened the kiss.

By the time he broke away, we were both breathing heavily. He pressed a kiss to my lips one more time. "I'm finished upstairs. Want me to help put away chairs?"

"Sure."

Evan turned around and muttered, "Crap."

I peered around him to find that Alaina had gone. I rushed to the front window to find her standing next to her car, her hand with the car keys waving in the air as she spoke into the phone. I didn't need to hear her words to know she was ripping Adam a new asshole.

"She left without us noticing." Evan rubbed his chin.

"She hasn't left yet." The front door was still unlocked, so I went outside to run after her. Evan was at my heels. We screeched to a halt in front of her.

"He's selfish, Adam. You knew that before you married him. He doesn't care about anyone but himself. He never has, and he never will. I forbid you from letting Zack be alone with Cameron or my parents. If you want them to continue to have a relationship, it needs to be under adult supervision."

As she listened to Adam's response, shades of confusion tempered the worst of her fury. She shot a frown at Evan and me, making it clear that we were the source of her bewilderment.

"I made my position on that quite clear many times. Don't pressure him to consent to meeting with them again. He's eight, Adam, and he's a good kid. He doesn't want to disappoint you." She covered the phone with one hand, which didn't mute anything, and said to us, "I'm sorry I can't stick around to clean up. Family emergency."

She meant to dismiss us, but we weren't going anywhere.

Turning away, she opened her car door. "Yes." She shot a look over her shoulder at me. "Hi, Zack. No, baby. I'm okay. I'm just worried about you. I didn't know Uncle Cameron and the Wepplers were being big jerks to you. Yes, he is."

This time, when she looked at me, she smiled. "Okay. Goodnight, sweetheart. I love you." She ended the call and slid her phone into her purse. "You told Zack that you would hug me?"

The day had been crazy busy, but I'd made sure to fill Evan in about what happened with Zack. It was one reason he'd stuck around so late. He'd wanted to be there for Alaina as well.

I strove for casual. "A friendly hug. He was afraid you'd get mad and sad, and that both emotions make you cry. He didn't want you to cry alone."

Up until that moment, she hadn't looked like she was close to busting loose. Now tears streamed down her cheeks. "He's such a good-hearted boy. I'm glad he won't be around Cameron anymore."

Evan and I flanked her, and we engulfed her in our dual embrace. She melted between us for all of ten seconds, and then she pushed us away.

"You guys are good-hearted as well. Thank you for looking out for me. I'm okay. I'm relieved to know what triggered his panic attacks. If I had known he was dining with my parents, I would have figured it out a long time ago. They give me panic attacks, and I'm a lot older than he is. Daniel, thank you for getting him to open up. He just idolizes you." She looked up, catching my gaze for a heartbeat, and she took a tremulous breath.

A hint of a blush stained her cheeks, and it deepened when she looked to Evan. "Thank you for the hug. I needed that."

He opened his mouth to respond, but nothing came out. Their gazes locked, and a poignant moment passed between them. I thought he might kiss her. His head tipped the slightest amount, but he stopped before he got anywhere.

She tore her gaze away and put distance between her and us. "Thank you both. I'll see you tomorrow night. Maybe bring something chocolate?"

"Absolutely." I grinned, happy that she'd carved out a recurring place for us in her weekly schedule.

We watched her go. I clasped Evan's hand in mine. "You didn't make a move."

"She's upset. I don't want to kiss her when she's vulnerable." He heaved a sigh. "But it's taking an awfully long time."

Chapter 19—Evan

"I can't believe you haven't practiced the new song." Bryn parked her hands on her hips and growled at me.

Used to her theatrics, I finished drying the plate in my hand, and I put it in the cupboard. "I've been working a lot. Business is good, and most evenings and weekends, I've been working on Daniel's place. I haven't had more than a handful of evenings to get out my guitar."

She huffed again, adding a foot stomp for good measure. "You're doing an awful lot of free work for Daniel."

I dried a glass and put it away. "You say that like he's not my fiancé and we're not getting married."

Daniel sauntered into the kitchen. We were planning to meet friends at a bar with an open mic night. It wasn't the one we usually went to, but Sophia had convinced us to give it a try. To that end, Daniel was dressed to impress. His dark, wavy hair was perfectly coiffed. His jeans hugged his lower half in all the right ways, and he paired that with a light green Henley shirt that brought out the undertones of olive skin.

He threw an arm around Bryn's shoulders and leaned in to whisper conspiratorially. "I pay him with sex."

"Oh, eww." Bryn made a face and shoved him away. "You could pay quicker and give him time to practice our song."

Daniel let her go and pulled me to him. "Finesse takes time, Bryn. If you're with a guy who doesn't take his time, trade him in for one that does." Then he kissed me thoroughly, showing Bryn exactly what taking his time looked like.

When he let me go, I went back to drying the dishes. Bryn was sitting at the small dining table, scrolling through something on her phone.

Daniel sat across from her. "Seriously, though, he did practice. But he's being a perfectionist about it. I think you could do the new song tonight, and he'll be fine."

"We haven't practiced the harmonies together enough," I protested.

"Practice now," Daniel said. "I'll tell you if you're ready or not."

I got my guitar, and Bryn and I sang the folksy song she'd written. We sounded great for most of it, though Bryn was definitely the better singer. My voice lent depth to hers, but that was about all I was good for.

"That's my favorite one yet." He clapped in appreciation. "Bryn, you're getting noticeably better at songwriting."

I knew Daniel wouldn't tell me the song was good if it wasn't. When he didn't like one of Bryn's songs, he refrained from commenting on it at all.

The bar was closer to Sophia's house, so it took a little time to get there. Bryn drove us in her brand new car. She'd just graduated from college, and she landed a job teaching music at the elementary school we'd attended. Right now, she lived with our parents while she saved for a down payment on a permanent place. I'd heard rumblings from my dad that she had her eye on my condo, since I wasn't going to be there for much longer.

Daniel absolutely hated the condo's small rooms.

Bryn picked up Kaitlyn, a teacher friend from work, on the way, and by the time we arrived at the bar, the four of us were laughing and chatting like longtime friends.

Laskies Bar was situated at the end of a block of mixed retail stores and restaurants. The inside was moderately lit and decorated in metal and neon. A rectangular bar dominated the back. Tables were scattered through the room, though a small dance floor near the tiny stage had been cleared. People danced on the floor and on the stage.

"It's more like a club than a bar," Daniel noted. "I don't see a sign advertising open mic night."

I wouldn't be upset if I didn't have to perform a song I wasn't a hundred percent certain about in front of a roomful of strangers. A lot of people didn't care if they sounded good or not, but I did. Whether it was crown molding or a song, I aimed for perfection.

Bryn squealed. "I see Sophia and Drew." She grabbed her friend's arm, and the pair took off.

Daniel and I watched them wind through the crowd while we figured out where they were headed.

"I see them." Daniel took my hand, and I followed him to where his sister was sitting.

Sophia hugged Daniel, and she kissed my cheek. Then she handed me a token. "I signed you up already. The sheet filled up quickly, and I had to arm bar someone just to get the last spot."

Having seen Sophia kick ass in the studio, I had no problem picturing her taking out a slew of people just to get me a spot, though I knew she was kidding about being violent. "Thanks. I appreciate you looking out for us."

She laughed and ordered a pitcher of beer.

As we were last, I settled in to socialize with friends and watch two hours of diverse performance offerings. I tuned out during a banjo performance to listen to Drew relate an experience he had with a weird catering request.

Time passed, and soon Bryn was tugging on my arm. "It's time to tune your guitar."

The song she'd written was optimistic about finding love, and it had a catchy refrain. As Bryn started singing, people took to the dance floor. That had never happened before. She glanced back at me, a huge smile on her face. Then she gave her full attention to the audience.

I looked out there to see Alaina on the dance floor. Shocked to see her unexpectedly, I messed up the rhythm for a couple measures. She held a colorful drink in one hand as she swayed in time to the music. A flowing black dress draped down her body and swirled around her thighs. It was sleeveless, and the neckline veered down enough to reveal a tantalizing peek of her cleavage. Clara was next to her. As the tempo of the song picked up, Clara and Alaina danced together, twirling each other around the small space. I could tell Alaina had a little too much alcohol in her system because she stumbled into people three times.

Twice, she fell against the same man. The second time, he laughed, and he joined in with the way she and Clara were dancing. I didn't know who he was, and I didn't care for the way he was trying to make a move on her. The guy did a move where he curled her in his arm and spun her out. She went flying into a chest—Daniel's chest.

Relief flowed through me.

Her head fell back as she looked up, and a huge smile broke out on her face.

He took the drink from her hand and gave it to Clara, and then he took over dancing with her. I sang the last chorus with a lot more enthusiasm. When we finished, the crowd roared their approval with laughter, whistles, and cheers. Bryn beamed as we left the stage.

I abandoned her to Kaitlyn, and I pushed through the throng on the dance floor to get to Daniel and Alaina. The bar had switched to house music, and a pulsating song blared through the speakers.

When I found them, Alaina's arms were wrapped around Sophia's neck. She hugged Sophia tightly, and then she said something. I couldn't hear over the music, but her lips seemed to be forming a declaration of love. She did the same thing to Drew, then Clara, and then she came to me.

Her face lit up. She jumped as she threw her arms around my neck, so she landed with her legs around my waist. I caught her with my hands firmly planted on her luscious little ass. She smacked a kiss on my cheek and said, "It's my birthday!"

I had no idea. We'd taken an apple pie over to her place last night, and she hadn't said a thing about her impending celebration. A slow grin spread over my face. "Happy birthday, Lainie. I'm happy to give you a spanking."

She laughed as she wiggled to be set down. Once she was on her feet, she shook her finger in my direction. "You're a naughty boy."

"Oh, honey, say the word. I'll be as naughty as you want."

Though she heard me, her attention went to Bryn. She hugged my sister and kissed her cheek. "I loved that song, Bryn. It was so good! What a great way to end open mic night. Clara wouldn't let me read my poem."

Clara intervened. She pried Alaina away from Bryn. "You're going to thank me for that later, when you read it over again and see how bad that poem is."

I knew Alaina liked writing bad poetry, but it was the funny kind of bad, so I didn't see why she shouldn't share. "Aww, Clara. You should've let her. After all, it's her birthday."

"Not until midnight," Clara said. "And no, that poem needs to not be shared. Not only was it awful, but it was about all the things she shouldn't have done in her life. She needs positivity moving forward, not another night to drunkenly dwell on the negatives."

Alaina bounced up and down, clapping. "It was called *Shouldn't've*. I like that word because it's a double contraction for *should not have*. I got it from the Buzzcocks' song. You know the one?"

I had no idea what she was talking about. "I've never heard of the Buzzcocks."

Rolling her eyes, Alaina made a sound of disgust. Then she sang— badly. I made out some of the words, enough to know it was about falling in love with someone you shouldn't've fallen in love with. The lyrics hit me hard.

I looked to Daniel to find him similarly affected. He grasped her arm and leaned down to make his comment private. "You wrote a poem about how we shouldn't've fallen in love with you?"

Her eyes widened. "No. It's about how I shouldn't've fallen in love with you. I started off with Adam, but then I took him out because he gave me Zack, and that little boy is the light of my life. I wouldn't trade him for the world. So, I took Adam out even though he was the first guy I shouldn't've fallen for."

Daniel's frown didn't ease.

"But—" She slapped her palm against Daniel's chest. "You shouldn't've either. You have Evan, and he's dreamy."

Even though she was reiterating all the reasons she thought we shouldn't be together, I liked that she called me dreamy. "Do you dream about me, Lainie?"

"Only when I'm awake." She glanced around the immediate area. Sophia and Drew danced on the other side of Daniel. Bryn and Kaitlyn had drifted off and were surrounded by admirers. Clara stood off to one side, giving us some side-eye.

Alaina didn't seem to notice her friend's disapproval. She grabbed Clara's hands. "My drink is gone. Let's get another one with a pink umbrella—ella—ella."

Once she left us, I slid my arms around Daniel so we could dance together and discuss a strategy for tonight. "She said she's fallen in love with us."

Daniel didn't look very impressed. "She's told everyone tonight that she loves them."

"But she didn't put them in a poem."

"She's inebriated, and she doesn't seem inclined to want to change that status," Daniel observed. He parked a hand on my hip and the other played with my hair.

"Yes, but this unique opportunity has afforded us valuable insight into her psyche."

With a curl to his lip, Daniel tilted his head and chuckled. "Who the fuck *are* you?"

"You're attracted to intelligence. I'm trying it on."

He pulled me closer and brushed his lips across mine. "I already know how smart you are, Ev. I don't want you to be anybody but yourself because that's the man I love."

Being with Daniel had always felt good, but now that we were together, he continually surprised me with how romantic he could be. I kissed him, taking control with the masterful slant of my lips and my larger-than-life presence. He melted against me, submitting to my erotic demand.

Before things escalated to indecent, Sophia and Drew bumped into us. Given the force used, I knew Sophia had done it on purpose. Breaking off, we gave her our attention.

Drew lifted a sympathetic shoulder, but Sophia scowled. "I don't know what you two assholes are doing, but I will find out."

Daniel grinned. "It's called kissing, and I feel sorry for Drew if you haven't figured out how to do that yet."

She punched his arm. He saw the full force coming at him, and he countered the move, shoving her trajectory away.

"Geez, Sophia. What the hell is wrong with you?"

She stabbed a finger at me, and then she did the same to Daniel. "I saw the way Alaina greeted both of you. It was far from innocent. So help me, if you two fuck things up with her, I will murder you both in your sleep."

Daniel sported a bigger grin, and I knew I wore one as well. Alaina certainly hadn't hidden her affinity for us beneath her usual professionalism.

"Don't sweat it, Sophia. We're friends. Didn't Daniel tell you we go over to her house every Thursday and have pie?"

"Pie?" Drew threw his head back, roaring with laughter. "That's what you're calling it?"

Channeling his best facsimile of indignation, Daniel drew his eyebrows into a sharp V and scowled. "It's literally pie. Yesterday was apple pie. Last week was cherry pie. The week before was chocolate mousse. Sometimes we have it with milk, and sometimes there's wine. Evan is getting pretty good at rolling out a crust. We've been doing this for a couple of months."

Sophia blinked, her expression both incredulous and suspicious. "You're both up to something. This isn't a game."

Daniel dropped all pretense, as did I.

"No," I said. "It's not a game. We're both in love with her, but she's not on board with being a thruple. So, we're settling on friendship—for now."

Sophia sputtered, starting and stopping several sentences, but nothing came out.

Drew said, "I think what Sophia is trying to say is that she's not sure what you're doing is wise or in the best interest of the therapy program you both run."

"Yeah," Daniel said. "She keeps saying that. Sophia, we're not pressuring her for anything. We're moving forward with our life together, and we've extended an open invitation for her to join us. That's all. Alaina's fine with our current situation. She writes us into her schedule and everything."

"Okay, warning given and received," Drew said. "My Queen, may I suggest we head home, and I can give you a full body massage?"

Sophia didn't look at all placated, but she went with Drew.

"Let's go find our lady fair and make sure she's not a damsel in distress."

Daniel laughed at my description, but he led the way to Alaina's table. It turned out that she was not out with just Clara, but with several friends from the University. She introduced us, but I didn't catch all their names.

We hung out for a while. As the night wore on, and she indulged in her fourth Mai Tai, I slung my arm around the back of her chair and leaned closer for a private conversation. "Lainie, how are you getting home tonight?"

She pointed to Clara. "She was the designated driver, but we're just gonna call for a ride. We'll come back tomorrow and get my car."

I held out a hand. "Give me your keys."

"Yes, Sir."

I started at her use of my title, coming out of nowhere like it did, but I saw no sign she was attempting humor or sarcasm.

She handed them over without a second thought, and she went back to discussing strange things graduate students had requested.

"Stay here," I ordered Daniel. "We're driving her home. I'm going to let Bryn know."

While I could text my sister, I preferred to tell her in person. I'd already confided in her about Alaina. Always loyal, Bryn was cheering for my success.

Not that tonight was a move toward success. No moves would be made while she was intoxicated.

Daniel drove home. Alaina and Clara occupied the backseat, which was a constant source of laughter, slurred speech, and declarations of love and adoration. Listening to them, we found out how they'd met and many of the adventures Clara scheduled for Alaina.

We dropped Clara off at her house. She lived in a neighborhood near the University. It was full of smaller family homes marked by meticulous landscaping and, owing to the late hour, dark windows. I helped her out of the backseat, and I walked her to her door. "Are you okay to go inside alone?"

She giggled, and I caught her as she tripped going up the porch steps. "I'm fine. Just a little tipsy still. Alaina is freaking trashed. You're gonna need to put her directly into bed."

"We will."

As she dug in her purse for her house keys, Clara chuckled. "That's not what I'm talking about. You give her an aspirin and a glass of water, and make her go to sleep. Do not try to make your move tonight."

Since I didn't know Clara very well, I forgave her for thinking I was that much of a jerk. "Clara, I would never make a move on a drunk person."

"Good." She unlocked her door. Just before she went inside, she said, "Alaina tells me everything. We both know what you're doing."

I hadn't known Alaina was aware of our stealth campaign, but I didn't bother to deny anything. "You don't approve?"

Clara inhaled deeply. "I don't disapprove. As long as she's happy, I'm happy."

"Her happiness is our ultimate goal."

"Yeah. Well, you're closer than you think." She squeezed my wrist, and then she went inside.

I returned to the car with a doofy grin on my face. I opened the front door to hear Alaina protest. "Nobody is back here with me, and now I'm all alone. I don't wanna be alone on my birthday."

"It's after midnight," Daniel reasoned. "Your birthday was yesterday."

"Nope. I was born at midnight. Tenacal—Teni--Tenicly, my birthday is today." She paused. "Ten-ta-cle-ly. No. Thas not the word. What's the word?"

"Technically," Daniel supplied.

"Yes." She unbuckled her seatbelt to lean forward and pat him on the shoulder. "Tenicly. Not like a squid. Thank you."

"Anytime." To me, he said. "You should sit in the back with her so she doesn't try to climb into the front seat."

She bounced and clapped as I slid into the seat next to her. *Technically*, I had to pick her up and scoot her over because she was somehow sitting in all three seats at once. Daniel drove off as I was trying to get her back into a seat belt.

She grabbed my hand, touching her palm to mine, and let loose with a gleeful laugh. "If I was drunk all the time, we could hold hands."

Grinning at her uncontained delight, I stopped trying to get her to settle down. "I guess that's looking on the bright side."

Her lips mashed into mine, and our teeth collided. I hadn't seen the kiss coming, so I was unprepared for the attempt.

"Ouch."

"Alaina, you've had a lot to drink tonight."

"I know. I feel great, and I wish you'd call me Lainie."

Calling her by that name was supposed to signal the start of a scene, or at least that she was my submissive. "I wish I could call you that as well."

Somehow she catapulted from her seat to mine, and she landed straddling my lap. Her face was inches from mine, and she trailed her fingertips from my temple and down my neck. "How about just once? You can whisper it."

No part of me wanted to deny this temptress. "Lainie."

Before I finished uttering the endearment, her lips brushed mine. A spell held me captive. I knew I should stop her, but I didn't want to. She was making the moves, and I was sober.

The kiss continued as she ran her lips lightly over mine. I felt the barest trace of a caress as her fingertips skated over my face, head, neck, and chest.

With a groan, I capitulated to her magic. I wrapped my arms around her as I tilted my head and parted my lips. I meant to take control, but she was beyond reason. Her touch was everywhere, untucking my shirt from my jeans while somehow tickling behind my ear and guiding my hand under the hem of her dress.

I did my best to keep her from taking off my shirt, but I didn't have anywhere neutral to redirect her energies. She ripped her lips from mine to trail wet kisses and stinging bites down my neck, and she rocked her core against the bulge in my pants.

"Sir, oh, Sir," she murmured as she kissed.

"Ev?" Daniel said. "You know she's not sober, right?"

"Yes. Somehow, she's grown tentacles, and I only have two hands."

"I thought you were a Dom?"

My first thought was to tell Daniel to fuck off, that I couldn't dominate her now, but I realized he'd made a good point. I gathered her wrists in one hand, and I pinned them behind her.

Eyes closed, she threw her head back and ground against my hard cock through the denim of my jeans. Binding her wrists only served to make her hornier.

But she was a sight to behold. Shrouded in darkness, she seemed to glow with an internal light. Her chest heaved as she rocked, displaying her breasts like an offering. I wanted very badly to touch her, but I knew I couldn't.

So I slid my free hand between us. She settled onto it, pressing her clit against my thumb while my fingers stimulated the rest of her pussy. Her panties, the only thing separating my flesh from hers, were sopping wet.

She thrust faster and harder, and then her whole body went stiff. Her mouth opened, but only a tiny squeak emerged. After several moments, she slumped against me. Her heart hammered against mine, but her breathing was even.

I let go of her wrists.

Daniel handed a wet wipe to me. "Lainie?"

"I think she's asleep."

"Did she climax?"

"I'm pretty sure that happened." I finished cleaning her juices from my hand, and then I brushed her hair out of her face. "Or she got really close before passing out."

"I wouldn't have stopped her, either," he said. "Plus, she said she gets there fastest when she's on top."

Chapter 20—Daniel

I carried her inside, but she didn't stir until I laid her down on the bed. Her eyes squeezed tighter, and she made a small noise.

"Shhh," I said to soothe her. "It's all right, Lainie. I'm here. I'm going to put you to bed."

She made another noise, and her hand groped the covers on her other side.

"I'm here, too." Evan unbuckled the strap on her shoe. "I'm taking your shoes off so you can sleep more comfortably."

Now her eyes fluttered open, but just for a second. "Need to brush teeth."

I couldn't see how she could do that while she was mostly asleep and as limp as a rag doll. "You might not be awake enough for that."

Ignoring me, she rolled out of bed, landing on her feet with her torso still horizontal on the mattress. I helped her achieve vertical status, and she lurched off in the direction of the bathroom.

I looked to Evan for guidance. He gazed after her thoughtfully. "I guess we're helping her brush her teeth. She's going to want to change into pajamas as well. You go supervise teeth brushing, and I'll raid the dresser in her closet for pajamas."

Bothering a woman in the bathroom wasn't something I'd done to a woman who wasn't my sister before. Sophia and I had a running contest where we did stupid and annoying things to each other. It was part of our bond, though it was harder now that both she and I lived with other people. I wanted to make Sophia's life harder, not Drew's.

The bathroom door was open, but I knocked anyway. Alaina stood in front of the sink. Her electric toothbrush was in her mouth, her eyes were closed against the light in the room, and she swayed on her feet.

In my supervisory role, I positioned myself where I could catch her if the swaying turned into toppling. The hum of the toothbrush filled the air. When it stopped, she bent over to spit and rinse.

I took the toothbrush from her, rinsed it, and set it on the counter. She did not react to my presence at all. Instead, she reached into a cabinet and came away with makeup remover.

It looked like I was going to be there for her entire going-to-bed ritual. The domesticity of it all made me smile. Midway through washing her face, she stopped abruptly and looked at me.

"You would think, if I was going to hallucinate you being here, that you would at least be shirtless."

That explained why she didn't react to anything I did. Since I was a hallucination, I lifted my shirt over my head. "Anything for you, Lainie."

She checked me out for a long moment, and then she finished washing her face. I handed her a towel, which she accepted without comment. She patted her face dry, and then she tossed the towel on the counter next to me. Stopping in front of me, she slowly reached out and poked my stomach with her finger.

Finding out I was flesh and blood, and not a figment of her drunken imagination only caused her to frown. "I must be asleep." She walked her fingers up my chest and down my arm. "Mmmm, I like this dream."

Then she took one step closer, and she pressed her body to mine. Automatically, my arms wrapped around her, and I had a better understanding of how hard it must have been for Evan to hold back as much as he had in the car.

She set her fingertips across my cheeks, and guided my head down, and then she devoured my lips. Passion exploded, stinging like so many sparks between us. My hands sprang to life, wandering over her body, greedily touching that which had been denied for so long. They landed on her ass, and I lifted her so that she straddled my thigh.

Her mouth slid away from mine, and she trailed light kisses down my neck. Then she burrowed her face into my chest, and her whole body went slack.

Evan came in then. He found me, gripping the ass of a woman asleep in my arms. His face asked a question, and I felt a little judged.

"I swear, she started it, and she was awake five seconds ago."

He chuckled and motioned for me to bring her into the bedroom. "I found a nightgown."

Together, we changed her out of her pretty dress and into a long sleep shirt that had a cat curled around a cup of coffee.

"At least she likes cats," I said. Evan had two of them. A year ago, he'd found them abandoned at a construction site, and he'd adopted them. His niece had named them Sebastian and Ariel, though they were both male cats. I didn't think cats cared about gender.

We tucked her under the covers, and then we looked down at our sleeping princess.

"So," I began, "are we staying the night or stealing her car to get home?"

Evan thought for nearly half a second. "I think I saw one of those warehouse club packs of extra toothbrushes under her sink."

"She doesn't have a guest room," I observed.

"She has three sofas downstairs."

I was up, bright and early the next morning. While Evan and Alaina slept, I scrounged up enough ingredients to make a birthday cake from scratch. She didn't have anything I could turn into frosting, so it was going to be a naked cake. I found sprinkles and arranged them to resemble words.

Evan waved as he headed to the main floor bathroom to wash up. He'd never been a morning person, so I didn't expect anything from him until after his first mug of java. When I heard water run upstairs, I whipped up pancakes and a banana-walnut topping.

"Why are you in my kitchen?"

Wearing my most welcoming smile, I glanced at the entryway. Alaina had showered and dressed. She wore yoga pants, a black shirt with two skeletons dancing, and a fuzzy sweater. Her damp curls flew free, springing in all directions, and her eyes were bloodshot and bleary.

To my lovesick eyes, she looked like a slice of Heaven.

"Good morning, sunshine. I have pancakes and coffee to get you started. Did you take something for your headache?"

She shielded her eyes from the glare of the morning sun streaming through the windows and from the overhead lights. "I don't have a headache. I just feel like shit."

"Comfort food and caffeine will help you feel better." I set a heaping plate and a mug at the table, and then I took her arm and guided her there. "Sit."

She sat.

"Eat slowly." I leaned down and pressed a kiss to the top of her head. "Happy birthday, Lainie."

Evan came into the kitchen. He headed to the coffee maker, but I motioned for him to sit down. I brought him pancakes and coffee, and then I joined the two people I loved for breakfast.

"Happy birthday, Lainie," Evan grunted. In his defense, he tried to inject some joy into his greeting, but gruff was as gentle as he got until after coffee. He tried to make it better by kissing her cheek.

Alaina eyed us each with a high degree of suspicion. Then her gaze settled on Evan. "Did we have sex last night?"

"Define *sex*." He sipped his coffee while cutting a wedge of pancake.

"I'm not in the mood for games."

"No clothes were removed, though you did give it a valiant effort."

I watched the ire in her expression morph to panic, and I set my hand on her arm. "He's not playing a game, Lainie. Evan has no sense of humor first thing in the morning. He wants clarification on what you'd consider to be sex."

The panic receded, and some of the bleariness cleared from her eyes. "Penetration?"

"No. Kissing, groping, and if you orgasmed, it was the result of friction. I couldn't tell because you passed out."

Now her gaze swung to me. "We made out?"

"A bit. I wasn't sure you were quite awake. You called me a hallucination and asked me to take off my shirt, so I did." My grin grew. "And then you snuggled into me and fell asleep in my arms."

Her eyes widened, and she put down her fork. "I'm so sorry. I want to apologize to both of you, and I can't say anything to excuse my behavior. I've never done anything like that before."

Evan chuckled, which was a landmark occasion because his mug was still mostly full. "It's okay, Lainie. We didn't mind."

"Not even a little bit," I echoed.

"You should," she whispered. "What I did was wrong on so many levels."

"Name one." Evan perked up and ate with more enthusiasm as he challenged her misconception.

"You're engaged. If anyone knows how devastating it is to be cheated on, it's me."

I chuckled. "Lainie, if you're involved, it's not cheating. Evan and I are both in love with you. We want to be with you as much as we want to be with each other."

She put her head in her hands, holding it with the tips of her fingers, and she sniffled.

Concern wrinkled Evan's face. "Lainie? Are you crying?"

Wordlessly, she nodded.

"Baby, why?"

"Because I don't have the courage to do this." Her voice emerged as a thin whisper, screeching anguish at top volume. "I'm in love with both of you, but instead of feeling joyful about that, I feel nothing but panic and fear."

I lifted her into my lap and wrapped my arms around her. "You feel like everyone in your life who you've loved has hurt you. Your parents are assholes. Your brother is a narcissist who targeted you your whole life. Your ex cheated on you."

She nodded as her hand fisted in my shirt, and she kept her face buried in my chest.

Evan pulled out the chair next to me, though he was close enough to also be on my lap. He stroked her hair back in an effort to soothe her. "Lainie, think about the people you've let get close to you since you broke away from those toxic relationships. Clara is an amazing friend. You have Zack. And now you have Daniel and me."

She hiccupped. "I barely know you or Daniel."

I chuckled. "That's not true. In the past couple of months, we've become friends. Real friends. We meet up every week just to hang out. We talk all the time. You've met my family. You know my sister pretty well. You've met Evan's family, and you've even become friends with his brother, Alec, and his family. Family is everything to us, and I know it is to you as well. You just had to work harder to find one that fits."

Tilting her face up, I kissed her cheeks, brow, and temples.

"We want to be your family." Evan continued my point, and he did a good job. Words weren't his thing—he preferred to take action—but he came through when it mattered. "You and Zack won't regret taking a chance on us."

She pushed away from my tender affection and sat up on my lap. As she'd done before, she rested her fingertips on my cheek and on Evan's.

I held my breath because the last time she'd done this, she'd shown us the door.

"I want this." No more tears streamed down her cheeks. "But I—I've never done something like this before. You're both so much younger than me, and you're going to throw my schedule into chaos."

Evan grasped her wrist and turned her hand so that he could kiss her fingertips. "For a little while, until we find a new normal. I'm not saying integrating our lives will be easy. It's going to require a lot of honesty and open communication. But we're committed to making this work. It's going to be epic, Lainie. I'm sure there will be days when you want to kill us, but mostly, you're going to love having us around."

She laughed at his description. "I suppose you want to have a D/s relationship with me?"

"As I do with Daniel, though he's only submissive in the bedroom. I'm fine with that, but I have a feeling that you'll sometimes want more, which is also okay."

She lowered her gaze, looking at his mouth. "You keep calling me Lainie, so we'll have to look for another way to start a scene."

Evan grinned, but it was the gloating kind he tended to use whenever he got his way.

I needed clarification. "Is that a yes? I'm going to need to hear you say that you want to be a thruple with us."

A brief frown turned down the corners of her mouth as she considered my request. "Thruple. Hmm. I think I like that word. Yes, I want to be a thruple with you."

Evan jumped up, picking Alaina up from my lap, and twirled her around. "Ha! I told you it was a word."

He set her down, and I crushed her to me. Evan joined on her other side, and his lips met mine, tenderly communicating the love and joy he felt.

Chapter 21—Alaina

"Mom?" Zack stood in the open doorway of my office. He wore his winter coat, but it wasn't zipped. I noted the missing hat and gloves as well.

I'd been working on edits to my book while Evan helped Zack with a science project. I closed my laptop and got to my feet, smoothing my skirt down as I stood. "You finished?"

"Yeah. It's epic. Dad's almost here to pick me up. He texted."

Due to Adam's divorce, our custody schedule had changed. Zack came to my house after school every day because there was always someone here to supervise him. Most days, Daniel or Evan picked him up from school. He still spent three-and-a-half days each week with Adam, but now I saw him most days, which I really liked.

After deciding to take a huge chance with two amazing men, I'd had a heart-to-heart with Zack. He'd been surprisingly understanding. His main concern was whether he'd be allowed to practice martial arts with Daniel at home or not.

I'd consented, and Daniel had set down some rules around using martial arts at home. He did not mess around with that stuff. It reminded me of the rules Evan had imposed about the D/s side of our relationship, like we had to use code words or signals when Zack was at home, even if he wasn't in the room. I'd been nervous that I'd have to spend a lot of time training them on how to behave in a household that contained a child, but in retrospect, I shouldn't have worried. Daniel worked with children every day, and Evan had a passel of nieces and nephews around all the time.

Since they'd moved in, I frequently arrived home to find extended family members visiting, and my phone constantly had messages from their family members. They'd accepted me without batting an eye at our unusual arrangement. Zack and Ashton, Alec's son, had forged a solid friendship, and he was growing used to having a bustling household.

Evan had also confiscated my list of home repairs. He'd reordered it so that it made sense from a construction standpoint. So far, he'd fixed the plumbing issues, and he'd built Zack a loft bed that doubled as a tree fort. He'd also finished remodeling Daniel's studio, which now boasted a gym and a kickboxing ring.

I was learning kickboxing. I'd found I liked kicking and punching the sandbag quite a bit.

I went to the doorway and hugged Zack tightly. Then I kissed his forehead. "I love you very much."

The doorbell chimed. Zack and I went to answer it. Adam stood on the porch. He stomped snow from his shoes.

"Do you want to come in?" I always asked, but Adam usually declined. He wasn't keen on my living arrangement.

"Sure." He stopped in the entryway, which let me close the door and stop letting out the heat. He hugged Zack. "Did you finish your project?"

"Yeah. Evan helped me."

Just then, Evan brought out a large cardboard box. "I had to take it apart to pack it up, Zack. I put some extra glue and dowels in there in case anything breaks when you put it back together." He handed the box to Adam. "Hi, Adam. How are you?"

I loved that Evan and Daniel were unfailingly polite to Adam even though Adam was so stiff.

Adam peered inside the box as he took it from Evan. "I'm well. Wow. This is very detailed."

Evan lifted a shoulder. "Once a structural engineer, always a structural engineer. Zack has a great eye for angles. Now he just needs to learn the math."

I smothered a smirk. Adam had assumed neither of my men had attended college, so Evan and Daniel like to work mentions of their degrees into every conversation.

Once my son and his father were safely away, I leaned against the closed door and witnessed the subtle changes as Evan shifted from my helpmate to my Dom. He stood a little taller. His shoulders somehow were broader, and his presence filled the space and my senses.

I lowered to my knees, and as I settled into position, submission overtook me. My brain shut off, blocking out everything but Sir.

He began by caressing my neck, and then his fingers wove into my hair. "Did you finish your edits for the day?"

"I didn't get as far as I'd planned, but I'm at a good stopping point. I'm ready to serve you, Sir."

"Daniel will be home any minute. Help me clean up the mess Zack and I made, and then you can go take your test."

We were trying to get pregnant, so I'd been taking ovulation tests before we had sex. "Yes, Sir."

The moment I stood up, Evan swept me off my feet. His mouth devoured mine with a searing kiss. I wrapped my arms around his neck and my legs around his waist. If he wanted to carry me upstairs for a quickie before the scene, I was on board with that plan. But after the kiss, he set me down.

Daniel came home while we were still cleaning. He went upstairs to shower away the sweat from teaching his advanced MMA class without coming to see us first. I noted the frown on Evan's face.

"Do you want to go up and surprise him in the shower?"

Evan grinned. "Are you saying you're willing to finish picking up all by yourself?"

I surveyed what was left of the mess. "If you can put away the glue, I'll sweep the floor, and I'll meet you upstairs after I take my test. Does that sound okay, Sir?"

"That sounds okay." He gathered the three kinds of glue and headed toward the utility room.

"And, if I come upon the two of you having sex, I get to masturbate while I watch." I shot him a devious smile as I got the broom from the closet.

The three of us had negotiated a pattern that allowed us each to have time alone with the other. We'd put Daniel and Evan's bedroom furniture in the two rooms across the hall from mine, so we each had our own space. Technically they were guest rooms, but on the nights the three of us weren't together, the one or both men were banished to another bedroom.

I really liked having two nights each week to myself.

Last night had been Evan's night with Daniel, but I'd come upon them having sex in my office instead of one of their bedrooms. Since they were in my domain, I'd masturbated while I watched them like they were my own personal porn channel.

"If you come without permission, you'll get a spanking." Evan threw that over his shoulder as he left the room.

That wasn't much of a deterrent.

I swept the floor. The ovulation test confirmed that today was a good day to make a baby. I washed my hands and headed upstairs, removing my clothes before stepping foot in the bedroom, which functioned as a dungeon tonight.

The bedroom looked different since my lovers had moved in. The whole house did, really. Daniel's grandparents' dining table occupied the dining room. The other living room had furniture. The books in the library had multiplied. Daniel's crime books were there. Evan had contributed favorite books he'd collected his whole life. He'd added everything from Dr. Seuss to Suzanne Collins to Michael Crichton, and he had a whole collection of books about fixing things.

Zack had seized upon some of the middle level books Evan had contributed, and the two of them chatted about characters and themes as Zack read through them.

The bedroom now had a sofa, two wingback chairs, and several tables. One long table had kink equipment set out on it. The photographs and flowers normally there were underneath, but the candles were still in place.

Voices came from the direction of the closet that was the size of a small room. Evan had built a bench seat in the center of that room. I sank to my knees and folded my arms behind my neck.

I'd meant to stay that way, but they came out wearing green. Not just any green—a bright, vibrant green that bordered on neon. My gaze rose of its own accord, taking in their striking—not in a good way—green body suits.

They were form fitting, leaving nothing to the imagination. On top of their heads, they wore headbands with two springs that had green balls perched on top of them.

Aliens.

They'd dressed as aliens. I teased them about alien abduction role playing, but I'd never actually done it. Well—not like this.

Evan pointed to me. "There's a prime specimen. Let us collect it and return to the ship."

Daniel nodded. "Yes, boss. It will be perfect."

He scooped me up, carried me to the bed, and set me down gently.

Evan buckled leather restraints around my wrists and ankles. In short order, I found my wrists bound together above my head, and my legs attached to a spreader bar.

"Wh-Who are you?" Belatedly, I realized I should be acting like a terrified woman who'd been kidnapped by aliens instead of a submissive excited about scening with her Dom and their lover. I stammered, but it only made my acting comical.

"It's making noises, boss," Daniel noted. "Should I plug that orifice?"

Evan peered closer at my mouth. "Let me try an oral treatment." His mouth devoured mine with a wet, sloppy kiss that was more gross than romantic. He ended by licking my lips.

"Eww," I said. "Aliens are disgusting."

"Are we tilting your pelvis up after?" Evan broke character to whisper in my ear. He wanted to know the results of the ovulation test.

"Yes."

With a grin, he nodded to Daniel. Then he said, "Assistant, let us begin the physical inspection."

Daniel rubbed his hands together. "I've been wondering about these bumps on its chest."

"I have, as well," Evan said. "Let's inspect them."

Daniel climbed on the bed opposite from where Evan stood next to it. He reached out and poked my breast. When nothing exploded, he widened his exploration into a light caress. Soon he was kneading the globe and pinching the nipple. He knew exactly how to touch me to get me going.

Moaning, I arched into his skillful hand.

"Favorable reaction," Evan noted. He inspected my other breast.

Soon groping turned to tasting, and they both sucked and bit my nipples. Evan's torture was always more painful than Daniel's, and the dual sensations sent pleasure through my body and moisture flooding my pussy. They inspected until I writhed and shouted from the overstimulation.

Evan handed something to Daniel, and I braced myself for the clover clamps.

Without being told, I inhaled, and exhaled slowly. It didn't work to stop the scream from both clamps biting my tender skin at the same time.

Before my wits gathered, a vibrator slid into my pussy, and Daniel put it on a pulse setting.

Evan crossed his arms. "We must let this simmer for a little while." He looked to Daniel. "Assistant, it is time for maintenance to your form."

"Yes, boss." Daniel laid down next to me and lifted his arms above his head.

Evan went to the other side of the bed, and he opened a panel in the crotch of Daniel's outfit. Despite the pain in my nipples and the intermittent vibration in my pussy, I wanted to watch them play with each other very much.

Daniel wore a cock ring that gathered his balls and cock into a ponytail. His cock was already engorged because playing with my boobs excited him.

Evan began by stroking the length of Daniel's cock. "This part looks like it's in good shape." He leaned down and licked the crown, and then he took it in his mouth.

As I strained to lift my head for a better viewing angle, Daniel reached over and stuck his fingers in my mouth. He fucked them in and out as Evan's head bobbed on his cock. I figured, if I'd really been abducted by aliens, I'd probably bite anything they tried to stick in my mouth, but this was the erotic edition, so I sucked and moaned and scraped my teeth along the pad of his fingers.

Evan lifted away from Daniel's cock, and Daniel let his fingers slip from my mouth.

"Assistant, are you prepared to receive your plug?"

"Yes, boss." Daniel shimmied to the edge of the bed and bent over.

Evan put on a latex glove, and he squirted lubricant onto his fingers. Then they disappeared behind Daniel. I couldn't see Daniel's face, but I heard his moans, and I knew he was getting a prostate massage.

That didn't last long enough to give him a happy ending. Evan produced a very large plug, and he fed it into Daniel's ass. Daniel gasped and swore.

Evan slapped his palm against the base of the plug. "I've given you the new, larger size to protect you against contamination by the test subject."

"Thank you, boss," Daniel grunted. He crawled toward me, and Evan came back around to my side of the bed/test table

He turned me onto my left side, facing him. With the spreader bar, my right leg was high in the air. He eased my legs forward, bending at the hip, which brought my foot off the bed and gave us more room to maneuver. He held onto my top leg, and he eased the vibrator from my pussy.

Daniel's fingers probed my vaginal opening.

"Do you need help, Assistant?"

"No, boss. I can get it." Daniel pulled my ass back, and his cock eased into my pussy.

The position meant he filled me. He rocked slowly, feeling out this different angle, and every time he surged forward, his cock hit my sweet spot. My breath caught, and I canted my hips back even more.

In no time, he established a rhythm that had me moaning and whimpering.

Evan turned on the vibrator and pressed it to my clit. Electric sensations rioted through my body. The noises I made grew louder and less coherent. Evan closed his hand over my mouth, restricting the airflow to my nostrils.

Behind me, Daniel jackhammered into my pussy. It was too much. With a muffled scream, I climaxed. My eyes rolled into the back of my head.

Vaguely, I heard Daniel's roar as he came inside me. I was aware of them shoving pillows under my hips to elevate my pelvis and help the semen travel deeper. Limp and spent, I didn't bother trying to open my eyes. I rode the waning waves of my orgasm.

Until something cold touched my anus.

My eyes flew open.

Evan and Daniel knelt between my knees, holding them up. Both wore a latex glove on one hand. Daniel eased a lubricated finger into my ass. He sawed it in and out.

"This hole appears to have many of the same properties as the other one, but it's tighter. Do you think it's another breeding hole?" Daniel's smirk betrayed how hard he was working not to laugh.

Evan made a thoughtful noise. "Let's see if we can both get a finger inside it." He reached forward, and I felt his finger join Daniel's.

They played for a bit, rubbing me the right way while they made comments and suppositions about the breeding capabilities of my species. Then Daniel pressed a bullet vibe to my clit while the two of them finger-fucked my back entrance.

With my hips raised on pillows and my feet planted on the mattress, I thought I'd have the leverage to lift myself, but I'd forgotten about the spreader bar they were holding down. The constriction conspired to work as a strict restraint. I couldn't wiggle to meet or escape the onslaught.

This orgasm took longer to build, but it slammed into me with tremendous force. I begged, pleaded, swore, and shouted, but they ignored it all.

While I was insensible, they lifted me and turned me onto my knees and face. My arms were free, but my body was a limp noodle, so it didn't do me any good. Evan's cock slid into my still-pulsing pussy. The intrusion was greeted with enthusiasm, and my orgasm lengthened.

It was too much; I reared up, fighting against the sensory overload.

Daniel forced my head back down, and Evan's strong hands wrapped around my wrists. He folded my arms behind my back, and he used them as a handle to force my hips back every time he surged forward.

Tears dripped from my eyes as I sobbed and begged for mercy.

White-hot pain tore through my breasts as Daniel removed the clover clamps. I screamed so hard, my voice went silent. Wonderful agony seared from my breasts straight to my pussy. My senses fried from the overload, and the world went dark.

I woke to find myself sandwiched between two warm, strong bodies. Hands stroked soothing caresses through my hair and down my back. Light kisses pressed to my temples and shoulders.

Inhaling deeply, I urged myself to full consciousness. "How long was I out?"

Daniel chuckled. "Long enough for me to recover. I'm ready for a second round of alien impregnation."

My body ached, and my limbs weren't on board with being awake. I chuckled, and it sounded utterly pathetic. "How about you impregnate Evan while I watch?"

Evan lazily caressed my thigh. "I'm up for it, and if you change your mind, we can always incorporate you into the scene."

I'd been afraid of what accepting them into my life would bring, but I wasn't afraid anymore. Giving in to their invitation had brought joy and love, and I'd removed them from my 'Shouldn't've' list.

My arms recalled how to work. I bent them to bring up my hands to caress their faces. "I love you both so much."

Daniel kissed my cheek. "And I love you both so much."

Evan laughed. "And I love you both so much more."

A Note to Readers:

Couples from previous novels appear in this book. You can read more about Sophia and Drew in Serving Sophia (Awakenings 3).

Evan mentioned that Sophia had a mentor, Ellen. Ellen is a supporting character in Letting Go (Awakenings 1) which follows Jonas (Ellen's best friend) and Sabrina.

Ellen also appears in Owning Up (Awakenings 2) as a supportive friend for Samantha, as she falls in love with twin Doms, Alexei and Stefano.

At the end of this book is a preview of Serving Sophia.

Michele Zurlo

Michele Zurlo is the author of the Awakenings, Doms of the FBI, and the SAFE Security series and many other stories. She writes contemporary and paranormal, BDSM and mainstream—whatever it takes to give her characters the happy endings they deserve.

Her childhood dream was to be a librarian so she could read all day. Some words of wisdom from an inspiring lady had her tapping out stories on her first laptop, and writing blossomed from a hobby to a career. Find out more at www.michelezurloauthor.com or @MZurloAuthor.

Lost Goddess Publishing

The Doms of the FBI Series

Re/Bound (Doms of the FBI 1)
Re/Paired (Doms of the FBI 2)
Re/Claimed (Doms of the FBI 3)
Re/Defined (Doms of the FBI 4)
Re/Leased (Doms of the FBI 5)
Re/Viewed (Doms of the FBI 6)
Re/Captured (Doms of the FBI 7)
Re/Deemed (Doms of the FBI 8)

The SAFE Security Series

Treasure Me (SAFE Security 1)
Switching It Up (SAFE Security 2)
Unlocking Temptation (A SAFE Security Short)

The SAFE Security Trilogy: Mercenary Hearts

Forging Love (A SAFE Security Novella: Mercenary Hearts prequel)
Drawing On Love (Mercenary Hearts 1)
Broken Love (Mercenary Hearts 2)
Shards of Love (Mercenary Hearts 3)

Awakenings

Letting Go
Owning Up
Serving Sophia
Giving In

Safeword: Oasis Series by Michele Zurlo

Wanting Wilder
Mina's Heart

Paranormal by Michele Zurlo
Dragon Kisses 1-3
Blade's Ghost

MM Romance by Nicoline Tiernan
Nexus #1: Tristan's Lover by Nicoline Tiernan
Nexus #2: The Man of His Dreams by Nicoline Tiernan

Anthologies
BDSM Anthology/Club Alegria #1-3 by Michele Zurlo and Nicoline Tiernan
New Adult Anthology/Lovin' U #1-4 by Nicoline Tiernan
Menage Anthology/Club Alegria #4-7 by Michele Zurlo and Nicoline Tiernan
Discovering Desires Anthology by Michele Zurlo

Bear's Cove Series (MM/MPreg) by A. J. Stone
Dak's Omega
Tanzil's Second Chance
Perfect Blend: Kofi's Omega
Swept Away

Draco International (MM/MPreg) by A. J. Stone
Amaricio's Omega
Koren's Omega Neighbor
Zeke's Reluctant Omega

You can read about Sophia and Drew's story in Serving Sophia (Awakenings 3). Here's a look at Chapter 1.

Chapter 1

Sophia

I held him tightly with one arm as he sobbed against my shoulder, and I skimmed my hand lightly up and down his spine to soothe him. His silky skin seemed to caress me back, something Chris never did consciously.

He dragged the edge of the blanket closer and used it to wipe his eyes and the moisture on my skin. "I'm sorry, Mistress."

Now I shushed him. "We've talked about this, Chris."

"I know. I'm sorry." Realizing what he'd done, he chuckled and shook his head, and the tears leaking from his big brown eyes ceased. "There I go again."

By day, Christopher was a high-powered attorney, but here, in my dungeon, he was my submissive. I'd spent the last hour breaking him down, a process that enriched both our lives, and now he was a quaking mass tucked into my side.

I loved the power and control I had over my subs. Nobody could give Chris what I gave him—a safe place to come apart and the impact play necessary to facilitate his healing. It was a heady feeling, being in control of such a handsome, virile man.

He sat up next to me. "It's habit. The way I was raised, men don't cry."

I sat up and rubbed his shoulder. Defined by slim, strong muscles and streaked darker brown from the marks my flogger left, he was a study in perfection. "Christopher, men cry, and there is no need for you to apologize for having emotions, for feeling things deeply. You're human. Embrace your humanity."

Christopher came from tough stock. Outside of my dungeon, he was a man's man. He drank hard liquor, ate his steak rare, and didn't blink when faced with a DA who had a solid case. He was methodical and unemotional in his approach to defending his clients, and he was the same way in his personal life.

The only place he felt safe enough to let down his rock-solid wall was with me, and even then, I had to force him to drop the façade.

I thrived on the challenge. I loved breaking him down. I treasured the deep well of trust between us. We had something special.

He snorted. "You never cry."

Though he was wrong about that, I didn't dispute the claim. I'd never cried in front of him. I adored Christopher, and I prized his submission, but I'd learned to keep my emotions stowed safely away. Instead, I basked in his display, soaking in the purifying power of his tears.

In lieu of an answer, I traced my fingertip along his full bottom lip. I loved his lips. Chris was a fantastic kisser, and under my tutelage, he'd become skilled at eating pussy as well. That was one skill women needed to be more vocal about. There shouldn't be a participation prize for that sport. More men needed to learn how to please a woman with their mouth, and they weren't going to become proficient without feedback and practice.

Lots of practice.

He turned toward me, following my caress, and he brushed his lips across mine. His foray was tentative, asking for permission. I'd trained him well. When I didn't give it, he pulled back. "Have I displeased you, Mistress?"

I scratched my nails through the short, fuzzy black curls that dotted his head. Breaking him down had been a satisfying experience for both of us, and now I was very horny. "You pleased me, Christopher. Now lick my pussy and show me how much you appreciate me."

"Yes, Mistress." He lifted me easily to remove my shorts, and then those wondrous lips closed around my clit in an erotic caress. The flat of his tongue swiped and teased through my folds as he patiently urged me to completion.

Tension built and released, and he moaned as he slurped evidence of my orgasm. The small climax left me hungry for more.

"Get a condom, Chris. I need you inside me."

He snagged a condom from where I'd dropped several on the edge of the bed, and I grabbed the riding crop from where I'd propped it against the headboard. Excitement sparkled in his eyes, and his erection seemed to strain toward me as he rolled the condom over the thick length. I tapped the flap of the crop on the underside of his balls, and he moaned. I tapped harder, and he gasped.

"Mistress, I want to please you."

Meaning he was close to coming. My Christopher was a masochist. He couldn't achieve orgasm without pain, which was why I'd flogged him until his mind floated away, and then I'd brought him back with five cane strokes. I hadn't broken the skin, but he was tender and bruised.

He entered me roughly, another clue as to the tenuousness of his control, and he set a frantic pace.

I brought the crop down across a cane stripe on his thigh. "Slower. If you come before I do, I'll torture your dick."

Chris wasn't a fan of CBT—cock and ball torture—so it was definitely a punishment he didn't relish. Taking a deep breath, he slowed his pace. "Yes, Mistress. I'm sorry, Mistress."

As that was an appropriate action for which to apologize, I let him have that one. My orgasm built anew. Chris found my sweet spot and concentrated on hitting it with every thrust. I brought the crop down on his ass and thighs. It wasn't a punishment or warning. I got off on his pain, as did he.

He cried out, moans and pleas as he fought for control.

But control was mine. His body, his orgasm—these things belonged to me. Aiming for a bruise, I hit harder. He trembled on top of me, his moans turning to desperate sobs. More than his cock, his pain and desperation drove my climax. Seconds before my orgasm hit, I dropped the crop and pinched a welt with vicious intensity.

"Come," I commanded as delicious bliss washed over my body. "Now."

He threw back his head, buried his cock deep, and howled as he came.

Then he collapsed next to me, his chest rising rapidly as he moaned and whispered my title reverently.

I closed my eyes, a pleased smile curling my lips. This had been a great scene.

Tightening the belt of my robe, I watched Christopher wince as he put on his pants. I'd rubbed arnica into his welts, but he was still going to be pleasantly sore for the next few days.

"Do you want a robe instead?" I motioned to the cabinet where I kept his things. Hanging in there was the crop I'd used on him when we'd fucked, as well as the floggers and cane I'd used earlier. I'd clean them tomorrow. "It's late. You can sleep over."

"Thanks, but I can't stay the night. I have an early meeting."

Though I adored my submissives—I currently had two subs I saw regularly—I rarely invited them to stay the night. We weren't romantically involved, and so it was often easier on everyone if we parted after a scene. Sometimes when Chris stayed, we did a short scene in the morning.

"We need to debrief. You can dress afterward."

"That's okay." Chris wasn't submissive outside the dungeon, and his mind was already halfway up the stairs. "I like this kind of sore."

Scratch that—he was most of the way up the stairs. He'd stopped using my title.

Rather than call him on it, I opened the door. "I'll meet you in the kitchen."

My house was small, a little under a thousand square feet, but it was the perfect size for me. On the main floor I had a kitchen, living room, two bedrooms, a tiny office, and a good-sized bathroom. In the basement, I had a laundry room, a storage room, and a dungeon.

I hopped up the stairs, an extra spring in my step because I was sexually and emotionally sated, and then I got the coffee maker going. As it wheezed and spilled my favorite elixir, I heard the creaking of the stairs.

The door at the top of the steps opened, and Chris poured himself into the nearest chair.

Chuckling at his amorphousness, I got out two mugs. "I can set the alarm to get you up early enough to be home in time to change. You can shower here."

He tugged at his collar. "I met someone."

In the midst of pouring scalding hot java into a mug, I frowned. We weren't romantically involved, and we were by no means exclusive. But something in Chris' tone gave me pause. "Someone special?"

"I think so. We've been out twice, but we've been talking and texting every day for the past two weeks. I really like her."

I added liberal amounts of sugar to my mug. "If you want cream and sugar, you're going to have to get it yourself." He was too picky when it came to doctoring coffee. After that first time, I'd required him to do the honors himself.

"Black is fine."

I set the mug in front of him. "If you complain, I won't beat you next time."

"Sophia, I'm trying to tell you that there won't be a next time." He sighed. "Jennifer isn't into this sort of thing. She wouldn't understand."

Nonplussed, I sipped my coffee. Though it was late, I didn't mind the caffeine. Once Chris left, I planned to shower and do some stretches so that my shoulders wouldn't be sore in the morning. Chris might like muscle pain, but I didn't.

"Christopher." I said his name every bit as crisply as he'd said mine. "Does Jennifer know you need pain in order to orgasm?" He had trouble achieving an erection without at least a few sharp pinches.

He chewed that delicious bottom lip for a moment. "I've been researching this whole phenomenon. The brain is the largest sexual organ."

Skin was the largest sexual organ. The brain was the most important. I noted the correction, but I didn't voice it. "Are you planning to fantasize about being flogged and dominated while you're with her? Or did you get some of those erection pills from TV?"

Uncomfortable with the direction of the conversation, he shifted. "I'm not sure I get off on being dominated as much as from being flogged."

By way of response, I lifted a brow. Chris went through this every few months or so. Being submissive and a masochist clashed with the macho upbringing he couldn't seem to come to terms with. I wasn't a shrink, but I'd advised him to see one on several occasions. In the meantime, I liked to think our sessions helped him process some of his emotional trauma.

"Yeah." He ran a palm over the top of his head, petting himself as a calming mechanism.

I was bothered by this because spending time with me usually left him with an inner peace that was sorely lacking right now.

"You're right," he continued. "You're always right. But you know what? I need to do this. I need to try to have a normal relationship with a woman."

"Normal is overrated," I muttered. Leaning forward, I nailed him with a direct look. "You never said if she knows you're a masochist."

"Not yet." He pursed his lips. "I think she'll be okay with it. I don't think she'll be okay with me having a Dominatrix."

"Okay," I said. "If that's what you want, then I'm no longer your Domme."

He seemed simultaneously crushed and relieved. "Sometimes I resent that you're so understanding. Sometimes I wish I could be the man you think I am."

I wasn't being understanding. Chris and I had been together, on and off, for a little over four years, and though we didn't have a romantic relationship, he meant something significant to me. I'd given him so much, and in my dungeon, he'd given me everything. At best, I was being a passive-aggressive bitch. "On any given day, you're the man you want to be."

He shook his head. "I'm still trying to figure out who that is."

"Well, good luck. I hope you find happiness with Jennifer." I knew he wouldn't. He was too much of a fucking chicken to ask for what he needed. The only reason we'd met was because he'd come to the club where I worked as a service Top. I'd charged him top dollar—ha, ha—

to flog him until he was a sobbing mess for almost a year before he'd asked me for more.

I had a strict policy about not having sex with my clients, so I'd forced him to relinquish his membership to City Club before I'd consented to anything. For the past three years, we'd engaged in a fairly steady D/s relationship punctuated by his attempts to have a vanilla girlfriend.

We'd never developed a romantic association, though I hadn't been opposed to it. Chris had only ever wanted domination from me. Even with all the talking and the number of times he'd poured out his heart and soul to me, he still didn't see me as a viable candidate for a relationship.

I used to be perturbed about that, but I mollified my emotions by taking them out on his ass, which he loved. Since then, I'd cemented armor around my softer emotions, tucking stray wants and wishes away behind a thorny barrier.

And yet, I wasn't lying. My wish for his happiness was as genuine as it was bitter.

Deep down, I wanted to find happiness like that, but I'd learned the hard way that my path didn't lead in that direction.

CPSIA information can be obtained
at www.ICGtesting.com
Printed in the USA
BVHW032307181220
596095BV00008B/249

9 781942 414650